evening's empire

Tor Books by David Herter

Ceres Storm
Evening's Empire

a tom doherty associates book

new york

evening's empire

david herter

EVENING'S EMPIRE

Copyright © 2002 by David Herter

This book is printed on acid-free paper.

Edited by David G. Hartwell

A Tor Book
Published by Tom Doherty Associates, LLC
175 Fifth Avenue
New York, NY 10010

www.tor.com

Tor® is a registered trademark of Tom Doherty Associates, LLC.

Library of Congress Cataloging-in-Publication Data

Herter, David.
Evening's empire / David Herter.—1st ed.
p. cm.
ISBN 0-312-87034-5
1. Oregon—Fiction. I. Title.

PS3558.E7938 E94 2002
813'.6—dc21
2002019001

First Edition: June 2002

Printed in the United States of America

0 9 8 7 6 5 4 3 2 1

To

s. a.

*a*cknowledgments

I'd like to thank Mr. Harry W. Herter and Edith Scott; Arinn Dembo, who guided this book through its early drafts; my patient editor, David Hartwell, who resurrected the project; Caitlin Blasdell, for important under-the-wire suggestions; and the lovely Susan Adams. Also, many thanks to Bill Tuttle, Lael and Zach, Susan Draeger, Dawn and Issac, Ted Chiang, Becky Morris, Therese Littleton, Russell H., Lucius Shepard, Charles Harness, Brooks and Blaise, Scott Herman, C. Trull, Chris Schelling, Moshe Feder, Ed Chapman, Tom Pace, Duane Wilkins, A. P. McQuiddy, Ray Gallardo, Melissa, Jarrah, and Justin.

Apologies to Jules Verne.

Janacek's *Osud*, Stravinsky's *Persephone*, and Martinu's *Julietta* were somehow crucial, as were the novels of Blaylock, Powers, Wolfe, Flann O'Brien, and Brian Moore.

The late Stephen Albert inspired my early drafts; I attended many of his lectures and concerts at the Seattle Symphony, where he was composer-in-residence.

part one
the reign of the vertical

Just then I heard vague chords, sad harmonies with an undefinable melody, the wails of a soul which wanted to break its ties with the earth.

—*20,000 Leagues Under the Sea* by Jules Verne

*e*vening, oregon

He followed the road to Evening through stands of alder and weeping spruce.

For six days he'd been driving west from Boston, slowed by snow in the midwest, across the Rockies, into Montana, Idaho and eastern Washington, all of it ending as he crossed the Oregon plain, where autumn had returned with the gold-leafed trees surrounding the highway, and a pall of rain.

And here on the coast, even the rain was gone. This three-mile stretch, weaving from 101 to the main street, looked as it had during their first, and last, visit to town.

He remembered Anna sitting silently beside him, still upset over their argument; how, as this forest thinned and the first houses appeared, in grottoes of rhododendron, sunflower and ivy, her mood had changed. She'd been charmed by the architecture along the downtown stretch, by the brick shops, the wrought iron benches, and the elegant Queen Anne mansion aloof on its basalt bluff above the sea.

"Look at it!" Leaning into the breeze through the open window. Brushing damp hair from her eyes. "It's lovely!"

A short wooden sign rushed past him:

WELCOME TO EVENING, OREGON
HOME OF EVENING CHEESES
POPULATION 310

Suddenly, the forest was left behind.

The main street stretched before him, as it had more than two years earlier, the single and two-story brick buildings with awnings and overhanging plastic signs, under mostly blue skies.

To his left was the inland hill, with houses that seemed to float in the pine; to his right, a coastal bluff.

Russ pressed the brake pedal, looking for—finding—the mansion on the bluff, with its steep roofs and octagonal tower.

All as he remembered.

As he reached the first of the buildings—a red brick barber shop, a gas station with antique pumps—he recalled those days spent in a room made of music, scraps of notation taped to the walls, shelves, windows, spread across the floor; the struggle to capture that elusive sound, from a nightmare.

Another sign appeared, framed in lacy black iron:

Evening–by–the–Sea's
Chamber of Commerce and Visitor's Center
Open from noon till five.

Behind it, a three-story Victorian stood against hemlock.

He pulled over to the curb, parked, and shut off the engine.

In the near silence, against the faint ticking of the engine, he set about straightening the mess on the passenger seat, refolding the Oregon map, putting pencils in the glove compartment, his comb, Kleenex, sunglasses in the dash tray, closing his notebook, aware of the town beyond the windows.

He slipped the notebook into his breast pocket.

Reaching up, he turned the rearview toward him, studied his beard, his chapped lips, his thick brown hair. He didn't look too haggard. Distracted, perhaps, but he'd often been told he looked distracted. Anna had said it was his gently rounded Welsh nose, his slight, bearded chin. Both conspired to give him a furtive look.

He drew a deep breath, then exhaled.

Now he simply resembled someone who'd spent five-and-a-half days on the road. A tired man. Distracted, perhaps.

In a real town, not a nightmare.

Only as he pulled on his sweater, lost within the heavy folds, did he realize his heart was pounding.

He stepped out into a cool breeze.

Ahead, people were walking by the storefronts; a dairy truck, its brakes squealing, was turning left; but this nearby stretch was quiet. He climbed the stairs to the porch. A door of rose-red glass admitted him to a foyer, and a large office. He stepped inside. A woman looked up from behind an oak desk. She was in her late forties or early fifties, wearing a blue blazer and matching skirt. She had short auburn hair, and plump cheeks that were attractive only when she smiled. And when she *did* smile, striding around the edge of her desk to shake his hand, he remembered her. She'd been at the house where they had taken him. She'd fetched a blanket for him, and spoken of shock.

"You look familiar," she said.

He shook her manicured hand. "Russ Kent."

"Mister Kent, yes. Of course." Though it was subtle, recognition froze her smile. "I'm Peggy Chalmers, head of the City Council and Visitor's Center? I must admit, it's a surprise to see you."

She gestured to a chair, then resumed her place behind the desk and a nameplate reading *Peggy C.*, carved from a piece of driftwood. "How long has it been? Two years? It was in September, wasn't it?"

"August," he said.

"Oh, it was awful. Just awful. I can only imagine what it's been like for you. How are you doing?"

While he told about getting over it, about getting back to work, he could sense behind her compassionate demeanor the obvious question: *why have you come back?*

"I've been given an important commission, for an opera. And I haven't been able to get much work done back home." He paused. "I need time to myself, to get it under way."

"But come back to Evening?" she asked, courteously enough. "I'd think this would be the hardest place for you to work."

"I had to see the town again." He paused, trying to remember what he had planned to say. "I had to . . . put some bad dreams to rest."

She smiled gently. "My only thought is that you should have called. We could have made arrangements for you. That's what a Visitor's Center's for."

"I wasn't sure I'd go through with it. Not until I reached the exit off 101."

She lifted the pencil, then tapped her rounded chin with the eraser. "You realize we have no motels? The nearest is ten miles north in Port Rostov."

"Last time here . . . I saw a sign for a bed-and-breakfast."

She nodded. "Miss Sumner runs it. But you know, I think she's closed now?" She glanced to the wall, and a gold-framed portrait of an old, white-bearded gentleman. Her grandfather? Or the town founder . . . what was his full name?

A placard below it read *Joseph Evening 1876–1959*.

"Only because we never *get* any tourists in the winter," Peggy said. "Let me call her. It might not be a problem. How long were you wanting to stay?"

"A week. Maybe a little longer."

She wrote something down. "A price range?"

"Anything reasonable."

She patted the folders and loose papers on her desk, then lifted a slender black book. "Give me a couple minutes." She stood. "I'll use the other office."

Russ half-stood. "Do you mind if I make a call here?"

"Not at all. Dial direct."

She left the room, shutting the door softly behind her.

Somewhat relieved, he sat down, pulled the notebook from his pocket, flipping open the cover. On the third page, Ellie—Anna's former student and now his part-time assistant for the project—had written her phone number, and underneath: *Call me every night!*

She'd been upset about his decision to drive alone, and through such bad weather.

The line rang, clicked.

"Hello?" It was Brian, her boyfriend.

"Hey, Brian, is Ellie there?"

"Sure. Just a sec, Mister Kent."

It must be around 7 P.M. on the east coast. He'd probably caught them after dinner.

"Here she is, Mister Kent."

"Hi. So, you're there?"

"I've arrived."

"How're you feeling?" Her voice held a note of concern, and restraint.

"Like I need to stretch my legs."

"That's not what I meant."

"I'm okay. A bit tired."

"Did you find a place to stay yet?"

"Right now I'm at the Visitor's Center. I should know pretty soon. Listen, is there any news?" He forced his shoulders to relax.

"Not really. I photocopied those contracts, mailed them off to Schirmers and your agent, and sent a copy to Santa Fe. Oh, and Malcolm left a message. Hold on."

Russ nearly told her not to bother, but she'd already put down the phone.

Through the door he could hear the murmurous rise and fall of Peggy Chalmer's voice. Positive, pleasant sentences. Night would be here soon, and he didn't look forward to driving north to Port Rostov—though he *would* rent a room there, if he had to, and drive down to Evening, at least for a few days.

"Russ? He said to tell you 'spear carriers have been added.' He left his number. You're just supposed to call him. Do you want it?"

"I think I have it. The 219 number, right?"

"Yeah."

"Anything else? Anything from my Dad?"

"Nope. But I'm seeing him tomorrow."

"Well, if I get a room, I'll call you later tonight with the phone number. I'm sure he'll want it, too."

"Okay."

"It might be late, so turn the ringer down."

"I will, Russ. Take care."

"Thanks, dear. Bye."

He hung up, and tucked the notebook back into his pocket, wondering if he should've asked her for supplies. What had he forgotten? He'd brought blank score sheets, pencils, gum erasers. What else did he need?

Scores for inspiration? The Verne book?

The door opened. Peggy Chalmers strode back in, smiling. "You're in luck. Megan thought it would be just *fine* to put you up. She's asking a hundred a week. That's twenty-five off the normal rate, considering it's the off-season."

The relief was physical: he relaxed his shoulders and straightened in the chair. "Good. That's great."

"Megan Sumner's not a native, but she's still one of my favorite people in town. And the house is one of our most grand. It's at the south end of town, at the top of Alder. A Second Empire with a view of the sea. Here . . ." She wrote directions on a slip of paper—left-handed, holding the pen at an extreme slant—and passed it up to Russ.

He stood up, eager to leave, eager to get this room, this place in town.

Coming around the desk, she shook his hand again and said, "I hope you enjoy your stay, Russ. We're being given a chance to start over. We the town, I mean . . . to prove ourselves again."

She walked with him to the front door. "The sea gets quite moody. We get wonderful storms. Blustery, but not destructive. And the perfect inspiration for an artist." She reached out as if to touch his elbow. "You should come to our Winter Gathering. Or at least consider it. It's this Saturday, up at the Evening mansion. Don't decide now, just keep it in mind. Your new landlady will have all the details."

Thanking her again, he turned away and walked down the stairs, into a cool breeze and flecks of late afternoon sun.

In the most vivid reoccurring nightmare, he finds himself in the mansion, overlooking the town where Anna had died.

The exact location varies. Sometimes it's a room of dark wood and carpeting, with a desk and sofa, bookcases, cordoned off from a hallway with velvet rope; sometimes a high-ceilinged dining room, likewise restored to the 19th century; sometimes the tower.

The remnants of First Street stretch below, lost in blackberries and wild flowers. Seagulls wheel above an inland hill dense with spruce and hemlock. The town has been deserted for years. Yet if he stares toward the hill—and he always does—there will be a flash of yellow, a sly sidewise movement between the houses.

Anna, in a yellow dress, stepping out against the distant spruce.

She's too far away for him to see her face, but everything about her is familiar. The blond of her hair, the set of her shoulders. She stands tentatively, as though she might vanish as easily as she appeared. And she will.

Through the glass comes a sound, something between Anna's real voice and a cor anglais, murmuring in B flat. Music has been color for Russ since he was a child. Her voice, like her dress, is yellow.

She steps back and disappears.

In a sudden overwhelming silence, he resists the urge to look for a door, a way out; there is none. Eventually he finds himself at the western windows. Below, the cliff drops to a basalt shore, which terraces down to pools of green and silver; a drained seascape, stretching out and down, in jagged tiers, to the blue-black mountains of the ocean deep.

Nothing moves. But he watches, listening. Then the windows hum with it. No color, every color. Elusive.

Stepping close to the window, he looks down to where her body lies broken on the rocks, her limbs laced with seaweed, her head crowned by a luminous band of water.

The downtown was a half-mile clutter, with a bank, a hardware store, a beauty salon, a grocery, other shops passing too quickly for their signs to register. Compared with the quaint seaside towns he'd visited, like Astoria, or Pacific, Evening was low-key. The side streets were lined with modest Craftsman-style houses and cottages, while the main street offered wares and services for the town itself, rather than for the tourists; though the *Evening Cheese Outlet* store was quite visible in the center of town, its windows decked with bright yellow crepe and posters proclaiming the various brands of Evening cheeses.

Toward the south end, beyond the last of the town's three flashing red lights, he paid closer attention to the street names. Spruce. Burle. Aberfoyle. Alder.

He turned left on Alder and accelerated up the steep hillside. As Peggy Chalmers had promised, the house was at the top, on the corner of Alder and Seventh, and easy to spot—a dark green Second Empire with a mansard roof and bay windows on either side of a porch.

He parked the Volvo by the curb, pulled out the keys. Stepping out, he was aware of the hillside behind him, roofs and trees dropping away, and the sun sitting just over the sea.

An old blue Suburban was parked in the driveway.

He followed a path of stepping stones across the lawn, between modest flower beds, and climbed the porch stairs. A fanlight of green glass crowned the door, which stood open. He knocked on the edge of the screen. "Hello?"

There was movement inside, far back.

"Megan Sumner?"

"Yes. Just a sec." A glancing voice. "It's open. Come on in."

He opened the screen and stepped into an entry hall, facing a staircase. Flagstone underfoot. The air smelled of moist earth, with a hint of cinnamon. He called out: "Thanks for taking me without notice."

To the right was a rec room occupied by a Ping-Pong table stacked with clay pots and vases, bags of topsoil and bark.

"You must be Mister Kent." She appeared in the living room to his left, wiping her hands on a towel.

She was nearly as tall as him, slender with long, dark brown hair tied back; she wore a beige shirt with the sleeves rolled up, jeans and tennis shoes.

"Russ. Thanks again."

"Well, I never completely close down." She was younger than him, late thirties, perhaps. "Things are a little messy. I apologize. I had kids from the school over to help with the garden. C'mon, let me show you around."

He followed her into the living room, with its plush green carpet (Russ almost remarked aloud on the theme) and a brick fireplace. Couch, chairs. Filigree shelves stocked full of seashells, sand dollars, glass globes, gleaming bits of bronze and silver.

The room looked quite comfortable.

"I wish *more* people would pass through in the winter," she said. "The land looks its best now, entirely green and lush. Kitchen's back there, but . . . this way, let's go upstairs."

At the top of the stairs, five doors opened onto a landing. Four bedrooms and a small bathroom with a claw-footed brass tub. "That's original. From the 1890s." She ushered him to the right, to the front left corner bedroom. "The view is gorgeous from this one."

The room was small with a hardwood floor. A bureau was immediately to his left, and farther along the wall, set in the corner, were an old oak desk and a spindle-back Queen Anne chair; beside them was a not-too-small bed.

He walked to the desk.

Two windows bracketed this corner. One faced south, and the other west, so that someone sitting here could look over the crest of Alder Street at the sea.

With the rheostat beside the door, she dimmed the overhead light, bringing out a sunset in ribbons of pink and purple that faded halfway up the sky.

"I love it," he said, to say something.

Across the street was a blue and white Italianate, its top three windows rounded like sedate eyes. While he watched, a gull alighted onto the iron cresting. It shuffled back and forth then drew in its wings, and in that moment seemed to disappear, to transform, its silhouette just another decoration on the fanciful roof.

During a simple spaghetti dinner, at the pie-crust table between the living room and the kitchen, Megan told him about teaching part-time at the school. "I help out with reading to the younger kids. I'm also the school bus on Mondays and Fridays."

"Just one school for the town?"

She nodded, sipping some water. "Some of the older kids go up to Rostov. Otherwise it's K through 12." A moment later she added, "Or K through 11. There's nobody in grade 12 this year."

Eating, Russ was happily aware of how comfortable he was, how different things were from what he'd expected, during the long drive. How different from the nightmares, those long nights in snow-bound motels.

"So what's it going to be about?" she asked, adding, "Your opera?"

The question momentarily surprised him.

"If you don't want to tell me . . ."

"Captain Nemo," he said. "It's *20,000 Leagues Under the Sea*."

She smiled. Her brown eyes warmed with it. "Really? Sounds like perfect material."

"I agree." A moment later, he added, "Though I probably wouldn't have chosen it on my own."

"Who did?"

"It was a conspiracy." He took another piece of garlic bread, dipped it in thick sauce. "My dad suggested I start a new project, and a composer friend of mine, Ollie Knussen, said I should tackle an opera. He mentioned doing Poe, Hawthorne—I'd set Hawthorne before. I thought of Verne, and decided on *20,000 Leagues*. What I'm going to call *Nemo*." After a sip of satisfyingly cold water—pleased again, at how well things had gone—he said, "My dad helped get me the commission. And Malcolm Moore, who's another friend, a novelist, playwright, is doing the libretto. I'm glad for them now."

"So how long till it's staged? Where?"

"The premiere's in Santa Fe, four years from now, March 17."

"So it's set."

He nodded. "I already have a seat assignment."

She laughed.

Smiling, he added, "Now I only have to write it."

While they finished their meal, she pulled out a laminated list of rules and recited the particulars. They were all sensible enough, easy to agree with.

After dinner, and the first awkward pause, she offered him coffee with optional brandy. "To celebrate the beginning of your work," she said. While she prepared them in the kitchen, full strength, he wrote out a check for the first week's rent.

Signing his name, he sensed a conclusion to the last week's feverish preparations; his father's and Ellie's worries, the long tiring drive.

He tore off the check and set it by her plate.

"Let's toast," she said, "to the success of your project."

"And to the picturesque, and very real, town of Evening."

He saw a momentary discord in her eyes, as they brought the china cups together; soon forgotten.

At 7:15, tired, warmed by the brandy and the meal, he excused himself and walked upstairs to his new room. He pulled out the fold-up clock, set it, wound its stubborn key, then dimmed the light by half.

The ocean was barely visible, dark under the dark sky.

Tomorrow, he thought, when I begin the work, it'll be there. I can look up from the desk to the sea.

He opened one of the suitcases, pulled out his clean T-shirts. Stuck between them, fluttering now to the mattress, was a sheet of yellow paper containing a single line in Malcolm's jagged hand:

Mobilis in Mobili.

He called Ellie, left his number on her voice messaging, then finished unpacking. The closet smelled of mint and roses: there was a potpourri on the overhead shelf.

He stowed the suitcases in the closet, then turned to the small box on the bed.

His name and address were written on the top and sides in magic marker, in Ellie's neat cursive. Inside were the drafts that had been taped to the walls and windows of his father's study, two hundred forty-some-odd random sheets full of chords, tone-clusters, notes in colored pens and pencils. He hadn't used color in years but needed it now, to help capture the peculiar tonal combination, the sound that wasn't quite sound, from his nightmare.

Ellie, who was a year away from her masters in music education, had insisted on organizing them by predominant key and note values, and numbering the sheets.

The sheet numbered 213 had seemed to capture it, a twenty-note cluster on a twelve-line stave, quarter tones and semitones in mingled colors almost soaking through the paper, with desperate annotations along the side. A cloud of tones that was also—somehow—the crown of seawater shimmering over Anna's head.

Whether it would inspire something in the opera, Russ couldn't say.

The libretto was on the desk. Ninety-five pages and far too wordy. He resisted the urge to look through it, wishing he'd brought the book, though it had proved too difficult a read in Boston, too slow for his mood.

How did Malcolm's version start?

With the report of a monster at sea, spoken aloud.

"Composers are never entirely satisfied with librettos." His father had said that, the night before Russ's departure. "It's a rule of sorts, Russell. You can use what you want and throw the rest away. I know other writers, don't I?" William Kent had added, "Though I suppose Malcolm is ideally suited to Nemo, isn't he?"

Russ stepped to the desk, leaned toward the window. Lights were on in the Italianate across the street and the other houses, too, behind rhododendron and pine, dropping out of sight. Darkness and scattered sodium lamps, the further darkness that was the sea.

He looked north, along the shore.

He would go there tomorrow.

Russ leaned back in the tub.

The light was turned low. He shut his eyes, listening to the soft plashing, the drips, and the echo in the brass.

A remote, fearful thought: the complexity of an opera production, the commitment. Writing for voices that hadn't yet been cast.

He'd composed for the stage before, a chamber opera, *Dr. Heidegger's Experiment*, performed a half-dozen times by a student company, recorded but never released; and three song cycles, the second of which had been a finalist for the Pulitzer in 1996. But he'd never tackled something as complex as *Nemo*. Four years of work, writing for an unfamiliar house, as-yet-unknown singers, with a full orchestra, two-hours plus, through-composed. And he wouldn't hear what he'd written until the sitzprobe, the first rehearsal with singers and orchestra, years from now.

He let his hands float on the surface.

Malcolm's opening wouldn't work. Instead, it would begin with orchestra, with the waves. The double bass. Four of them. A muddy sound, more felt than heard.

Portamento.

He ran his hand just under the water, realizing the victory today. A successful return.

And the town was real.

Tomorrow, he would visit the bluff. And start work.

He rapped his knuckles against the side of the tub. It rang in A flat. Purple, like dark blood.

He sprawled in the ocean depths, in a tweed jacket, shirt, trousers, shoes. Behind him, or below, as he struggled upright, were patches of green and turquoise, and stretches of sand—the sea floor.

He kicked, swam down, awkwardly at first, the water chiming as he picked up speed, as the features on the ocean floor became cottages, Craftsman-style homes with silted roofs and coral yards, and pine trees burdened with seaweed, all of it threaded by roads and sidewalks that glimmered in the dark.

A town beneath the sea.

He wondered at it, no longer swimming but dropping—being drawn down to a cottage on the corner, and a corner window.

The glass was cloudy, algae-stained. And something was imminent, he knew. If he only looked long enough. And listened.

For this was a dream, he realized.

And the sudden sound, the murmuring, was a *cor anglais*.

Through cloudy glass a white arm, a hand, beckoning.

In the dimness, Anna's face made of sand, with silvery eyes, a wounded stare, as the currents tugged him into swirling trumpets and trombones, into trembling bells, that woke him.

He reached blindly to the bedside table, shut off the alarm, collapsed against the pillow. For a long moment he pondered the image of Anna made of sand, with wounded eyes. But the dream faded, leaving just the morning light on the ceiling.

And this morning was different.

Remembering, he pushed himself up on his elbow and squinted at the clock. 8:40. He added it up. Nearly nine hours of sleep.

Throwing back the covers, he swung his legs out and down, then stood, stretched, taking in the contents of the room, everything from last night made somewhat unfamiliar, drably exposed in the daylight. The desk, with its small lamp and old rotary phone. The straight-backed chair. Overhead, the milky globe with bronze fittings, controlled by the rheostat beside the door.

He moved to the windows.

The world below the hill was lost in fog. The trees along Alder Street faded from green to a diffuse gray, like watercolor portraits as they dropped from sight. The Italianate, with its iron cresting and cupola, rounded windows, looked like a cardboard cutout, while the other houses, the shrubs and larch trees were bled of detail. Everything was still.

A *picture* of silence.

Feeling like an intruder, he descended the stairs.

He found Megan in the living room. She was sitting lengthwise on the sofa, in a woolen sweater, jeans and wool socks. She looked up from her magazine. Immediately he felt comfortable.

"Good morning. You're up." She sat up and dropped the magazine, *Atlantic Monthly*, on the carpet. "Hungry?"

"Yeah. Good morning."

"I made some waffles earlier. Too many."

All the windows were uncurtained; the lamps were off. A bay window looked onto the foggy front lawn, while the narrow, tall windows on either side of the couch were nearly blocked by larch trees, leaving the room in morning stillness.

"I love the fog," he said, as she stood up.

"Mornings are my favorite, this time of year." She walked toward the small dining room—really a nook formed by the half-wall of the fireplace. Over her shoulder she said, "Usually it burns off by noon, then it rains. But sometimes it doesn't go away. It just stays like this."

Like the bottom of the sea, he thought, glancing past her, to where a smaller window in the kitchen seemed to glow.

"Sit down. Breakfast is served."

The waffles were in the oven: the smell was wonderful. While she pulled on mitts, he stepped to the sink and looked out the window, to pine trees, a white fence under the press of fog, a patch of lawn and, closer to the house, so that he had to lean forward to see it, a rowboat. In the peeling hull were flowers: yellow, blue and white.

Looking at them, he recalled how *Nemo* might open. The double bass in their lowest compass, bowing in glacial slowness back and forth, a rumbling rise and fall, portamento, in deep currents.

And he remembered the dream.

"The dark blue ones are *sisyrinchium bellum*," she said. "Don't ask me to spell it. And the albino ones are bleeding hearts. They're quite rare, thank you. I pamper them quite a bit. I'll even bring them inside when the weather turns really rotten."

He saw Anna and her wounded eyes.

"It's a challenge," she said.

He shrugged it off, turned his attention back to Megan, to her smile.

"My nemesis is the strawberry-root-weevil."

"Strawberry-root-weevil," he repeated, stepping back. "It has a ring to it."

She smiled again. "Always thought so. And there's salal that loves to take over the backyard." With a spatula, she scooped up the waffles and stacked them on another plate. "Last year it got into my rowboat. I was going to yank it all out, but it was attracting all kinds of birds. My little rowboat was full of starlings and doves. How could I evict birds from my boat?"

She set a tub of butter, a bowl of powdered sugar and a tureen of maple syrup on the table. "Here you go." Then the plate of waffles. "Sit and eat. You have to like them."

While he ate, genuinely enjoying, he listened to the double bass, in portamento, from E minor.

"Doomy, dreamy Nemo, standing on the deck of the *Nautilus*, sings these words . . ." Leaning forward, Malcolm Moore broke into a smile, and for an instant Russ expected him to sing the lines. " '*You can understand, sieur, why I treat you as enemies. Force me, and I'll put you on the hull, dive beneath the waves, forget that you existed.*' "

Malcolm brushed a tangle of salted black hair away from his eyes, watching Russ and the old man across the coffee table. "I've simplified it. Took out the excess you were complaining about. All the strophic settings, the traditional aria forms." He looked at Russ's father. William

Kent was silent, nervously fingering the carved handle of his cane. Malcolm said, "Any comments? Complaints? Russ?"

This had been the second meeting, two weeks earlier at his father's house.

"It's fine," Russ told him. "Really, right now I'm only interested in the broad shape. We can talk about changes once I start sketching."

"Can I see it?" William Kent lifted a hand from his cane.

Malcolm was hunched over the stack of pages, blunt fingers lightly tapping the edges into alignment. "Let me read to you, Mister Kent."

Malcolm wore faded jeans and a sweatshirt torn at the neck. His hair was almost as shaggy as it had been in college, black salted with gray, and he'd begun growing a beard. "Affecting the Nemo look," he'd said to Russ's father, as he stepped through the front door.

"Please tell me," William Kent asked patiently, "whether you have a character refer to him as 'doomy, dreamy Nemo'?"

Malcolm grinned. "You don't think I would, do you?"

"I'm not quite sure with you, Malcolm."

"Maybe an early draft. I think I had Aronnax saying it."

"But Aronnax is too prosaic, too astounded with the mechanical wonder of it all." The old man placed both hands, once again, on the horsehead cane. "And it's an awful line." The fingertips of his right hand were smooth, while those of his left were thickly calloused: the stripes of a career violinist. "You're capable of brilliance, Malcolm, as much as I hate to admit it. Your second novel was compact and clever—clever in a good way. And you've always respected Verne, haven't you, since your college days. That's an extremely positive attribute. Now think back to those times. And think *simply*."

Malcolm countered: "Aren't operas supposed to go too far?"

William Kent shook his head, looking down. "I've read my share of Verne, and he never goes quite far enough. You'll just be compensating. Give us a *normal* sort of excess. As for the ending, I wouldn't suggest you wander very far from it."

"You're right, Mister Kent." Malcolm grinned again. "You're right. I'll make sure it's . . . economical. I just get . . . carried away with my Nemo, I guess."

Russ looked down at the notebook.

He'd listed some scores for Ellie to get him, for inspiration.

Stravinsky: *Persephone*
Knussen: *Where the Wild Things Are*
Busoni: *Doktor Faust*
Catan: *Rappaccini's Daughter*
Weir: *Blonde Eckbert*
Reimann: *Lear*

His father said, "I'd like to know your definition of economical, Malcolm."

"A light touch, word-wise, Mister Kent. No long arias or airs. Nothing to stop the drama. No sea shanties for Ned Land. Most of the glory will go to Russ and his chromatic chords, though I get the feeling the folks in Santa Fe want a real showstopper in the third act. You know, blood and flailing tentacles."

"I warned them today." William Kent raised his eyebrows in the wake of those gently-spoken words. "*Nemo* offers a chance for melodrama, in the truest sense." He smiled at his son. His eyes were a flat gray, but took on a blue, youthful fire whenever he played the violin. "I told Bert, *Russell won't double the pitches on any account.*"

"What if I want to?" Russ asked.

"As long as they're not expecting it, we don't care. I told them, the single concession we'll make is to put some female voices into it, but only because Russell was planning to already. It certainly makes sense to us from a business point of view. Opera companies love their sopranos. And you want to get a second production, remember. An opera isn't really alive until till then."

Malcolm nodded, tapping the pages. "I'll work on ideas. Russ mentioned putting some women in the crew. More spear carriers, right? Since it's Verne, maybe spear carriers from the center of the earth? A bout of mistaken identity? Amnesia? I'm being facetious."

"Just be *subtle*, Malcolm."

"There's subtlety in the new draft. Prosody, too."

"But we can't read it?"

"Let me read it to you. What part would you like to hear?"

Russ looked up from his notebook. "How does it end?"

Malcolm scratched his beard. "I'll read you the last few pages, then."

"I don't want the last pages. I want the *ending*. The final words. How do you finish it?"

"Simply," Malcolm said.

William Kent shook his head. "Read us the words."

"Without context, they lose their charge. You can't just blurt them out."

"Don't blurt," William Kent said, with a mischievous smile. "Sing!"

Malcolm lifted the stack and slid out the last sheet. "Well, Mister Kent, they're not sung. They're spoken. Just like the opening. This is out of context, you understand?" Malcolm looked at William Kent, who nodded. He cleared his throat. "We end with Nemo's final words, do you remember them? 'Enough, enough.' A whisper. 'Enough, enough,' fading off. Silence."

NEMO

AN OPERA LIBRETTO

ACT ONE: MAELSTROM

[We open on a dark stage. As the words are spoken (not sung!), a pale green light blossoms on a scrim across stage front, while behind it, made into a ghostly figure, we see PROFESSOR ARONNAX, prone on some jutting rock. The light reaches a peak in the middle of his speech, to slowly die to darkness at the end, for the overture.]

ARONNAX (spoken)

These words he said:
 "The world began with the sea,
 And will end with the sea
 There reigns tranquility, supreme.
 For the sea does not belong to tyrants.
 Thirty feet below their power ceases,
 Dies out, their domination
 Disappears.
 Ah, Sieur, one must live within the ocean.
 Only there have I no masters!

There I am free!"
His motto, fixed to the Nautilus hull
In raised bronze letters:
MOBILIS IN MOBILI.
Mobile within the Mobile Element.
(beat)
The year 1866 was marked by a strange event.
A sighting at sea of an enormous creature
A monster, quick and merciless.
Hunting the ships of Man.

MUSIC BEGINS.

It would begin with the double bass. Four of them—perhaps six—in a staggered opening, mostly from E. A muddy sound, more felt than heard.

He knew the first measure. Yet he lingered.

The basses break free of that lowest note, back and forth in a glacial tremolo that would unwind in four or six separate voices, crossing and recrossing, articulating a sluggish rise and fall, portamento, as overture.

He focused on the top of the oblong page, on the first stave, his eyes finding hierarchy in the five lines. A moment later, with quick flicks of his pencil, he drew a bass clef, then the accidentals.

He held the sound in his ear, the compass points of rise and fall.

Portamento, like a sea wave. Dense, lying close to the stage, to draw down the ear then startle with scurries of brass.

As he placed his pencil above E—an octave higher than the instruments would sound—the stave under his pencil was now to some extent his ear, and the lines were the steps of the diatonic scale. He dabbed the first note, timbre and tone remaining as his pencil came away, and dabbed a second, joined it with a third.

"Russ, you have a call."

For an instant, her voice was in deep strings, part of the pencil sketch.

"You want to take it up here?"

He looked at the black rotary phone in the corner of his desk. The ringer must be off. "Sure. Thank you."

"Give me a sec. I'll hang up downstairs." She left the room, shutting the door quietly.

Somewhat dazed from the interruption, he glanced at the score sheet, the complete measures, the cross-outs, eraser smudges.

He lifted the handset. "Hello?"

A click, as Megan hung up downstairs.

The morning fog had cleared, and the ocean lay sharp and gray to the horizon.

"Nemo here."

"Malcolm." Russ sat back in the chair. "How'd you track me down so soon? Ellie?"

"She refused. Didn't want to tell me till tomorrow. So I dialed Oregon information, got the number for your visitor's center. Peggy Chalmers. Quite pleasant, cheerful voice anyway. I hope I didn't wake you. It's oh, one-fifteen there, huh?"

He turned to the fold-up clock. "Twenty to ten. My clock must have stopped."

"Ominous."

"Not really, it's a wind-up. I think I knocked it too hard."

How long *had* he been working?

He thought of the walk he needed to take.

"Listen, I don't want to interrupt your work, but I thought I'd tell you I've stopped re-writing the old draft, and started *re-conceiving*. I actually dug up that Verne play I wrote at college, for inspiration. I'd like to send you some updated pages in a few days."

"Okay," Russ said, vaguely alarmed. "But remember, everything's rough right now."

"Sure. I've had a few more Vernian insights, is all. Listen, I'd like your address if you have it handy."

"They use PO boxes down here. I don't know the number. Just address it care of Megan Sumner, S-U-M-N-E-R, Evening, Oregon."

Malcolm said, "Quaint."

"I'll call you later with the number, but I think that should work."

"I'll send you some of this new draft when it's done."

Staring at the score sheet, at where he'd stopped, Russ said, "Right now I'm only concerning myself with general sketching."

"Of course, Russ! It's your party! Now I'll let you get back to work."

"Bye, Malcolm."
"Arrivederci."

Pencil in hand, he read over the sketch. The double bass in six long portamento lines, a seasick ostinato taken up by the cellos marked con sordini, divided and muted. A second subject of growling tubas and contrabassoons. Then the ostinato again, messily sketched, from cellos to violas to violins, the surface of the orchestra, more quiet, in eerie harmonics, to wake the piccolos in the last measure.

A three-note motif, marked *faint*, *shrill*, like the gulls outside.

It was complete enough, and far more detailed than he'd intended; or perhaps needed. In any case, it didn't beg more work.

Looking back at the clock, remembering only then that it had stopped, he decided he'd worked long enough.

It was time to take a walk.

He tucked his notebook and a pen into his breast pocket.

"You're missing a wonderful day," Megan said as he stepped out of the house. She sat on the top porch stair, cradling a book on her lap, and now she smiled. "You're on Peggy's social list. She just dropped by and told me I had to mention our Winter Gathering to you. It's this Saturday night. The big seasonal get-together at the Evening mansion, if you're not too busy."

Still thinking of the walk ahead, he said, "I'd love to." A breeze rushed in the evergreens, a vast sigh over the fainter surf. "I'm going to take a walk. What sights do you recommend?"

"Drop by the Warp and Weft, just round the corner on First. That's Bennie Dreerson's bookstore. He's one of my favorite people in town. Buy a book from Bennie and he'll be your friend for life!"

3
the warp and weft

The modest homes down Alder Street resisted the steep hill, their yards enclosed by low, leaning fences, with gardens of rustling rhododendron, morning glory and fern, pleasantly overgrown, decorated with driftwood, old glass bottles and glass fishing floats.

Trudging down the sidewalk, he listened to the rustling gardens and the breeze making the sound of the surf in the trees. Distant traffic, and gulls farther out, shrilly crying.

The sidewalk was buckled. The walk was hard on his knees, a perfect reason not to go all the way to the bluff. He might have to drive tomorrow, or the next day.

He stared down at his shoes, then beyond them.

Remembering Anna in the car—*"It's lovely,"* she'd said.

Remembering further back, earlier that day, up in Portland, where they'd visited the Bowers Music School so Anna could interview for a possible teaching job. The weather had been in the mid-seventies, warm for the coast, and the matron had warned them this wasn't the rule in weather. "I don't mind the rain," Anna had said.

"But what about Mister Kent?"

"Grew up on the northeast coast," he told her. "I'm used to it."

On the corner was a dilapidated gray Victorian. *Warp and Weft*, read the porch sign. He wondered whether he should meet Megan's friend, or continue on.

Inside the nearest window was a placard, *Open till we Close*, while beyond were dim shelves packed with books. It promised diversion. If he wished, he could meet Megan's friend and stay long enough to make a walk seem unwise. There were clouds in the north, and the sun might not last after all; it might rain. There would be time to visit the bluff tomorrow.

A dog barked, startling him. It stood tied to the porch that faced First Street, a white husky with cold blue eyes, peering through the posts. As Russ raised a hand in greeting, the dog began growling, settling the question for him—*onward*— when suddenly the door opened and a garrulous voice said, "Up, Ody! Move your butt!"

An old man with wild white hair stepped onto the porch. "Oh, you were bored, were you?" He tucked a sack under his arm, fumbled with the zipper of his down vest. "Keep your head, dog." The dog pulled against its chain, and the old man scowled, blinked irritably, then spat over the rail into the strip of grass. "Jump up and you'll make me fall down these stairs. Think it over." He bent down to free the chain, the wind whipping his hair.

"Get moving." He nudged the dog with his boot, then followed as it picked its way down to the sidewalk. "Home, Ody!" The dog trotted off downtown, tugging the old man behind him with a faint *clink-clink* of the chain on the sidewalk.

Russ watched them for a moment—the old man nearly stumbling into a rose planter, righting himself, and being led around the corner out of sight—then climbed the stairs. As he opened the door a tiny foghorn sounded, a piercing G that dropped half an octave. A blast of heat, smelling of old newspaper, cigar smoke and Mentholatum.

The sunlight didn't get much farther than the windows; the place was lit by a dozen or so library lamps, bronze fixtures shaded with green glass. To his left, bookcases faced the front of the store, interrupted by an overstuffed chair.

Down this central avenue of shelving, the front of a desk could be seen; a lamp lighting a vial of white flowers.

Russ called out, "Hello?"

In response, a chair scraped the floorboards. "Yes. I'm here."

The voice was a bland baritone.

Walking forward, Russ could see more of the desk: an antique cash register with $1.59 showing through a scratched window, an ashtray stubbed with two cigar butts, a block of cheese on a plate, and two tumblers, one half-full.

"A good afternoon to you."

Beyond the desk was a battered armchair, where a plump man sprawled. He wore a black cardigan that hugged his belly, and was bundled in a gray woolen scarf, a book on his lap. His face was rounded, a double chin, a flattened nose with expressive nostrils. His hair was thick and gray, and uncombed. His eyes were gleaming. "I thought I would let you look in peace, perhaps settle on an item, before announcing my presence." He set the book on a low table, then, with a grunt, pushed himself up, walking the single pace to a high stool behind the counter, where he sat. "I'm Bernard Dreerson," he said. His eyes were a pale blue; the left wandered slightly. "This is the Warp and Weft. And you must be the visitor."

"*A* visitor," Russ said.

"No, no, *the* visitor. The one staying at Megan's house. My dear friend Megan, who supplies me with flowers for my store." Dreerson nodded at the vial. "You're Russell Kent, the composer."

"Pleased to meet you, Mister Dreerson." Russ extended his hand.

Dreerson straightened up and gripped it firmly, gave it a shake and let go. "Call me Bernard, or Bernie, or Bennie, anything but 'Mister Dreerson.' And it *is* a pleasure to have you in town, Russell Kent. Though you don't quite sound as east coast as I expected."

Russ smiled. "I've been mostly away for fifteen years."

"Well, the mystery is somewhat clearer. Please, look around, buy something!" He lifted a butter knife. The smell of bourbon was quite intense. "Can I offer you some cheese?" Dreerson smiled amiably and set down the knife. "Then I hope I can offer you a book. My stock is bountiful and catholic. Please, look. Go ahead."

"Do you have *20,000 Leagues Under the Sea?*"

"Hmm. Captain Nemo? Look in Science Fiction, past Aberrant Psychology, to your left. Good luck."

At the bookseller's urging, Russ began to wander leftward down the central avenue. Film and Television, Maritime History, Aberrant Psychology. Had he missed it?

He backtracked. The section was small, several dozen well-thumbed paperbacks, and no Verne.

Russ continued on.

Remembering Anna in the car, and the aftermath of the visit to the

Bowers school. An hour south on 101. "Why'd I even bother going for the meeting?"

Though just a preliminary, the interview had gone well; or had seemed to go well. She'd have to fly out again in January, and afterward, back in the car, Russ had encouraged her. Not that he was entirely sure Portland was the best place to settle.

"Hmmm?" He had rolled down the window.

"I can tell you've decided on Boston."

"Nothing's been decided."

"You're always arguing for it, in little ways."

But she was the one who wanted an argument.

He tried saying nothing. The silence had stretched, and she shook her head, turned away. "What little ways?" he said, evenly. "What was the last way?"

"This morning. You were saying that you wanted to see your Dad more next year."

"I wasn't arguing to move there. Just to spend more time visiting."

"What's for me back on the east coast, Russ?"

It had been more than a year since she'd played the cello in concert, since the tendinitis, or perhaps carpal tunnel, had made her turn to teaching.

She had wiped blond curls from her eyes, and looked out her window.

"Well, nothing's been decided, Anna. Not till after January, when you fly back out. Right?"

She didn't respond.

Aware of battlements being raised, Russ focused on the road.

Some minutes later, in a clear but unobtrusive tone of voice, Dreerson called out, "I heard all about your arrival from the grapevine. Not that I'm a member. Well-placed sources, let's say. I was once a newspaperman here in town."

At a hardback titled *Sere Salmon*, Russ asked, "Was there ever enough news?"

"You'd be surprised. In a way, I'm still experiencing the effects of it. Do you realize you're the first viable customer I've had in a week, not counting my friend Tom Carver, who just left?"

"You probably do better during the summer."

"Not much better. Most find our town by accident, and then they want a beach, or a hotel. They don't stay long."

Russ recalled Anna's excitement at coming upon First Street. *Let's stop, Russ.*

"How's browsing?" Dreerson asked cheerfully. "Any luck with the Verne?"

"None."

"Do you have any other particular interests? Perhaps I could point you to them."

Russ mentioned music, though he had no urge to read such books.

"Over here, Mister Kent, this way."

He walked back along the avenue until the drunken bookseller was revealed.

"Over here, on the seaward side of the store." Dreerson gestured with an empty tumbler. "Take your time." He smiled and gently shook his head. "I'd like to sell a book to you. I won't lie and pretend this doesn't interest me."

Russ turned right at the corner and walked down the front aisle, toward the overstuffed chair.

"Past the chair," Dreerson said. "In the final cul-de-sac to your right. Watch out for the traps."

"The what?" Russ stopped, gazing down at the sunlit carpet. In the first alcove, atop a threadbare fleur-de-lis, was a mousetrap baited with bright yellow cheese.

Dreerson appeared behind him. "We're having a rat problem" he said, and chuckled. "Rats in a cheese town! Don't want them chewing up my books, but they have my sympathies when it comes to our cheese, actually. Have you ever tasted Evening cheese?"

"Not yet," Russ said. "But you offered . . ."

"No, I offered you the good stuff. Tillamook cheese, from farther up the coast, where the motto is 'tree, cheese and ocean breeze.' It's the only brand I'll eat. Any opportunity to upset Burle and the others . . . but don't let me keep you from browsing. Go ahead, peruse, but watch out for the traps."

Russ stepped around the chair, then turned a corner down a short aisle, then another corner, reading titles, noting textures, not caring whether he would find books about music or not. The section didn't matter; any would do. In the filtered daylight, he found himself calmed by these colorful and dusty spines.

Horse Sense at Dawn. The Calhoun Cherry Cereal Story. Give Me Something for the End of the World. Perhaps his selection was the reason Dreerson had so few shoppers.

How many people would want to buy *Dinosaurs of the Oregon Interior*?

He pulled the small hardback from the shelf. The jacket was frayed at the edges, but the cover painting was still luridly colorful. A gold brontosaurus stood before a thicket of vivid evergreens, clenching a stripped tree trunk in its maw. A subtitle in tall letters read: "The amazing alternate history of the state! by Dr. Lewis Sensamall."

He opened the cover, which creaked faintly, and found a price written in pencil along the upper corner, $3.95, with the initials BD underneath. He was about to return it, about to slip it between *Backyard Barbecue for All Your Neighbors!* and *Simplified Roman Architecture*, when he opened it again, curious to see if there were more illustrations.

There were. Facing the title page (with both the subheading and author's name printed in red ink) was a painting by the same artist: a hunchbacked dinosaur stood on an otherwise empty beach, against a primeval sun. As he flipped through the book about ten of these paintings were revealed. Dinosaurs and evergreens, dinosaurs and swamps, and in those primordial illustrations seemed to be born a whistle that rose to a shriek.

He looked up, listened, and recognized a teapot. Dreerson's stool scraped the floor and the whistle died.

For three dollars and ninety-five cents, he thought, *I'll make him my friend for life.*

Island by Aldous Huxley. *How to Freeze Dry Foods. Encyclopedia of Donnelly.* The entire section was crazy, a mishmash. He found a label marked *hesperus* on top.

Hesperus, he remembered: the *Evening Star*.

He was about to continue on when he spotted a trap several inches from his shoe. From here the cheese looked dark green. He decided to take this as a warning: buy the book and continue his walk.

At the front desk he found Dreerson clutching a bronze pot, pouring hot water into his tumbler. The air became sharp with the scent of bourbon and instant coffee. Resting his elbow on the desk, Dreerson stirred the stuff with the butter knife. He looked up. "Ah, yes. I have a nerve in my neck that begins to twinge when a purchase is imminent. It's never been wrong."

"I'd like to buy this." Russ set the book on the counter.

Dreerson straightened, and lifted the book carefully. "What made you choose this one?" He deftly peeked at the price.

"Dinosaur."

"Of course." Dreerson turned to the cash register and pushed three stiff buttons with his thumb. Leaning forward, he gripped the crank and gave it a turn. Fifty-nine cents slipped down while 3.95 jutted up, then the drawer popped out with a broken-spring sound and a rattle of coins.

Russ pulled a five dollar bill from his wallet and passed it into Dreerson's waiting hand.

Dreerson took it, retrieved the change and passed back one dollar and a nickel. He watched as Russ put away his wallet, his left eye slightly wandering.

"Mister Russell Kent, would you forgive an old man a crass question?"

"Sure." Russ smiled amiably.

"Well, from the grapevine comes word—surely not to be trusted—that you're in town for reasons other than writing an opera. That you might, in fact, be researching a legal proceeding against the town, due to your wife's tragic accident."

Surprised, Russ shook his head. "No," he said, adding, "No, that's not true. I'm here to work."

Dreerson almost looked disappointed. "Another rumor says that you are perhaps intending to open an artistic colony one day, here in our lonely town by the sea."

"Yeah." Russ laughed. "Maybe. Who knows. It's a charming town."

Dreerson scratched his rounded chin. "Yes, a charming sea, a charming sky, a charming bit of land. It's only some of the people who tend to grate on one's nerves. I could write you a list of people to avoid, but I'm afraid that I wouldn't be believed. It's something that must be experienced." He sipped some coffee, then grimaced.

"Megan mentioned something about a party this Saturday."

"Yes. The Winter Gathering, yes. If I can rid myself of this damned cold, I'll go." Dreerson sipped some coffee and made a face. "That's the reason for the scarf, you realize? And the firewater. Remedies I've found in my labyrinth of books."

He lifted the tumbler and gestured in an expansive, lingering arc.

Russ walked down First Street, the sack tucked inside his jacket and held there by his pocketed hands. When he left the store, Dreerson's foghorn had sounded again, the tones conjuring up Nemo's ocean, the deep, watery glissando of the waves.

He walked, aware of the task now at hand. Remembering that day, and retracing it. His eyes were drawn to the mansion atop the bluff. Unaware he was doing so, he slowed his pace to accommodate her own, as he had done so often when they held hands and walked and said nothing, or when, if the weather was cold, as it was now, she would link his arm with hers.

"Look at it!" she said as the town appeared, and her voice, mostly silent this last hour, startled him as much as the view.

Ahead, sunlight dazzled off the pavement, the storefronts and wrought-iron benches along Evening's main street. All of it was bright and active beneath the hillside of darker green.

"It's lovely! Queen Anne Revival. See?"

On the right, atop a seaside bluff, was an ornate mansion with a busy roofline and a tower.

"Yeah. Impressive."

They passed a barber shop, and a gas station with antique pumps. The town didn't seem the usual sort of tourist trap. And the traffic was sparse enough. Except for a small sign on 101, there was nothing to attract your average vacationers. Only those interested in mundane detours, like the Kents, not eager to arrive early at the motel in Blake Beach, or to allow tired arguments to return.

"Let's stop Russ," she said. "My legs could use a stretch."

"Sure."

Passing a pharmacy and a Laundromat, he admired the peeling paint, the pedestrians in blue jeans and T-shirts going about a day's work, old men on sidewalk stools.

He parked the car along the curb and shut off the engine. In the sudden silence he turned to her. She looked tired, a little heat-dazed. But she smiled. A good mood had returned, as suddenly as the town had appeared from out of the forest.

That morning he'd watched her sleeping, a flicker of motion under her eyelids as she tracked some dream. He'd been jealous of it, had wanted to share it, and upon waking her, had asked about it. "The sea," she'd whispered. "I can only remember the sea."

.   .   .

He met her at the back of the car and took her hand.

Anna shut her eyes, tilted her head against the breeze and allowed herself to be drawn forward. "Step," he said, and she followed him onto the curb and down the sidewalk, her thongs slapping the cement.

She wore a yellow cotton dress. As the wind surged, the fabric smoothed against her full hips and gently rounded breasts.

Her fingers loosened in his hand.

"Where's the ocean?"

"Past the bluff," he said, letting go. "We should walk the other way. South."

"I want to see the mansion. Look, there's the top of it over the trees."

Beyond the combination Chamber of Commerce/Visitor's Center they found a road leading up. A signpost read, *The Evening Mansion: Oregon Historical Landmark*, with the tour hours listed below.

"We've missed the last one, Anna."

She brushed blonde curls from her eyes. "Let's walk up. We can see it, at least."

"Grounds might be locked."

"You're so lazy. Listen, the ocean."

"We could drive up."

"The ocean's hidden behind this hill, but the hill ends farther on. See? There's an intersection. I bet the road goes down to the beach. We can walk down." Anna took his hand, pulled him forward. Smiling, Russ followed.

A street sign named it Oceanview—she read it excitedly before they turned the corner—and then the sea was revealed, between the bluff and a hillside of pine. Sunlight glittered close to shore, leaving the more distant ocean untouched, a teal blue that blended from water, to horizon, to sky. The road was a modest slope bordered with brown lawns and bungalows, ending in a cul-de-sac of curb. Beyond it, a stand of evergreens blocked from sight the breakers and the coastline.

As they walked down, he could sense Anna's impatience. Smiling, she tugged him forward. She might have run, if he weren't holding her hand.

At the bottom of the hill, an old man with sparse gray hair paused in the act of sweeping his porch. He looked up at Russ, giving him an amiable smile.

The air smelled of damp earth and the sea, interrupted by brief, startling interludes of flower.

They emerged on a narrow bluff. Madrona trees grew hunched against the wind and water, their orange bark curling and cracked. Morning glory covered the ground, narrow white blossoms and heart-shaped leaves. Ahead, the ocean unleashed long white combers toward the coast.

Her hand tightened on his, then let go.

Less than two yards away was the drop, down to basalt far below, curving out to a shingle with barnacled boulders and greenish-black puddles of polyps and seaweed. Farther out, the combers crashed into the rocks, throwing great sheets of water into the air. He felt it on the wind. Glancing at Anna, he saw the water gleaming in her hair.

She smiled, watching the sky. She seemed about to speak.

A sea gull had appeared from the south, soaring through the otherwise empty blue sky, and he watched with her the white flicker of its wings as it began to wheel above the water, gaining altitude in a dizzying spiral.

*o*ld crick

Standing at the edge of the bluff, he remembered her pointing at the gull, the sleeve of her summer dress rippling in the breeze, and her voice, amused and calm, speaking the last words that he never quite caught.

"Mister Kent!"

An old man was walking through the morning glory—the old man from the house, who'd been sweeping his porch that day. The wind tossed his sparse gray hair, pressed his dungarees against his narrow frame.

"Sorry for interruptin', Mister Kent." He stepped cautiously, as if he were treading the deck of a ship.

Russ said, "I . . . I can't remember your name. But you're the fellow . . ."

The old man stopped a yard away, shoved his hands into the pockets of his dungarees, then nodded. "I'm the witness. Saw you walkin' here, too. Same way as I saw you then. Looked up from my yard work and there you were." The man's teeth were oblong and yellowed; he offered a plaintive smile.

As the wind surged, Russ thought of the drop behind him. He stepped farther inland and clutched the book beneath his jacket. He couldn't recall the book's title, or the reason why he had bought it.

"I'm Charles Crick," the old man said, blinking against the wind. His eyes were a bleary blue. "Caretaker for the Evenin' mansion." He tilted his head to the left.

Russ looked up the bluff, to the mansion's upper floors, the chimneys and octagonal turret.

"I'd like to thank you," Russ said. "I wouldn't have made it that day, if you hadn't been there. And afterwards, with the sheriff."

"Mister Kent, you got my deepest sympathies. When I looked up from my sweepin' and saw the two of you walkin' by, I could tell you were in love. By the way you walked, you realize? You were in step."

Russ nodded, remembering the argument that had brought them to town.

The sun was level with his eyes, hidden behind clouds.

"I should've made more of an effort. To stop your sightseein'."

Russ shook his head.

"Can I offer you a warm drink over at the house, Mister Kent? I'm sort of semi-retired now and my son Pete does most of the work at the mansion."

"I . . . I don't think so." Russ realized that Crick probably couldn't hear him, so he turned, repeated himself and added, "I'm going to head back."

"Let me least give you a ride."

Russ looked beyond Crick at the evergreens. He recalled the solemn procession of Anna's stretcher to the ambulance, whose lights had glowed between the trunks.

"Thanks, but I need a walk, Mister Crick. Especially after visiting here. I didn't think I'd have the nerve."

"You approached it bravely, Mister Kent."

"Thank you."

While they walked back across the bluff, Crick was glancing over at Russ, peering up.

The old man cleared his throat and a few strides later said, haltingly, "Did anyone ever tell you, Mister Kent, that you look like Dylan Thomas the poet? With a beard, of course?"

"No." Branches rustled above their heads, and the ocean lost some of its fury, receding into a constant rush like the wind. Searching for something to say, he added, "Maybe if I were to shave, people would notice it."

"I'm a big fan of Mister Dylan Thomas. Some folks here in town figure I'm a uneducated man, seein' as how I'm just a general good hand when somethin's broke. But I've always been a reader. Always loved Mister Thomas's *A Child's Christmas in Wales*."

They stepped over the curb, onto the asphalt of Oceanview.

" 'When I was a boy, and there were Wolves in Wales,' " Crick said. "That's the way it goes. One of my favorites." Upon reaching his driveway the caretaker stopped. He shoved both hands into the pockets of his overalls, looked at Russ then looked away, as if casting about for words.

Condolences, Russ thought.

"I've heard, Mister Kent," Crick ventured, "that you're workin' on an opera of *20,000 Leagues Under the Sea.*" He smiled. "That was one of my favorite stories as a boy. Tried to interest my son Pete when he was younger. Anyways, I didn't stop with that single book. When I grew older I tried to read everythin' of Mister Verne's, so I fancy myself now as sort of a Verne *nut.* I've even read the hard-to-find ones. You ever heard of *Michael Strogoff?*"

"No, I haven't."

"That ain't a person, you know; it's one of his books. Not many people have read it, but I have. So I guess that's really why I snuck up on you. Saw you walkin' and thought I'd re-introduce myself and tell you 'bout my knowledge. In case you have any questions that need answerin'." His smile now blazed into a toothy grin.

"I appreciate it." Russ found his face numb from the wind. "You'd like the libretto I'm working with. A writer friend adapted the book. He's a Verne fan, too."

Crick raised a hand. "I wasn't meanin' to infer that you don't know what you're doin'. I was only suggestin' . . . if you needed any help." He wiped his nose with his thumb and nodded once more. "Well, it's been an honor to meet you again."

"Actually, Mister Crick . . . could I get a drink of water before I go?"

"Surely."

He drank two cups, sitting down at a table in Crick's small kitchen, while the old man spoke about the mansion, and all the damage done regularly by the ocean winds; fifteen minutes later, Russ bid him farewell. Halfway up Oceanview, with his thighs and calves aching from the climb, he half-wished he'd taken Crick up on his offer of a ride. But he needed some more time. It was a duty, of sorts, to remember; to say goodbye at last. Then back to Malcolm's libretto and the dream music, to push against the silence where the notes had stopped.

Beneath our boots as we slog through forest, dinosaurs wait. Beneath our glorious spruce, Silurian glories slumber in bedrock. Beneath our very homes lie the bones of ectotherms. In this land that was once the sea, bones of the ancient air-breathers have been found. Did they lose their way along the shore? Did they like lemmings march off the edge of a cliff, great brontosaurs tumbling down into the surf, one by one by one? Or were the textbooks wrong, and your house, which is above the sea, has always been above the sea? Did the Ordovician, the Silurian, the Cambrian, the Jurassic, the Age of Chivalry and the Age of Roosevelt, all walk upon the same stage? Did the world fool the scientists, and offer up only to those who truly looked, the bony evidence?

Listen as I tell you what I found. . . .

After dinner, there came a tentative knock upon his bedroom door.

He was lying on the bed, with only the desk lamp on, reading his book. "Come in."

Megan opened the door. "You have a visitor, Russ." Her voice was amused.

He set *Dinosaurs of the Oregon Interior* upon the bedside table, next to the broken alarm clock and the lamp, then pushed himself up so he sat on the edge of the bed. His lower back and legs ached from the walk.

Megan led in Charles Crick. The caretaker's hair was combed back. He wore dungarees over a white dress shirt buttoned to the collar, and a slightly nervous smile.

Russ stood. "Hello, Mister Crick."

The visitor looked shyly about, then nodded at Russ. "Evenin', sir."

Megan said, "I didn't know you two were friends."

"Met at the bluff, Miss Sumner." Crick gazed at the libretto and score sheet laid out on the desk.

"I brought you a present." The old man held something dark, shaped like a bristling rock. He lifted it carefully.

Russ hesitated taking hold. It was some kind of fish, round and puffy, covered with spines, with paper-thin fins sprouting from the sides and a mouth ending in a frozen pucker. The scales were mottled blue and purple.

"A hycopathius, Mister Kent. Dried out. Quite harmless. The spines ain't sharp."

Russ presented his open palms. The fish weighed only a few ounces.

"It's a rare fish, a favorite of our town. Nearly our mascot. You can see it don't have eyes."

It didn't. Just the wide mouth, vaguely grinning. The scales had the texture of rice paper.

"I was thinkin' it might inspire you, sir."

Russ studied the spines along the arch of the back, the fins resting lightly against his palm. "Thanks. It's inspiring me already."

"You're welcome, Mister Kent."

Again, Crick looked over at the desk, while Russ set the fish atop the bedside table. The lamp lit up the scales.

"Is that, sir, your opera?" Crick leaned forward from where he stood, peering at the oblong paper covered with dots and slashes, minutely-lettered words.

"A sketch," Russ said. "Mostly the vocal line and a few instruments."

"And how are you likin' the words?"

"Malcolm's done a pretty good job."

Crick seemed to want to approach the desk, but he stayed where he was, looking from the music, to Russ, then to the fish.

Megan asked, "Could I offer you something to drink, Charles?"

Crick shook his head. He peered at the clock. "I can see it's gettin' close to ten. Later than I thought. I gotta get on home." He nodded, then waved, and the gesture reminded Russ of a benediction. "Hope you enjoy it, Mister Kent. Hope it adds somethin' to your opera."

The old man turned and said to Megan, "Got to see what the boy is doin' with his chores. The wind does a lot of damage to that old mansion. Sometimes folks don't appreciate the job we do."

"You know that's not true, Charles. I think they do."

"See you later, Mister Kent."

"Goodbye." Russ added, "Thanks for our talk today, Mister Crick."

Megan was studying Russ. She looked as if she wanted to say something, but then the old man was pushing past her and she followed.

Before closing the door she mouthed a goodbye to Russ.

He listened to them walk downstairs, heard muffled words of farewell below, and the front door opening.

He turned to the fish. He sat on the edge of the bed and studied it, recalling his dream of the ocean hillside, the endless windows. He tried to fix the clock, knocking it with his knuckle, winding it, shaking it, then gave up.

Later, when he turned out the lamp, the last thing he saw was the fish's blind, ridiculous snout.

(Around the Captain, the crew clambers over the bristling backswept fins, and the glistening armored scales that seem more fish than ship. Our castaways huddle, shivering.)

NEMO (calmly, coldly):

 I could leave you all
 On the watery deck
Russ leaned over the libretto, pencil in hand.
He crossed out *all*.
 I could leave you ~~all~~
 On the watery deck
 (Nemo's voice is colder still).
 Dive down
 Beneath the crashing waves
 Forget you ever existed!

As he read, trying to parse it out, he reminded himself that this was only a sketch, that he shouldn't linger too much over details but push onward. He circled *you ever*, certain the lines could be better.

Russ had already thrown out the first five pages of libretto—Ned Land, Professor Aronnax and his assistant Conseil boarding a frigate to hunt the monster.

Nemo would open with the aftermath of the sinking. In the waves—the cellos, violas, violins, played *con sordini*. Victims foundering in the water, calling out. Then the *Nautilus* rising to flurries of contrabassoon, trombone glissandi, and tuned percussion.

 Dive down

Beneath the waves

Forget you ever existed!

He'd jumped ahead to this, Nemo's entrance.

The Captain sings in calm, cold tones, *sostenuto*, over murmurings in the brass and strings that boil up as he threatens them. With a returning motif of trailing diatonic seconds—a seagull, in the piccolos.

He crossed out *beneath the waves*. Wrote a question mark, and ASK MALCOLM: REWRITE. EXPAND?

He straightened in the chair, set down the pencil.

In the notebook he'd written *Reign of the Vertical*.

It was a phrase from *20,000 Leagues*. To Verne it meant the underwater world, of sea flora growing upwards in the current. But to Russ it suggested dense yet transparent harmonies, in many layers. A complete immersion. And in this different element, a different musical scale to some extent—not the normal half-tone and whole-tone steps, but *quarter* tones in the strings, articulated beyond the glissandi. Queasy, seasick. For the underwater scenes, a density like something out of Aribert Reimann's *Lear*; though often hazy, in upper partials. Here, in the aftermath of Nemo's aria, Russ could use it behind Nemo's voice.

I could put you all

On the watery deck

He read the line and wrote a question mark beside *watery*.

He set the libretto next to his cold coffee, picked up his pencil and returned to the sketch, the troublesome lines. Scratching out what was there and drawing an arrow down to an unused stave, writing *Take Two* beside it. He drew an alto clef—a quick backward C. Listening to the idea, the possible curves and angles the words might follow, he dabbed the first note, then—his pencil point hovered a few millimeters above the page—a second, a third, setting aside all worries about the libretto, about projection, tessitura, balancing the singer with the orchestra, making the texture heard in the hall.

Just a sketch.

Nearly a page later, his hand cramping, he stopped.

He set down the pencil. The side of his second finger held the impression of the pencil. He rubbed it, aware of empty stave lines waiting beyond that last note. Resisting it.

Looking up from the page, he felt dazed by the silent room. Outside, morning sunlight glinted off the ocean in varied yellow and steel; the sky was a deeper blue.

"Did I wake you?" Megan asked as he reached the bottom of the stairs.

"No." He turned left, into the rec room. He realized he was quite pleased to see her. "Good morning."

"Want some breakfast?"

"I woke up early. Around six. I had a big bowl of cereal then."

She sat on a stool behind the old Ping-Pong table. The sleeves of her denim shirt were rolled up and her hands were dirty. "You're a very quiet boarder, Russ."

"Except for pencil scratchings," he said, watching her eyes, intent on work. "Sometimes I swear under my breath."

She smiled.

Laid out on the table before her, in the light from the bay window, were unearthed flowers, wrapped in damp paper towels, beside bags of soil.

She lifted a bag and shook several inches into a green plastic pot, then dug a cavity in the soil, unwrapped a flower from its paper towel and buried the root. She was methodic and careful, consumed in the task, and only when the yellow bud stood upright did she seem to remember he was there. "These are refugees from my garden," she said. "A winter storm has been predicted, so I'm bringing my favorites inside. Where do you think I should put them?"

"I'd like one in my room." He sat on the stool, propped his socked feet on the rung. He liked the idea of a winter storm.

"To keep the fish company," she said, unwrapping the second flower. "I didn't even hear you moving around upstairs. I think composers should be required to sing and bang away on a piano." She studied the flower for a moment, tipping it toward the light. "So how's it going?"

"I'm writing a vivid first draft." He added. "More detailed, more . . . illustrative than usual."

"Like what?"

He told her about the underwater scene he'd written. How he'd begun thinking of a percussive motif for the *Nautilus*'s engine, with celesta, vibraphone, cimbalon, as well as wood blocks and untuned gongs, against the sea-wave portamento in the strings.

"I think it's the view," he said, smiling. "It's *over-inspiring* me."

"But that's the sort of thing you need for an opera, right?"

He nodded. "I hope so."

"I've been to one. Back in Washington, before college. That must have been, what, the mid-seventies? Seventy-six or -seven. It was one of the Ring operas. Can't remember the name."

Russ leaned forward, elbows on his knees. "Horned helms? Dwarves?"

"Yeah. The whole nine yards."

"Flying horses?"

"Yeah, I remember horses. And that famous bit of music." She hummed the first notes of *Ride of the Valkyries*.

"You went to *Die Walküre*," he said.

"That was it. My parents had to *drag* me. I'm embarrassed to say it now." She tamped the soil around the transplanted flower, then regarded it, revolving the pot. "They thought they could force culture down my throat, before I left for college." She seemed to share a smile with herself. "The experience stayed with me. It was captivating, and ridiculous somehow. Bravo for my parents."

"Did you feel enveloped by it?"

"Well, yeah. It seemed like we were there for days."

"Wagner worked toward an ideal," Russ said. "It was called, if you're ready for it, *Gesamtkunstwerk*."

She repeated it, unwrapping another flower, this one with blue-specked yellow petals.

"It means *total work of art*. He envisioned opera as something that would encompass music, painting, acting, ballet, architecture, all the arts."

"There you go; that's what I saw."

"But even *Die Walküre* wasn't the ideal. I guess if you were to take it to its extreme, everyone would sing. Everything would be a piece of art. Every natural event would be planned for effect and absolute drama. There would be no audience. We would all be performers."

He looked to the end of the rec room and her open bedroom door. A mirrored dresser sat against the far wall, reflecting light from the bay window behind him.

"Guess what?" she asked, resting her hands on the table. "I've decided to stop playing the ignorant hostess and fess up." She paused. "I know about your last visit to town. I remembered your name when Peggy first called me."

He nodded, at a loss for words. He pretended to study the flower.

"I wasn't sure when to bring it up."

He smiled. "Now's a good time. Her name was Anna, and we were married for sixteen years."

"So you were visiting . . . where it happened?" Megan's tone was gentle. She looked down at her hands. "Out at the bluff? Where you met Old Crick?"

He nodded, and instead of answering, said, "Old Crick?"

"They've always called him that. There's Old Crick, and there's his son, who's twenty-something, does most of the work at the mansion."

"Young Crick?"

"Exactly."

"Evening has its share of colorful characters, doesn't it?"

Smiling, she poured a layer of soil into a new pot. "We're a small town. It's a rule." She unwrapped another flower. "You know . . ."

He was staring at the mirror again. Snapshots and cards were tucked into the edges, framing the silhouetted man who sat rigidly upon the stool, trying to look relaxed with one hand in his lap, one casually on the Ping-Pong table.

The image blurred, and began to shimmer.

He felt the first vibration through the stool, then through his hand. The stack of pots tipped, swayed and—as they both stepped off their stools—fell with a clatter onto the hardwood floor. "Tremblor," she said. The ground jolted, then the house settled around them.

"Shit," she whispered, walking around the edge of the table, arms outstretched, ready for another jolt. He followed her through the entry into the living room. At first he thought it had been spared, then noticed the tipped whale shelves, a scatter of decorations on the carpet.

She walked carefully to the fireplace and knelt beside the brass spars, fishhooks and a tiny ceramic whale.

"Let's hope it's over," he said, heart pounding.

"I used to love quakes when I was a kid."

Nothing lay broken on the kitchen floor; no windows were cracked. "You were lucky, Megan. But I wonder about the rest of the town."

In the next hour she phoned several people around town. Bernard Dreerson's store had a few collapsed shelves, and the diner had some broken dishes, but otherwise the effects had been minor.

"Have you had a lot of quakes out here?" he asked, helping her clean up knickknacks that had fallen onto the carpet in the living room.

"Nothing too disastrous. I guess we have to expect it. The Pacific Rim, all that."

She seemed uneasy, and jumped when the phone rang, smiling at Russ as she answered it.

"Hello?" She brushed loose bangs from her eyes. "Oh, hi Peggy. . . . Yes, we're fine."

Russ went into the kitchen and checked the cupboard; a mug had shattered on the floor. He threw the pieces into the garbage. When he returned to the living room Megan had hung up. She said, "Peggy Chalmers says 'hi.'"

"Was the Visitor's Center damaged?"

"Nope." Megan laughed. "She really called to make sure I remind you about the Winter Gathering. She mentioned it three times. So, remember: Saturday, at the mansion. Eight o'clock."

"Sure."

"Some folks really dress to the nines, but they allow the rest of us to wear nice informal clothes."

"I'll keep you company in my sports jacket."

"Now . . ." She searched the coffee table and end tables for her keys. "I have to help drive the kids home." She found her keychain on the carpet. "They weren't scared by the quake. They actually thought it was fun, but we're going to see them home anyway. I'll be back in a couple hours."

She left.

Russ fixed himself some coffee, carried it upstairs, and took his place in the diamond-cushion chair. For several minutes he studied the last sheet, and his notebook. *Reign of the Vertical.*

Beside it he now wrote *Descending. Quarter tone? Dense layers?*

He listened to the dense mostly descending strings, down and down. It might serve as a fanfare to a set piece: the underwater walk.

Then the floor swayed beneath his chair, and the desk beneath his hands.

Or rather—he sat still for a moment, listening—he had *imagined* it.

Nothing had moved.

Across the street, on the Italianate's porch, a woman in a brilliant blue and yellow pantsuit was watering a hanging flower basket. Her brunette hair was swept up into a perm, riffling now in a gust of wind. Megan had referred to her as Mrs. Nelson.

Dinosaurs of the Oregon Interior, he found himself thinking.

But nothing else out of the ordinary.

He'd imagined the room tilting like the deck of a ship at sea, silent beneath Nemo's voice.

A gift from this afternoon.

He stood up, unnerved, and happened to glance out the south-facing window.

Two men stood on the sidewalk below, gazing up at him.

Both wore dark coats, the hems flapping in the breeze, and black boots. One man was nearly bald except for a fringe of black hair that stirred behind him, while the other had thick blond curls, and their eyes and mouths were set in rounded faces. Though it was hard to judge a person's height from this angle, they seemed unusually short.

As Russ watched, the balding one spoke from the corner of his mouth, nodding to this upper floor. The other raised his eyebrows and appeared to reply.

They stood with their hands clasped in front of them. And their wide faces were smudged with dirt, or soot.

As if they'd crawled out from under a house collapsed by the quake.

Had they been injured? Were they surveying the houses for damage? If so, they did nothing but gaze at this window, sometimes speaking asides to one another.

Staring down, he began to feel as if they had seen him all along.

Dwarves, he thought. Dark dwarves.

Russ stepped back, found his shoes. While he struggled with them an explanation occurred. Perhaps they were here to offer condolences?

Had he seen them, during his first visit?

Forcing himself not to hurry (aware of a shiver down his neck, the wire of adrenalin), he walked out of his room, slowly walked down the stairs to the flagstone entry, opened the front door and stepped onto the porch.

A breeze rushed at him. Mrs. Nelson had gone inside. Upon reaching the side of the house, he looked without surprise at the deserted lawn and sidewalk.

Standing where they had stood, he gazed up at his own window, which reflected the bright clouds.

the winter gathering

I step outside and witness the ebb of the Jurassic age.

Notebook in hand, I watch the great oreganosaurus dip his head down toward the spruce. I see the tree's spire tilt toward him as he tugs, eager to dislodge the green needles that serve as his nourishment. Farther away, through a veil of hibiscus and rhododendron, a sartopatus gazes into a pond, peering perhaps at its reflection, or a fish—the bristling hycopathius or the slender, needle-nosed tark. Above, a pterodactyl glides serenely through the reddening Oregon sky.

Let us talk, fellows, about the great lost worlds of yore. Atlantis and Mu and Hyperboria. Let us talk of wonders invisible to the inquisitive eye of the "moderns." Wonders of a strange past lie beneath our feet, beneath our beds of foxglove and fern, beneath basalt and sandstone, beneath a glaze of winter snow. And who among us will dare dig through this veneer, will dig and scoop and brush away the accretion of time that is only an accretion of inches, and who will behold the mysteries?"

—*Dinosaurs of the Oregon Interior*

"It's rare to have an out-of-towner," Megan said, as they left the house on the eve of the Winter Gathering.

"I'm honored." He climbed up into the Suburban, made sure the edge of his tweed jacket was inside, then shut the door.

"I remember my first Gathering, back in the mid-eighties." In the dark, her black leather jacket, black dress and stockings were almost invisible, leaving a moonlit profile, lips parted, a glint of teeth, as she searched the key chain. "It was *quite* the big deal."

"Now you're making me nervous. Does everyone show up?"

"If they didn't, I'm sure Peggy would let them hear about it."

"Even a couple of little guys in dark coats?"

She laughed. "Yes, Russ, even your little guys in dark coats. If they live in Evening, they'll be at the Gathering tonight."

As they neared the top of the bluff, the Evening mansion lifted into view. First the octagonal tower—windows blazing—then the slender chimneys, the bustle of steep roofs and gables in green, white and yellow, with ranks of luminous windows shimmering like the paper lanterns strung below the eaves.

She had to drive twice around the gravel lot to find a space, and park. "Are we ready?"

"Ready."

Outside, they followed a picket fence to the yard, where kids in suits and dresses were swatting balloons beneath lanterns, beside a grand thistly tree that owned half the lawn. "That's our Korean pine," Megan said. "And everyone's so pleased with it. Just wait. Someone'll ask if you like it."

However large the tree, the mansion dwarfed it. It sprawled in three directions from the turret, with lanterns at various heights swinging in the breeze, casting light and shadow on the green walls and shingles cut to resemble long low ocean waves and crescent moons.

"Megan!" a girl called out.

"Hi!" Megan waved. "Is that Jana?"

"Yes!"

"Hi, Jana!"

Others waved as Russ and Megan crossed the grass to a yawning arc in the center of the trellised porch, called a *horseshoe entrance*. All the party's activity seemed concentrated within: elegant figures, laughter and excited voices, the bright *ting* of china plates, and music. A tuba, violins?

He followed her up the stairs, across the porch and through the open doors.

To his left, pillars framed a glowing green ballroom. Ahead, a hallway led farther into the mansion.

She said, "Let me drop this jacket off."

Watching the figures move past the ballroom entrance, he wondered if he'd under-dressed.

"Russ?"

He turned back, smiling.

"This way."

The hallway was carpeted in green, sided in green-striped wallpaper, lit by soft yellow lamps. Dozens of portraits lined the walls on either side.

"This is the Hall of Founders," she said.

"Capital letters?"

"You bet."

Framed in brass, each portrait was a sepia photograph, its subject caught in the sort of stiff, earnest pose common to the day. Nearly all the eyes were squinting, inquisitively, and following them down the hall.

Russ tried to imagine these people alive, circa 1900, blinking after the phosphorous exploded, standing up from their straight-backed chairs in living color.

"Halbert Chalmers." She pointed to a particularly portly gentleman. "He was Joseph's original partner. And that's Arnold Renworth, our first dentist and blacksmith. That one with the thick eyebrows is Clement Parker. His great-grandson—same name—runs the Laundromat. That's an Aberfoyle. I can't remember his first name. His great granddaughter Judith should be here tonight; she owns the diner. There's Barbara Crick. And the Clarksons. The Yarrows. Nells. The Ryans. Old man Burle, the first cheesemaker. Can you tell I used to work the tour when they were shorthanded?"

"Yes. You're very good."

"And here's Joe," she said.

The final portrait was larger than the others, set in an oval frame out of which radiated the silver rays of an idealized, surrounding sun. A plaque affixed to the frame read, "Joseph Evening, 1933."

Unlike the other photographs, this one had more space around its subject. The town patriarch stood in some hazy field. He wore a black waistcoat and flowing claret tie. His cheekbones were sharp, accentuated by a narrow white moustache and a beard whose silver strands were tapered to a precise point. But what dominated the image were the eyes, almond-shaped with white lashes, both expressive and reserved.

He recalled the modest version of this portrait hanging in Peggy Chalmers's office.

"Bennie Dreerson was a teenager when Joe Evening died," Megan said, continuing on. "Imagine that."

The Hall ended on a solarium, or an indoor patio. Tonight, it served as the coatroom. One wall was double-glass panes, looking onto a rock garden lit with lanterns, and the dark of the sea.

Megan removed her jacket, revealing the supple line of her waist above the black knee-high flounce skirt.

"You look lovely, Megan."

Searching for an empty coat hook, she smiled and said, "Thanks. But wait till you see some of the other dresses. This'll look like bargain basement." She finally hung her jacket over a denim coat, then clasped her hands. "Okay. Are we still ready?"

"Ready as ever."

A girl in a white dress blocked the ballroom entrance. She offered up a fishbowl full of yellow pins.

"You have to take one!"

"Is it the new logo, Merilee?" Megan took two of the round pins, passing one to Russ.

The girl nodded. In the ballroom light, her hair shone green. "They made a thousand of them!"

Russ examined his. An inch in diameter, the pin was meant to resemble a loaf of cheese, with a wedge of black in the center and another eating into the right-hand side, forming a lower case "e."

Megan looked down and carefully pinned the yellow "e" to her left shoulder strap.

"It's cheese!" said Merilee.

"Very nice. I hope you're taking time to enjoy the Gathering, Merilee."

"I am. Bye!"

Russ pinned his to his lapel, then followed Megan into the ballroom.

Six crystal chandeliers, each stocked with green-tinted bulbs, filled the heights of the room with a watery glow. Women wearing long skirts and men in tuxedos danced in the center, or gathered along the edges of the jade-like floor. Children, equally groomed and attired, wandered politely among the appetizer tables.

"Their dresses are handed down from mother to daughter," Megan remarked. "To be worn only at the seasonal gatherings."

There was music. A violin, a viola, a clarinet and a tuba. What was this melody? After another phrase he recognized the largo from Dvorak's *Ninth Symphony, From the New World,* transcribed for this strange quartet.

"Everyone's here tonight," she said.

Evening Cheese Association, Founded 1917, read the banner stretched above the door. Each chandelier cast a refraction on the ceiling, a Catherine wheel of yellow light in the green.

Idly, he gazed about for any short men.

Then Megan was touching his arm, saying, "This is Russell Kent, the composer." He found himself being introduced to an elderly couple, both resplendent in white, the woman's dress decorated with hand-stitching in floral patterns along the neckline and the hem. Evie was her name. Russ didn't catch the gentleman's, but he resembled one of the portraits in the Hall of Founders: a narrow face, aquiline nose, bleary brown eyes, all very prominent as he nodded excitedly during the introduction.

Megan said, "He's in town to write an opera."

"Writing an opera! Hey-oh! Imagine that!" The gentleman licked his lips and vigorously shook Russ's hand. "Evie here can sing some, Mister Kent!"

"Arthur, shut up. Pleased to meet you, Mister Kent." His wife smiled graciously, revealing pearly dentures.

"And if you need a crooner, why I've been known to *out-Sinatra* Sinatra in my day."

Evie said, "I'm sure he doesn't want a crooner."

Arthur shushed her, softly patted her hand and led her off into the crowd. As if this were the proper signal, more people approached, reciting their names, familiar from the Hall of Founders, more Aberfoyles and Yarrows and Ryans, exchanging tipsy smiles and clammy handshakes. Everyone wore a cheese pin, and Russ found his attention diverted trying to spot the yellow "e" on sleeves, on collars, pinned to the bottom hem of skirts.

Soon the Dvorak ended to vigorous applause, and the crowd around them dwindled until he and Megan were once more alone.

"Bennie's supposed to be here," she said, looking at the opposite side of the ballroom.

"Let's find him."

"Russell Kent! Megan!" Peggy Chalmers, wearing a sparkling silver dress with a yellow corsage at the shoulder, stepped out of the crowd. She looked heat-dazed, her plump cheeks aglow, auburn hair slightly mussed. An "e" pin was affixed to each shoulder strap.

"How wonderful, you both deciding to come." She pushed aside the one broad bang that tried to hide her eyes.

"Like I told you, Peggy."

"That's a beautiful dress, Megan." She touched Russ's arm. "And how's your opera?"

A bit surprised, he said, "It's going well, quite well," then fell easily into professional forecasting, speaking of the sketches he'd completed. "The town's inspiring me."

"Wonderful!" Peggy exclaimed. "And the weather must help, too! There's something about the ocean, something pure and vital, especially when it storms. Are you aware you're talking to one of the original members of our town's *Storm Watchers*?"

"A club?"

"Yes! We like to sit by a fire on a stormy night and tell stories. And sometimes, the next morning we'll scour the beach to see what the storm brought up. Glass floats, agates. Why, here's one of our number!"

Peggy grabbed at a woman walking past. She was an older woman with a long face, platinum hair in pleats, arranged as carefully as the "e" pin on her right shoulder strap, and the yellow corsage—an azalea bloom—on her left. Her face suddenly brightened with a yellowed smile. "Hello, Miss Peg!"

"Patsy! Have you met Mister Kent, our composer?"

"I've not had the pleasure!" The woman turned to Russ, offering a limp hand. "Patricia Burle-Clarkson, Mister Kent."

He gently shook it. "Russ," he said.

Perusing him up and down she said, "Would you mind me asking, what is your *alma mater*, Mister Kent?"

"You're oh so direct, Patricia!"

Russ smiled. "Well, mostly the New England Conservatory, and Richmond Central High School. And IRCAM—capital letters—just for a semester."

"IRCAM?" The woman's long face seemed to get longer. "Sounds like a government agency."

"It is indeed." He smiled.

Peggy stepped closer. "Russell—did you hear the music? Oh, they've stopped for a break, but did you hear it?"

"Yes. I loved it. An eclectic arrangement."

Megan was looking into the crowd around them. She adjusted her pin, brushed a hand along her skirt.

"It's Andrea Yarrow's group. I call them the Cheese League Orchestra. Oh, you really have to meet Andrea. She's a *marvelous* music teacher, and she's very excited to have a composer in town!"

"Pegs, chow for now!"

The woman—Patricia—wandered off into the crowd.

"Is Bennie here, Peggy?" Megan asked.

Peggy shrugged. "I wouldn't count on it. I haven't seen him. Listen . . ." She touched Megan's forearm. "You two have fun. Go get something to drink and stay awhile. Charles Crick has really outdone himself with the buffet table. The Hangtown Fry is delightful! Now, there's Charles, and I *must* corner him while he's still *all here*, if you understand."

She rushed off.

"Shall we, Megan?"

"Yeah."

He nearly took her hand as they walked together into the crowd.

"Peggy's a very animated woman," Russ said.

Megan laughed. "She's on her own wavelength, for sure. Especially during a town function."

A bust of Joseph Evening, sculpted from cheese, presided dourly over the abundant appetizers. As large as life, the face was similar to the portrait in the Hall of Founders, complete with eyes rendered with irises of Camembert, chiseled cheekbones, a tapered beard and top hat, its shoulders draped with leaf lettuce.

"Look at it," Megan said, grinning. "Yes, it's finally happened. I'm embarrassed for our town."

"It's impressive," he replied, noticing the cavities and depressions where cheese had been taken: curious indentations along the shoulders, the hat, with choppy half-circles along the brim.

"Now comes your real indoctrination, Russ." She handed him a plate.

"Are you going to wimp out and take some cookies, or go for Joe's head?"

"The hat looks tasty."

He found a knife, grasped the hat's brim (wary, for an instant, that he not block the old man's eyes), and sliced off a strip. Dropping it on his plate, he wondered who'd be the first to remove Joe's nose. Was that ever good etiquette?

"Why are you laughing? That's authentic Evening cheddar."

"Thanks."

"I'd like some of the Brie on his collar," she said, "but I'm afraid the whole thing is going to collapse. That's going to happen, you realize. Look at him. How can that neck support him?"

"There must be some sort of internal structure?" Russ offered. "Be brave."

"I'm wimping out." She picked up a plate and turned to the rest of the fare, to platters of applesauce cake, potato salad and beggar's pudding, silver tureens of cinnamon sauce, bottles of Oregon wine, a tray of nearly depleted ginger cookies, and more cheese arranged in layered ranks of red, yellow, white and orange.

"It's a tough choice," she said.

Russ ate some cheese, found it cheddary but plain, perhaps a bit too waxy. "So, are there any Evenings in attendance?"

"Huh?"

"Evenings? Relatives of Old Joe?"

She shook her head, mouth full. Then, after swallowing, she said, "The last direct descendant died a few years back. You should ask Bennie about it, he'd know."

On the other side of her, a young man set down a flat of champagne bottles. He was dressed casually in a white shirt with the sleeves rolled up to the elbows, jeans and tennis shoes. His blond hair was tied back, revealing a sharp jaw and acne-scarred cheeks. He worked quickly, grabbing the bottles by the neck and unloading them onto the table.

"How're things, Pete?" Megan asked.

"Hey," he replied, pulling a pocket knife from his pocket. He pried out the blade with his long, grimed fingers, then twirled each bottle against the edge and peeled away golden foil.

Megan said, "Hope you plan to take some time off, to enjoy the Gathering."

The young man, perhaps eighteen, perhaps twenty, laughed halfheartedly.

"This is Russell Kent, Peter. He's the composer who's renting a room at my house. Russ, this is Pete Crick."

Young Crick, Russ remembered. "Glad to meet you, Pete."

"Same here," said Pete.

"Oh, more champagne!" Peggy said, appearing behind him. "Peter, I was just telling your father that you're a *jewel*." She gave him a half hug.

Grinning uneasily, he finished the last bottle, wadded up the foil and after a sheepish "see you later" walked off into the crowd.

"Russ, you've got your cheese, now you *must* have some bubbly, both of you." Peggy lifted a bottle and gestured at Joseph Evening's head. "Terrific centerpiece, don't you think? We've been so lucky with the food and the music—oh, and the crowd is in such a great mood!" She twisted off the wire muzzle, then turned away from them. Grimacing, her cheeks puffed out, a wing of hair falling into her face, she pressed at the cap with both thumbs. *Pop!* the cap flew off, up toward the tall windows to bounce against the glass and fall down, down against the reflected ballroom and the night beyond.

As it struck the floor, the musicians began to play.

From the first shimmers of violin and cello, he knew it. Strauss's *Blue Danube*.

Peggy exclaimed, "Oh, my goodness!" Champagne foamed over the rim of the first glass. She set it down and wiped her hand on the tablecloth, then lifted the glass to Megan, poured one for Russ, and poured a third for herself.

"Strauss," Russ said.

Megan nodded. "A waltz. The Danube, right?"

"Joseph Evening always intended our town to be artistically strong," Peggy said. "Of course, he never wanted to attract *bohemians*." She spoke this last word in a hushed, half-amused tone. "We had a few try to come up here in the sixties, and had to discourage it. In a way, I guess you were one, weren't you Megan?"

"From a later generation," Megan said. She shared a glance with Russ, harbored a smile.

"Oh, and you worked out so beautifully. The kids just adore her, Russ. I don't know *what* we'd do without her!"

From the other side of the ballroom the tuba lumbered into the Danube's familiar theme, and almost simultaneously, in a squeak of dress shoes, a large man rushed up alongside Peggy and offered his hand.

"Peg! Let's take a whirl!"

Peggy jumped.

The man bowed, displaying his dark widow's peak and broad forehead.

"Bob! You scared me half to death!" She reasserted her cheeky grin and set down her drink. "After you *mon chere*!"

They walked off.

Megan wasn't hiding her smile anymore. Watching her, Russ felt an almost nostalgic impulse, mental pathways that hadn't been engaged since college, or junior high. "Megan?" he said, aware of his throat clenching. "How'd you like to dance?"

Looking into the crowd, she nodded. "Sure. It's almost like Vienna in here."

He took her glass, set both down, then they walked out among the dancers, her shoulder brushing his, to an open space. She stopped, turned and smiled. It was a slight, suddenly shy smile, as he stepped close, placed one hand above her hip, and with the other clasped her own outstretched hand. They hesitated, waiting for the top of the slow ¾ beat, then began to waltz. How long had it been since he'd done any dancing? Not since the early days with Anna, he was sure; and even then, not much.

They were careful at first, paying attention to the music, watching their feet—his brown shoes and her black flats—but within a half-dozen bars they fell into the stepping, swaying rhythm and allowed their attention to shift, gazing idly at the other dancers and the crowd.

"Who's Bob?" he asked, into her warm hair.

"Bob Burle, our Master Cheesemaker."

"Ah. The guy who carved the head."

"The very same." She laughed; he felt it under his hand.

She adjusted her hand on the small of his back while they turned, beneath the glorious chandeliers, and spindles of brighter green on the green floor.

"There's Bennie," she said.

"Where?"

"Back by the windows." She gestured with her chin, then guided him in a half-revolution. He could see flowing skirts and the crowd, the windows along the far wall, but couldn't see Dreerson. "Glad he showed up," Russ said nonetheless, while another part of his mind tracked the music, the bellicose tuba, wondering how long he would be allowed this guiltless pleasure.

Surely not for long. . . .

"Do you see any short, sooty men?" he asked.

She laughed. He could feel it beneath his hand.

"You're on your own there. And you're not keeping in proper step." They both looked down at the floor, their foreheads briefly touching.

"There is no proper step," he said.

"Hey-oh, Mister Kent!" Engaged in a frail embrace, Arthur and Evie see-sawed slowly past, smiling as they revolved out of sight.

Russ and Megan danced for a time without speaking, their gaze connecting, breaking away to watch the crowd. She recited the names of the other dancers. He was aware of her warm breath on his neck, aware of the subtle jasmine fragrance of her perfume. Soon he heard the approach of the final bars, and with a triple groan from the tuba, the orchestra expired into silence.

She let go his hand; he let go her waist.

"I'll be back," she said. "So why don't you look around for Bennie. Tell him to stay put." She pointed out the area near the windows where she had seen him, then walked off toward the entrance.

*t*he view from above

Interesting, he thought, standing nearly dumbstruck in the middle of the dance floor. *That was interesting.*

People passed by, nodded, smiled; some greeted him by name, though he had forgotten theirs. He forced himself to walk in the direction she'd pointed. Halfway there he caught a fleeting glimpse of the musicians through the crowd: three adults with violin, viola and clarinet, and sitting apart from them, a fat boy with a tuba.

Dreerson wasn't in sight near the windows. In fact, this was one of the few pockets of free space. He decided to stay for a bit and ponder the dance. Facing the window, he studied his reflection, while behind him the elegant figures milled against the green, faintly transposed over the dim features of the rock garden.

Had she been surprised? he wondered.

And what would happen next? A return to the formal relationship of landlady and tenant? Nothing at all?

Glancing leftward, he saw a familiar face, now gazing vaguely down at the garden, or at the reflection of his own tight black suit. It was Old Crick, looking over, eyes widening.

Russ raised his hand. "Mister Crick!"

Crick blinked. Then, grinning, he shuffled over. "Why . . . why here's the spittin' image of Dylan Thomas, the poet."

"You set up a great buffet."

Crick bowed, hands behind his back. "Can't claim the cheese head. Mister Burle carved that. Our Master Cheesemaker these last twenty years." Crick was trussed up in suspenders and cummerbund. His sparse hair was slicked back, a rose jutting from his lapel, next to an "e" pin. "Though it looks like old Joe's been in the sun too long, don't it?"

"It has to be difficult to work with, I'd imagine."

With a blare from the tuba, the music began again.

Crick nodded, shifted in place, then stared at the crowd.

Reflected in the window, couples moved onto the dance floor. Russ looked over at the entrance, for Megan.

Listening as the clarinet joined violin and cello, over the tuba outlining a two-four beat. Fourths and fifths. Americana. On the verge of being familiar.

The musicians were hidden behind tables and a sprawling arrangement of flowers, but their conductor was partly visible—a woman in her early thirties, with short red hair, conducting them with exaggerated lifts of a slender arm.

Simple Gifts was the music.

The clarinet outlined the familiar melody, against the eddying strings and softly blurting tuba.

Crick cleared his throat. "Mister Kent, you mentioned the other day you got some expert to handle the facts?"

Russ turned to the caretaker.

"You got someone that knows what he's doin'? On your opera?"

"Yeah," Russ said, half-listening to the music. "Malcolm Moore. He loves Verne. Actually, when Malcolm was in college he wrote, directed and starred in a one-man show, all about Jules Verne."

Crick looked doubtful. "Has he read *Mystery Island*?"

"I'm not sure. I think so."

"Can't claim to understand Nemo without reading *Mystery Island*. He's a prince, you know. You don't find that out in the first book."

"Actually, that's good info, Mister Crick." Russ looked to the entrance.

"And there's other books Verne wrote nobody thinks to read, but I read them. All of 'em that's in English, at least. Not every one of them's translated."

"Well, when Malcolm and I were in college, I remember he had a shelf in his dorm room packed with Jules Verne."

Would she see him here near the windows? Had she found Dreerson, and remained with him? "But I didn't know the other, about him being a prince."

Crick nodded with his entire upper body. "Well, I'm your man for Nemo facts. Happy as a clam to be a consultant."

From out of the crowd stepped a short, brawny man with an exuberant flush. "Hey, Charlie! Would you mind if I just went and grabbed some more soda pop? The tub's been empty for near a half hour!"

Russ appraised his messy brown hair, prominent eyebrows. No soot-covered man, here.

Crick nodded vaguely. "Where's my boy? He shoulda' seen to that."

The man shrugged.

Russ offered, "I saw Pete a while back, stocking champagne."

Crick didn't seem to hear. There was a puzzled look to his eyes. "Sure, go get it. But my son shoulda' seen to it."

Russ turned back to the window and watched the reflected crowd.

"Mister Crick, maybe you can help me find two men who were standing outside Megan's house. I don't know their names, but I can describe them. They were short, and heavy set. One had curly blond hair, the other had sparse black hair. They wore dark coats down to their knees, and boots."

Crick ran his palm lightly along his greased hair.

"I had the impression that maybe they'd been roughed up in the quake. Faces and hands were smudged with dirt, or soot."

"Soot, huh?" Crick seemed to mull it over, then raised his hand, waved to someone behind Russ.

The reflected Bernard Dreerson, carefully holding a full glass of wine, sidled through the crowd toward them. "Well, well. Charles. Russell Kent."

Russ turned. "Bernard."

"Hey, Bernie."

Dreerson wore a brown corduroy jacket over a striped shirt and paisley tie. The elbows of the jacket were patched, the sleeves frayed. The tie was tight enough to make his chin flap over the knot when he looked down at his wine.

Russ couldn't find an "e" pin.

"Didn't think you'd show, Bernie!"

"Not show? And miss this celebration of all things cheddar?" Dreerson glanced sideways at the crowd. "You've ingratiated yourself with the very best of our town, Russell, while surrounded by the very worst."

Crick grinned, shook his head.

"Charles has done a marvelous job keeping the mansion in shape, as well our favorite Korean Pine."

"Bernie, you know any short fat men in town?"

Dreerson took a small sip of wine. "Besides myself?"

"Shorter. How short, Mister Kent?"

"Shorter than both of you."

"Mister Kent here saw a couple short fat men standin' on his sidewalk."

"Goodness," said Dreerson.

"Well, I didn't have a good view. I was looking down from my windows, so I'm not sure about their size. They seemed short. Standing on the sidewalk gazing up at my windows, after the quake. Both in long dark coats. And dark pants and boots. Maybe they were uniforms. And their faces and hands were sooty."

"Hmmm. Well, look around." Dreerson gestured with his glass, which was still nearly full to the top. "There are several other short men among our towering ladies. Like Georgie Aberfoyle from the service station, there by the dance floor? He's rather short. Perhaps the soot was oil?"

"What about it, Mister Kent? Was it that guy just walked through here lookin' for soda?"

Russ shook his head. "Rounder. And shorter." Though exactly how short, he couldn't say. He'd only seen them for a moment. "Maybe they were out-of-towners."

Dreerson said, "It's a puzzle." He sipped his wine, almost chastely.

The three watched the crowd, and listened to the music, *Simple Gifts*, which was into its grandest iteration, note values doubling, promising a close.

Russ asked Dreerson, "Have you seen Megan?"

The bookseller shook his head. "Not since your dance. For heaven's sake, Russell, don't let us keep you if you want to find her."

"I'd get lost myself." He glanced at the entrance.

The music finished up to halfhearted applause, which Dreerson augmented by setting down his glass and clapping enthusiastically. Russ joined him at a more reasonable volume. Those nearby turned, then glanced away.

Dreerson smiled. "Look at them all, such a *colorful bunch*."

Peggy Chalmers was gliding ebulliently along the edge of the dance floor, with Patricia Burle-Clarkson at her elbow; both heads turned as they passed, and their eyes latched onto Dreerson, then away.

He raised his glass, and the index finger of his other hand. "One!" he shouted at their backs, over the din of china plates and conversation.

He shook his head. "Ah, Peggy is looking as lovely as ever. Patsy, too. And here's another. Hello," he said, nodding to an austere lady in a green dress, a yellow corsage at her shoulder. "First and only," he said, and saluted her retreating back.

Dreerson chuckled. "They think I only showed up for the free drinks."

Old Crick snorted. He was looking into the crowd, toward the dance floor, where Pete stood with a girl in a yellow dress, both laughing. Crick walked off toward them.

Dreerson sipped his wine. Swallowed, and smiled.

"So, Russell, how do you like the book?"

Russ nodded, and tried to remember it. "I've read the first few chapters. Very entertaining."

"Yes. Strange to think of all the wonders that lie beneath our Oregon soil, wouldn't you say?"

"Sure." Russ smiled.

"You know whom you should meet, Russell? Tom Carver, our local amateur archaeologist. Another of the worthies in our town, a man who has held his head high around the uninformed and narrow-minded folk. He lives a few blocks from the Weft."

"He here tonight?"

Dreerson shook his head. "As things stand, I'm here as a sort of fringe observer. Like the UN during a touchy international incident. I'm afraid Tom Carver is less impartial than myself. The feathers would fly, if he were to show up. Hello, Clement!"

A man with fiercely thick eyebrows was hurrying past, didn't stop to chat.

"Clement Parker, runs our Laundromat and lawn-supply store," Dreerson said, adding, "But you *would* like to meet Tom?"

"Yes. I would."

"How about tomorrow night? Do composers toil in the evening hours? Say, around seven P.M.?"

"Seven P.M. is off the clock."

"Excellent."

"Watch the tubs! That simple!"

Old Crick's voice rose above the din. Heads turned to where the elder Crick stood beneath the Cheese Association banner, angrily raising a fist at his son. "Service for the townsfolk! You keep an eye on things!"

The younger Crick stood his ground for a moment, then stormed off through the entrance; the older shook his head and followed, while those nearby, after whispers and murmurs, returned to their conversations.

"Hmmm." Dreerson's left eye was wandering, and he tipped back his head and sniffed the air. "Ah, beggars pudding. It calls to me. How about some honest Oregon fare, Russell?"

Anxious for Megan to return, he said, "Maybe later. I just had some cheese." Once more he scanned the crowd. Remembering the feel of her waist under his hand, as they moved.

"Would you do me the honor of accompanying me, then. Otherwise I'll have nobody to talk to." As they walked across the ballroom floor, a few people greeted Russ, but none spoke to Dreerson. "Repercussions of my journalistic days," he said over his shoulder.

Indeed, he might have been invisible.

"Oh, my," Dreerson said, as they reached the buffet table. "Look at him."

What remained of Joseph Evening resembled an abstract sculpture. Gone were the brows, the tapered beard, the top hat, with only sliding, jagged recollections of their structure.

Dreerson picked up a cracker. Using it like a spoon, he reached forward and plucked off what remained of the nose. "Now he's anonymous," he said, regarding his cracker. "Rendered faceless by the masses. There's a lesson in that, though I doubt anyone else here would agree."

"So, what happened in your journalist days?"

"My crimes, you mean?" Dreerson ate the cracker, and his attention settled on three women standing near the windows beyond the table. Each wore a long green dress, a yellow corsage at the shoulder.

"My crimes are of the fourth estate, of course," he said. "Reporting on various frauds and infelicities. A public works project rife with mismanagement. Refusing to kowtow to the local government."

From the trio came mention of Dreerson's name, amidst whispers, then giggles.

Dreerson raised his glass of wine, and sipped. Without looking at Russ, he said, "Excuse me, Russell. I'll return." He walked over to the women.

Russ watched Dreerson engage them in murmurous conversation. He glanced back to the corner windows: still clear, and she wasn't to be seen in the crowd.

The dancers were slowly waltzing to a transcription of *Beautiful Dreamer*.

Another older woman with a yellow corsage, and an "e" pin nearly hidden below it, hurried past, smiling at Russ.

He turned back to the buffet and asked himself if he was hungry. The rolls, the jam, desserts all looked good, as did most everything not made of cheese. But he decided to wait for Megan.

At the other end of the table, a large man was working his way along the fare. He wore a brilliantly white smock, white pants, polished black shoes. His head was bald and gleaming at the crown, with a receding hairline shaved to a charcoal shadow. And his head was slightly inclined, while his hands plucked.

Keeping an eye on the entrance, Russ watched as the man loaded his plate with slices of cheese and apples, a bowl of beggar's pudding, bread with jam, slices of meat, and more cheese, strawberries, salmon.

The chef, Russ presumed, or kitchen help in general, then noticed the chrome loops in his breast pocket, and the comb beside it.

A barber.

Russ looked back at Dreerson.

The ladies were arrayed in a half-circle in front of him, and speaking quietly, almost in unison, like some elegantly sinister chorus. One was Patricia Burle-Clarkson, her long face unsmiling as Dreerson rebutted, raising his arms in emphasis, the padded shoulders of his jacket jutting up level with his ears. His wine came dangerously close to spilling.

A stink of lanolin wafted over the scents of chicken and cheese.

"Four twenty-five," said a quiet, somewhat wheezy voice behind Russ. "Plus tax."

Russ turned.

The barber stood close by, a gleaming, meaty face and surprisingly tiny black eyes that now perused Russ's beard.

"Sorry?" Russ put on a smile, wanting to step back from the smell. "Didn't catch that."

"Four twenty-five for the cut. Free shave, too."

"Sounds reasonable," Russ said. "But I think I'll keep the beard."

The barber, still appraising, nodded. Then wheezed, "Have to go sooner or later." His eyes lingered on Russ's chin.

"Later, rather than sooner," Russ said.

The barber shrugged.

"Shit!" Something clanked on the table. Pete Crick was pushing a flat of soda cans farther onto the buffet table. "Sometimes he just don't know what he's sayin'."

His pony tail had come loose, hair falling forward as he arranged cola and creme soda. "How'd he like it if I just left, huh?"

"You're the only one running things here, Pete?"

"Not supposed to be, but I am." He wiped his hands on his jeans. "Pretty soon I might just take off."

Russ looked back, expecting to find the barber, but the barber was gone. Russ looked for a blob of white in the crowd, wondering if the barber had been a soot-covered man.

Too big, and too tall.

"Looks like Mister Dreerson's raising hell with the Storm Watchers again."

Russ turned to Dreerson and the chorus.

"They're Storm Watchers?" He remembered what Peggy had said about her group. These women didn't seem the sort to get up early, and wander the storm-blown beaches in search of agates and fishing floats.

Russ allowed a pause. "Pete, have you seen Megan? She left a while back."

"Yeah. She was in the atrium, with a couple of the teachers from school."

"Where's the atrium?"

"If you hold on a sec I'll show you."

When the soda was deployed, Pete took up the empty flat, gestured to Russ, and walked off toward the entrance.

Following, Russ noticed the red-haired woman, the band leader, watching him from the corner.

The Hall was mostly empty.

"Atrium's down by the coatroom," Pete said, leading him past the brass-framed portraits on the green-striped walls, the antique visages gazing, squinting, peering out.

"I get to dust all these," Pete said.

"Sounds like a good time."

"Oh yeah."

They walked to the end of the Hall, and the coatroom, where a couple was gathering up their belongings. The Atrium was off to the right. Like the coatroom, it had a glassed-in ceiling, entirely reflecting the room, except for some paper lanterns.

"Looks like they've moved on. Maybe the library upstairs."

Impatient—striving for patience—Russ said, "Where's that?"

"Come on. I got a shortcut."

Back down the Hall—Aberfoyle, Crick, Parker—then Pete suddenly stopped, approaching the green-striped wallpaper on the right.

He grinned at Russ, then slipped his hand into the wall. Something clicked: a latch camouflaged in green-striped wallpaper. A door popped free, six feet high and two feet wide. Cool air rushed out.

He pulled the door wide on darkness and stepped inside.

Turning sideways to fit, Russ followed, smelling oil and old rags.

At the opposite end hovered an oval of silvery light, like a low moon.

Its light trailed down the spiralling rail of a staircase.

"Spiral stairs?" Russ whispered.

"Yep," he said, shutting the door. The latch clicked. "They were popular back when this place was built. We have 'em all over town."

Barely aware of the racks and tables on either side of him, Russ walked to the staircase.

Each stair was die-cut with an ornate pattern of moons and stars and streaking comets. He touched the cold rail. He gazed up into the circle of dim light and saw the celestial pattern back-lit, a silhouette that multiplied as the staircase rose through the ceiling.

"This leads to the tower?"

"Sure does. I call this the maintenance level. My office. Library's two floors up." Grinning, Pete reached between brushes and bottles on a nearby shelf, feeling for something. He pulled out a bottle of beer. "Want one?"

Russ shook his head. While he walked the perimeter of rail, he heard the fizz of the bottle being opened, a dull plink as the cap hit the ground.

"Watch out!"

Russ stopped, looked back.

With his bottle, Pete gestured at the ground near the stairwell.

A mousetrap lay in wait a few inches from Russ's shoe, baited with cheese.

"They're all around. Guess I should've warned you." Pete sipped his beer, then walked over to Russ. Without a word, he grabbed the rail and began to climb. His tennis shoes rang out on the stairs as he turned and turned again, disappearing up.

Russ placed a shoe on the first stair. He gazed down at the moons and stars, then began following, jogging up with one hand on the rail.

The staircase swayed as he passed up through the oval of light, up through the sectioned floor and frayed carpet, into what might have been a sitting room, with parlor chairs and a fireplace in the distance. They continued, up and around, past another room of bare wood, with a table—perhaps a dining table, now entirely covered with sheets. Up and around, then shelves of books surrounded him, oil paintings of seascapes, a panelled door, a curtained window. The air was warmer, smelled of wood polish.

"Library," said Pete, pausing above. "Guess they're not here."

The muffled sounds of the party could be heard. Russ was ready to turn around, walk back—she must be back in the ballroom, perhaps waiting at the windows—when Pete said, "Hey, you want to see their clubhouse?"

"Whose?"

"Storm Watchers."

"In the tower?"

After a pause, Pete nodded. "We're almost there anyway."

"Sure."

Russ followed him up, over stairs polished to a dim gleam from the tread of many shoes.

Beyond the rail the library revolved past, dropping away. They emerged in a dark dining room. A tea service glittering below moonlit windows. He quickened his step, left this room behind for another, a narrow niche with a sofa and an antique radio, then two more rooms too dark to see.

Above him the stairs corkscrewed into a luminescent oval. Made of moonlight, he presumed, glowing through the windows of the tower. Round and round he climbed, dizzy, slowing down until the final sectioned floor rushed past and he found himself staring at a plush burgundy rug, at the knobbed foot of an old chair.

His heart pounded in his throat as he climbed the last spiral of stairs into the tower room.

All the walls had windows. Eight walls, eight windows. Directly ahead, lights twinkled on the hillside.

For some reason he'd expected to be facing the sea.

He became aware of shapes beneath the hill, easy chairs sitting in front of the panes. Stepping around the brass rail encircling the top of the stairs, he approached the chairs, moved between them (noting a pair of eyeglasses on the patterned cushion, binoculars hanging from the teak wing). Stepping up against the glass, he was afforded a dizzying view of the mansion below: steep roofs, brick chimneys looming above yard, and lanterns swinging.

He looked at the hill. He could make out Cheddar Street rising directly ahead, a band of gray up the hillside.

Though the Visitor's Center was hidden, there was the dark barbershop, and farther south, the grocery store beside Dreerson's shop. Above it, the evergreens hid most of the houses from view. He wasn't certain which might be Megan's, but picked out a light among the trees and imagined it was his window, and pictured the desk within that window, and the music on that desk.

Pete stood against the opposite windows.

Russ straightened. "I'm surprised the chairs aren't over there."

He moved between chairs and crossed the stretch of bare carpet. Here, the ocean glittered gray on black. The sky was wisped with cirrus clouds, draping the half-moon.

"They don't care about storms off the ocean," Pete said. He raised his bottle and gulped.

Town gossips, Russ presumed.

He stepped close to the window. To his right, below, were dark ever-greens, the bluff at the end of Oceanview.

He recognized the madrona trees.

Remembering Anna on the edge of the bluff, pointing at the gull, as it flew a perfect circle over the water, somewhere out there. He looked. There.

And felt very little. Dark, and the moonlit trees, the stretch of rock and water, and it was all simply what it was.

He pressed his forehead to the cold glass, and looked.

Dispassionately, he wondered if this proved the trip had served its purpose. This sense of distance, without the nightmare aura. More than the height of the tower and the remoteness of that stretch of rock, there in the dark.

Instead of nightmares he was thinking of Megan, and her jasmine per-fume.

He looked around at the elegantly worked wood sill and the plush car-pet underfoot, and Pete Crick, who in the half-shadows, staring out at the sea, might have been one of the portrait sitters in the Hall, come alive after the phosphorous exploded to climb up here and brood. The same stillness in the scene, as though in a picture frame. Years swinging like the paper lanterns.

Russ stepped back, blinked. Pete Crick was once more Pete Crick, gulping down the last of his beer, wiping his mouth with his sleeve.

"Ready to go?"

He looked back toward the spiral stairs. "Yeah.

Thanks, Pete."

"Any time, Mister Kent. And the party's almost done. Anyway, till next year."

He found her with Dreerson in the lobby. The bookseller was chatting, holding a now-empty glass, while she leaned down to tug at her black stocking. She wore her jacket, unzipped.

"I've sighted him!" Dreerson said loudly.

Megan straightened. She smiled, though not as brightly as he'd hoped.

"Pete was giving me a tour," he said.

"Sorry about losing you, Russ. I had to rescue Bennie from an argu-ment."

Dreerson chuckled. "Right when I had them where I wanted them."

Megan stretched her shoulders. "You both ready? Bennie?"

"Certainly, my dear. And thank you for the ride. The party has definitely peaked."

Russ followed them onto the porch, where some of the teenagers were gathered in the shadow of the trellis, smoking cigarettes. They nodded, waved. Megan said, "Bye."

The wind was cold and brisk.

During the drive, Dreerson reminded him of the appointment at Tom's the following night. "I'll call if the time won't work out for Tom, though I can practically guarantee it!" She pulled over at the corner of First and Alder. "Megan, you are an angel! Russell, see you tomorrow evening! Seven-thirty at the Weft!"

She was silent as she drove them up the hill, pulled into the driveway. As they parted in the entry, he upstairs to his room, she to hers, she said, "Did you enjoy it?"

"Yes, very much."

"I'll be out by eight, and back late tomorrow. I'll leave numbers where you can get in touch with me."

"Maybe see you late, then."

"Okay."

The next night, walking down Alder Street, he was walking into a fog from off the ocean. It haloed the lamps, dampened the sounds of surf and traffic, and rendered the houses as vague facades, decorated simply with fishing floats, netting and fern.

He might have been walking down the inclined stage of an immense theater.

A bad day at work, he decided.

Russ slipped his hands into his coat pockets.

Megan had been up before him. She'd left a note saying she was teaching at the school today and afterwards going to Claire's—one of the older ladies he'd met at the Gathering. *Back late, after eleven*, it read. *Sandwiches and soup to heat in the fridge.*

Russ had tried to stay away from circling thoughts of the Gathering, and the waltz with Megan, how pleasant that had been. The waltz, and whether things had soured toward the end, and whether they had any significance at all.

All of it was incidental, *should* be incidental. Work on the opera was the important thing.

And work hadn't gone well. Even with all the inspired settings of the past few days, Malcolm's adaptation—or the source material itself—had seemed weak today. Too much talk, and too much Aronnax and his lackey Conseil; not enough Nemo.

Russ was ready to accept it was his mood, not the libretto. He knew enough about the process to take the day off. Alone in the house, and later walking along Seventh, to Cheddar, down to Sixth and back home, he'd brooded on his choice of Malcolm. His father had argued against it, but Russ had insisted, and still believed, that Malcolm brought to the project something the other nominees couldn't: a genuine enthusiasm for Verne, a respect for old-fashioned storytelling, and no preconceived notions about opera.

In any case, it was only the first draft. The real test would begin after the sketches, after Evening. Would Malcolm be able to supply scenes, lines, words, on demand?

He remembered his father saying, *I know other writers, don't I?*

As he neared the bottom of the hill the Warp and Weft materialized above the sidewalk, prominent at stage right. Its lighted windows were burnished by the fog, framing the figure of Bernard Dreerson adrift among the multicolored books like an aquarium fish among its coral.

"I love the fog," Dreerson said, leading Russ down the stairs to the side-walk below. "What we need is a real lighthouse nearby. Just the sound of it. Though on some nights you can hear the one up north, in Rostov."

Dreerson had complained of his cold, and wore a sweater and scarf under his overcoat, gloves, as well as an old brown fedora. He carried an umbrella.

"All the moles are safely ensconced in their houses. And the town lies peaceful."

First Street was deserted. Past Dreerson's store was a vacant lot, fenced in. Then the Evening Diner, in gloom, with a half-dozen empty booths and the lighted kitchen, where a cook was scraping down the grill. The Laundromat was closed, as was the hardware store.

Only themselves and the fog, and one of the three stoplights, vaguely blinking.

Russ said, "When is it *not* peaceful?"

Dreerson chuckled.

"I apologize, Russell, for abandoning you last night. I really didn't intend to, but the sight of those three Graces, lined up. It was too much to resist."

"No need to apologize," Russ said amiably. "I had a good time. Pete showed me around the mansion."

"I so rarely attend the official town functions. I'd not seen them in a while. Therefore it was a chance—a sober chance, you realize—to settle a number of civic and personal issues."

"Did it work?"

Dreerson shrugged. "Not at all, of course. I got in a few choice insults, and I even managed to spill some wine on Patsy. Very fulfilling."

At the intersection with Cheddar Street, Dreerson motioned them right. Cheddar was twice as wide as the others. Fogbound, it seemed emptier, climbing up and out of sight.

To either side were more facades, behind gray alder, and glass globes shining in the gardens.

"This will be perfect timing. They'll have finished with the dishes by now."

"We're expected?"

"Yes. Though its likely Hillary's attitude might suggest otherwise."

"What's her attitude?"

"Keep in mind that she's lived with Tom for the last twenty years. That could wear any woman down. And at times, her disposition is slightly south of a harpy's." Dreerson smiled. "She loves Tom, but doesn't have the patience for him and his hobbies anymore."

"*Hey-oh!*"

It might have been a mannequin, sitting in a folding chair on a porch to the left. Waving. "*Hey-oh!*"

"Good evening, Arthur!"

If Dreerson's voice was flattened by the fog, Arthur's reply seemed miles away. "*Hey-oh, it's Mister Kent!*"

Russ waved. "Arthur!"

"*Start spreadin' the news. . . .*" The voice, returning in warbling, drawn-out tones, was singing, off-key. "*I'm leaving ta-day!*"

Arthur raised his arms.

Quietly, Dreerson said, "Arthur was once our dentist. These days his son runs the practice. A much kinder, steadier hand, and not as stingy with the gas."

Russ looked over his shoulder; the figure was already lost in the fog. "I met him at the Gathering."

Past the intersection with Second, they arrived at a white bungalow encircled by a chain-link fence. Small signs on every post read: *Absolutely No Solicitors!*

A dog barked, low, gruff. It was the grayish-white husky Russ had seen a few days earlier, now on the bungalow's porch.

"Ody!" Dreerson unlatched the front gate and walked through. "What a good boy!"

Ody wagged his bushy tail.

Dreerson allowed Russ to pass, shut the gate securely, then led the way through waist-high sunflowers nodding grayly in the fog.

"Friends approaching!" Dreerson called out. "No foes tonight, Ody, but keep the guard up! The coast is never clear!"

Six creaky stairs brought them to the porch. The dog's ears sharpened. Dreerson petted him, and the dog back-stepped and sniffed Russ's hand.

"Hey, boy." Russ scratched the back of his head.

Ody sat, staring up with pale blue eyes.

The lights were on behind curtained windows to the right and left.

With his knuckles, Dreerson knocked twice on the door.

Waiting, Russ heard a faint patter in the sunflowers. The first drops of rain.

Dreerson said, "Here he is. Tom has a signature limp these days."

The door opened.

"Greetings, Tom."

"Bern."

Russ recognized the man who'd stepped from the Weft a few days earlier. Today, Carver wore denim overalls and a plaid shirt. He was taller than Russ had realized—six feet two inches at least—with a bulbous, veiny nose, and wiry white hair thinning atop his speckled pate.

Dreerson said, "May I present Russell Kent, the esteemed composer of modern music. And Russell, Tom Carver, esteemed scientist and gadabout."

"Mister Carver."

Carver squinted. "Call me Tom." They shook. Carver's hand was large and leathery. "Bern tells me it's an honor to have you in my house, and I've no reason to dispute him. Get in before I lose my heat." He stiffly waved them inside. "Stay put, dog-dog."

The living room was small, with a couch, coffee table, a console stereo, a console television, and recliner. The air smelled of fish and steamed vegetables. Two archways opposite the door led to a hallway, and a bright kitchen, where a dishwasher was churning.

Russ said, "Bernard told me you're the man to meet."

Dreerson removed his hat. "Yes, the town sage."

"Sage?" Tom's voice was a basso rumble. He shoved his hands into his waist-high pockets and walked farther into the room. Travel posters covered the walls—Paris, Istanbul, Monte Carlo—along with a few framed watercolors of Ody. "Bern's just fooling with you."

"Russell, you can't really tell much about Old Tom by his living room. His real soul is to be found *downstairs*, in the basement." Dreerson laid his umbrella and the fedora on the coffee table. "Isn't that right, Tom?"

Carver mushed his lips, glancing down at the carpet, and shrugged, hands still stuck in his pockets. "What do you know about our town, Kent?"

"Not a lot," Russ said, adding, "Everything a tourist should know."

Carver lowered himself onto the red vinyl recliner, knees jutting up to either side. "Go ahead and sit." He waved at the couch. "*Everything a tourist should know*," Carver repeated, as Russ shoved aside some magazines and sat down. "That ain't much, is it Bern?"

"I'd like to know more," Russ said. "I'm told you have some interesting finds."

Dreerson, still standing, added, "And stories."

"Not in the best mood for stories tonight."

Dreerson's eyebrows rose. "Did you hear from the council?"

Carver nodded once. He leaned forward and rubbed his knees.

Dreerson said, "The outcome wasn't surprising, I suppose."

"What about?" Russ asked.

"Aww." Tom shook his head. He looked up at Dreerson.

"Tom wants to dig on the town's property, a certain area of the backwoods. And our town council denies his request simply to deny it."

"Bastards," Carver rumbled.

"Quite." Dreerson unbuttoned his coat.

A voice, both sour and playful, said, "That Dreerie?"

It came from the kitchen.

Carver rubbed his knees more vigorously.

"Dreerie and friend?" An old woman shuffled into the kitchen light, in wooly blue slippers. She wore a matching house dress, and clutched a jar of gleaming eggs to her apron, twisting the lid shut as she looked at Dreerson and Russ.

"Greetings, Hillary," said Dreerson. "How goes the canning?"

"Who's this, now?" She looked at Russ. Wilted eyes, under wilted gray bangs.

"This is Kent, Hilly. Russell Kent."

Russ nodded. "Hello."

She squinted, and muttered, "Husband who brings over company, says nothing at all."

Carver raised his hand. "Aww . . ."

She levelled a glance at Dreerson. "That your wet umbrella on my coffee table?"

The bookseller smiled. "Dry as a bone, Hillary. As am I, alas. Mind if I fetch us some brew? I think I'll find it in the fridge, correct?"

Scowling at the bookseller as he stepped through the archway, she said to Tom, "You plan to smoke, too?"

"Aw, go back to your work."

"Aw, aw, aw. You sound like a bird. Like one of those things you have in your basement. Quit rubbing your knees. Take some ibuprofen if they hurt." She looked at Russ. "Watch what they tell you. Don't believe everything you hear."

Russ smiled. "I'll try not."

The bookseller reappeared, clutching a six-pack. Hillary scowled again, then shuffled back into the kitchen.

With a last pat on his knees, Carver pushed himself to his feet. "We'll be in the basement, dearest! Ody's on the porch!"

The stairs were steep, with a single rail on the right. A switch at the top tripped a lightbulb below.

"Watch the fifth, Kent," Carver called back mysteriously, then pointed down at the stair he'd just completely climbed over. "Loose."

"That's your burglar alarm, isn't it, Tom?" said Dreerson, stepping over it. "You'll hear them tumbling down and down. Maybe a crunching sound when they reach bottom."

Russ carefully followed.

On the left, against the wall of the house, were crude shelves braced between the tacks, descending along with the stairs. Each shelf had a saucer holding what appeared to be a cube of cheese. Green cubes, gray cubes, each stuck with a toothpick and a small slip of paper, all of it pelted with dust.

Evening Cheddar 1972 read one, in careful block letters.

The next lowest was, *Evening Havarti 1968*.

Russ could smell a faint cheesy tang, along with the oil and warmed wood-dust smell of the basement now opening out to his right, in a shadowy sprawl of clutter.

The lightbulb shone above a concrete floor and the foundation; farther to the right was a worn ottoman in faded green, and in the corner opposite the stairs, a workbench.

Carver walked along the edge of the clutter to the bench, snapped on three segmented lamps.

Shelves on either side were packed with jars and cans, brushes, magazines, old lightbulb boxes.

"There's some stools, gentlemen."

As Russ grabbed them, Carver climbed onto a padded, rolling high chair, and flipped a switch on a small bookshelf stereo. He plugged in a tape.

Distantly, from under the bench, or through the racking, a tenor trumpet rang rising thirds, up from C.

"Hope you don't mind Satchmo, Kent."

"Not at all." Russ climbed onto the stool. He looked over the contents of the nearest shelf. A framed portrait was turned to face the wall—perhaps another of Joseph Evening, like the one on Peggy's wall, and at the Gathering.

Beside it were more little plates of cheese: *Evening Blue, 1979*, and *Evening Cheddar, 1975*.

"Part of an experiment," Dreerson said, handing Russ a cold bottle of beer. "Right, Tom? An experiment in the durability of our product."

"Durable as rocks." Tom accepted a bottle from Dreerson, twisted off the cap. "After 1965, Kent, you get bargain basement rennet, artificial coloring in all your varieties, and detectable amounts of mouse turds." He tipped the bottle to his lips and gulped.

The label read *Lighthouse*, illustrated with a surf-tossed promontory and lighthouse shining its beam down toward a turbulent cove.

Opening his, Russ said, "Local stuff?"

"Regional," Dreerson said. "I think you'll like it."

Russ sipped, and the beer was a cold tingle across his tongue, the flavor pleasantly full and dark.

Dreerson was waiting.

"Great stuff," Russ said, appraising the licorice-like aftertaste. "Bravo."

"It's from Port Rostov, of course."

On the farther shelves, jars held what might have been more cheese samples, or chunks of green rock.

He took a longer sip.

Pipes were gurgling overhead. The dishwasher was a vague, rattling roar.

"Tom . . ." Dreerson leaned forward. "I thought of introducing you two when Russell bought a certain book from my store. By the great Lewis Sensamall. The dinosaur book."

"Dinosaurs of the Oregon Interior," Russ recited, and sipped another mouthful, slowly swallowed. He looked for somewhere to pitch the bottle cap; finding none, he surreptitiously slipped the cap into his coat pocket.

"Sensamall, huh?" Tom nodded, glanced at Dreerson. "Smart fellah. Knew his stuff, on a certain level. But he's usually a *right turn* from the truth."

"Right turn?"

"Never there, Kent. Never really *at* the truth, but always close enough to peer around the corner. If you close one eye. If you squint."

Carver set his empty bottle on the bench, patted his knees then stepped down from the stool. "Well, what I got's nowhere near as dramatic." He walked into the clutter, along a narrow path between a bureau draped in a dusty quilt and stacks of antique chairs. He stopped at a stack of oblong containers.

Carefully, Tom lifted off the top container. It was made of durable plastic, or Tupperware.

Bernard offered Russ an encouraging smile.

"What we got here," Tom said, stepping sideways toward them with the container clutched to his stomach, "was dug up . . . oh, early 1970s. Bern, could you put the dropcloth down?"

Dreerson opened the bench's drawer, took out a bolt of black cloth which he spread and twitched into place with his free hand. Tom set the container down beside the cloth, peeled off the lid, then reached in and began removing shards of rock, each several inches long. Pale blue rock. He laid them on the black, having trouble grasping the smallest pieces.

Eight. Ten.

He aimed all three lamps on the shards, or bones.

Russ had never heard of bones with this bluish cast, though they were too uniform to be rocks.

"They're bones?"

"Go ahead and touch."

Russ ran his finger down one shard, doubtful. Smooth with tiny pits. Ice cold. Perhaps his fingers had been numbed by the beer bottle. "How'd they get shiny?"

"Yeah." Carver's voice had lost some of its heft. "Hilly went over 'em with her jewelry buffer, a few years back." He grunted. "Woman."

Dreerson said, "She meant well, Tom."

"Can't say for certain if they're bones, Kent. Not sure. Wouldn't trust any eggheads at a university with this." He wiped his mouth with the back of his hand, and burped under his breath. "Wrote the date on this box here. January 16, 1973, about a half-mile outside of town."

Draining his bottle of beer, Russ realized he was already on the verge of being pleasantly drunk. And happy to be here, he decided, with these two eccentrics, and the trumpet very distant and melancholy, in sinuous lines, like arabesques of smoke.

Russ said, "So . . . what do you think they are?"

Carver mushed his lips. He glanced at Bernard, then shrugged. "Bones of an extinct animal, Kent. Been in the ground a long time. Millions of years."

The basement door creaked open. Hillary called down, "Disposal's clogged again!"

A laugh struggled from Carver's throat. He shouted up, "Use the god-damn broom handle!"

"You think I'd interrupt his Majesty without using the broom!?"

He stepped down from his stool, shaking his head. "Gentlemen, I'll be back with the second round."

"Hoo-rah," said Dreerson.

Carver tromped up the stairs.

Dreerson finished his third bottle of beer, set it down.

Russ moved his stool closer to the bench. He touched the rocks, or bones. They had been laid down in a pattern, he realized, perhaps Tom's attempt to show these shards as they'd once been connected, with two fragments laid vertically end to end, and four more fanning out below. Like a claw. A bird claw.

"Well, Russell, how goes the rooming house?"

He began take another sip before remembering the bottle was empty. The licorice taste lingered pleasantly.

"It's going well. Megan's a great lady."

"Yes, she is." Dreerson nodded into the scarf bunched up at his chin.

"Peggy told me . . . she's the only non-native in town?"

"Yes."

"How'd that happen?"

Regarding Russ from beneath gray curls, Dreerson said, "She hasn't told you?"

"Not yet."

Russ tried to read Dreerson's expression, the flat mouth, the beaming eyes now glancing down at the floor.

Dreerson, like himself, was *lit*.

Russ said, "I didn't want to pry, at least, not too quickly."

"Megan met one of our own while at university. Jack Sumner. George and April's kid. They married, and she moved here about fifteen years ago. Jack, sad to say, died four years ago."

A husband.

Russ nodded, not surprised.

"What happened?"

Dreerson looked up at Russ, or past him. "An accident. Up at the factory. Horrible thing. She was devastated. It's been a rather slow healing process." Dreerson straightened. "I'm sure she intends to tell you in her own time. No doubt she thinks it too . . . melodramatic a revelation." Dreerson looked at his empty bottles of beer.

"Did she ever think of leaving?"

Dreerson shrugged. "She might have gone back north, to Seattle, though she was never very close to her parents. I think she's grown too fond of many of us in Evening. Everyone dotes on her. She *transcends the cliques.* She even gets along with Peggy, which I find quite extraordinary." Dreerson stared down at his hands, and his plump face looked suddenly very sad. "It's good for her to have boarders in the winter. I hate the idea of her staying there all by herself."

The door opened. Tom was tromping back down the stairs. Behind him Hillary called out, "Smoke and drink! Drink and smoke!"

"Aw! We got a real human *conversation* going on down here!"

The door shut behind him.

Dreerson glanced up, eyes twinkling.

"Ready for another one, Kent?" Carver clutched a new six-pack in one hand, three cigars in the other. "Bern don't smoke much, but I got a *see-gar* for you if you want it."

the a.c.l.

After Carver handed him a beer, Russ reached for the portrait turned to the wall, and turned it back. It was a black-and-white photo of Joe, but not the familiar one. Here he was slightly younger, beardless, with a silver tinge in his dark hair, seated in an armchair before the wide windows of the tower. He was in shirtsleeves. Standing beside him was a gangly man in his twenties, in a checkered jacket, suspenders, messy brown hair, a long face.

"Yep," said Carver, taking his seat. "Me and Joe. God bless him."

Dreerson tossed his cap into a cardboard box beneath the bench. "That was a while back."

"Fifty-four."

Russ said, "Want me to turn it back around?"

Carver shook his head. "About time I let Joe look in on things."

The younger Tom held a dirty shovel—incongruous in the Victorian finery of the room. And Joseph, staring directly into the camera, had a looseness to his features that suggested he might break into a smile.

Carver studied the photograph, mouth half-open. "You remember, Bern? What old Joe said to me then?"

Dreerson nodded.

Russ twisted the cap off his bottle, and tossed it under the bench.

He could hear rain drumming in the garden.

"That day, Kent, when the shutter clicked, Joe nodded toward the camera and he says, *'Tom, I sense you looking back at me that time, from that lens. You're an old man, out there, beyond that flash that pricked your eyes. And that old man, looking back at us, has made some great discoveries.'*" Carver mushed his lips. "Then he was smiling. Remember, Bern? And Joe had that look about his face, that he knew things he wouldn't ever tell about."

"Yes, and you didn't believe him. You said, as I recall, *What is there left to discover? I* took the picture, Russell. With my old Brownie."

Carver hunched his head, cursed under his breath. He grabbed a fresh bottle of beer.

"And you *did* discover great things, Tom. Don't forget that."

The old man shook his head, scowled. "Before the Cheesers took over, Kent, Bern and me were always up seeing Joe, talking over weighty matters. Stuff that flew right over their goddamn heads." He gulped down half the bottle, smacked his lips, while Dreerson nodded, and both seemed to fall into reminiscence.

Not wanting to think of Jack Sumner, Russ said, "So, who runs the factory today? Joe's relatives?"

Dreerson shook his head. "Joe never had any direct descendants, though some in town claimed to be that. The factory's owned collectively by nine of the families, with the others having their shares."

"Coup in seventy-two," said Carver.

"Yes, in 1972, Peggy's late husband and some others took over running the factory. That was my banner eighty-point headline in the newspaper: *COUP IN '72.* One of the last issues I put out, I'm afraid to say. Peggy Chalmers and her next-door neighbor Patsy—now known as Patricia Burle-Clarkson—grew up wanting to take the reins of the town, by which I mean taking over the factory. And they did."

"Harpies."

"Yes, Tom, but how many of us get to live out our childhood dreams?"

Russ asked, "What about Jack Sumner's dad? What'd he do?"

"Good man," said Carver.

"George worked at the factory, in charge of shipping. He was also— like his father, and his father's father—a geologist, and loved nothing more than haunting the hills around town, in search of interesting rocks."

Russ stared at the portrait. Then he grinned and lifted his bottle, gesturing. "Been there."

When they seemed to not understand he added, "Up to Joe's tower. At the mansion."

Carver's eyebrows jutted up. "Truthful?"

"Ah! Young Crick took you there, on your tour. At the Gathering. Right, Russell?"

Outside, a dog barked.

Carver straightened.

"Yeah," Russ said, looking over his shoulder, into the clutter. A second bark, more aggressive, came from that direction: from the porch.

"That's his goddamn prowler bark."

Carver stood up, shuffling out of the lamplight, down a narrow path between the bureau and stacks of boxes. Metal pails were kicked aside. Carver climbed some steps. Chains rattled.

Dreerson exchanged a glance with Russell.

From outside, Carver's voice, faintly: "Ode?"

"Probably a cat," Dreerson assured Russ, just as Carver poked his head into the side door and shouted, "Think it's time to retire to the porch, Gentlemen!"

Standing, Russ said, "Do we have to?"

"Fresh air." Dreerson looked as though his legs might buckle.

Russ followed him, and it was like walking on stilts, looming over the clutter that loomed to either side.

"Lighthouse always packs a wallop," Dreerson remarked.

They found Carver crouched at the top of three concrete stairs, a shadow against the peaked roof of the house next door. Rain was coming down, beating tendrils of fog inside. Windchimes sounded up and down the hill.

"Careful walking over the sill," Carver said under his breath. "Drops down into my wife's hibiscus."

Dreerson followed, then Russ, through shivering sunflowers, into the rain.

"Had a visitor," Carver said to Dreerson.

Rain sparkled under the streetlamps. The fog was dissipating in an off-shore breeze, but was still thick in the distance, as backdrop to the street.

"You see 'em, Ody?"

Ody stood at the top of the stairs, ears sharp, regarding the empty sidewalk and street.

"Bite 'em in the butt next time."

Russ followed Dreerson up the stairs, both having problems with balance.

Wiping the water from his hair, Russ saw a crumpled piece of paper between the dog's front legs.

Carver stooped and picked it up.

"A communication!" said Dreerson, nearly out of breath. Grunting, he fumbled for the folding chairs. "Strangely timed."

Russ leaned against a corner post and listened to the chimes, faintly spangling, like various crotales and cymbalum.

"Hold on, Russell. There! I've set up a chair for you."

Russ carefully lowered himself down, next to Dreerson.

As Carver unfurled the paper, something clattered to the porch: a yellow pin. Two black wedges forming the lower case "e".

Russ pointed. "Got one of those. At the party. The Gathering."

"God damned Storm Watchers," Carver pronounced. He flattened out the paper between his hands.

Dreerson leaned forward. "What does it say, Tom?"

Carver spat. A moment later he turned the paper toward them. They could make it out in the window light, handwritten in block letters:

HERE'S A PIN FOR YOU, TOM!
SORRY YOU COULDN'T MAKE IT TO THE GATHERING!
HOPING YOU AND HILLARY ARE WELL!

"Scoundrels," Dreerson said.

Russ gazed at the street. Rain lashed the asphalt.

The idea of someone running out of that deserted street scene to toss a note on Tom's porch . . .

"Strange thing . . . to throw at your door," Russ said. "Isn't it?"

Carver held up the paper. "Not strange at all, Kent, if you can read between these lines." He shook it, then grunted.

"Sit down, Tom."

"Moment." Carver opened the front door and stepped inside.

Dreerson hunched, pulling his coat tighter to his throat. "Enjoying yourself, Russell?"

Russ grinned, nodded. "Too much."

The lights behind the windows clicked off; the porch was in darkness.

When Carver returned, he clutched another six-pack, and sat down on the other side of Dreerson. "Hilly's gone to bed."

Taking the proffered bottle, Dreerson said, "Perhaps we shouldn't have come over on such short notice."

"Aww, she's fine." Carver popped the cap on his bottle, slurped. More quietly, he said, "Kent, you've been to the tower. What'd you see?"

"Not much, actually."

"Smoke?" Carver offered a cigar.

"No, thanks."

Shrugging, he chewed the end of his cigar, then spat. He fumbled for an old butane lighter, sparked it, and slowly puffed the cigar to a cherry glow.

Russ said, "Actually, what was strange was. All the chairs in the tower were set up overlooking the town, not the ocean. And when I asked Pete why the chairs were set up that way . . . he said they were set up for the Storm Watchers."

Russ coughed.

"Hmmm. Pete tell you anything else?"

Russ began to take a sip of beer, then stopped himself.

"He said they weren't . . . uh, interested in the sort of storms that come off the ocean."

Carver's cigar glowed bright.

"How the town has fallen," said Dreerson, in dulcet tones, and his voice, on the long vowels, struck a resonance with the wood of the porch. He was gazing out at the rain. "You can measure how much by the character of that room, Russell. Once a place of deep thought and reflection, and now a place for schemers."

Carver leaned forward and scratched Ody under the collar. "Tell me, Kent. How'd you like to be a member of *our* club?" His face was level with his knees as he gazed up at Russ, grinning past his cigar.

"Let's not get . . . Russell involved. He's here for important, even *noble* tasks. Perhaps the most . . . *worthwhile* thing that's ever been done in our town. An opera. Imagine that!"

"An honorary member, then." Sitting back, Carver saluted Russ with his beer bottle. "You're looking at the founding members of the *Anti-Cheese League*."

"The *A.C.L.*," Dreerson said.

Ody raised his head, ears sharpening.

Russ said, "And what does the . . . ACL do?"

Ody was gazing out toward the street, then began to growl.

Dreerson raised his hand. He whispered, "Can you . . . hear them? There's someone *coming down the sidewalk*."

Carver sat up straight.

Amid the rainfall and the chimes: boots scuffing the asphalt. Splashing through puddles.

Ody renewed his growl. Carver touched the dog's neck, silencing him. "Sounds like a big 'un."

Dreerson scooted his stool forward. Carver swore beneath his breath. Beyond the fence at the far corner of the property, a sheen of yellow materialized from out of the rain.

A large figure in a bright yellow raincoat, rubber boots, holding a yellow-and-black umbrella, walking under lamplight. The umbrella partially hid a broad bald head.

A moment later, Russ recognized the barber, remembered him at the party, and the stink of lanolin. Beady eyes roaming Russ's beard. *It'll have to go sooner or later.*

The barber, out for a walk, staring down at the sidewalk in front of him. And either he didn't see the three of them on the porch, which was likely, or he was pretending *not* to see them. Which suddenly *seemed* likely.

Carver was hunched forward, with one hand on Ody's collar; Dreerson sat rigidly, one hand at his collar: mimicking statues.

As the barber strolled past the gate, Russ tried not to laugh.

Then Carver came to life.

"Bastard." Grunting, he leaned forward, grabbed the balled-up paper then struggled to his feet—almost keeling over backwards, startling Ody. He clamped the paper in both hands, then wound his arm back in an awkward pitcher's stance and tossed it through the rain, in the barber's direction; it fell short in the grass. "Bastard!"

The barber was past them now, the yellow raincoat losing itself in the fog.

"There, there, Tom. That was a brave stand, nonetheless. I'm sure he couldn't help but hear it fall."

Carver's cigar was on the porch. He picked it up and, swearing beneath his breath, lowered himself into the chair.

"That was the barber, right?" Russ asked.

Carver spat. "Root of all our problems."

"If not the root, Tom," said Dreerson, "then one of the main tendrils."

"The barber?"

"Yes, Russell. The barber of Evening is also its mayor."

"Really?"

"For the last fifteen years. Except for a dreadful term in the eighties, when the office was held by Peggy."

Russ mulled that over.

He tried to remember what Dreerson had said about Jack, about Megan, but it was momentarily lost. To say something, he said, "So who else is in the ACL?"

Carver looked to Dreerson, who replied, "Peter Crick and his father, Charles. We also have some other honorary members around town, Russell, like your landlady. Though Megan probably would be embarrassed to admit it."

"She puts up with us," said Carver. "Great gal."

"And what does the A . . . the Anti-Cheese League do?"

Dreerson grinned. "Civil disobedience, Russell, of a subtle variety. Only Tom and myself can be considered full-timers. And that's because we have nothing else to do." He raised his eyebrows, and drank some more.

Russ did likewise, finishing the bottle, though he knew he shouldn't have. And he'd need to visit the bathroom very soon. Once more he declined Carver's offer for a smoke, and looked out into the rain. He would arrive home drunk, smelling of cigars.

Carver and Dreerson were talking about the garden, Carver remarking that Hillary would have to re-stake some of the sunflowers, and Dreerson saying that rain had been predicted through the week, with worse weather on the way, and murmuring about something else, but Russ was mesmerized by the rain striking the steps, as was Ody.

Finally, Carver said loudly, "Well, let's make some quick pit stops. Then, if I drive slow, I can drop both of you off home."

The house was dark, the driveway empty. Russ was as much relieved as disappointed. Where was she? He grinned, stumbling inside, told himself this was for the best. That he needed to go to bed. Drink some water— some aspirin—and go straight to bed. He struggled to remember what Dreerson had said, about Megan and Jack, and Jack's accident.

He turned on the living room light.

According to the clock on the wall it was ten past ten. She wasn't due home till after eleven.

He collapsed on the couch and waited for the room to steady.

It might be good to step outside, just for a while. Let the rain wake him up, wash the cigar smoke from his clothes.

He made himself rise and walk into the kitchen. He drank a glass of water, then another, staring at his reflection in the window.

Bedtime.

Pausing at the stairs, he looked into the rec room, suddenly curious.

If Megan were to arrive home, he'd hear the Suburban pulling up the driveway.

Cautiously, he walked into the rec room, holding onto the Ping-Pong table for support, stepping to her open bedroom door.

Reaching around the jamb, he found a rheostat knob and slowly turned it.

Russ Kent was revealed in the bureau mirror, startled, with a drunken grin, his shirttails out.

He smelled perfume, the jasmine scent she'd worn at the party.

Immediately to his right sat an old four-poster bed with ruffled green fabric, sheets and a blanket tangled near the baseboard. Beside it a nightstand with a push-button telephone, a window looking onto Alder Street. A bookshelf, a chest of drawers made of blond oak nestled into the corner diagonally opposite from the door.

Where was Jack?

He focused on the pictures tucked into the left-hand side of the mirror.

He stepped inside.

Scent of jasmine intensified.

There were three photographs.

The first was a color snapshot of an old couple. The woman possessed Megan's striking eyes and slender figure; the man had a squarish face, was bald, and lifting a glass of champagne. Parents.

The second was a picture of Seattle, with the Space Needle illuminated against a dark sky.

The third . . .

There he was. Russ was certain. There, in the third photo.

It was a small black and white image, yellowed at the edges. The type of thing usually spit out in a strip from a coin-operated photo booth. He looked mid-twenties. Short, dark hair, an easy smile, as he gazed to the right of the camera.

Russ looked a moment longer, then turned away. For a strange instant he saw a woman lying above Megan's bed, receding to a print of a woman lying on a bed, tacked to the wall above Megan's mattress, framed by the four-poster.

Russ stepped closer.

It was a painting he'd seen before, somewhere. A woman, nude, asleep, face lost in the pillow, the barest hint of a smile, arms up against her body, legs stretched out, one foot crooked behind the other. The colors were bleached out. Tempura. Drybrush. Andrew Wyeth, he remembered. One of the *Helga* series, though for an instant it had seemed a woman floating over Megan's bed, held up by whatever she was dreaming.

Russ woke with a headache, a sour stomach. 11:05, according to the clock. Sitting up, he realized he'd forgotten to set the alarm. And, of course, the clock was broken.

Clouds, and light rainfall, against the spruce.

Ignoring the hycopathius, he climbed out of bed—winced at pain behind his right eye—and pulled clean clothes from the closet and dresser. He tried to recall the night before. Visiting Tom Carver, and drinking too much. Seeing the strange shards of bone or rock. Carver and Dreerson telling him about their club, the Anti-Cheese League.

And the barber—the Barber Mayor—walking by.

More importantly, Megan's husband, Jack.

What had he done in her room? Stumbled in, smelling of cigars, and looked at the photo tucked in the mirror. The painting behind her bed. Had he touched anything? Closed the door behind him? Turned off the light?

In the bathroom, he listened for any noise from downstairs. He turned on the shower, got the water steaming, and sat under a spray.

Jack Sumner. Killed at the factory. Isn't that what Dreerson had said?

He dressed in a warm shirt and jeans, took three aspirin with a tall glass of water, then, after listening at the top of the stairs to the silent house, walked downstairs.

There was a note on the dining room table.

Hi Russ!

I'm at the school today. There's cereal in the cupboard, milk in the fridge. I fixed you some ham sandwiches for lunch, and soup's in the plastic bowl on the second shelf. See you around 6 for dinner.

Bye—Megan.

ps: here's my number at the school.

After breakfast, he returned upstairs to the desk, and *Nemo*.

The corner windows were dappled with rain, and pleasantly cold. Just the thing to clear up his headache.

He sat down, arranged the libretto, the blank score sheets, pencils, erasers. Instead of picking up the threads of Tuesday's work, he skimmed ahead in the libretto, trying not to be critical, uninterested in page after page of dialogue, in the chemistry of the characters, until he reached the underwater walk to the island of Crespo.

The first set piece.

We begin with a green frieze, and perhaps the murmuring of your orchestra. In slow motion the four divers descend from the ceiling, our Captain, Professor Aronnax, Conseil, and Ned Land, all looking like bipedal creatures of the sea in silvery green, with only the odd Victorian filigree to mark them works of Man. Their faces are open and pale. In their voices, a sense of solitude; none can hear the others, and only Captain Nemo's soliloquy achieves a coherence, as he limns his kingdom.

Russ already doubted the setting. But it was a sketch, only the first draft. Such decisions would be finalized with the director. He read back a page: Nemo talking to Professor Aronnax as they are

suited for the sea as a medieval knight is suited for battle, with strange procession, and a hint of ritual more alchemical than scientific.

NEMO (boastful):

"Professor, these forests of mine/ask neither light nor heat from the sun. There are no lions, tigers, or panthers."

Conseil, mistaken as to Nemo's intentions, is excited to go ashore on dry land, to Crespo island. Nemo counters:

"Ah, but these islands are known only to me./They grow only for me/Their forests are not on land/but under the water!"

Russ glanced at his notebook. He'd written, in regard to the first underwater scene, *Descending. Quarter tone? Dense layers?*

He remembered that the scene might start with quarter-tone layers in the strings, articulated beyond the glissandi, mostly descending. And colder timbres. Woodwinds instead with the strings, adding a late-Stravinskian chill to the tones, mostly descending, as the principals entered the underwater landscape. Half-tone, quarter-tone steps, against a slow crescendo in the double bass as their boots touched the sea floor. He listened to it in the cold air off the windows, against the glittering rainy sea.

He set a fresh sheet before him, drew a line down the left-hand side, connecting six staves. Wrote clefs, and key signs, sharps and flats. Then, holding the initial sounds, the vertical compass, he dabbed notes, added stems and barlines, two measures, three, assembling in layers, erasing, brushing away the shavings, continuing on, until the page was the music in his ear.

Russ sat back, flexing his hand. An hour or more had passed. He set down the pencil, becoming aware of the messy desk, the spruce marching down the hillside and the rain, the foggy sea. His aching knuckles.

Nonetheless, his headache was gone.

And the section was surprisingly complete. Not a sketch in short score. A page of long score.

How to project voices? Which were most important? He remembered the dialogue—Aronnax's excited cataloging of the fauna, Conseil's anxious remarks, Ned Land's bluster. These could rise and fade from the fabric, but Captain Nemo's would have to stand out, as he pontificated over his realm.

A whole-tone line, to anchor the rest.

He stretched and stood up, and walked downstairs.

In the kitchen, he heated the bowl of soup she'd left him, ate the sandwich, and thought of adding an obbligato instrument to Nemo's voice. Brass, to help it stand out from the woodwinds and overwhelming strings. To ring fanfares behind Nemo's words, or swim opposite his voice.

As he slurped the soup (it was delicious) he looked around at the kitchen. Notes tacked with magnets to the fridge. A shopping list. An ad from the factory, for bulk cheese. A film festival schedule from Portland several years old.

The appliances were from the 1970s, or older. No doubt they'd belonged to the Sumner family. The china plates, too, and the silverware. How much more in this house was theirs? What was Jack's?

And were there other Sumners in town?

The older friend of Megan's—Claire?

Resisting the urge to explore, he washed the dishes, cleaned the counters and kitchen table, took a can of soda from the fridge and went back upstairs.

At the now-dim desk he switched on the lamp. The hycopathius's scales gleamed blue and purple. Sitting down, he read over what he'd done, was pleased to find the fabric of the underwater scene still viable, the ideas still interesting.

He pushed on.

When he stopped, the windows were dark. The clock said 1:14; it must be at least six. Headlights moved up and down Bluff, cars coming home. People with umbrellas walking along Seventh. Shortly afterwards, the crunch of tires on gravel pulled him from the music.

Headlights flared on the wet windowsill.

Russ sat back, remembering the waltz, the doubts.

The front door opened. He listened to boots stamping on the flagstone, and a moment later walking through the rec room into her bedroom, then out and back across the hall into the living room, to the kitchen.

He tried to continue work, but couldn't. He stood up, sat on the edge of the bed then lay down, staring at the ceiling.

A while later, the scent of spices and baking bread reached him.

He washed up, changed into a clean shirt, then went downstairs.

"Hi, Megan."

"Well, there he is." She was at the oven, mitts in hand. She smiled, and Russ relaxed a bit. "Tonight the cook's taking it easy. Noodles and bread, and green beans."

"Sounds great. Smells great, too."

Her hair was loose on her shoulders. She wore a thick wool sweater, jeans and wool socks. "Be just a few more minutes."

He said, "Can I help?"

"Do you want to clear off the table?"

She'd brought home a stack of drawings, now with her purse and car keys on the dining room table; the first was a pine tree beside a giant block of cheese, the yellow crayon so thick it gleamed waxy in the overhead light.

"Like my kids' work?"

"Very nice. I like the cheese especially."

"That's Cathy Burle's. Her dad's the master cheesemaker, you know. I think he makes her draw cheese-themed pictures."

He set the sheets, purse and keys on the counter, then wiped down the table, and laid napkins and silverware.

Garlic bread was baking in the oven; he realized how hungry he was.

She asked, "How'd your visit go last night?"

He laughed.

"What?"

"I made the mistake of drinking with Tom."

"Let me guess. Lighthouse."

"Yeah. A little more kick than I thought."

"I should have warned you. So did you like Tom?"

Russ nodded. "Quite a colorful character. His wife, too."

She turned down the oven, took off the mitts. "I agree. Believe it or not, they're also quite lovable, once you get to know them."

"What can I help with? How about the salad?"

"You don't need to."

But he gently pressed, and she directed him to the bowl in the cupboard, the romaine lettuce, tomatoes, sprouts. "I have two specialties," he said. "Pasta and salad. But I do them well."

The clock on the oven said 8:10, confirmed by the clock in the dining room. He was surprised it was so late. Rain spattered against the windows.

"If you're feeling really industrious, you can mix the oil and vinegar, too." She took a bottle of wine from a lower cupboard. A pinot noir. "I was going to serve red with the pasta." She held out the label for his inspection. "It's from Rex Hill. Claire—you met her, I think—we go up there a few times a year and visit a winery."

He mixed the dressing, and uncorked the wine. When it was time for the salad, he poured them both a half glass, as she sat down opposite.

She complimented the salad. He offered small talk about the rain.

"So," she said, tucking strands of hair behind her ear, "how would you describe your music?"

"Hmmm." Thrown by the question, he sipped some wine. "I've always had a tough time answering that."

"Pretend I know something. Don't dumb it down."

"It's chromatic. Sometimes neotonal, sometimes—I wrote some atonal pieces. Early on. How's that?"

"I recognize neotonal and atonal. But not chromatic. Is that colors?"

"It's all the notes in the scale. More than *do re me fa so la ti do*. The notes between them. So, there's technically dissonance, but only to make the tonality interesting."

"Did you always write in that style?"

He shook his head. "I started out . . . well, when I was a kid, I saw music as colors. So you were sort of right about chromatic. It's called synesthesia."

"I've heard of that."

"I wrote with colored pens, and crayons. But it was diatonic—normal—music. My father taught himself to read my stuff. He'd play these little pieces I wrote for violin." Russ sipped some wine. "But I had all that color stuff educated out of me."

"What about CDs? Do you have any available?"

"A few," he said, adding, "I had more on LP, and cassette. There's a label called CRI—Composers Recordings Inc. They had six of my early works, sharing the flipside with another composer. I have a couple out right now on CD, on a label called New World."

"I'd like to hear one."

"Sure. I'll get something mailed out."

Megan sat back. She set down her fork, clasped and unclasped her hands, then hooked her fingers on the edge of the table. "I have something I should have told you before now." She exhaled. "But . . . Bennie says he told you last night." She looked down at her plate, then back. "About Jack."

After a pause, Russ nodded.

She said, "I guess I should've mentioned it. Especially after you told me about Anna. That was the perfect time. I mean, how chicken is that?"

"Not at all. I can understand your motivations."

"Well . . ."

"And anyway, *now* was the perfect time to mention it, right?"

She smiled, and raised her wineglass. "Okay. Salut."

"Cheers."

They touched glasses, and sipped.

While he wondered whether to say more, she stood, taking her plate to the sink. "Stay put," she said, and returned with the tureen of noodles and the garlic bread.

"So, has your music been performed nationally?"

"Coast to coast," he said, smiling, taking some bread. "Though not much in between."

"Is it hard to get orchestras interested in new stuff?"

"Well, you need a champion. Some rising conductor, maybe in a metropolitan orchestra, or maybe a small regional orchestra that could record your stuff."

"When was your last concert?"

He thought. Remembering before Anna's death. "The last was at the Aldeburgh Festival, in England. Three years ago. That was a big deal. A month before that I had a piece performed down in Ojai, California."

He served himself a plentiful portion of noodles; they were delicious. He complimented them, and they ate for a time in silence.

"What's the busiest this place has gotten? You ever filled all the rooms?"

"Once. Hard to imagine, isn't it? In summer we get more visitors who wander down from 101." She poured herself a half glass more wine. "I've been here since . . . since nineteen hundred and eighty-two. I opened the house in eighty-seven. It was busiest, I guess, in the early nineties."

The lights flickered, died.

In the dark, he felt the floorboards roll under his shoes.

The china clinked.

"Megan?"

He half-stood.

"Another tremblor," she said.

Behind him in the living room, metal chimed and crashed—knick-knacks tumbling from the shelves.

A pot clanged into the sink.

One moment she was sitting in the dark, staring up at the ceiling, then she was up, moving past him. Unsure of his step, his heart beating in his throat, he followed, through the dining room.

Faint light from the bay window.

"Oh, damn." She was walking across the carpet.

"Be careful, Megan."

"I have candles," she said. "In the drawer."

"It may not be over."

She walked to the bureau and pulled open the bottom drawer. He heard a clacking as she withdrew the candles. Then she turned toward him and they stood listening, waiting.

"It's over," she said, a gray figure in the dark.

Then the papery slide of a matchbox being opened; and a scratching.

The match tip flared, went to the top of the candle. As the wick caught, she shook the match out, lifted the candle, holding it at arm's length. The light quivered across the room.

The carpet, sea green, was littered with coins, seashells, sand dollars. A green glass globe sat on the fireplace flagstone, uncracked, a piece of driftwood beside it.

Somewhere outside, a low siren groaned once.

"The volunteer fire alarm," Megan said.

What about the power lines?

"Megan, I'm going to check outside."

"I'll call Bennie."

The street was pitch-black.

Bundled in his coat, he nearly tripped down the slick stairs, looking for the sputter of downed lines or fires.

The neighborhood was quiet in the rain.

He walked through wet grass to the curb. The electricity was out along Seventh, and down Alder.

Across the street, the door of the Italianate opened and a figure hurried down the stairs, in a white raincoat, crossing the lawn to the driveway. It was the lady with the bouffant hairdo—Mrs. Nelson. She opened the door of her station wagon.

Another siren blast sounded up the hill, echoing off the windows.

"Mrs. Nelson!" he called out.

She startled. "Oh, goodness! Mister Kent! The rumbler's put me on edge!"

"Think there's been damage?"

"Second siren should be the all-clear! I think everything's okay! But I have to check on work!" She ducked into the station wagon, backed out of the driveway and headed north along Seventh.

He stood listening for other sounds—cars, voices, police sirens—but heard only the rain. As his eyes adjusted he could see candles glimmering behind windows next door, then curtains twitching in the house next to Mrs. Nelson's, a face peering out.

The rain was falling harder.

He returned inside, shed jacket and shoes, in dim candlelight. Two small candles burned on the dining room table. She sat by the coffee table, lighting a third, setting it on a small dish. The match jumped.

"Power's out all over," Russ told her. "And Mrs. Nelson just ran off to work."

"Bennie thinks it'll be out for a while." She shook the match out. "Maybe I shouldn't have lit these? If another one's on its way?" There was tension in her voice.

"Do you have a radio?"

She nodded, with the back of her hand wiping strands of hair from her eyes. "Somewhere." She stood up. "Ummm, in my room, I think." She took up one of the candles and walked carefully into the rec room.

Russ stepped around a sand dollar and a scattering of coins, to the dining room table.

With a slightly shaking hand, he poured himself some more wine, drank it down, then stood waiting for the adrenaline rush to subside. He could hear Megan moving around in the bedroom, and a car driving past along Seventh—someone else off to check on their business, perhaps. He picked up his glass and, after a hesitation, Megan's, which was half-full. He carried them into the living room.

There came the faint sound of staticky music, pop, then Mozart or Haydn, as the candlelight pooled in the entrance: louder, as she walked back into the living room, clutching the portable radio. "This is the Rostov station." She knelt down beside the table, setting the candle on the table, and the radio beside it. "We're not big news in Rostov."

"I guess not."

She noticed her glass. "Thanks. She lifted it, gulped a mouthful.

"You're missing the bouquet." Smiling, he likewise gulped. It burned down the back of his throat, up his nostrils.

"I hate quakes," she said, sitting back on her heels. She laughed, though it sounded forced. Her shoulders dropped. "I've decided it. I hate them. I don't want to be in another one."

"Then let's not think about it."

"Sorry, Russ. I'm a wimp."

She pushed her shoulders back, a shiver going through her. She shut her eyes.

Russ looked at a gray sand dollar and pieces of worn green glass on the carpet. "So how long have you been collecting those knickknacks?"

"To distract me, right?"

"Of course."

She drank some more wine. "Hmmm. Those are all a few years after college. Eighty-five?"

"So you and Jack took trips to the coast a lot?"

She nodded. "Not to here, but over to the Washington coast." Watching her glass in the candlelight, the wine-colored reflection on her jeans.

Then, nearly spilling her glass, she stood up. "A sec," she said. Unsteady, she set down the glass and took up the candle and walked carefully across the living room, into the rec room, to her bedroom.

He leaned forward, set down his wine. Tiredness was replacing the adrenaline, and he yawned.

"This is Jack," she said, returning to the living room.

She knelt down.

She held the small photograph from her bureau.

He squinted up, pretending to study it for the first time.

The young man with black hair, glasses, turtleneck, smiling, gazing at somebody to the right of the camera.

"Where were you in eighty-five, Russ?" Slowly, she set the candle on the coffee table, and the photo beside it, then sat cross-legged on the carpet.

She switched off the radio.

"Eighty-five?" Startled by the new silence, he watched the candle. "I was in Santa Fe, serving a residency program. My first. Anna was a student teacher at college."

She drank some more, blinking blearily. Squinting, now, noticing something on the carpet. "Look at this." She leaned back on her heels and held up something between her index finger and thumb. It was a gold tube.

"What is it?"

She turned it this way and that, so it caught the candlelight. He hadn't a clue.

"You don't know?"

"No."

She laughed, then brought the tube to her lips. C, faint as the candle flame, and just as orange.

"A recorder," he said, surprised. Or was it a penny whistle?

She conjured three more notes, in an ascending scale, the last one causing the flame to flutter. "How do you like my music?"

"Nice."

She held it in front of her eyes and regarded it, then reached for her wineglass.

"Where did you get it?"

She didn't answer for a long moment. Her eyes were unfocused.

"Hmmm?"

"The penny whistle? Where'd you get it?"

"Can't remember. Had it a long time. From a street fair, I think."

"So . . . if you and Jack met at college, why did you decide to settle here?"

She set down the glass, looking at the recorder. "If you'd asked me then where I'd be twenty years down the line . . ." She watched it for a long moment, then brought it to her lips and conjured a faint C, G, A.

Her eyes, looking at something beyond the music.

Faintly smiling, she set it down on the table. "Jack came back when his father died. It would only be a few years, long enough to repay his debt to the town. Only a few years in a wonderful mansion on the Oregon coast. I didn't complain. Sounded like a strange sort of paradise to me."

She shook her head, drank the rest of her wine. She stared at the candle. A moment later she stretched, then turned partly away from him, and laid herself slowly back on the bare carpet near the table.

"A few years," she murmured, shutting her eyes. "And here I am."

Brown hair pooling in candlelight. Her upside-down face, and smile, and the pale curve of her throat, under the sweater.

Russ leaned forward, picked up the whistle. Weighed it in his hand. A duct flute. Tin.

The tip was warm, and tasted of wine. He exhaled a faint C, and allowed it to fade into the rustling crackle of the candles and the rain.

Then sensed a presence.

Here and gone, as he conjured another C, and watched the candle.

In the dark to either side, Anna, in silence. Solemn and gray, and nothing more, since he refused to look directly. The shape like Anna made of sand. A wounded stare.

He let it grow, in the dark of the room, to either side, in the blood beating in his ears. The ghost of Anna made of sand, made of grayness. Holding those last words never spoken in her open mouth.

As the very air itself took on the dim green shimmer of underwater.

Anna, somewhere on this hillside, among the overgrown houses. Here.

He shut his eyes and rode the pounding blood, as his skin came alive to it, ready to feel a hand on his face, his neck. Then it subsided, to rain tapping the windows, and Megan breathing deeply.

He opened his eyes, and watched her in the candlelight; eyes shut, lips half-parted, one hand below her breasts, rising and falling.

Asleep.

He moved his hand, then his leg. Sat forward, stood up.

He found a blanket in the rec room and gently draped it over her, then blew out all the candles but one, and brought it upstairs.

. . .

Sometime in the early morning he was startled awake when the lamp flashed on. Squinting against the glare, heart pounding, he saw an after-image of blood-laced water, and recalled it hovering like smoke over a distant city on the bottom of the sea.

No ghosts in sight.

He stood in morning glory, near the edge of the bluff, squinting into the breeze.

It was cold and smelled of the sea, and was a balm, along with the tidal roar, and the sight of combers hurtling in slow motion, gray and white.

Gulls wheeling above the surf.

During the walk he'd mulled over the night before. The quake, and their anxious reactions to it, and the wine. Too much wine, and the nightmares. It could all be explained.

Russ looked up over his left shoulder, at the mansion, green and gray against the clouds.

From up there in the tower, this stretch of ground had seemed anonymous. He had decided, two nights ago, that the nightmares were over, and the dire reasons for the trip had been overcome.

He glanced back down, stepped closer to the edge.

The inquest decided Anna had lost her footing on loose rocks here at the edge of the bluff, had fallen into a head down position, striking the rock, then the shingle, and barnacled boulders.

Due to the nature of the injury, they said she'd suffered little.

He looked down to where her body had come to a rest. The drop looked less dangerous than it had seemed that day, or the last time he was out here.

Resisting a sudden—quite gratifying—wave of dizziness, he walked along the edge until he found the trail that Old Crick had followed, a gentle switchback down the rock. He stepped over a fringe of scotch broom, over the edge, his shoe dropping down until it found the damp rock slope. He shifted over, crouching to clutch the rock until both shoes were on the slope, then began to climb down. With his weight thrown

back, his palms steadying himself on the rock, he reached the more modest slope and was drawn, jogging, down to the rocks.

Here was more immediate sensation.

The stinging air, the rush of water, the noise, reverberating off the
cliff-face. Yes, this is what it had been like.

A dozen paces away, the tide spilled over dark stones, seaweed and
driftwood, hissing its retreat. He was level with the water, surrounded
by cliffs which intensified the sounds, gave them a shrill edge.

He forced his eyes to the rock beneath his shoes.

This was the place. Kicking away some dried polyps, and gravel, he
recognized it. A flat shelf some eight meters wide, among the bumpy
shingle.

Her head had been tilted toward her left shoulder while she stared at
the sky, a slack expression slowly stealing across her otherwise uninjured
face. One arm had been scraped and bloodied, her left leg bent outward
at the knee. A viscous fluid covered the rock beneath her head, became a
bright red on the barnacles, laced with her blond hair.

When he had touched her shoulder, she seemed to find a last bit of
awareness. Her eyes had turned to him, and through the mask of her face
communicated a vague ease, an acceptance, perhaps.

Or something like surprise. Amusement.

Then her stare had slowly hardened, remaining fixed on the sky when
he stepped back.

The sound must have occurred to him then, the watery crown. And
the nightmares, born in that awful silent stretch of time before Charles
Crick appeared above, shouting down about having called the State
Patrol.

He looked up, around. Shook off that silence.

On either side stacks of basalt pushed out from the cliff face. Beyond
were more barnacled boulders, driftwood, and ropes of seaweed tussling
in the current.

Something winked there, a brief gleam as the tide withdrew.

Again.

He relaxed his clenched fists, then began to walk along the shore
toward it, idly curious. Another gleam, turquoise. A glass fishing float?

Whatever it was, it would supply him with a reason for such a morbid excursion, after the fact. In case Old Crick was home when Russ climbed back up, and happened to see him.

Hi, Charles! I saw something in the waves. Had to check it out.

He rounded the edge of the basalt stack. He kicked through polyps and driftwood. Backed against rock, with only a few yards of shore between him and the tide, he stood for a moment gazing down at the rushing green and silver water.

The smell of brine was thick, oppressive like the mist in his hair, his eyes. When the tide rolled out he saw the object in his periphery. A narrow glint, tangled in seaweed.

He stepped toward it, trying to keep his shoes away from the water. The object looked rectangular. It shimmered.

Pushing up the sleeve of his jacket, he waited for the tide to withdraw. As it surged out he leaned forward to grab the object—suddenly dizzy as if the ground were sliding out from under him. His fingers grasped nothing, and the icy water rushed back in, submerging his hand, rolling forward to soak his shoes. He swore. He stepped closer, leaning farther forward—water up to his ankles now—until his fingers touched a smooth surface. He seized it, lifted it out.

It was cool and heavy, more complex than a simple rectangle. Its shape had ten flat sides, of what looked like iridescent pearl.

Stepping back, he tilted the box, and tiny blue flecks danced across the surface. He shook it, and felt something shift inside.

Whatever it was, it hadn't been in the water for long.

Something to show Tom Carver, he thought, touching the smooth edge.

He shook it again, and the motion seemed to conjure voices out of the air.

For a moment, he stood still. The voices continued, emerging from the tidal roar. They seemed to be coming from behind him, from the lookout point at the top of the bluff. He hadn't seen a soul during his walk along First and down Oceanview. With its scrim of trees, the bluff had always seemed to be an unlikely place for townspeople to visit. And now here were voices, two of them, arguing, shouting in flat, gloomy tones, as if they were fighting about some old and exhausted topic. He couldn't make out the words. After listening a few moments, he approached the edge of the basalt stack.

Holding the strange box close to his chest, he peered around the rock.

Two figures stood at the top of the bluff. They were short and plump, and wore black coats. They held their gloved hands cupped in front of them as they gazed soberly out at the sea.

The dark dwarves.

Not sooty anymore, no, but it was unmistakably them. One had thick blond hair, the other a sparse fringe of black.

Without looking away, Russ stuffed the curious box into his inner coat pocket and buttoned it shut.

The blond one began to cry. He pulled out a yellow handkerchief and blotted his eyes, while the other continued speaking in a deadpan tone. The blond one shook his head and turned away, while the other remained, still talking, though his voice was now quiet enough to be lost beneath the surf.

Russ felt a chill from his soaked shoes, but he was hesitant to step forward. The men might disappear, figments from a dream.

But anger made him step out, walk three paces into the cove.

He raised his hand.

The black-haired one froze, and gaped. Starting, the blond one turned around, clutching a yellow handkerchief to his chest. When he saw Russ he pantomimed a frightful scream and lumbered out of sight.

The other remained for an instant, then stumbled after his friend.

Confusion kept Russ rooted to the beach. He nearly called out, then—charged with adrenaline—he ran toward the trail, began climbing, using hands as well as feet as he scrambled up the wet rock, intent only upon seeing the soot-covered men when he reached the top. If he was quick enough, they couldn't disappear.

And upon scrambling over the fringe of basalt and scotch broom, he saw black coats dwindling in the evergreens.

"Wait!" he called out, hoarse, gasping for breath. Blood pounded in his temples. He began running through the tall grass toward the trees, faster than he'd run in years, expecting to snag his foot yet somehow keeping pace, dodging through the hemlocks, branches whizzing past, his eyes set on the vague black forms in the sunlit street beyond.

When he reached the cul-de-sac he spotted them lumbering up the sidewalk near the top of the hill. He doubled over for a moment, tried to gain his breath, then continued, jogging slowly up Oceanview. They disappeared over the crest and he was alone, winded, jogging up past the bungalows and hoping that nobody would notice, or call out to him.

They'll disappear, he thought. They'll run into a house, hide behind a hedge.

On reaching First Street he spotted them stumbling along in the middle of the road.

Blinking against sweat, he crossed First to the other sidewalk—the black-haired one casting glances over his shoulder, dragging his friend around the corner, onto Cheddar Street.

Again, Russ thought they had vanished, yet when he turned that corner he saw them near the intersection with Second. The blond one stumbled with his free arm outspread, as if ready to grasp something should he fall.

Ignoring the burning in his chest, the numbness on the soles of his feet, he maintained his pace through the intersection with Second, past Tom Carver's house, slowing as he reached the hill. His gait faltered as he reached Third, but he was closer now, close enough to see their terrified faces when they glanced back.

The factory. They were heading for the cheese factory.

He pushed himself, lengthened his stride, knees aching. Not far, now. Gasping. Through the trees ahead, a yellow building.

He tripped. He sprawled forward and struck the pavement with his forehead. A blizzard of stars engulfed him, his ears rang, and he lay there for a moment—for minutes?—until the stars winked out one by one by one.

He spit dirt from his lips. The concrete was icy against his hands. He pushed up, struggling to his knees, ignoring the burning along his chin, the warm trail of blood that now soaked into his shirt collar.

He was up, walking, barely running toward the great yellow building with the twirling sign *Evening Cheeses*, toward the double glass doors that were slowly swinging shut.

"Where? Where . . . are they?"

The receptionist—it was Mrs. Nelson from across the street—gawked. She raised her eyebrows. She touched her bouffant hairdo, and lifted a snack tray of cheese. Then, "Do you need first aid?"

We Provide the Cheese! read a poster behind her desk.

He turned to the empty lobby. He wiped sweat from his eyes. "They . . ." It was marbled with blood on his hand. "Where . . ."

Was he making sense?

He doubled over and tried to catch his breath. Something burned along his chest, damp between the shirt and skin.

When he straightened, he saw a door directly ahead, inset with a crystal swan-winged handle, and stumbled toward it.

Mrs. Nelson cried out, "You can't go in there!"

Just before losing his balance, he grabbed the handle and swung with the door into the room.

"What's the problem?"

Russ straightened, tried to say something imperative, but nothing came out.

"Are you hurt?" A brawny, balding man stood behind the desk, shirt-sleeves rolled up. His receding hair formed a sharp widow's peak. His lips were small, his nose flat and wide. His eyes didn't waver.

Russ swallowed, tasting blood. He cleared his throat, wiped his mouth. "You're . . . hiding them. Two men. In black coats. They came in here. I want to know where they are." He suddenly noticed—and accepted quite easily—the mansion made of cheese sitting on the man's desk. It was a replica of the Evening mansion, about three feet tall, impeccably detailed with horseshoe entrance, patterned shingles, and a tower jutting up from the corner. The smell of it permeated the room.

"You're bleeding, did you know that?" The man's voice was gentle; he held a surgical scalpel in his right hand. He gave a slight, embarrassed smile, set the scalpel down beside the trellised porch, and rummaged through the contents of his desk. He pulled a tissue from a tissue box and stretched across the gabled roofs to offer it to Russ.

Russ took it, remembering him now from the Gathering: the man who'd asked Peggy to dance.

"You really look upset," the man said. "Have a seat. Please." His eyes darted toward the door.

Russ gained his breath. "Where are they?"

Behind him, Mrs. Nelson said, "It's Russell Kent. He pushed his way in."

"That's all right, Gloria." He addressed Russ, renewing his smile. "Please sit down. I'm Bob Burle."

A piece of driftwood sat on the corner of his desk. *Bob B*, it read.

He motioned to the chair. "Please."

Russ moved around to it, and sat down heavily. Pain stabbed at his knee. He blotted the cut, and when he brought the tissue forward it was bright with blood.

"Here's a few more." Burle slid the tissue box around the mansion, then reached into the drawer again. "I had some antiseptic in here, otherwise Gloria can . . ." He brought out a bottle and a large bandage. "Here we go." He pushed them across the desk to Russ. "Tell me, Mister Kent, did you fall on company property?"

"No."

"I couldn't hear you. I'm sorry."

"No," Russ repeated.

"Did you hear that, Gloria?"

"Yes, Mister Burle. Do you want me to phone Megan?"

"Yeah, do that. And you can leave us now. Shut the door, please."

Russ heard the door click shut. He pulled some more tissues from the box.

"Use that wastebasket down there near your foot," Burle said, sitting down. He studied Russ around the side of the mansion.

"Where are the two men?" Russ asked. His hand shook as he held the tissue to his forehead.

"Which two men?"

"They ran in here right before I did." He tossed the bloody tissue into the basket, then pulled out a fresh one. His forehead burned. He felt blood or sweat trailing along the edge of his beard.

"What did they do, Mister Kent? Are they the ones that hurt you?"

"No, I fell. I was chasing them, and I fell."

"Why were you chasing them?"

"Because they were running away from me," Russ said, grimacing as he realized how ridiculous it sounded. "I just want to know who they are."

Burle leaned back in his chair. "Why?"

"Because they were standing in front of my house four days ago. Watching my window. And they disappeared before I could talk to them."

Burle laughed. He leaned forward and lifted the scalpel, then ran the blade along the slanted tower roof. A flake of cheese fell to the blotter with an audible tap. "This is a small town, Mister Kent. People feel safe enough to stroll and sightsee; it doesn't mean they're watching you. Megan Sumner's home is a refurbished Second Empire. It's worth a look now and then."

"Why did they run? Just now, out on the bluff?"

Burle shrugged. He slouched to peer up at the tower, then smiled. "Okay, Mister Kent. Okay." Dropping the scalpel, he reached forward and fumbled for an intercom button. "Gloria?"

There was a rasping, buzzing pause. "Yes, sir?"

"Who were the two gentlemen that came in prior to Mister Kent?"

"It was Misters Danace and Obolus," she said, and after a moment's hesitation added, "They told me Mister Kent was chasing them."

"Okay. Thanks." Burle leaned back, then shrugged. "They were two of my workers, Mister Kent. Stan Danace and Stan Obolus. We call them the two Stans. Quiet types, never had any trouble with them. They're probably cowering in the employee locker room even as we speak."

Russ blinked as some blood touched his eye. He dabbed at his cut, reciting the names to himself.

"I don't think you're going to need stitches for that, Mister Kent. Bleeding's the only concern now. How's it coming?"

Russ pulled away the tissue. "Slowing down."

"Did you fall out on Cheddar?"

Russ tried to nod. "Yes," he said. "Near the top."

Shaking his head, Burle turned his attention back to the cheese mansion. He leaned forward and peered up at the tower. "I've been carping for some time now about the condition of our sidewalks. But money's tight." Plucking up the scalpel, he knelt behind his desk, muttering "I need to get a grounds-eye view."

While the Master Cheesemaker was hidden, Russ reached into his jacket and unsnapped the inner pocket. He touched the peculiar box. It seemed intact, its surfaces cool and comforting.

A few minutes later, the intercom buzzed. "Megan Sumner is waiting in the lobby, Mister Burle."

Burle stood. "Take the tissue box," he said to Russ. "I'll clean up here. You go home and rest."

The door opened behind him. Megan stood there, keys in hand. Her lips parted. "God, Russ, are you okay?" She stepped forward, almost reached out for his forehead, then drew back her hand. "What happened?"

"I was ghost hunting," he said. With a wry, pained smile, he followed her out the door.

"This is going to sting." She dabbed antiseptic ointment along the cut above his right eye, pulling it away momentarily when he winced, then touched it to the bruise high on his forehead. She was sitting beside him on the couch. Arrayed on the coffee table were a bottle of hydrogen peroxide, a roll of gauze, some bandages and ointment, and the box he'd found along the shore.

She applied a sterile pad, taped it, then wrapped thin gauze around his head. "This is a temporary measure. We'll see how it looks tomorrow."

After securing it, she leaned back and gave him the peace sign. "How many fingers?"

He attempted a smile. "I'm fine." He stared down at the puzzle box. Even in the dim living room, its facets glowed, blue flecks shimmering across its many sides.

"They were your sooty dwarves, huh?"

He nodded, then said, quietly, "Yes." His legs were cramping up. He only wanted to crawl upstairs and soak in the tub before sleeping.

She lifted the puzzle box. "You should show this to Bennie," she said, shaking it gently. "He'll love it."

"I will." He shut his eyes, heard her shift on the couch beside him.

Quietly: "Hmmm. I know the two Stans, Russ."

He looked at her. She met his eyes, and a long moment later said, "They're honorary members, too. Of the ACL."

Confused, Russ tried to form a question, but she said, "Bob was telling the truth. They work at the factory. They don't go out much. But I'll try to talk to them. Find out why they ran. Okay?"

Russ nodded. "I think when the pain goes away, I'll feel even more a fool." Carefully, he touched the bandage. "I need a bath."

"Come on, let's get you upstairs."

His head throbbed as he stood. Megan wrapped one arm around his waist, held his forearm and led him across the living room.

"How is it?" she asked, as they climbed the stairs. "Bearable?"

"Yes."

She walked with him into his bedroom, turned up the light. Russ pulled out clean boxers and a T-shirt.

In the bathroom, he stood near the sink while she prepared the tub, plugging the drain and twisting the tap handles. Water splashed down, echoing in the bronze space.

He gazed into the mirror. Curls of brown hair fell over the top of the bandage. Tired eyes accented by crow's feet, deeper than ever.

"Maybe I should take your temperature."

"I'll be okay," he said.

"I have some codeine aspirin."

He gently touched the edge of the bandage. "That would probably help. Thank you, Megan."

"See you after."

She left. Russ nearly called her. He shut the door. He climbed painfully into the tub and leaned back in the water. His forehead stung, his skull pounded. The bandage wilted in the steam.

He had to rouse himself from near-sleep, get up and towel off. His wound ached as he leaned over to pull on his boxers. Carefully he pulled on the T-shirt, then walked across the cold hall into his room.

As he was climbing into bed, pulling up the sheets, she knocked at the door.

"Come in."

"Here's two little pills." She wore a robe and slippers. She handed him a glass of water then the pills. "How does it feel?"

"Better. Much better after this." He swallowed them down, and set the glass on the desk, beside the hycopathius. "I'm feeling foolish." He sank back against the pillow, grimacing.

"You're not, Russ." Then, quietly, she said, "And I'm going to prove it to you, tomorrow."

He watched her, nearly spoke, then, feeling the silence stretch, pulled back the blankets, moved closer to the wall.

She looked down at the bare mattress. "Are you sure?"

"I am."

She nodded, and after looking at the open door, pulled loose the belt on her robe, shrugged it off. Below the hem of her T-shirt, white panties, long supple legs. Then the surprising warmth of her as she moved under the sheets, the smell of shampoo, and her cold toes brushing the tops of his feet. "Get some sleep," she said. He smiled into her hair, a remote excitement mingling with something entirely familiar as she rested her head on his shoulder, and the codeine warmed his veins and fogged his thoughts, and he slowly drifted down.

part two
the celestial country

The musicians of the orchestra at last took their places. The first violin had gone to the stand to give a modest *la* to his colleagues. The stringed instruments, the wind instruments, the drums and cymbals, were in accord. The orchestra leader only waited for the sound of the bell to beat the first measure.

—*Dr. Ox's Experiment* by Jules Verne

Anna, in a yellow summer dress, walks beside him.

"It's called Oceanview!"

She points to the street sign as they round the corner, then the glittering sea is revealed. "Look!"

Her hair, her dress, are sunlit, in luminous B-flat.

As they follow the sidewalk down the hill, he listens.

"All the houses are empty, I think, Russ."

At the bottom, Old Crick appears, hands in the pockets of his dungarees. "Afternoon, folks." He nods. "Guess you're here to see it?"

"We are," says Anna.

"This way, then." He leads them over the cul-de-sac curb into the trees.

Russ tries to ask Anna what they're here to see, but she's hurrying ahead, after the old man with sparse brown hair, looking up at the branches. She reaches for one, grabs. Snaps off the end.

It twangs. E flat.

And Old Crick, glancing back, has become Joseph Evening in a sere black coat and cravat tie, and a grave smile. "*Give us more of this wondrous water,*" he says over his shoulder, in a peculiarly thin baritone, as they emerge onto the bluff.

"We don't mind the rain, do we, Russ? We grew up on the east coast."

Madrona trees hunch against the sea. The horizon visibly curves. And where the bluff ends is a vertical lattice of black steel and down-curving rail: the top of a spiral staircase.

Joseph Evening stops beside it. "*An acquaintance of mine, knowing my curiosity in such matters, has sent for both of you.*" His voice might have come from an old 78 rpm record, and a Victrola's horn. "*Watch your steps, sir and miss.*"

The air resounds with the cries of seagulls, echoing against the cliffs, though there's not a gull in sight.

Joseph Evening gestures at the staircase. "*Tours cease at dusk.*" Smiling, for an instant he becomes his portrait, complete with sunburst frame.

Anna laughs and hurries ahead. Russ tries to stop her but she's already climbing down. He follows, onto black iron crescent moons and stars, around and down, looking past them to a shape in the water below. Hard to see through the railing and stairs. Something massive, bristling white and gray.

He stops, leans over the rail.

Flecks of gray and white, a nervous motion. Thousands of gulls shoulder to shoulder, shuffling, and Anna is climbing down toward them, around and down, skirt whipping in the breeze. She waves the alder sprig. She shouts. The effect is wind on water—whitecaps, and thousands of wings shrugging, the air trembling as the gulls take flight, in every direction.

He crouches, waits for them to pass.

What remains below is a ship. The shape of it, against the glittering green tide, is hard to hold. Ovoid, a frozen roil of silver and green filigree, over a hull like black lava. Sunlight skitters over furrows, over scallops, silver to black to green, to a brilliant yellow on the spine, a glowing emblem:

Mobilis in Mobili
"*N*"

Rustling sheets, a weight on the mattress beside him.

He opened his eyes.

Megan was watching him, close-by, a tangle of hair across her face. "You were smiling."

He stretched, became aware of a dull ache throughout his body, an itch across his forehead and scalp, beneath taut gauze. "I was dreaming," he said, carefully turning his head toward her. "Of the *Nautilus*."

"A good dream?"

Smiling again, he tried to remember it. "Weird dream." He pushed up against the pillow, wincing at a slight pain above his left eye, and in his shoulders, his legs. "I think Captain Nemo was nearby."

The corner windows were full of sunlight.

"How does the head feel?"

"Hmmm. Bearable."

She leaned toward him and gently touched the edge of the gauze. "The bandage looks great. I did a splendid job, if I do say so."

"You should say so." He hazarded another stretch, and mused over the night before, and this strange contentment.

She lay back on the pillow. When she spoke again it was quiet, almost a whisper. "We're going to tell you everything." She brought her arms over her head, against the bright light, and tangled her fingers in her hair. "All our silly secrets. Would you like that?"

He nodded. "Yes."

"We'll go see Bennie after breakfast."

"Bennie, you have visitors!"

They walked down the Weft's gloomy aisle. Russ was slow, his thighs and hamstrings aching from yesterday's run.

Ahead, somebody yawned.

They found Dreerson slouched in the plush chair behind his desk. His eyes were puffy, and he blinked twice, looking up. He stretched. "Morning." He pulled down the hem of his cardigan. "Megan. And Russell." He rubbed his eyes, and stretched again.

A pistol lay on the table beside him. A .45 Smith and Wesson.

He noticed the direction of their gaze. "Tom's. Loaded with blanks." He pushed it aside, yawned, then heaved himself to his feet, and sat down on the stool beside the register.

"We have something to show you," she said.

"Really. I'm tremendously excited, though I may not sound like it." Dreerson blinked again, then peered at Russ's forehead. "Good lord. What happened?"

"A stupid accident," Russ told him.

"Is it the town's fault?"

"No, Bennie. It was his own fault."

Dreerson's gray eyebrows drooped. "Is it serious?"

"A nasty cut and a bruise," she said, looking at the bandage. "Bled a lot, but I don't think it's too serious. We'll keep an eye on it."

From his inside coat pocket, Russ pulled out the linen-wrapped object. He uncovered the glimmering box.

Dreerson leaned forward, scratching his belly.

"Flotsam," Russ said. "I found it in the water, beneath the bluff at Oceanview."

Dreerson bit his plump lower lip. He looked up at Russ's forehead. "Did you hurt yourself climbing down to it?"

"Later. I was chasing my sooty men up the hill. I tripped."

Megan said, "The Stans, from the factory, Bennie."

"Stan Danace was one."

"Oh." Dreerson's eyebrows raised. "Of course I know Danace. A good, little man. But to tell you the truth I've never seen him here in town, actually."

Dreerson offered no further enlightenment, but turned his attention to the box. "May I hold it?"

Russ passed it into the bookseller's hands. Turning on the nearest library lamp, Dreerson brought the box under the shade. The sides faintly glowing with blue flecks.

He turned it over, watching the flecks flow across the surface.

"Bennie, I've told Russ we're going to let him in on everything. I think he deserves to know. And you're a better storyteller than me."

With a smile, Russ said, "Somebody needs to tell me something."

Dreerson tilted his head. The lamplight gave green highlights into his wild gray bangs. "Yes, we don't fear the Cheese League, do we?" He lifted the box in both hands. "But not down here. Let's go up to my apartment." He stepped out into the aisle, and glanced at the front door. "If anyone drops by, we'll hear the foghorn."

"Watch yourselves."

Russ followed Megan along a narrow hallway on the second floor of the house. Hardbacks were stacked waist high on either side and the air was warm, tinged with Mentholatum. "I still haven't managed to entirely straighten up after the quake."

The upper walls were hung with striking Indian artifacts—carved cedar masks, a ceremonial rattle, portions of hide covered with pictographs of owls and suns—as well as watercolors of Ody, signed *Tom*.

"Here we go," Dreerson said, ushering them into a workroom crowded with two tall desks, boxes, and a row of file cabinets, each labelled *MORGUE*. Like everywhere else in the Weft, the surfaces were cluttered. Light from a hexagonal window spilled onto books, magazines, coffee cups, empty liquor bottles, and a dusty hycopathius, nestled in the keywell of an old typewriter. It was larger than the one Crick had given Russ, with some of the spines broken off.

"Look for seats," Dreerson told them. Russ found a canvas chair beneath a pile of blankets. Megan found another folded up and stuffed between two file cabinets, while Dreerson rolled out a stool.

They took their places, Russ and Megan side by side in the channel formed by two desks, facing Dreerson, who, for the moment, stood in front of the little window. He lifted the box into the glare, smiling at the flecks of blue that danced in the surface. A moment later he turned to Megan. "So. You want me to tell the impossible history?"

"Please." She folded her hands.

"And Russell, you'd like to listen?"

He nodded, setting aside his questions, and that word *impossible*.

"Hmmm. I always wondered how I would tell it. I think we all have here in town. I actually wrote down a narrative some ten years ago. Very secretly, hush-hush, in candlelight, in the dead of night—for others who attempted such insolence have suffered very early, entirely reasonable, accidental deaths. I put the only copy in a safety-deposit box, in Rostov." He smiled uneasily, and looked back at the puzzle box.

"There's something inside," she said. "We shook it."

Dreerson raised an eyebrow. "What happened?"

"Nothing."

He lifted it to his ear and, carefully, his face tight with trepidation, he shook it. "You found this *in* the ocean?"

"Yes."

Dreerson looked around at the nearby shelves, then walked to one of the file cabinets, grabbed a small fishbowl full of rubber bands and paper clips, and dumped its contents onto the cabinet.

"Would anyone like some coffee? I'm being an awful host."

"Sure," Russ said, shifting on the stool. Trying for patience.

Megan asked for a glass of water. Dreerson squeezed past them with a murmured "pardon me," disappearing down the hallway. A moment later, running water could be heard.

Megan nudged Russ with her foot, and smiled. "Okay?"

"Okay."

"How's the head?"

He gently touched the edge of the bandage. "Itchy," he said.

Dreerson returned holding the fishbowl against his stomach, the puzzle box bobbing in cloudy water. "I've tried to approximate the sea," he said, setting the bowl down beside the typewriter. Light from the window glowed and spun in the water, and cast a faint rainbow onto the desk.

"The history should be prefaced." Dreerson ran a hand through his dishevelled hair. "An illustration, or illustrations. Give me a moment, please." He walked to a file cabinet, and leaned close to read the faded labels. "These drawers hold the remaining archives of my newspaper career." He thumbed a catch and slid the second drawer open. "Not a vast career, Russell. The newspaper was never more than ten pages an issue, printed because Joseph Evening himself asked me to. He would say, 'What's a small town without a newspaper,' and reply to it, 'A town with a secret, Bernard.'"

He pulled out a handful of photographs, looking down at one—a 5×7—as he walked back to his stool.

Sitting, he handed the photograph to Russ.

It was a head-and-shoulders portrait of Joseph Evening, in a dark suit. He lay against a knitted pillowcase. His beard was long and snowy white, the top of his head bald and freckled. His eyes were closed.

This was a dead man. The burial suit was similar to the outfit that Russ had seen in the earlier portrait, without the claret tie.

"How long after he died?" Russ asked, noticing the stillness in Joseph's drawn face, the eyes and eyelashes.

"A few hours," Dreerson replied. "They told my father not to shoot it, but he did anyway. Would you say it's a respectful picture?"

"Yes."

"Memorial photographs were common at the time, especially when the subject was such a great man."

Russ studied the face, the remoteness of it, vacated.

"This was the moment, crystallized. We like to think the town continued prosperously, and by all accounts it did, for two decades, before the cheese clique took over. But here is the moment of its death. Our town, our dreams, with him."

Russ tilted the photograph. Sunlight flashed across the head and shoulders.

"As with most of history, Russell, it's a tale of upstairs and downstairs. Though in our case the term must be taken quite literally."

Dreerson handed Russ a mug of coffee. "It's not too hot for you in here, is it?" He reached into the drawer, came back with a bottle of bourbon. He splashed some into his mug. "Instant coffee requires this," he explained. "It only improves the taste." He offered some to Russ.

"Tiny bit," Russ said.

"My bones are succumbing to age and winter. I dull my aches with Mentholatum."

Megan said, "You should see a doctor, Bennie."

"Perhaps." He saluted her with his mug. "But it's not too bad yet, dear. On with the story."

Dreerson blew on the coffee, and the steam swept up and over his face. He inhaled. "Russell, the first time you came into my store, you bought a book. Did you happen to notice where it was shelved? The section name?"

Russ thought for a moment. "Hesperus."

"You're familiar with it? It means the Evening Star, of course. I've had visitors think it was a pun, somehow. Or ask why the section is such a mixture of titles, and I've always managed to bluff my way out of it. I'm always hoping I'll fail, and that the visitor would demand a better answer. My own subtle brand of civil disobedience." He smiled to Megan. "Hesperus is the Evening Star. It's also linked to *Hesperius*, which means 'Western,' and *Hesperia*, which means 'the land of the evening star,' or 'the western land.' Joseph Evening came up with the name, as he came up with his own surname. So I suppose I should tell you something about him. This gentleman, caught in everlasting sleep."

Russ looked at the dead man on the pillow.

"He was born in 1876, in Wilmington, Delaware, as Joseph Harriman Silfax. His parents were moderately wealthy, the father—named Harriman—was a successful surgeon, and planned a prosperous medical career for his son. But Joseph had no interest in medicine, or whatever future his father had planned; his passions were outside the classroom. You could find him wandering the coastlines or the forests, or in the company of women with bad reputations. The books he read were the ancient histories, philosophy, astronomy, and some of the more crackpot sciences of the day. His tutor in these matters was his paternal grandfather, Joseph, Sr., the eccentric patriarch of a dairy farm in Salem, Mass. where Joe would stay during the summers. Harriman had been Joseph, Sr.'s only son, and when he left the family business for doctoring, it broke his father's heart. That he became a wealthy doctor only worsened the pain.

"Subsequently, Joseph, Sr. saw in his grandson a like mind, and steered him through subjects that interested Joseph, Sr. the most. Dairy farming, of course, since he hoped Joe would take over the farm one day. But also the sad histories of the eastern coast, especially of the Salem forefathers, and the witch trials, with vivid trips to Gallow's Hill, what had become the most lovely of spots for Joe to sit and read.

"The Visitor's Center has an exhaustive display of his belongings at the time, including ancient train tickets, and rock specimens, pinned butterflies, and Joe's books. Descartes, Homer, Plato, of course. Samuel Pepys's diaries, and the collected Hawthorne and Thoreau. Joe was catholic in his tastes, and was soon to attain a touch of Transcendentalism in his philosophy. Mankind didn't know all there was to know, in this industrial age. The present world was not Fallen, nor was there a need to look back on ancient Greece or Napoleonic France or what have you, for the Golden Age. Joe, Jr. was certain it was waiting out there, yet to be discovered.

"And New England was seeming smaller every day. Life at home became more and more difficult, even at his grandfather's farm. He began to disappear entirely for stretches of time, up and down the coast. Again, Russell, you can look in the Visitor's Center display for train tickets and souvenirs. Up to Concord and Essex, and to various universities where he lurked, and learned. In a pub in Essex he met a man named Halbert Chalmers, who was of a like mind, though nowhere near as brilliant, and actually somewhat of a thug. Halbert introduced him to the works of Francis Bacon, LePlongeon and Ignatius Donnelly, author of

Atlantis, the Antediluvian World, whom Chalmers claimed to have actually met. By then Joe was all but estranged from his immediate family, and an infrequent guest at his grandfather's farm. Indeed, he wouldn't return home to Wilmington until 1903, when both his parents died in a boating accident on Lake Erie.

"Russell, have you read Sleepy Hollow? The headless horseman?"

"Yes," Russ replied, surprised by the turn. "Long time ago."

"Washington Irving wrote it, and it's Irving who set Joe on the road to Oregon, indirectly, through a book he'd written some forty years before. I have the original edition, on the shelf up there. Two volumes." Dreerson pointed. Russ, sipping his whiskey-laced coffee, pretended to look for it.

"The red bindings. Its title is *Astoria, or Anecdotes of an Enterprise Beyond the Rocky Mountains*, and it tells a folk history of Astoria commissioned by John Jacob Astor. Astor, I'm sure you'll remember, was America's own Midas. His ambition had been to extend his American Fur Company to the west coast, through two expeditions, one by land, one by sea, and both failed quickly and utterly."

Dreerson stopped to drink, his eyes measuring Russ, and Megan. "There's another book up there, more tattered, in green binding. A town history written by Peggy Chalmers's grandmother, though it's actually a thinly veiled hagiography. In it you'll find mention of a dream the young Joe supposedly had on the dairy farm. Of a shining city on the western sea. It's nonsense. Absolutely. I know the truth through Joe's own mouth—that it was Washington Irving who lit the fire under him, and got him and Halbert thinking about Manifest Destiny, of the unexplored western lands, wherein all the wonders of Francis Bacon and Donnelly could perhaps still be discovered.

"In 1903, when Joe's parents died, Joe was suddenly quite wealthy. He wasted no time in using these resources to set out west by rail, accompanied by Halbert. By the year's end, they arrived in Portland, and Astoria. There's a picture . . ." Dreerson began paging through the photographs on his lap, old sepias, crimped and creased, though Russ would rather hear more of the story, while he still had a measure of patience. "Somewhere . . . in here. In any case, they had arrived, and for Joe it was everything he was hoping for. He and Halbert fit in with the rough and tumble—Joe because of the promise it held, and Halbert because he was as much of a thug as any of the trappers. They each met a woman of ill-repute, and took up cheap lodgings. Joe made exploratory trips, sometimes with Halbert and local Indian guides, sometimes by himself, down the northern coast of Oregon, studying the local legends, visiting the tribes—the Tillamooks, Chinooks, the Clatsops, the Coos. He heard legends of strange happenings, of other worlds, other mediums of life, of . . . peculiar transformations. Tales of cities under the sea. Of a Chinook who went to the land of the dead and came back to tell of it. All of which struck a chord with Joe. Here it is. . . ."

He pulled out a worn, small print, and handed it to Russ. Two bearded men in fur stood against a sooty hut, with the sea behind them. Russ recognized the first man as Joseph, younger, beardless. The other was stockier, with a long face. Halbert Chalmers. A thug indeed. But both were grim-looking, in the way only sepia portraits from the pioneer days could be.

Dreerson sipped his coffee, then set the mug down beside the fishbowl.

Russ handed the print back. Megan had not looked at it.

"Joseph and Halbert, and their brides, settled in Astoria for about a year. Around this time Joe cast off his last name in favor of Evening, a name redolent in his mind with the west, and western dreams. News of their interests spread, and they gathered a motley group of like-minded crackpots, including my grandfather, an astronomer who called himself an astrologer, and whose own father had been a trapper in California. Joseph recorded and indexed the folktales he'd collected, and created a huge chart of pins and threads, complex and color-coded, indexed by theme and variations. And they noticed an interesting lacuna in one area, along the southern coast. The legends never once mentioned this particular stretch. Further interviews with the natives produced strange responses: that they had simply always known to avoid the area, which wasn't hard, since it was so indistinct. In one account it was termed *land of the gray owl*, meaning, perhaps, land of bad dreams.

"Joseph set out, alone. To those left behind in Astoria, it was as if he'd disappeared without a word. There were rumors that he'd fallen victim to a gambling debt, or to the natives. Some spotted him up in a Vancouver brothel. But Joseph returned two months later, a little worse for wear, bedraggled, you might say, but with a peculiar light in his eyes, and that light never left him.

"He was mum about his findings, but immediately filed a plat in Oregon City for a stretch of coast. Perhaps inspired by Ignatius Donnelly, who had tried to establish his own town on the west bank of the Mississippi, Joseph now wanted to start one. He was not surprised to learn that the area was unclaimed, and he easily secured a donation land claim for hundreds of acres. Armed with this, he asked Halbert and the others to journey with him, and start a new town. A month later, Joseph and eighteen of his followers set off in ox-driven carts, arriving, after an arduous springtime journey, on this stretch of coast.

"There were no large rivers nearby, no brilliant views other than the coast, and the inland fields weren't too promising. But, still, the people stopped with him, and settled. You know their names. Vinson Burle, our Master Cheesemaker's great grandfather, was one of them. And Gerald Sumner, of course, who was a woodsman. Garrison Aberfoyle, a wealthy geologist, and his wife Audrey. And so on.

"It was tough at first, but they reached the four years of continual occupation necessary to earn incorporation from the state of Oregon. And so *Evening*, as Joseph decided to name it, was now a proper, if rather small and rather out-of-the-way Oregon town. He eventually began the dairy, and served as our first master cheesemaker, with the cheese culture shipped all the way from his grandfather's farm on the east coast.

"Eventually the town would have to buy their milk elsewhere. And survive without any good-sized river from which to ship, and no suitable roads. But all that mattered little, since the real focus of the town was something else entirely. Something Joseph had discovered on his own excursion along the coast, the secret of the land of the gray owl, which Joseph now elucidated for them. A fabled island city, as yet uncataloged. Beyond the margins of history, something Plato and the rest had only caught glimpses of, around corners, and which now lay buried beneath volcanic basalt, beneath the very crust of the coastline of Oregon. And Joseph would call it *Hesperus*."

Dreerson lifted his mug. As he sipped, he glanced at Russ, who tried to maintain an attentive, open-minded expression.

Megan was staring down at her hands.

He continued, "The ground in these parts is a smattering of sea-floor basalt, sandstone and shale, quite a hardy mix. In 1914, Joe purchased slant drilling equipment from a bankrupt oil company, and announced that he was entirely certain where to dig and how far. It took twenty years to reach it, but reach it we did, in 1937."

With the heel of his shoe, Dreerson tapped the floor twice.

"Below?" Russ said, shifting in his chair.

"More or less," Dreerson said. "We like to term it *downstairs*."

The windows rattled as a truck drove down First Street.

Russ looked at Megan. The seriousness in her eyes stopped him from saying anything.

Dreerson hesitated, then handed across another photograph. Russ set down his cup of coffee.

A coal mine, and coal miners, peering up at the flash. "That is from 1922, when the pioneer tunnel was well underway. From '17 until about '37, the town of Evening patiently dug, and did its normal work upstairs. An architect named Gerald Crick, who had built all of downtown, now indulged himself at Joe's expense, and built the grand Queen Anne mansion on the bluff. The town attended lavish parties there, and the first seasonal Gatherings, funded in part by rather profitable gold veins we stumbled upon during our dig. We basked in Joseph's eerie confidence. And in 1937 our sandhogs reached what my father termed a 'dull golden wall.' Here . . ."

He gave Russ another photograph, faded, on brittle paper with wavy edges; five figures in dark clothes, hard hats, gloves, crouched before a gleaming surface, which in sepia tones looked golden.

"My father is the fourth on the left."

Russ found him, shorter than the others, bespectacled, looking a little lost. And all of them with remote expressions.

"Jack's grandpa, too," Megan murmured.

"Yes, there, second from the left," Dreerson said, and pointed. A tall figure, though hard to see his face under the brim of his hat. He held one hand against the wall.

"It wasn't gold, of course. It was icy cold to the hand, and was nearly impossible to break. Though they tried. At every seasonal festival, Joseph would unveil some new scheme to break through, and the town would be gung-ho to try it. And all the while, of course, we had to keep the secret from the outside world. Which wasn't so hard. The highway had been built, but Evening was largely ignored, as Joe told us it would be. The cheese factory did fair business, mostly by mail order, but our other, subterranean income of precious metals bolstered those figures on the tally sheet. To the world at large, the cheese company was modestly prosperous. Tourists ignored us. The view wasn't too enticing. There were no beaches to speak of, no hotels."

Dreerson leaned back, stretched out his legs again. "We sold our cheese, harvested our cranberries, pocketed our gold under the table, and carried on as a small town of the United States. Four young men were lost in the First World War, eight in the Second, three in Korea. By now we had a professional-looking civic structure, with city managers and aldermen, and elections for mayor and so forth. We did business with Port Rostov and Tillamook and the rest. And Joseph lorded over the town from his castle. You could sometimes look up from where you were in town, and see him up there, under a blazing lantern.

"Of course, there were some in town who did not have the patience for Joe, or who thought to exploit Hesperus to their own purpose. And here the story becomes sinister, Russell, and hard to pin down. They are very careful, those thugs beginning with Halbert Chalmers and his son. Not trigger-happy, at all. Anyone who threatened the town might end up in collapsed tunnels below the hill, or struck by a truck in road accidents. I know that Megan doesn't entirely believe me on this point, and perhaps it doesn't need to be stressed. And true, these incidents of bullying didn't always end with death. Some troublesome citizens might merely require little threats, or none at all. Hesperus broods into our town, you see? Into our dreams. To some extent, we are gratefully in thrall to it."

Dreerson's voice became subdued. "There were entirely natural accidents as well. In 1952, there was a terrible one. Clyde Crick—Charles's older brother—was killed in an explosion, along with young Ozzie Renworth. Both had been taking their turns drilling into the wall, when it broke open under their jackhammers. I remember seeing Charles, then in his mid-twenties, running out of the Town Hall—what's now the barbershop. There'd been an explosion, and injuries, and it was only later we learned of the deaths, and in the same breath of Hesperus being reached. The funeral was a strange affair, of course, both horrendously sad and triumphant. And it took four patient months before the opening in the wall could be widened enough to crawl through. Tom Carver, back from college with half an archaeological degree, supervised the process.

"Everyone wanted old Joe to be the first inside, but he was too ill. A bout with pneumonia had left him bedridden. They brought him over and set him in a lavish bed beside the entrance, and he spoke to the explorers on the telephone, and assured them that they had reached the top portion of a tower, part of a vast city.

Dreerson leaned forward, and spoke more quickly, as though to hold Russ's attention. "As it happens, Charles Crick and Tom were the first to step through, and found a circular chamber, with a strangely-vaulted ceiling. The air was cold, but not damp. The walls were of an unknown material, and would glow where the flashlights touched them, and remain glowing. On the floor were two circular designs, a large one in the center, another smaller one along the edge, suggesting doors of some kind. The men were too occupied with the simple wonder of this room to worry immediately if there was a way to proceed down."

Bernard Dreerson flipped through the photographs. "You're doing very well, Russell."

Russ nodded. "Thanks."

"Joseph died in 1959. A happy man, I daresay. Fulfilled. His body was interred on the mansion's grounds, though he had always hoped to be buried in Hesperus, on a catafalque in one of the grand temples he'd seen in his dreams. His bones are still waiting.

"Since his death, a schism developed, if I myself and Tom, and several others, are enough to warrant that term. Nonetheless, there were those that were open-minded to the realities of Hesperus, but not to the close-minded tactics of Halbert Chalmers, his descendants and hangers-on, whom we shall call the Cheese League. I suppose the town wouldn't be here without them; certainly not if it were full of Bernards and Toms. In 1972—Coup in '72, remember—Peggy's late husband built an addition that completely enclosed the tunnel structure, which had been city property before. They had complained about lack of security, and the need to consolidate the structures on the hilltop. Now, whoever controlled the factory, controlled all access to Hesperus."

Again, Dreerson paused to sip some coffee. He grimaced.

"I used to have silent eight-millimeter films I shot down there. Is your head hurting, Russell? I have aspirin somewhere."

Russ had been touching the area below the bandage. "I'm fine," he said.

"There's only a little more. Charles is the man who discovered how to open the doors in the floor. A series of percussive sounds, his hammer tapping in a certain area, causing the doors to drop to the chamber below, where they had to be heaved to the side. And so on, which took a while, finding the code to each chamber, until they reached the vast last chamber, as large as a train station, though with no visible way out." Dreerson nodded to his typewriter, and the dust-glazed, eyeless visage. "Lately, there's been whisperings, through sympathetic insiders like Charles Crick, that our sandhogs, Obolus and Danace, have had better luck with the latest pioneer tunnels in the walls of that last chamber, and are close to breaking through to that fabled city. The most momentous of events, and Peggy and her Storm Watchers want to deny Tom and me access." Dreerson turned to the fishbowl.

"Now you've found something. The first new artifact that I've been allowed to touch in . . . many years. And I'm certain it *is* from there, Russell. Though why it would be in the sea is a mystery."

Dreerson leaned back, drank the last of his coffee and set down the cup. "Well, how impossible does all that sound?"

Russ searched for a response. "I guess I'm having a . . . rational reaction."

"Understandable. As I'm sure Megan will agree. Best to think of it as a legend, for the time being. So we'll end it as the great Chinook storytellers would end their sessions." Dreerson tapped the photographs back into a pile, and intoned, *"Now let us separate and go our ways to the rivers, the mountains, or into the air."*

Megan was looking at the puzzle box. "Bennie, are we going to open it?"

"Well." Dreerson leaned close to the fishbowl, and gently tapped the glass. "Tom's in bed today with the *flu*—Hillary's code-word for a hangover. And in these sorts of situations, I'm not allowed to see him until the following day—Hillary's law—meaning my phone calls will not be answered, nor will the door. Perhaps tonight, or by tomorrow night, most certainly. Tom should perhaps be very well rested when I drop this bombshell on him."

She nudged his shoe with hers. "What are you thinking, Russ?"

"I'm not sure I believe all this."

Dreerson nodded, and folded his arms. "That's the best reaction we can hope for. Really."

Pencils sharpened and laid out above the oblong score sheet, the libretto beside his erasers, a fresh cup of coffee: with the ritual complete, Russ looked down at the score for the Underwater Walk, dense with chords and string lines, and the voices, with words messily written below.

He tried to carry it forward, but his thoughts snagged on Dreerson's story.

He sat back, stared out the window at the sea. A few minutes later he stood up and lifted the box of Boston sketches onto the bed. He opened the flaps and began taking out the numbered sheets, laying them like tiles on the comforter. Scrawled chords and clusters in colored pencil, pen, random notes, page after page that he'd plastered to the walls and windows of his father's study, attempts to capture that musical object from his nightmare. What he had were glimpses, imperfect. None entirely right.

Or maybe they were something more.

He resisted an undertow to his thoughts, something like panic.

Maybe he should take a walk. Get out into the cold air and the rain, and let it wash away this nonsense.

The hycopathius gaped silent.

Russ lifted it by one spine. It looked more than ever like papier mâché, something manufactured by small towns for their roadside shops.

"You're ridiculous," he told it, remembering it in his dream, swimming through the drowned streets of Evening.

"You get one of the lobelias." Megan set the vase of blue flowers down beside the fish. She wore a sweatshirt, jeans that were dirty at the knees, and wool socks. "It's one of my favorites. You have to be nice to it."

"I will."

"The starlings almost ruined them last summer. They went for the salal and got the lobelias too."

Her hair was loose on her shoulders, her cheeks were pink.

"Cold out?"

"Yep. Down to low forties. Too cold." She looked at the scraps of music covering the bed.

"Mind if I sit?"

"Please."

She picked up six sheets and set them on the others, then carefully sat down, propping her heels on the frame. "So how's it going?"

"It's not." He leaned back in his chair. "Not at all. But that's understandable, I guess."

"Maybe you should take the day off."

He shrugged.

She looked down at the scraps surrounding her.

Russ watched her eyes, remembering how Anna would read scores, sometimes nodding to herself, fingers of her left hand stopping strings on an imaginary fingerboard.

"When Jack told me the secret, maybe two months after we'd come back to town, I refused to believe him. Simply refused. Even after he showed me some of the artifacts. It was just . . . well, I was just too realistic."

"Bernard says it . . . broods into the town."

After a moment, she looked up, nodded. "Yeah. I'm not sure I entirely believe him. But . . . I remember weird dreams my first nights here. Of something living on the hill. Something alive. Something under the hill, that came up through people's basements." She shook her head. "But maybe they were just dreams."

She began to lean back on her palms, and almost crushed a sheet. She took up the paper and smoothed it against her thigh. She turned it toward him: sixteenth notes, in a chromatic melody.

"Strange. That this is music. From a lay person's point of view, I mean." She was trying to hold Russ's eyes with her own, and smiled now as he looked at her.

Russ said, "What does it look like to you?"

She studied it, and Russ found himself studying her brown eyes, the gentle turn of her chin, her supple neck, vanishing into the sweatshirt's collar. It billowed as she leaned closer to the page, on bare skin. The white curve of her breast. Russ felt an pang in the back of his throat. He smiled.

"Barbed wire," she said, tracing the line of notes with her index finger. "And little black footballs." Smiling up at him.

"Very good. You show promise."

"Do I?"

"Definitely."

She turned around, began picking up the pages. She gathered them into a pile and set them on the box beside the bed, then lay back, the sweater riding up her stomach as she stretched down to her toes.

Russ pushed out of the chair, dropped carefully onto the mattress beside her, the pain, a dull throb in his forehead. The scent of jasmine and sweat, her warmth, as he leaned into her, hair tickling his face as he kissed her, teeth clicking. She smiled. He kissed her smile, her neck, tasting salt, a soft pulse beneath his lips. She giggled from his beard. Then they kissed again, hungry. "Slowly, Russ." She slipped her cold hand beneath the waistband of his jeans.

Later, in the dark, with the sodium lamps on Seventh casting watery trapezoids on the wall, he asked her about Hesperus.

Quietly, she said, "What in particular?"

"Anything."

"Hmmm. Anything." She stretched, her warm skin sliding against him.

"If I were to go on the tour, would I be able to see the door. Maybe a sign, *Hesperus*?"

She laughed lightly. "Not a chance."

"What if I were to break in, and run past Mrs. Nelson?"

"There's three doors you'd have to get through, all with alarms, a security camera and intercom." She was staring up at the ceiling, or past it. "Once you get through, the first part is just a tunnel. Two sets of stairs, one for up, one for down. And there's a . . . wide ramp between the stairs, where you can pull up pallets on chains. The tunnel leads down to the gold wall. You walk through into a chamber, with the large opening in the center of the floor, and a smaller one on the side. The smaller ones change their position with each level. Clockwise. And they've put an elevator in the center portal, so there's this cage, dropping down. In the smaller portals there's spiral staircases that Joe'd bought back in the twenties. You can climb down, if you want. And the smell, the old iron." She was quiet, and Russ listened to her breathing, and was just about to speak when she said, more quietly, "And the further down you go, the echoes get . . . strange. A few months ago they put Christmas tree lights on some of the stairs, winding down. And everybody with little mining hats and flashlights. All these people you know from town, like coal miners."

Staircases, elevators. He remembered visiting a mineral cavern, clunking down wooden planks into the hollow dark. Now, he imagined a similar world below the house, below the hill, and—briefly—pictured it. As real as the pillows beneath his head, these blankets, the chipped wood wall behind him.

She whispered: "He died down there."

Russ looked over. Her eyes were shut.

"He . . . was working with Tom and Charles Crick. Digging a side tunnel. And they struck . . . an opening. It didn't look natural. Had corners to it. And they could hear strange sounds coming from it. Jack didn't want to wait. He'd always wanted to be the one to reach the great city." She cleared her throat. "There was a cave-in. Five others were hurt. We never found a body.

"But others have died, too. I mean . . . can't complain too much. Everyone in town, pretty much, has lost someone down there."

She stretched again, moved closer. "That's just the way it is here."

When he woke, she was sitting up in bed. Messy hair, a pale shoulder, goosebumps. "Morning," she said, bleary-eyed.

"Good morning."

"Clock's wrong. It can't be almost ten." She yawned, then shivered. "Brrr."

He was pleasantly tired and warm, even as the impossible stories welled up in his thoughts. Underground cities, downstairs, upstairs, the Barber Mayor, the Cheese League—chased away by the hard winter sunlight, and the sight of her nakedness as she tossed back the blankets and stood up, and turned to him, lovely white breasts with dark, pebbly aureoles.

She found her panties, stepped into them, tugged them up. "So how's the head?"

"Hmmm. Better." He touched the edge of the gauze. Only an itchy numbness above his eyes.

He watched her gather her T-shirt and robe. Her hips still bore crimps and creases from the sheets.

"You should get some more sleep, Russ."

"Have to leave so early?"

"Yeah. My first class is at ten." She squinted out the window. "God, it's like winter."

At the door, she hesitated, with sunlight across her thighs. "Well . . ."

"You look beautiful, Megan."

"And you're not awake yet." She smiled, and hugged her clothes to her chest. "Bye."

He sank into the pillow.

Sometime later, he woke again. Carefully, he stretched, and found his body sore but not as bad as he expected.

The clock insisted 9:50. Sunlight streamed across the desk to the carpet. Near noon. He touched the gauze. Aspirin, not codeine, could handle the pain.

In fact he felt quite good.

He climbed out of bed.

The baseboard register roared with heat that mingled with the window cold. Frost had formed on the panes. The trees looked more gray than green, and entirely still. The ocean, in winter cold, looked more green than gray.

He stepped back, glanced down at the box beside the bed, the scraps of paper hurriedly set inside.

Megan's whispering came back to him. Of the tower, its elevator and staircases, of Jack, lost in the cave-in, whose body was never found. While he showered—careful to keep his head from the spray—he pondered Hesperus. As unlikely as it seemed now, in the daylight, he couldn't dismiss it. Parts were undoubtedly true and the rest was exaggerated, in the manner of local legends and tall tales. *Things aren't entirely what they seem*, he told himself, standing at the bathroom mirror. He peeled up the gauze, wincing. The scab was darker, and stung when he dabbed it with peroxide and applied more antibiotic creme. He redressed it—a smaller bandage looking less dire—took three aspirin, and decided to go for a walk after breakfast. Cold air, sunshine. The everyday normal town. Though he didn't particularly want to climb the hill on the way back.

He decided to drive down to First, and park.

On the dining room table was a note from Megan: "Will this one do? See you after 4 P.M." An electric clock stood beside the note, bundled in its cord.

After breakfast he pulled on a sweater, his jacket and woolen cap, and stepped outside. The air was cold. Not east coast cold, but cold enough. His breath was visible. At the curb, he unlocked the sedan and climbed into the crisp interior, wondering whether the engine would start. Maybe it was sabotaged—if Dreerson was right, and there really *were* Cheese League thugs.

At night, no doubt, under cover of darkness.

He maintained a grin for several seconds.

The engine started easily.

He glanced down at the passenger seat. His Oregon map as he'd left it, partly unfolded, its lilliputian color-coded roads and dotted towns in a splash of winter light. Sunglasses and comb toppled in the dash tray, atop a pack of Kleenex.

And Seventh Street looked the same as always.

At the edge of Mrs. Nelson's yard a tawny cat trotted the curb, watched by a gull on the mansion's cupola.

He backed the car into the driveway then drove the short distance to Alder Street, and down the hill, slowly, looking for ice. When he parked and climbed out, he left the car unlocked.

The gray Victorian looked deserted. As always. *Closed till we Open* read the Weft's sign. Rounding the corner, he decided it was best not to go in. No need to hear further arguments for Hesperus. Not right now.

And Dreerson had said he'd call when Carver was up and around.

Beyond the Weft, parked in front of the vacant lot, was an eighteen-wheel dairy truck with *ROSTOV DAIRIES* on the side. Walking past it, Russ wondered what the driver—and Port Rostov in general—thought of Evening. The Diner door flashed open, a figure stepped out, huddled in a long jacket and baseball cap, and walked north.

The air near the door was warm, and redolent of coffee and charred bacon. Most of the dozen booths were full.

Russ looked at the crowd. Familiar faces. Some noticing him. Some not.

While at the corner booth, staring down at a spreadsheet spread across the table, was Peggy Chalmers. She wore the familiar blue blazer. Reading glasses were tucked high on her auburn hair. And though her eyes were reading columns of numbers, he expected them to dart up as he neared, and her slack expression to inflate with a smile. He looked down at the sidewalk. Passing, he caught a hint of movement—her head or hand lifting—but the diner was behind him now, traded for the Laundromat's vaporous windows, where a man with bushy brown eyebrows stood among hanging garments, and paid no attention to Russ at all.

Nonetheless, he listened for the Diner's door behind him, and the *clip clop clip* of Peggy's shoes.

Ridiculous as that was.

To his right loomed the inland hill, dark pine with silvery highlights, and windows glaring in the sun, as Megan's whisper once again recounted the factory, and the tunnels.

Christmas lights trailing down and around the spiral stairs.

It *brooded* into the town, Dreerson had said. Into their dreams, too, and Russ remembered his sketches from Boston, and felt the undertow of panic.

At the second blinking stoplight, the intersection with Cheddar, he decided to cross First and start back. Cold was getting under his jacket, into his shoes. He didn't want to stray too far from the car.

And just ahead, the Evening Cheese Outlet store was trumpeting its wares, with the barbershop visible in the distance.

No need to see the Barber-Mayor.

Waiting for a minivan to pass—somebody inside waved—he hurried across First, and started southbound, past the Evening Bank, which looked empty of customers, and the Aberfoyle Fixit Store. More black-iron benches, and concrete planters, one wrapped in a tarp, perhaps to protect it from the weather.

Dreerson had shown him old photographs of this area. Platted lots roped off for archaeological survey. The main street growing in the mud, those early days of the century, and the mansion rising on the bluff: funded by subterranean gold, if Dreerson were to be believed.

While Evening dug into the earth, and Joe oversaw the proceedings from the tower.

Here was an empty storefront, its glass windows pasted with flyers: notices for baby-sitters, and yard work, and for van trips to Portland dated some three years old, and a poster for Real Smoked Salmon Cheddar and Evening Havarti.

Have Havarti? read the slogan.

He shoved his hands into his pocket, squinting against the chill, and his thoughts circled back to the Boston sketches, to sheet 273, which had captured it, that elusive sound, from his nightmare.

The cluster of twenty tones had inspired *Nemo*'s opening measures—the sea-wave portamento in the deep strings.

But why *20,000 Leagues Under the Sea*?

It was Ollie Knussen who had offered to help with an opera commission, recommending several companies—Santa Fe among them—and also some books to consider, including Poe's *The Adventures of Arthur Gor-*

don Pym, which Russ had read and found not quite right, too dependent on its literary voice, too sprawling. But portions of it had seemed ideal, especially the sea storms and the eerie maelstrom at the end, and Russ had remembered a similar atmosphere in *20,000 Leagues Under the Sea* (both the book and, perhaps more vividly, the James Mason movie). A consultation with his *New Grove Dictionary of Opera* had revealed no other versions of the story. The plot was properly dark and somber, with Captain Nemo as a perfect operatic protagonist. The material was copyright-free, and free of any literary pretension that might work against him. And the ocean (this had seemed most important) could permeate the score, sometimes ominously so.

Music of depths, and dreams.

It was shortly thereafter that Russ had recalled his old college friend Malcolm Moore, and Malcolm's memorable, somewhat bizarre play about Jules Verne.

But *Nemo* had certainly been born from depths and dreams, and that twenty-note cluster. From sheet 213, as the crown of seawater shimmering over Anna's body.

And—he sensed it now, and immediately rejected it—from the hillside and what lay below, under the leaden Oregon skies.

Plodding up the porch stairs, he heard the phone ringing inside. He had some trouble with the lock, then rushed inside, stepping over a manilla envelope.

He hurried to the phone, grabbed it. "Hello?"

"Hi, Russ."

"Ellie . . ." He was out of breath. He looked back at the flagstone, and the envelope, and tried re-orienting his thoughts for Ellie and the east coast.

"You all right?"

"Yes. Just getting back from a walk when I heard the phone." *R. K.* was written across the envelope, in large black letters. "Nice to hear from you. What's up?"

"Well, I bring dire news, Russ." Her voice was cheery, not dire. "Just saw the weather report on CNN. A winter storm is *barrelling down* on the Oregon coast. Those were the exact words. Did you know?"

"It's cold out." He tried walking back to the entrance, but the cord wouldn't reach. "Maybe we'll get some freezing rain."

"So how's the project going?"

"I'm taking the day off. Don't tell my dad."

"I think you should take *two* days off, Russ. Or three. Don't push yourself."

"Just a day for now."

"So here's some news from your Brit composer friend."

"Knussen?"

"Yeah. There's been rumor that the ENO might pick up the commission, or Adelburgh. And they're trying to interest Philip Langridge. He'd be great for Captain Nemo, don't you think?"

"Perfect," Russ said, sensing, after all the fantastic worries of the last few days, the machineries of the opera production still grinding away. Like a splash of water in the face. "That's great. I'll have to call both of them when I get back."

"What's up, Russ? Something's up. I can tell."

She had done so well, those months after Anna's death, in sussing out his mood.

Blame lay easily at hand. "Hmmm. The libretto, I guess. It's not perfect."

"How bad is *not perfect?*"

"Workable, for now. We'll see. It just needs a focus."

"Use a red pen, Russ. And scissors."

"I will."

"But take a few days off. Drink some hot chocolate and stay warm. What was her name? Your landlady?"

"I'll be calling you, Ellie. Tell my Dad not to worry."

"Done, Russ. Talk later. And watch out for the storm. The anchorman sounded concerned."

He could hear her smile.

"Will do, dear. Bye."

"Bye."

He hung up the phone then walked back to the entrance. He stooped, picked up the envelope.

It was heavier than he expected.

R.K., with his own bootprint on top.

The flap was sealed with masking tape.

Resisting the urge to open it right away, he set it down on the coffee table, then fixed himself some hot chocolate in the kitchen, trying to decide who might have dropped it off.

A few minutes later he sat down on the couch, and ran his thumb under the seal, tilting it. A stack of photographs spilled out, dozens.

Vague, dark colors.

Colors as forms, crowding the margins. A sense of straight and curved shapes. He turned to the next.

The same shapes, from a wider angle. The shapes were a dim color, and he sensed an organization, repeated shapes, sharp and curved, and colors mingling into different hues.

He looked in the envelope for a note; finding none, he continued on to a third photograph much like the first two except for the glare of a flashbulb across the surface, which shone like rock.

More dim shapes, dim colors, and he turned to the next, sensing more beyond the margins.

(Depths.)

Tiny specks or flaws tracked and curled across the surface. Maybe dust on the negative—too tiny to see.

He remembered the photo of Dreerson's grandfather in the tunnel, blinking up, mole-like. Depths, and dreams.

Who had brought these? His dark dwarves? Peggy Chalmers? The Barber-Mayor, skulking along the street.

Heart pounding, he turned to the next photo.

Ancient colors, designs.

Here the camera was closer to the surface. What had seemed like dust or imperfections on the negative were many squiggles of silver—symbols, like letters or ancient ideograms. Or something more. Each a bustling single line, complexly formed and suggestive of movement.

In the next, taken from farther back, the colors now suggested a chordal procession. Too massive for the photo to capture.

He sat back resisting the urge to stand up, walk away, out into the cold air of the porch.

He cautioned himself, *I'm reading too much into this. I'm a composer. If I were an electrician I'd see ancient schematics.*

Yet the symbols reminded him, vividly, of notation. They wended among the blocks of color, as though on invisible staves. The shapes were like medieval *neumes*: graphic signs to represent a musical gesture.

He turned the pages, more glimpses of color, and strange melody.

On the last page was written a phone number.

"Hello?" The voice was female, light, hesitant.

Russ relaxed his grip on the phone. "This is Russ Kent."

"Yes. Hi. Hi, Mister Kent, this is Andrea Yarrow."

Andrea, from the Gathering. Tall, with red hair and slender arms. The bandleader.

He remembered her lingering stare as he left the ballroom with Pete.

"I found the package, Andrea."

A pause. "I'm glad. I'm sorry for just leaving them."

Did she know that Megan, and Dreerson, had told him about Hesperus?

"The images are quite interesting," he ventured.

"Did you . . . did you *hear* them, Mister Kent?"

He felt a tingle down the back of his neck. "Why don't we get together to talk about it? How about tomorrow?"

Another pause. "Yes. How about seven *p.m.*?"

"Okay. Seven."

"My address is 453 Cheddar Street. And thank you, Mister Kent."

"I'll see you at seven tomorrow."

After hanging up, he spread the photographs across the coffee table, and listened.

When Megan came home he was copying down the reoccurring signs in his notebook. Only a few photographs showed them large enough to be discerned. So far he'd found only twelve unique symbols, each seemingly too eccentric to be pictographs, or letters, though they might be diagrams of complex melodic movement. Or not.

Messine Neumes? he'd written, *10th century?* and had tried to list the names of the eight variants he vaguely remembered—*punctum, porrectus, torculus* . . . .

At any rate, these were much more elaborate, with several so convo-

luted he was doubtful about the accuracy of his drawings. He'd need
more photographs.

Neuma: gesture. The signs signify?

He looked up. She stood in the hallway, stamping her shoes on the
flagstone. "It's begun to snow," she said.

He looked out the bay window. "No kidding?"

"Yep." She kicked off her shoes and padded into the living room.
"What's that?"

"Something Andrea left for me."

"Andrea Yarrow?"

"She slid it under the door while I was out."

Megan sat down beside him, a chill on her clothes. She lifted a photo.
"Oh, yeah. I know this. From one of the chambers, on the way down."
She squinted.

"I'm meeting her tomorrow, for dinner."

Megan set down the photo, then sat back, combing fingers through
her hair. She grinned and took his hand. "C'mon. You've got to see the
snow." She stood up and pulled him to his feet, and to the entry. "This is
an event here on the coast."

She opened the door. The cold air possessed a weighty, almost physical presence. Following her onto the porch he gazed up, looking for
snow, finding only gray sky.

"There . . ." She pointed.

He noticed a flake, white and gray and white, floating down to the
lawn. And another, and then more, slowly settling in the grass.

"Hooray," she said, smiling.

The town was quiet. Even the distant surf was muted.

"It hasn't snowed for years," she said.

"Can we take it as an good omen?"

She reached out: an instant later a flake lay on her palm. "Of course."

The phone rang during dinner. She answered it at the kitchen counter. "Hello?"

Russ hesitated, a biscuit at his mouth.

Out the kitchen window, snow was really falling.

She laughed. "I know, Bennie. Isn't it great? I'm sure Russ sees enough of it in Boston, but I love it." She smiled at him, leaning against the refrigerator, setting one socked foot over the other. "Yeah, hold on, let me check." She cupped the mouthpiece. "Tom wants to look at the box tonight. Bennie figures we should be there, if you don't mind venturing into the snow."

"Sure." Though he'd wanted to spend the night studying the photographs.

" 'Sure,' he says. We'll meet you there. At eight. Bye. Go build your snowman."

She hung up. "Is that okay?"

"That's great."

"How are you feeling?"

Truthfully, a little muffled around his ears and eyes perhaps due to the change in barometric pressure. "My head's better. Haven't needed an aspirin since noon."

"Could you walk to Tom's? Through the snow?" There was pleasure in her voice.

"Looking forward to it," he said.

He wore his jacket, a sweater, jeans, and boots. The cap fit snug and warm around his head.

Walking, holding Megan's mittened hand, he gazed up at the flakes of snow tumbling out of the dark, yellow under the lamplight, white to blue in his periphery, striking his eyelashes, his beard. Russ decided he was glad for it, if only for distracting him from the photographs, and from what believing in those images implied: a tacit acceptance of Hesperus.

Around them, the snow was obliterating green from the hilltop.

Megan wore a red cap pulled down close to her eyes, and a ski jacket zipped up under her chin. "I never got enough of this when I was a kid."

"In Washington state?" he asked.

"Modesto." She made a face. "Till I was ten."

But for the faint creak of trees, the hill was quiet. The surf was a seashell held to the ear, behind her voice.

"I remember waking up once, middle of the night, and there was this glow in the backyard. It was snow, covering everything, and still coming down. A new land. We had a slide and it was caked with it. I couldn't wait to go outside. I snuck out, two o'clock in the morning, and starting chucking snowballs at the house. I got in big trouble, let me tell you." She swung their hands. "It's cold, Russ!"

"Slightly," he said, and smiled.

"You Easterner!" She zipped her coat up higher, the collar covering all but her smiling eyes.

At Carver's door, she pulled off a mitten and knocked. Then brushed snow from Russ's beard. "It's all over your hat, too."

Beyond the porch, snow settled in gray sunflowers.

As he pulled off his cap and shook it—a little blizzard on the porch—she knocked again.

In response came a low, friendly bark, then a muffled voice. The door opened. Hillary peered out, and up, under gray bangs. "Well, look who it is. Miss Megan."

"Hi."

"Dreerie said you'd be dropping in." Hillary opened the door. "You walk?"

"We did."

"Ah, the out-of-towner." She squinted at Russ's forehead.

"Hello, Hillary."

Ody gave a welcoming bark behind her.

"Inside. Don't bring the cold with you." She spoke down to Ody, "Hold your horses!"

Ody, ears sharp, tail wagging, moved back as Megan and Russ stepped inside. "Hi, Odysseus!" Megan said. "Bet you love the snow, huh?" She patted him between the ears, and scratched under his collar. Ody tilted his head, enjoying. "Has he gone out yet?"

"Inside, outside. Can't make up his mind. Can you?" She pulled her housedress tighter about her throat.

The room was hot, with a background hum of Mentholatum and broiled fish.

In the corner, the rabbit-eared television showed a weather report; a map of the coast with cartoon clouds and snowflakes. Faintly: "Three to five inches . . . Portland metro area alone . . ."

Hillary eyed it. "Folks going to be stranded on the hill. Poor souls. Reduced to cheese diets."

Megan stuffed her mittens in her pockets. "I don't think it'll be lasting long."

"Three days, the man says."

Megan shook out her hair. "I guess I should call Peggy. Offer my truck."

"Miss High and Mighty? Been all wrapped up in her own projects these days. Designing robes for all the town ladies. That's the latest. As if we needed robes to wear."

The floor thrummed, something in the basement—Carver's voice.

Hillary sighed, and clucked. "Oh, there he goes again. You'd think the blizzard would cheer him up, but not Tom. Not with Dreerie over." She took hold of Ody's collar. "He'll say I kept you here talking. Downstairs, but leave your coats on. It's like the Arctic down there."

Megan led Russ down the hall to the basement door, while Hillary said: "Not on your life, doggie. Sit right there."

Megan opened the door, started down.

Carver's voice could be heard, then Dreerson's bland baritone, under Megan's tread: "Careful, Tom."

"Being careful!"

Metal striking metal.

Over her shoulder, she said, "Do you know about the fifth stair, Russ?"

"Got it," he said, and stepped over it.

"Tom?" she called out. "Bennie?"

Shoes scraped over concrete, and a shadow climbed the wall: Dreerson, bundled in a dark coat, his pale face staring up. "Ah, here they are."

The stink of cigars mingling with that of cheese.

Hesperus Blue, 1976, read the label to Russ's right, stuck into the cube of cheese. *Evening Cheddar, 1972.*

"Megan, dear."

She hugged him. "Did you come over early?"

"Yes, I postponed the snowman till tomorrow." Dreerson looked up at Russ climbing down. "And Russell. Watch your step."

"How are you, Bernard?"

"Wonderfully cold." Dreerson wore a scarf, and his gloves. Two yellow "e" pins were fixed to his lapels. "A deep freeze on the coast. Rare as an intelligent inlander, as the saying goes."

A sharp sound startled them.

Carver, hunched over the worktable opposite the stairs, swore under his breath.

Dreerson murmured, "Tom's been losing his patience over the last hour. I'm reminded of the tower excavation, on which we labored for so long. If the box won't twist or snap open, then perhaps a particular sequence of tones is required. Another open sesame. At any rate . . . did you both walk here?"

"Couldn't keep him indoors," she said.

"This way, this way." Dreerson led them to the workbench. "Watch out for the extension cords and boxes and such."

Three articulated lamps shone on Carver's spotted scalp and tufts of white hair, as well as a nylon strap that fixed a little miner's light to his forehead.

An assortment of hammers and smaller metal tools were at his elbow, with tin trays, a plate with spent cigars, an empty tumbler, and the portrait of old Joe and young Carver.

"Tom?"

Dreerson leaned toward his shoulder.

Carver's head bobbed up. "Huh?"

"Russell's here."

"Kent?" Voice rattling the tin trays.

Carver turned around, shining into Russ's eyes, with a waft of alcohol trailing. Something stronger than beer.

"Tom."

"You made one helluva find." Carver's light had a magnifying glass attached, now over his veiny left eye, which widened as he noticed Russ's forehead. "What the hell . . ."

Russ said, "I tripped, fell. Stupid accident."

Carver grunted. "Well, your wound was worth it, Kent." He turned back to the table, and the puzzle box. Its faceted sides glowing under the lamps, swarming with blue flecks. "Bern's trying to tell me 'hold my horses.' But it's got a secret in there. I know it."

"I was merely arguing for the scientific process. No need to rush."

Carver leaned toward it, while fumbling among the tools to his right, passing over a hammer, pliers, tweezers. He lifted a small pick, like a dental pick. Then, gripping the box, he began to prod the edges. Dreerson made a noise, and said, "Careful, Tom," as Carver gripped more tightly—tight enough to drain the blood from his knuckles—then found purchase on the shimmering edge, and applied pressure, until his entire arm trembled with the exertion: the pick skidded off, struck the table.

Once more, Megan had zipped the collar of her coat up over her mouth. Her serious eyes studied the box.

"Isn't solid." Carver tapped it. "Something's in there. I plan to get it."

Megan said, "How about an X-ray?"

Carver let go of the box, set down the pick. He lifted the tweezers and set them down. Then laid his right hand flat on the desktop. "Don't got access to a machine, Meg." With his left hand, he turned the box. Scratches gleaming on moonglow pearl. "Damned if I'm going to let the cheesers in on this."

"Bennie was saying it might open up like those portals in the tower."

"Portals took years. Had that patience once. Not now."

"But if there's no other way . . ."

Dreerson exchanged a glance with Megan. "Tom, I believe we should take a break, eh? Return upstairs to some hot apple cider."

Carver grunted. Carefully, he picked up the box between a knobby index finger and thumb, staring down at it for a moment, then swivelled in his chair. Russ stepped back, to allow him to get up, but Carver only sat there, his eyes active, looking beyond Dreerson, Megan and Russ.

A faint smile cracked his lips, as he extended the box over the concrete floor and let go.

Megan lunged to catch it. Dreerson recoiled.

The box struck, rang in C flat, bouncing brightly; it rolled to Megan's boot.

She knelt.

"Careful!" Dreerson said.

Carver clasped his knees with both hands. "Had to!"

"It's still together." Megan lifted the box. "But it's cracked." Carefully she placed it in her cupped hand, then stood and set it on the bench.

"Had to do it, Bern."

Beneath the bright lights, hairline fractures could be discerned. Carver reached for the box, but Megan cupped her hands over it. "You're in a bad mood, Tom," she said, through the collar of her jacket. "I think you should wait till tomorrow."

"Yes, why don't we repair to the upper world, and warm our bones, eh?"

Carver brooded.

Dreerson glanced at Russ and Megan.

"I remember a similar time, Tom, many years ago, with Joseph. Soon after this portrait was taken." Dreerson lifted old Joe into the conversation. Carver briefly glanced over, then back. "And he said something along the lines of, 'Hesperus has waited for us to climb out of the pre-Cambrian muck, to raise ourselves to our feet and grow the brains and brawn necessary to understand it.' Remember, Tom? 'Waited while we shrugged off our ape-ish past and built the civilizations and sailing ships that would take us to the Oregon shores. And it demanded our patience while we dug into the earth, and further patience to break inside.'"

Carver mushed his lips. "Bastards. Want me to go to my grave not seeing it, Bern." Staring down, his eyes active. He spoke to the portrait as much as Megan, or Dreerson. "Gave my life to the downstairs." Carver shook his head, and seemed to be occupied with his tools, rearranging pick and knife and hammer. "Now they want to keep it from me. Want me to hole up these last few years, content with the goddamned tax break."

Dreerson said, "But here you have a piece of it in your possession. *Yours* to study. Not *theirs*. Careful study. Using common sense."

"Bastards."

Megan took her hand from the box, zipped down her collar.

A grunt, a flash of light and movement as Carver raised the hammer and swung it down on the box, striking its edge, the box twirling, knocking into the rack.

"Tom!" Megan reached out with both hands to catch it.

"This ain't drunken behavior!" Carver yelled. "Just short of patience! Long on questions!" He dropped the hammer.

Dreerson grabbed a lamp, and shone it down.

She reached for it.

"Careful!" said Dreerson.

The puzzle box had cracked open. As she nudged it back under the lamplight, there trailed a fine and silvery line of sand.

Pinned by the light were shards of puzzle box, a black interior, gleaming, and tiny bones in pointed shadows.

Carver stepped back. Dreerson, mouth half-open, was staring down.

The bones were a pale blue, nested in shreds of dry, translucent membrane.

Not real, Russ told himself. *Plastic*.

"Goddamn," said Carver.

Dreerson leaned closer. "It's intact, I think."

Carver reached for it. A tiny ribcage. Lamplight might have burned his hand: he withdrew. He poured some whiskey into his tumbler and gulped it down, his eyes wandering the air around him. "Forgive . . . an old man."

Without looking away from the pieces, Dreerson said, "Remove more of the casing."

Carver choked and swallowed. "Just didn't think, Bern. After all this time." He turned back to it. With a mostly steady hand, he lifted the tweezers and brought the gleaming points to the shards, grasped one and, gently, plucked it free. A glittering piece, midnight black on the inside.

He dropped it.

Lamplight found a blue oblong skull no larger than a fifty-cent piece, lolling against tiny shoulders, in a skirl of silver sand.

Megan, under her breath: "Bennie . . ."

"Fell off a ship." Russ heard his voice from the distance. His mouth had gone dry.

As Carver plucked away another shard, Dreerson said, "It's intact, Tom. You didn't damage it."

Tom grunted, then nudged another shard, plucked it off. Only the slightest tremor in his hand. He straightened, set the tweezers down. The blue bones—what *appeared* to be bones—resembled a human's in miniature. Though not quite. The three-fingered hand ending in slight yellowed claws, and claws for toes, too; the long, three-jointed legs draped one on the other.

And the orbitals of the skull too wide, at an angle to the sinus cavity.

Carver picked up a magnifier loop and leaned close, and moved it slowly across the tiny skull; wielding tweezers, he gently tapped it. He made a noise. "Lookit." Carver straightened, breathing loudly through his nose. "Ha, lookit, Bern. Skull plates're fused." He straightened.

"Full grown," Dreerson murmured.

Carver dropped the tweezers, then stood up. He looked at the nearby ground. He stepped past Russ and Megan, into the shadowy clutter beside the stairs.

Russ said to Megan, "Cargo, from some far east ship. Made of plastic. Right?"

Dreerson approached the bones, leaned close, and lifted the nearby magnifying glass. He peered. Made a sound in his throat. A laugh, or a shout, cut-off before it escaped his lips.

Then Carver was back with the Tupperware tub, and set it on a stool. He peeled off the lid. After fumbling among the contents, he lifted out two of the polished bones and set them—shakily—on the table. "Lookee," he said. "Femur. Look at the shape, Bern."

They matched.

Bones from some small animal, Russ told himself. Dug up and painted, and arranged like this, and put in this puzzle box.

Carver glanced at Dreerson, grinning.

"Tom, I believe you're right."

Carver's grin widened, and he fumbled for something among the shelves, saying, "Goddamn." He shouted, "Hilly!"

"This would prove, of course . . ." Dreerson's lips were curving into a similar-sized grin. ". . . would prove that Hesperus is to some extent still *alive*. At least with the psychopomp population."

"The what?" Russ asked, staring at the tiny, incurving claws.

"Celebration, Bern!"

The air clicked, whooshed in audible wow and flutter—an audio tape through unseen speakers. Then something droned, all around. A bag-pipe. Many bagpipes, and snare drums, in a Scottish snap.

"We did it, Joe!" Tom lifted the portrait.

Dreerson rocked on his heels to the music, gray bangs bouncing. "Yes, congratulations, Joe! And Tom!"

"Congrats, Bern!"

Dreerson raised his elbows. Still rocking on his heels, the bookseller began to dance an awkward, half-forgotten jig, lifting his knees, staring down blearily then glancing up, a smile lighting his face as Megan offered her hand. He took it.

"Ha, Kent! We did it!" Carver shouted over the din, and Russ gave a noncommittal nod and looked at the bones.

". . . racket!?" From the stairs: "What's that!" Hillary, crouching just past the fifth stair, peered to the corner. "You got Finn MacCool down there, and dancing?! Dreerie!"

Dreerson, now beaming and perspiring, stopped and turned, and flung wide his arms. "Hillary, it was a success!"

"Turn down that noise, Tom!"

Carver reached for the volume. Bagpipes receded. "Got us a psy-chopomp, Hilly!"

"You're breaking things is what you're doing!"

Carver shouted, "One of Joe's guides, bless its bones. Come down here and look, and show some respect!"

Looking, Russ tried to see a creature from Hesperus, entirely real, from somewhere under the hill.

The creature, the bones, sprawled with triple-jointed arms and legs, the tiny skull and its strange, hollow gaze, as oblivious to the skirling music as it was to the skirl of silver sand below it.

"Then you got something there I don't want to see." Hand at her throat, Hillary shook her head.

"Come on, Hilly!"

She ventured carefully down.

Russ said, "A freighter. Toys, or knickknacks. It fell overboard, washed up on shore."

Carver turned to him, shining into his eyes. "Huh, Kent?"

Hillary peered from a distance. "Looks like a rat."

Russ spoke more loudly. "I found it in the bay, at the end of Ocean-view. So maybe it fell off a ship, washed ashore."

"Rat with arms and legs, Hilly?" Carver laughed, then began coughing.

"Oh, there he goes," said Hillary. "Getting all excited." She shook her head. "You come upstairs. I'm making some hot chocolate."

"Bring it down, woman. We're working late!"

She shook her head. "You want pneumonia?" She walked back to the stairs. "Don't complain to me tomorrow!"

"Kent, you think this is something from the Far East maybe?"

Russ shrugged.

"Ha!" Carver stood up, nearly falling, and with a sideways glance at Dreerson stumbled into the clutter, into shadows.

Russ turned to Megan.

She stepped close, leaned over the puzzle box and bones. "Been a while since my college biology classes, but it looks . . . somewhat like remains. The bones . . . they might almost be bird, or animal. Strange coloring."

Carver, returning, said, "That's your basic psychopomp, Meg! Guide to the underworld of Oregon!" He was clutching an old framed painting. "Look at this here!" Carver knelt, and leaned it against the side of the bench, then angled a light downwards. "My pappa did this, by his own hand. Remember, Bern?"

Dreerson was looking at the bones—the creature. He turned back. "Oh, yes, that? Around that time, certainly."

An oak frame and foggy glass, enclosing a map seemingly hand-painted on parchment. A wash of green and brown ink forming a coast-line, and pale blue ink the sea. Russ recognized the bluff and the inland hill, familiar streets in strokes of india ink, and each minutely labelled. A legend in the corner, in ornate cursive, read *Evening and Under*.

"Pappa was an artiste, as well as one of your great amateur geologists. And did this hisself. From research and development. A map of the underground vents. Till 1972 this was hanging in the Mayor's office. Now, you point out to me where you found the box."

Russ knelt down, and located the Evening mansion, a profile in dim green atop the bluff, swimming in glare and shade as Tom adjusted the lamp again. With his finger, Russ traced the coast to Oceanview Drive, to the bluff and basalt stack which was decorated with a tiny, though entirely too large, seagull. He tapped. "Here."

"Hmmm." Carver readjusted the light, and knelt down, knees popping. He grunted.

Dreerson murmured something to Megan, who responded.

"Yep. Lookee." His gnarled finger tapped the glass. "See them tiny lines in yellow?"

Russ could not. Moving closer, he could, very faint.

"Pappa drew 'em. Each one, mapped out by him. Those're vents along the coast. From downstairs." Carver straightened, and said to Dreerson, "Bern, right near a vent! Direct mail from Hesperus!"

Russ straightened, and looked at Megan.

She raised her eyebrows.

"Vents is where this come from, Kent!" said Carver, stepping back to the worktable.

"Vents?" Hillary was tromping down the stairs. "Got no heat down here since you blocked them off, Tom. Protect your bones. Polar bear." She held a tray of four mugs, steaming in the cold air.

Dreerson said, "I'm not entirely sure I can accept that theory, Tom. At least not yet. In any case, what's important is we have discovered physical proof of what . . . until now . . . has been pure theory and hearsay."

Russ said, "Did Joe . . . describe a creature that looks exactly like these bones?"

"Yessiree, Kent!" said Tom.

Hillary handed him a mug of hot chocolate. "Don't believe it."

"Russell, he described a small humanoid creature with clawed hands and feet, roughly twenty centimeters in height. These bones are eighteen centimeters, which, since Joe's creature wore boots, comes pretty close."

"Bones and bones." Hillary shoved a mug at Dreerson.

He took it.

Dreerson chuckled. "I was just thinking I should snap a picture. This would have made the cover of my newspaper in the old days. Eighty-point bold headline."

"Bern?" Carver held a half-empty whiskey bottle.

"Absolutely."

Carver poured.

"Fine," said Dreerson.

"Meg? You want some?"

"No thanks."

"Kent?"

Russ declined as well.

Dreerson raised his mug. "Let's have a toast, at any rate." He intoned, "Here's to old Joseph Evening and his dream. And the empire that lies beneath our spruce and alder, our foxglove and fern."

"Drink to that," said Tom.

They brought the mugs together—all but Hillary, who stood shaking her head near the stairs.

Russ sipped, and winced at a pain over his eyes.

Megan saw it. "Feeling okay?"

He swallowed. Shook his head. "Might need another codeine."

"Tom, now don't you go getting drunk," Hillary said. "These folks aren't walking home!"

"Let's change the bandage."

She brushed droplets from her arms. Ripples in a brass timbre.

Russ leaned back against the curved edge of the tub. He was only beginning to lose the strange energy from the Carver's house.

In the last hour, since Carver had dropped them off, they hadn't mentioned the box or its contents.

"You'll have to sit up. Come on."

She carefully leaned down, grabbed the box of bandages and tape beside the tub, and turned toward him. Her face was freshly scrubbed and glistening, her eyes—suddenly careful eyes—regarding his forehead as she reached up, and peeled back the wilted tape.

"How does it look?" His hand, on her hip, brushed warm water from warm skin.

"It's healing, but the bruise is dark." She wadded up the bandage, flung it in the toilet. "Does it still hurt?"

"Not as much." Wincing again as she dabbed it with peroxide-soaked cotton.

"Maybe we should let the barber look at it. He's the closest thing we have in town to a doctor."

"No, thanks." Russ tried not to move his head. "Not the Barber-Mayor. Is it that bad?"

"Or we can drive up to Rostov." She applied the ointment, then taped the bandage. She tossed the spent cotton—which looked darker than he'd anticipated—into the toilet. "So," he said, relaxing his shoulders. "What did you think of all that?"

"All that," she repeated, then turned in the tub and lay back against his chest. "Hmmm. It was weird, wasn't it."

He dipped his hand in the water. "I'm trying to remember who it was who said, *The simplest explanation is usually the correct one?*"

"Somebody who wasn't born in Evening."

Coppery droplets, quarter, eighth, sixteenth, as she stirred the water with her hand. "I would have more doubts, Russ, if I hadn't been down there myself."

He persisted: "It's not too unusual for things to wash on shore after a storm? You get all kinds of ships off the coast."

Moving against him, she said, "Now you're being fantastical."

He could feel her laugh under his hand.

"We're like an opera, maybe. Operas have unlikely plots, don't they, Russ?"

His breath resonated in the fishbowl helmet. Stale air cooled his face.

Clad in the heavy suit, he trudged, gazing through foggy portals at First Street, at a sidewalk half-buried under pebbles, buildings lost in coral.

A school of brilliant blue fish darted over the Visitor's Center, past trees of green glass floats.

To his right loomed the inland hill, mossy green and undulate under the sparkling surface of the ocean, and he heard, beyond the rasp of the air circulator, a faint clockwork sound from outside, growing louder, what might have been a choir of alto flutes trilling up and down in microtonal steps, against a battery of chiming, clanging cimabalon.

Then the *Nautilus* soared over the top of the hill, silver and green over volcanic black, a roiling wake of skirling violins, snarling trumpets, as the water flew to silver.

*c*aptain nemo

"Russ? Are you awake?"

The room was dim, though the corner windows were bright with morning light. She stood in the doorway, dressed in a long T-shirt, her hair damp and loose around her shoulders.

"What's up?" He rubbed his eyes with the back of his hand, remembering snowfall and ancient music.

"I just got a strange phone call," she said. Her tone was amused, and when he opened his eyes again he saw her smiling, touching a finger to her chin. "I'll give you a moment to wake up." Still smiling, she walked to the window, squinting.

He pushed himself up against the backboard. Kicking away the covers, he realized there were many people who might be responsible for a strange phone call. He made a list.

"Who was it?" he asked, staring down at his pale, flabby legs.

"Charles Crick." She folded her arms. "About an hour ago, he found Captain Nemo wandering the grounds of the Evening mansion."

Russ brought his knees up. He scratched the underside of his thigh.

"Charles told the Captain that someone in town was writing an opera about him, and the Captain asked to see you." She leaned against the desk, clasping her hands in front of her. "Charles is going to drive him over."

"Captain Nemo?"

"The same. But don't worry, I told him to wait a half hour—to give you time to shower and dress."

"Shit." He rubbed his eyes.

"Yeah," she said, laughing. "You're awake. And the Captain's on his way."

"I'm getting tired of Crick." He got up from the bed, squinting at the glare.

The light spun rainbows at his eyes.

While he dressed in jeans and a sweatshirt, she stood watch near the windows.

"Humor him, Russ. He's a nice old man."

Russ ran his fingers through his hair, combing it away from his eyes, then pressed down the edges of the bandage. "I planned to spend the day examining the photos. I don't need these distractions anymore."

She leaned toward the windows. "Here's Charles's truck coming up the hill. And there *is* somebody in there with him. A man."

He found a pair of socks beneath the dresser, and pulled them on. "Does he have epaulets, a nautical hat? A world-weary face?"

"Wait. . . . Charles is parking now along the corner. And the other man *is* dressed like a ship's captain."

Russ stood up, stepped in beside her.

She pointed.

There in the blinding snow was Crick, struggling out of his rusted red pickup where Seventh met Spruce. He carried a suitcase. Coming around the hood of the truck was a stocky man in a dark blue blazer with gold buttons and silver-stranded epaulets. He wore a captain's hat, and stared at the ground as he carefully followed Crick along the sidewalk.

His boots were a polished black against the snow.

"Shit," Russ said, feeling his forehead throb. "What's Crick up to?" He looked away from the window.

Megan's smile was hesitant. She raised her eyebrows. "I'll go make sure we have refreshments for the Captain."

She hurried from the bedroom. Russ turned back to the window. His breath had fogged the glass. Instead of wiping it away—sure this would attract the pair's attention—he went downstairs to meet Captain Nemo.

There came a solemn knock upon the door.

He joined Megan in the kitchen. "You get it," he said. "I'll wait here."

"Chicken."

She walked off through the living room. A moment later, he heard the door open, then Old Crick's wheezy but excited voice. "It's Nemo, Captain of the *Nautilus*! And he's here to see your boyfriend!"

Another voice—a quiet baritone—said, "I brought cheese."

"Great. Just a moment, Captain. I'll fetch him."

Megan appeared around the corner, stepping into the glare from the bay window. She held up a loaf of Evening cheddar and called out, "Russ, you have visitors."

He shook his head. "Show them in."

Crick appeared, hunched in a raincoat, and set down the suitcase. Russ heard boots knock against the flagstone, then the Captain stepped into view. His suit was a silhouette against the glaring window light, but he looked the part.

"Russell Kent, I'm here to speak to you about your opera."

The voice was familiar. Russ wanted to laugh.

The figure raised a hand and lifted off the cap, revealing a tangle of salted black hair.

"Malcolm?"

"I'm *nobody*. And I am a King."

While Russ walked toward him, his features formed in the light: the bristling beard, wry eyes, the ugly grin.

"Russell!" Malcolm clapped him on the shoulder, while Crick stood with words of introduction dying on his lips, and a puzzled expression knitting up his face.

Malcolm grinned, showing crooked teeth. He squinted at Russ's forehead. "What's this? You get injured?"

"Tripped. I knocked my head on the sidewalk." He stepped farther back to appraise Malcolm's uniform. The double-breasted dark blue coat with gold buttons, dark blue trousers freshly-ironed, a white turtleneck, polished black boots. "Where'd you get all that?"

"Rented it from Carlheims's Costume Emporium."

The caretaker stared at Malcolm, lips moving as if words were sought but not found.

"Sorry to say I'm not the Captain, Mister Crick. At least, not usually." Malcolm stepped forward and lightly clapped Crick on the shoulders. The old man's eyes seemed a cooler, more pasty blue than they'd been before.

"This is Malcolm Moore, Mister Crick. The fellow who wrote the libretto I'm working from."

Crick gave a nod.

To Malcolm, Russ said, "Charles is quite a Verne fan."

Malcolm shot his sleeves, with their gold braid. "Indeed. His knowledge is superb, greater than mine. I've been rereading all my Fitzroy editions these last few months, Mister Crick. And I have many questions."

Crick reappraised the counterfeit captain. "I've been lookin' forward most greatly to speakin' with you on the subject of Verne, sir." He offered his hand, and Malcolm shook it.

"Yes, by all means. How about tomorrow, at the mansion? We can talk all about Captain Nemo and Prince Dakkar."

Crick nodded, seemed ready to say something else, then began buttoning his coat. He turned away, and Megan walked with him to the front door.

Sotto voce, Malcolm said, "Nice enough old guy. All the way over, he kept quizzing me about the *Nautilus*. Its crew compliment, its power source." While Malcolm ran fingers through his hair, pulling strands out of his collar, Russ was seized again with apprehension.

Malcolm grinned. "Surprised?"

"Sure," Russ said.

"I almost called. Then decided action was required."

Another suitcase sat in the entry, beside what looked like a familiar typewriter case.

Megan shut the door and walked back into the living room. She held up the cheese loaf. "I was hoping for Captain Nemo."

"Malcolm, this is Megan Sumner, the landlady. Malcolm Moore, the writer."

"Greetings, Meg." Malcolm stepped forward and hugged her. She grinned at Russ over an epaulette, then let go, stepped back.

Malcolm approached the whale shelves, examining the seashells, sand dollars, the gleaming bits of bronze and silver. "Wonderful weather you folks are having. Took everyone by surprise. Airport kept us soaring over Portland for hours. And when I landed, I still had one hell of an awful trip ahead of me." He picked up a green glass globe and turned toward the bay window. Lifting it to his eye, he peered out at the snowblind street. "Ended up ditching the car in your downtown."

With his uniform and ragged beard, backed by the shelves of bronze hooks and fishing floats, he suddenly looked the part of a sea captain; if not *the* Captain.

"Do you have anything to drink, Meg? Water?"

"Follow me." She led them both into the kitchen. "Would you prefer apple juice? Orange juice?"

"Apple juice, then."

Russ asked, "You wear that outfit from Boston?"

Malcolm nodded. "Stewardess thought I was Icelandic." He stepped over to the table, pulled out a chair, checked the tails of his coat then sat down heavily. He still held the globe. "This is a lovely town you have here, Meg. Especially the old mansion overlooking the sea."

"It's beautiful, isn't it," she said, handing him the glass. "We're all very proud of it here." She smirked at Russ.

"That's where Mister Crick found me, tromping in the snow." Malcolm drained his glass in four large gulps and caught his breath. "When I told him I was Captain Nemo, his eyes lit up. I knew I was in the right town." He glanced up at Russ. "So, how goes things?"

When Russ failed to immediately reply, Megan said, "He's taking some snow days off. Aren't you?"

Russ nodded.

"Actually, Russ, that's perfect. Perfect. Because I've come out to offer a change in direction. A *re-conception*. And most important of all, the story of Captain Nemo as Verne *intended*." He tapped his fingers on the table top, then briskly scratched his head. "I feel at home already. Poised for relaxation and serious work on the libretto, both at the same time." To Megan, he said, "Is there room at the inn?"

"I think I can find something."

"Excellent. So how are you doing, Russ? Other than the bump on your noggin? You look a little ragged."

"When I manage to get a full night's sleep, I'm sure I'll look better."

Fixing him with an intense gaze, Malcolm nodded.

Megan said, "You should lie down, Russ."

He nodded. "Later. Right now, I need some codeine. Is it downstairs?"

"Up," she said. "I'll get it."

"No, I'll be fine. Back in a minute."

As he walked toward the living room the sunlight intensified, bright yellow and full of heat, swarming with scraps of shadow now like birds flying in front of the sun.

Upstairs, in the bathroom, he decided against codeine and took three aspirin instead, listening to Malcolm's voice boom through the floor—the punchline to some joke, no doubt.

He went to his room, and the desk. Outside, sunlight struck a crystal street against the gray sea.

He forced his eyes on the photographs.

He spread them out, knocking the hycopathius, which fell to the floor, and bounced, but didn't roll far.

Symbols—*neumes*—against blocks of chordal sound. He looked and listened again, and doubted what he heard. Andrea would have more for him. Perhaps the images would be clearer. Louder.

Remembering that the dinner plans had been made before the snow, he decided to call her. He found her number on the last photograph, and dialed it.

She answered softly: "Hello?"

In the background, a violin slowly climbed a C scale.

"I have a question. Are we still on for tonight? I realize we made plans before the snow."

"I was presuming we would, yes. I mean, at seven P.M., if you can make it here. I have a car. . . ."

"I shouldn't have a problem with the snow. I'll be there at seven o'clock. For sure."

There was a pause. "I'll see you then."

"Bye."

"Goodbye."

He sat down on the bed, lay back, his forehead pounding.

"There he is." Malcolm grinned over the open suitcase on the coffee table. "Sit down, Russell."

Malcolm was on the right side of the couch, Megan on the left. She held the laminated list of household rules, and several twenty-dollar bills.

Russ sat down between them.

Malcolm said, "I brought presents. For both of you."

"Me, too?"

"Yes, Meg. You, too."

Inside the suitcase were two gold-wrapped packages surrounded by hardback books with lurid covers: *Mysterious Island, Robur the Conqueror, The Carpathian Castle, Michael Strogoff, The Demon of Cawnpore*—this last was a roaring metal elephant, bellowing steam.

"I want to read *Carpathian Castle*," Megan said. "Have you read it, Russ?"

"No."

"Here you are, both of you." Malcolm handed the first package to Russ. Heavy. A can. Russ tried opening it at the ends, but it was taped too tightly. Megan helped him, digging her fingernails into the paper, finally tearing it off. *Snow's Clam Chowder.*

"The real stuff," said Malcolm.

Russ hefted it into her hands.

"And secondly . . ." Malcolm lifted out the other package, and what remained—what Russ saw before Malcolm quickly lowered the lid—was a stack of manuscript pages as thick as a phone book, with ruffled yellow Post-it notes variously sticking out.

"There," Malcolm said, handing over the second package. It was much lighter.

Russ passed it to Megan. She tore off the paper. Grinning, she said, "Mmmmm. Sourdough bread. From Boston. That's great. Thank you."

"Yeah. Thanks, Malcolm."

"Through sleet or snow, however that goes. Who could rely on the postal service out here? How are you feeling, Russ?"

Russ shrugged.

Megan touched his knee. "His bruise has been healing, hasn't it. But I may drive him up to the next town if he keeps feeling rotten." Clutching the can, with the nape of the bread bag between thumb and forefinger, she stood up. "Okay. Six-thirty, with hot chowder and sourdough on the side. How does that sound? And right now, I'm going to make some tea for you, Russ."

He squinted up. "Remember, I'm having dinner at Andrea's tonight."

"I'd forgotten."

"At seven. Want to give me a ride over?"

"What's this?" Malcolm scratched his chin. "Going out tonight?"

Carefully, Russ said, "Andrea's the local music teacher. I promised a while back."

Malcolm sighed. "Oh, well. Meg, I'll just have a quick snack tonight and get some rest. Try to acclimate myself to the western coast. Nothing like an epic cross-country voyage to wear an old sea captain out." He donned his hat, and followed her into the kitchen.

Later, when Russ had bundled himself up in his jacket and wool cap—ready to leave—Malcolm said, "We'll talk tomorrow, Russ. Tackle this new draft, right?"

"Tomorrow," Russ replied, only because it seemed like years away.

"He only paid for a few days," Megan told him, driving slowly along Seventh.

"It's bullshit. He should've asked me. And I would've said no. Even without all the latest. . . ." Russ was clutching the envelope of photographs in his lap, and now relaxed his hands. He looked out at the lighted houses and the snow.

"Do you really feel up to this now? You could postpone for a day or two."

He shook his head. "I'm okay."

"Try to be nice to Andrea. She'd probably wilt away if you yelled at her."

"I'll be nice."

"I'm sure she practically worships you. A real composer, in her house. . . ."

He relaxed against the seat, ignoring Megan's sidelong glances, her smile. But his anger subsided anyway.

He pulled his cap lower on his head.

She opened the door, willowy and red-haired, in a powder blue sweater, white blouse, and a dark, knee-length skirt. She was a few inches shorter than he expected. Looking down, stepping back. "Hi, Russ."

"Andrea, hi."

"Please, come in."

He scraped his shoes on the wiry mat, then walked into a pale green living room cluttered with a diamond-patterned couch below a Picasso print, a coffee table, a bookshelf, small stereo and television, and in the far corner, a small upright piano with a metronome on top.

He wiped his shoes again on a softer mat decorated with a treble clef.

She shut the door. "May I take your coat?"

"Thanks." He unzipped it, took it off while holding on to the envelope. "What about shoes?"

"They're okay."

He handed her the coat. "Enjoying the weather?"

"Yes, but from inside," she said, smiling.

"Pretty rare, isn't it?"

She nodded. "We had a dusting a few years back. But nothing like this." Her hair was a short, glossy pale red, with bangs cut straight across her high forehead, emphasizing her narrow nose and solemn blue eyes. "Please, sit down." She gestured to the couch.

He walked across the immaculate beige carpet, and sat down.

From bookshelf speakers, Mozart's 40th Symphony was softly unwinding.

The familiar portrait of Joseph Evening watched from the bookshelf.

"Dinner's going to be a little late. It's chicken cordon bleu." She sat down, a cushion between them, and folded her hands on her skirt.

"Smells great," he said.

"Thanks. It's an experiment. I got the recipe from Hester Parker, whose husband runs the Laundromat. She prepared a lot of the food at our recent Gathering." She was looking at his bandage, then away.

"I wanted to say, Andrea, about your music at the Gathering, the transcription of Dvorak's *Ninth*. It was very charmingly done."

"Thank you." Staring down at her hands, looking up. "I was limited. To the instruments we have, I mean. I wasn't very happy with the arrangement, but the playing was lovely."

"Sometimes limitations make for more interesting music."

Had that made any sense? he wondered, still thinking of Malcolm barging into his life, ready to work.

"Could I offer you some cider, Russ? Hot apple cider?" She pushed the sleeves of her blouse, revealing freckled forearms.

"Sure."

She rose, and whisked off through the archway.

He set the envelope on the coffee table, and thought again of Malcolm, and of the work accomplished on *Nemo*—the pages of short score that now seemed somehow distasteful to contemplate.

Relaxing his shoulders, he looked toward the bookcase, and Joseph. The familiar almondine eyes, penetrating and cryptic, even from here. The portrait had handwriting along the side. Like an inscription.

Mildly curious, he stood up, walked over. In the empty space above the shoulder was written, in a spidery cursive, *To young Andrea, who will one day run our first town library—Joseph*.

Apparently, the man wasn't right about everything, Russ reflected.

Beside it were bound scores, mostly Dover editions—Beethoven's *Ninth* and Mahler's *First*, Bartok's *Microcosmos*, and piano pieces by Samuel Barber. CDs lined the shelf above. Arvo Part, Mozart. *Emmeline*, the recent opera by Tobias Picker, facing out. He saw none of his own works but didn't look too closely, stepping back.

He sat back down on the couch, just as she returned bearing a tray with two mugs and a plate of sugar cookies.

She glanced at the envelope, and set the tray beside it, lifting a mug. "Here . . . it's hot"

"Thank you." The mug had a painted seagull on the side. Apple-flavored steam tickled his nose. "Do you have private music students, Andrea? Outside your school duties?"

"Yes. Thirteen," she said, sitting down. "One was over when you called, earlier."

"A violin."

She nodded.

"That was Betty Nell, works at the factory. I have a baker's dozen, in the afternoons and on weekends. Adults and children."

"That's a busy schedule."

"Oh, it's not too much. And we've always been a musical town." She gazed down into her cider, through the steam. "Joseph Evening organized our first town band. And he wanted music at every town function.

A bandstand, too." She looked up. "I've been trying to get one of those built for years."

Regarding him over cup and saucer, there was a sense of holding back in the blue of her eyes, more prominent in the silence that followed, as she sipped, swallowed.

Carefully, she said, "You know our secret, Russ. Don't you."

He nodded, only a little surprised. "*From the New World*, as Dvorak would say. Hesperus."

She smiled, guardedly at first, then genuinely. Small white teeth.

"Though I'm not sure how much of the story I believe." Setting down the mug, he lifted the envelope. He drew out the photographs. Dim colors, a sense of harmonic procession, even in this single image. A sense of something immense, trapped in ancient stone. "But these are compelling."

"Did Megan tell you about the chambers?"

Russ turned to the next photograph; silver and gold symbols. Neumes.

The signs signified.

"Circular chambers," he said. "Portals in the center, and smaller portals along the sides. Elevator, and spiral staircases."

She nodded. "Yes, and most of the chambers have blank walls. Some have faint designs, like silhouettes of beings, of the ancient people. But one was unique." She looked down at the photograph. "The town council always thought it was abstract art. That's why they gave it to my family. Both my parents were amateur painters. But my father, ever since I was little, was sure it was more than just art. He spent years studying the color combinations, and the symbols."

She set down her mug. "The stone, throughout, is highly reflective. The echoes are . . . peculiar. The overtones—the upper partials— aren't quite right. Some in town hate it but I've always considered it the key to understanding those designs, those colors. And the silver and gold notes. That somehow, they described a music beyond our music."

She looked beyond her clenched hands, and smiled.

During dinner (chicken cordon bleu, green beans, potato and gravy) she asked about the contemporary music scene. She was well informed about the latest trends, and also of his last concerts at Ojai and Aldeburgh, from articles in *Gramophone*, to which she said she'd subscribed for years.

"I was wondering, Russ, about synesthesia. I read an interview with you, where you mentioned it. Does it help you as a composer?"

Resisting the urge for rote answers—about Olivier Messiaen and Scriabin—he simply said, "Don't know if it's helped me. Actually, once I started formally studying music, I lost a lot of it. I had it trained out of me, I guess."

"What was it like?"

He thought for a moment. "When I was a kid, we had this carpet installed in the house. Diamond patterns, alternating red and black. Whenever I walked across it, and looked down, I'd hear something like baroque music in it, a continuo. When I moved my eyes across it in different directions, it pulled the diamonds into something like a melodic line. Same way, I'd hear music and picture it as shapes and colors." He shrugged. "I've been back home, and the carpet's still there. Only now it's just a carpet, red and black diamonds."

He looked down at the photos.

"So do you *hear* those, Russ?"

He nodded, listening, staring down. Unsure of it. Then broke his glance. He set down his fork, and reached for the notebook in his shirt pocket. "The symbols are the crucial part. Maybe a sort of melodic map, or something much more complex."

He opened to the page where he'd sketched the symbols.

"I'd always thought of them as notes," she said.

"Are you familiar with *neumes*?"

"That's . . . a type of old notation, isn't it? From medieval times? Before measured notation."

"Yeah. A graphic symbol to *describe* a particular melody or gesture, instead of measuring it."

"Mensural notation, I meant." Her eyes studied the page, yet aware of him.

He said, "To draw any real conclusions, Andrea, I'll need to see more. Clearer photographs, of the whole chamber, if possible."

She nodded, and a moment later glanced up, directly. "I have more. I have the originals."

"Where?"

"Up at the school. My office." She touched a slender gold chain at her slender throat. Her eyes, looking up, were suddenly fearless. "It's closed down for the snow, along with the factory. But I could drive us up there."

After dinner, Russ bundled up in his jacket and cap. The snow had stopped, and the temperature had dropped considerably.

At the curb, they cleared a layer of hard snow from her car and climbed inside. She was quiet while the Subaru warmed up; her hair a dim copper against a black scarf.

Russ looked back, through the rear window, trying to see the mansion. He pictured Peggy Chalmers, Patsy, and the other elegantly gray-haired women huddled in dark, up in the tower.

Telescopes and tea.

Aloud, he said, "Wonder if the Storm Watchers are out tonight."

Andrea fumbled the car into gear. "I'm going to take a roundabout route, like I'm driving you home."

Her voice was smaller than before.

She drove slowly up Cheddar. The car bumped over furrowed snow that had refrozen and now gleamed under the sodium lights. At Fifth, she turned right. The houses under white pine, with lighted windows; along the sidewalk, a couple walking hand-in-hand, a few children building a snowman, and nobody paying extraordinary attention to Andrea's car as they reached Aberfoyle Street and turned left, climbing steadily to Seventh.

Then she doubled back to Cheddar, and drove up the rest of the hill. The surface was wind-blown, icy-smooth, and the car began to slide as it neared the top, wheels spinning, began to skate through loose snow, crunching, to finally bump against the curb.

"Can . . ." She pulled the brake, and parked, glancing into the rearview. They were into the trees, away from the houses. "Can you walk from here, Russ?"

"Sure. This should be okay."

He was careful climbing out, holding onto the car until he found his footing in the snow, then shut the door, climbed past the curb.

He looked toward the bluff, and the dark mansion.

She joined him. They followed the submerged sidewalk under the alder, with the smell of pine sap low in the cold air.

The *Evening Cheeses* sign stood motionless. The lot was an expanse of white, out of which the yellow building rose. They walked at an angle to it, passing a yellow dumpster, an *Evening Cheese Association* truck, and similarly white-topped wood pallets.

Just ahead was a patio, a flagpole, and the small red brick building that was the town's school.

Under the overhang, the concrete was dry. *Joseph Evening Memorial Schoolhouse, founded 1922*, read a plaque.

Russ knocked snow from his shoes, while Andrea unlocked the door and pulled it open. He followed—shoes squeaking—into a dim lobby, realizing only now how cold he had become, lips and fingers numb; toes, too.

Hands in his pockets, he resisted looking around, sure that Joe's portrait would appear in the dark, staring back.

"This way. It's not the fanciest room," she cautioned, down a hall pinned with drawings of cheese and trees. She walked into *Room 5*. A dozen desks. Green chalkboards. To a smaller room at the opposite side, her office. She flicked on the light.

A desk nearly filled the space, with two filing cabinets. A poster displayed the Circle of Fifths over the desk, next to another for the *James DePreist / Oregon Symphony Orchestra*.

"They've forgotten I took all these from the archive," she said, and opened a file cabinet with another key. She lifted out two thick folders. "I'll get you something to carry them in."

She laid the folders on the desk.

"Great."

While she rummaged, he flipped back the first cover. An image, vividly clear. More than before, a sense of three dimensions, with colors vibrating on colors, and the neumes winding through. The shape of it, the depth of it, sounding out to him.

She came back with a cardboard accordion case. "Here. This should work."

Hesitantly, he closed the folder, and loaded the batch into the case. "Thank you, Andrea."

They returned to the lobby, though he wasn't ready to face the cold again. With the case zipped inside his jacket, held against his stomach by his pocketed hands, he stepped outside.

A breeze stirred the trees, in faint crackles and chimes. Little dervishes of snow sweeping the lot.

Retracing their footsteps, Russ looked up at the factory, the dark windows, the bay doors decorated with the lowercase "e," and wondered at what it all enclosed.

Proof?

For all the stories offered by Dreerson and Carver? For the strange bones?

Could everything be confirmed, somehow, just by stepping inside?

He slowed, and she slowed beside him, looking over.

He gestured. "Is there any way . . . inside?"

Her hesitation was visible: a stutter in her vapored breath.

He added, "For just a quick look."

"I . . . have the key. And the codes. But not for getting downstairs."

He looked at the yellow wall, then downward. Past the snow, into what might exist, even at this moment, under the asphalt, under the hill. Entirely real.

"I just want to see inside," he told her. "See the door itself. To downstairs."

Just to know it's real, he thought.

a lecture about cheese

He followed her to a loading dock, and rusted iron stairs that led to a door marked *This is NOT a Customer Door*. Overhead, the clouds had a dim luminosity like pearl, and he remembered the puzzle box, and the bones, as the door clicked open and warmth rushed out.

He stepped into an immense darkened room.

When the door shut softly behind them, a brittle echo returned across the floor.

Fans whirred, gleaming, against the rafters. Skylights, faintly luminous.

A stink of cheddar and brine.

"Don't touch anything."

Something was beeping.

She stepped to the wall beside the door, pressed numbers on a keypad; another tone sounded; silence. She tripped a switch, igniting four halogen lamps over the mammoth stainless steel tubs and tables, the white floor and white walls, stainless steel doors, all of it growing brighter.

Along the right-hand wall were offices with wide glass windows, all dark.

As they crossed the floor—with the halogens buzzing, brightening— she pointed out the various equipment: the milling machines, the salt brine tubs. She explained that of all the people in town, she probably knew the least, but that everyone in town knew *something*, and went on to talk, distractedly, about the heat shock method of treating milk, about the handmade wheels of Jack cheese.

While the lights above grew steadily brighter, reflecting off the steel.

"This one holds 50,000 pounds of milk," she said, gesturing to a tank affixed with hoses and dials. But he looked toward the end of the room, to the far wall. A wide, yellow door, decorated with the lower-case "e" logo.

It looked heavy.

"Yes," she said softly, "That's it. Or, the first set of doors."

A sign beside the door read *Secondary Storage*.

He tried to project his imagination beyond it.

Something other than a storage room stocked with cheese.

Downstairs.

She was speaking, he realized. Almost a whisper: "When you first came to town . . ."

She was looking at the door.

"What?" He felt a rush of heat to his head, and something like nausea. He suddenly didn't want to hear her reply.

"That terrible accident," she said. "So senseless. Joseph had always taught us to believe in predestination. But your wife's death . . . it was senseless." She looked over, and her eyes caught the halogen glow. "But then you came back. To help us . . . to hear the ancient voices. The ancient music."

Somewhere, a door opened. The turning bolt echoed through the factory—the farthest office door opened, and a man in a white, short-sleeved shirt, stepping out. Waving. "Why, Andrea! Mister Kent! Fancy seeing you here!"

Bob Burle, the Master Cheesemaker.

Russ called out, "I was just getting a tour!" His voice thrummed in his head, awakening a pain behind his eyes.

"Well come on in here! Take a load off! I was just in the office putting in some *oh-tee*! Love to have some company!" He moved toward them.

Russ said, "Maybe some other time."

Then Burle waved, and the arc of his hand glittered and flashed. A scalpel. He laughed his wheezy laugh and called out, happily, "Andrea, grab your fella by the arm and drag him in here!"

"I'm ruining half the surprise by showing this to you, but what the hey?" Bob Burle sat down behind his desk, and the carved driftwood sign *Bob B.*

On the otherwise empty blotter sat a bust carved from yellow cheese.

A bust of Russ's head.

It seemed slightly larger than life—but how could one judge such a thing?

"What do you think of it, huh?"

Feeling for the chair behind him, Russ sat down. His forehead was aching. "Not quite sure," he said.

Burle's beady eyes darted from Russ to the sculpture.

"Come on, Mister Kent. Tell me what you think."

Russ looked.

Were his eyes so weary? Was his nose really such a soft curving line, his chin so slight?

Surrounding the bust were copies of magazines laid open to pictures of Russ Kent: an interview in *Gramophone*, a concert write-up in *Ovation*.

He was aware of Andrea sitting down beside him, and of Burle, on the other side of the desk, rolling up his sleeves; something raven-like about his widow's peak and sharp smile. The Master Cheesemaker leaned forward and peered at Russ, then lifted his scalpel and carved a wrinkle under the right eye.

Russ forced himself to speak. "You have an interesting factory, Mister Burle. I asked Andrea if I could see it. I hope I won't get her in trouble."

Andrea was staring down at her folded hands.

"Well, I offer no complaint, Mister Kent. It's great to have you here, yes sir. Who'da thunk I'd get my model right when I needed him. I'd like to just get those details that weren't captured in the magazine. I'll try to be flattering."

Peering at Russ, Burle leaned forward and rapidly carved another wrinkle. "But I *do* want to get all those laugh lines."

While the cheese dropped to the wax paper, Russ forced himself to speak. "Do you do a lot of these sculptures?"

"All the time, Mister Kent. All the time. I try to get everybody who stays here in our town. I might have to get that new guy at your house— that writer fella. If he stays here long enough." Burle shrugged. "Some people are great at making cookies, some at fruitcake, some at little wood totems. I make cheese busts. Whatever comes naturally, huh? Hold still, Mister Kent." Burle leaned forward. "I'm going to omit the bandage, you don't mind?"

Andrea looked over at Russ, and seemed ready to speak up, when Burle continued. "It's a medium all its own, I think you'll admit. Cheese tends to set after sculpting, get a sheen like candle wax. Over time the outer layer hardens. Grows a dull patina. Though certain climes give it a luster not unlike bronze." He turned the bust so that the opposite profile was revealed to Russ, then began cutting into the nose. "It's difficult, you realize, finding the right sort of cheese. Correct consistency is required. Perfect balance. Not too soft. Not too solid, or it'll flake. Hard cheese is no good."

Burle paused, exchanging his scalpel for a carrot peeler. Gently, he began to brush it against the bearded chin.

"The bacterial culture we use is the *same living strain* that Joe Evening had shipped all the way from the east coast in 1906. Imagine that. A thing of history, that culture. Retaining its own flavor and consistency."

Russ watched the peeler scraping, scraping. *You're taking away too much*, he wanted to say.

"The *preservation* of that culture, that's what's difficult. Must be kept pure. The right amount of rennet and milk, the right pasteurization— heat shocking is our method—the right amount of coloring to yield a yel- low like the color of baby ducklings." Burle straightened, then turned the bust, revealing more of its weak chin, its tired eyes. "Without the right culture, Evening would die as a town. Without the right culture, I couldn't carve anything. Why," here he chuckled, "you'd just be a crum- bly pile of cheddar on the wax paper. Not even fit for pizza topping."

Burle smiled. He leaned back in his chair, his glance darting between Russ and the sculpture.

"We were having dinner, Bob," Andrea said. "I wanted to show him my classroom. And since we were right next door, I . . ."

Suddenly, Burle leaned forward and carved a deep line between the eyebrows.

"Oh, is that it?" Burle smiled again, then shook his head. "I think I got you, Mister Kent." He tapped the bust on the crown of its head. "I think I got you here good as gold."

He stood in the entry of Andrea's house, leaning against the door. She'd phoned Megan several minutes ago. He held the case to his chest.

Andrea had asked him to shed his jacket and sit down on the couch, telling him he looked very tired. But he knew it was best for him to remain standing.

The encounter with Burle—and the almost as swift dismissal, back into the snow—had the texture of a dream.

From outside came a crunching sound as the Suburban pulled up to the curb. He stepped back and Andrea opened the door, admitting the cold air. "Thank you, Andrea. I hope I didn't get you into trouble."

Under her breath, she said, "He'll draw other conclusions."

He took her warm hand and shook it, then stepped out into the tumbling snow.

"Bye."

The Suburban idled beyond a white field. Megan waved from behind the passenger window, leaned over to open the door.

He began to walk along the path of submerged stones, favoring his left leg, conscious of the gleaming snow. She called out from the truck, or perhaps it was Andrea from the door, calling out, as he tried to follow the path. The snow became a curtain tumbling as he fell sideways, no pain, only softness, gentle stings on his face and neck as he shut his eyes.

For the second time that morning, he woke.

The bedroom was dim. Rain tapped against the window, but it wasn't the rain that had awakened him. Next door, the typing began again.

He tried to push himself up against the headboard, for a panicked instant unable to move his legs, then realized he was weighed down with blankets and a comforter.

The typewriter rattled on. He had recognized it immediately. Malcolm called it "Royal," a khaki-colored manual with a carriage-return shaped somewhat like a golf putter. In college, when Russ had leaned over the green keys, he'd smelled whiskey, ink and eraser shavings. He'd never forgotten it. In a way, it defined Malcolm.

Now, the two were together again, the performer at his instrument, the concert underway. Russ listened to them play into the afternoon.

"Move the toes on your left foot," Megan said.

The air was cool against his legs.

"Any pain?"

He shook his head.

She pulled the thermometer from his mouth and held it up to the window light. The rain had stopped. The typing, after a long pause, began again. "It's close to a hundred, Russ," she said, and shook it.

"But I can move my legs, no problems." A moment later he added, "And the cuts and bruises are looking better, right?"

"I still think we should take you to the doctor's." She set the thermometer on the bedside table, then pulled sheets and blankets up over his legs. "Rostov isn't far."

"Tomorrow," he said, lifting his mug. He sipped some mint tea.

She looked past him, at the wall. Listening to the typewriter. "Are you well enough to see Malcolm?"

He nodded. "I'm feeling much better."

"He wanted to barge in after you woke up, but I wouldn't let him."

Russ listened to the keys strike the platen, a metallic rainfall. Was Malcolm adding to those pages, or rewriting them?

"It's raining, warming up," she said, with a glance at the windows. "Snow's disappearing. You can see the roads again. It wouldn't be hard to get to Rostov."

"Let's see how I feel tomorrow."

"You passed out, Russ. Do you remember me shaking you? Do you remember the drive home?" Her voice had a nervous edge.

"I remember."

"Bullshit you remember! You were out of it." She sat on the edge of the bed, arms folded tight across her breasts. "It was serious, Russ."

"I agree."

She was quiet for a moment, looking at the wall, listening to the typewriter. "I can move him," she said. "Get him across the hall, into the spare rooms."

"That's okay. Only for a few days, right?"

He watched her eyes searching the wall, as though she were trying to silence the typewriter or make Malcolm vanish.

"Thank you, Megan."

She leaned over him, loose hair curtaining out everything but her eyes, her lips as they touched his own.

Russ was looking at the corner windows when Malcolm stepped inside.

"Greetings." He wore a black turtleneck, held a book in one hand, and a green glass globe in the other.

"Hey. Sit down."

Malcolm walked quietly to the desk, turned the chair toward the bed, and sat down. "Your landlady was worried, Russ. Said you passed out in the snow."

"I got dizzy. Exposure. Out in the cold too long."

Malcolm set the book on the blotter. "You certainly look better today." He stretched out his legs, relaxed his shoulders. Casually, he glanced at the desk. "But we don't need to talk about work till you're on your feet."

"No. Let's talk."

Malcolm reached for the hycopathius, lifted it into the window light, then turned it over, as if expecting to find a sticker on the bottom. A faint smile appeared, nearly lost within his bristling beard. "Charming," he said. He set it back down, then exhaled.

"So, what's the new *Nemo*, Malcolm?"

Again, Malcolm smiled. He sat back and said, in a sonorous, dramatic tone, "*Dakkar.*" Then, grinning, he lifted the book, held it out toward Russ: *Mysterious Island*. " 'Nemo,' of course, was what our Captain told the dull Professor to call him. But his real name is Dakkar, as we find out in this book. A brilliant man, and an Indian prince. And the opera—if you agree, Russ—will no longer be just *20,000 Leagues*. It will be the story of Dakkar's life, told through Dakkar's eyes."

Malcolm lifted the globe. "Sure you're up to hearing it right now?"

"I'm listening." Russ sat up straighter against the pillow.

"It begins in India, in the early 1800s, with Dakkar—a crowned prince, a brilliant young philosopher and scientist, already developing astounding new technologies. Fate or Faust, you could say. He's well-liked but aloof, and has a new bride he loves deeply. And Dakkar has enemies, of course. To convince the prince to do their bidding, they kidnap his bride. And Dakkar, through arrogance at his own abilities, tries to outwit his foes. But he fails. He finds her tortured to death, and is himself captured. His kingdom, overthrown. He loses everything, and is sold into a life of slavery on a remote south seas island."

Malcolm paused, and held the green globe up to his eye, gazing through.

"The sea, Russell. It forms the walls of his prison, yet it also offers Dakkar an escape, eventually. He harbors a thirst for revenge, and gathers around him a like-minded group, of all nationalities. Verne says they speak no language known to man; rather, it's one they've created in their years on the island, and it will be *my* creation for the opera, a language for the *Nautilus* and its crew. A singable, abstract language, barely heard, in the background. At any rate, there's a revolt. The slaves overthrow their oppressors and take to the sea. Dakkar finds his element, and works to build machines that will exploit it, to allow him to live in this unspoiled, undersea world. He finds an island well suited to his needs—deserted, and harboring a volcano. There he builds a base, and a fantastic undersea ship he christens *Nautilus*, and sets about wreaking his vengeance on ships of war." Malcolm paused again.

Russ tried to wear an attentive expression.

"The second act covers the events familiar to us, from *20,000 Leagues*. Nemo hunts the ships of war. The *Nautilus*, which has sunk many ships, is itself hunted as a monster. Nemo takes aboard certain survivors of a certain ship: our friends Professor Aronnax, Conseil and Ned Land. No longer the central characters, but foils for Dakkar. The act ends with the *Nautilus* sinking in a whirlpool. "Maelstrom!" says the crew, the only words we'll ever understand from them." A pause. "The third act . . ." Here, Malcolm again lifted *Mysterious Island*. Volcanic isle, storm clouds.

"The third act is Nemo's redemption. Alone, he raises what's left of the *Nautilus* from the ocean floor, and returns to his island home, Volcania, to brood. For a second time, a group of castaways stumble upon his province. It's almost a ritual pattern, we realize. An iteration in some grand scheme, grander than Nemo himself. He senses this. He keeps to the shadows, sings a tortured aria or two, resists the very idea of helping so-called civilized man. But then, finally, he must act to save them from yet another group of visitors to his island. Another iteration. He becomes their mysterious benefactor, and in the final act, as the Volcano erupts— praise Chekov—he reveals his presence to them. He atones, and dies. Dakkar, who mimicked Odysseus to Polyphemus the Cyclops, when he told Aronnax, *I am nobody*." Malcolm peered at Russ through the green globe. "Curtain falls." He smiled.

Russ, watching, realized that Malcolm's pitch was over, and a response was required. "Well, that's interesting. An interesting idea. Once I'm back in Boston, we can go over it."

Malcolm pressed. "But in regards to the general structure . . . viable, you think?"

"Maybe."

"Definitely perhaps?" Malcolm grinned.

"I can't make decisions one way or the other right now. The opera's on hold."

"Till when?"

"Until I'm back to Boston."

Malcolm sat back, raised his head, as though he were listening to the rain gusting against the glass, tapping in triple, quadruple time. He smiled. It was momentarily eerie. "Plot still needs some work, I admit. And I'll get plenty of work done here. Finding the town *quite* inspiring."

Russ said evenly, "Remember, no more than sixty double-spaced pages. Shorter the better."

The Captain folded his arms and wryly smiled. "Swift and fierce, Russell. Like a predator of the deep."

Moments later, when he departed, Malcolm left the book behind.

Russ threw back the blankets and stepped out of bed. He stood still for a moment to test his equilibrium, then stepped to the windows.

All that remained of the snow were white streaks along the edges of the road and under the trees, as though the sea had drowned Evening during the night, and left this spume upon the ground.

Next door the typing began, soon like the steady fall of rain outside. A promise that he wouldn't be disturbed.

Russ dressed in a warm sweater and jeans. He took out the manilla case, switched on the desk lamp, then laid out the first five photographs. Brilliantly clear colors. Majestic procession of chordal tones, threaded with neumes—some entirely new to him—that were also gestures in sound. He spent the next hour poring over the music, listening, trying to hear it anew, until a bell rang out downstairs, and Megan called up, "Dinner!"

But Malcolm wasn't staying for dinner.

"Mister Crick'll be by soon," he explained to her, pulling on his dark coat. "Sorry about that, Meg. Was wrapped up in my work. Later, Russ."

Carrying his notebook under his arm, he quickly drank a glass of milk and exited the house.

"Your Captain Nemo's beginning to piss me off," she said.

"So soon?"

She smiled.

Russ lifted the old bronze bell from the counter.

She smiled. "Like that? Usually that's my way of calling boarders to meals."

"Have you heard anything from neighbors," Russ asked. "About Malcolm?"

"Of course. Peggy called this morning." She opened the oven, pulled out a loaf of brown bread. "Very pleasant, cheerful. Wanted to know about the new boarder and I told her the truth. Crazy writer. Working on the opera."

She set it on the counter, then stepped behind him, encircling his waist with her arms. "So you're feeling better, huh?"

"Much better."

"Good enough to sleep downstairs tonight?" She kissed his shoulder.

evening and under

The jangling bell woke him. Remembering where he was, he reached for the phone on her bedside table.

"Hello?"

"Russell? Sorry to wake you." Peggy's voice, too cheerful. "Megan there?"

Still dark out. *6:03* said the clock.

He turned, touched Megan's shoulder, and she pushed up against the pillow. "For me?" she asked blearily. He stretched the cord across his chest and handed her the receiver.

"Hello?" Megan blinked, pursed her lips. She wiped hair away from her eyes. She listened for a moment. "Okay," she said. "What time is it?"

Another pause. She kicked her legs free from the blankets. "Okay." She handed the receiver to Russ.

He hung it up.

"Everything all right?"

She nodded, and rubbed her eyes, then stood up.

"Yeah. Just got to get up. Help at the school."

It was near noon when he rose, with an ache in his forehead, dizziness. He went to the toilet, waiting to see if he would throw up, but felt somewhat better, and better still after showering. He dressed warmly.

Malcolm was at the kitchen counter, fixing a sandwich. He wore a black lambswool sweater, cotton slacks and boots. His black coat was laid across the kitchen table, a notebook on top.

Two bricks of Evening cheese, cheddar and havarti, were peeled open on the counter beside him. Two bottles of Lighthouse beer, unopened, stood next to a lunch sack, and a copy of Verne's *Demon of Cawnpore*.

"Afternoon," Russ said.

Malcolm turned, with a gleam in his eyes. "Hey. Rise and shine. Feeling better?"

Russ nodded.

"You look better. Except for the bleary eyes."

"Seen Megan?"

"Not this morning. I slept late, though not as late as you." Malcolm smiled.

Russ poured himself some coffee, and resisted asking Malcolm about his dreams.

"Well, Russ, I'm off to Charles Crick's house. Did you know he owns a collection of Jules Verne, some in the original French? Had them since he was a kid, I guess. Got them from Old Joe himself. And he's promised to let me see them today. Quite wonderful inspiration."

Malcolm lifted the bottles of beer and lowered them into the sack. The glass clinked as he folded the top.

Moments later, without a further word, he donned his raincoat, gathered up his sack lunch and notebook, and left.

From the bay window Russ watched the dwindling black-clad figure, and lingering pools of snow.

Grimacing—a gleam painful to his eyes—Russ moved away from the window to the stairs, and climbed, with some difficulty, to Malcolm's room.

From the door he saw, for a strange instant, Captain Nemo sitting at the desk in the corner. Then recognized the captain's coat draped over a chair, epaulets gleaming, and the captain's hat atop the battered typewriter, against the brilliant larch trees beyond the window.

The room was a mirror opposite of his own. Lighthouse bottles lined the window sills. The walls were tacked with pages of manuscript and maps. One, over the bed, was of an island. *Volcania*, it read, jagged like the drawing. And underneath: *Mobilis in Mobili*.

The desk was cluttered with manuscript pages—heavily pencilled—a half-eaten sandwich, and the green glass globe from downstairs. Beside it, a black notebook.

Russ limped toward it. His right knee was aching.

He gripped the chair through the worn material of Nemo's jacket, and stared down.

The book was open to a page. There, in pencil, was Malcolm's handwriting, line after line, and at the bottom of the page, in darker pencil, as
though traced and retraced, were neumes.

He blinked, found them again, the symbols from Andrea's photographs, in Malcolm's hand. Not exactly the same as those recorded in his
notebook—more jaggedly drawn—but close enough.

Above was written the day's date, then:

> Dream. I'm standing in the mansion, looking at the sea. Old Crick there
> but was young again. Tells me I look like Captain Nemo. I gesture to the sea,
> realize I'm dreaming. I say, Look upon my domain. But the sea is gone.
> Drained. Though I sense it trembling out of sight, at the edges of the world.
> Below, among black and silver rock—fields of glittering fish. Closer to
> shore, canted on the rocks, is the *Nautilus*. I turn, look back into the man-
> sion's room. Old Crick's gone. Jules Verne stands there, circa 1880. Jules
> Verne, looking just like his photo. Arms folded. Smiles. Quite affable. Ges-
> tures to the floor, to strange symbols in gold and silver. Here they are:

The globe threw a quivering green light on the paper.

Russ glanced up. A breeze in the alder, throwing shadows. The houses
and road in wintery blue, and he was suddenly aware of a knocking
sound, random, soft, felt faintly through the chair, heard through the
open door behind him.

He opened the front door.

They stood side-by-side on the porch, staring up. They might have
stepped out of the ground itself, two dwarves in dark dusty coats.

Their faces wide and solemn.

"Sir," said the nearly bald one, in a cracked voice.

The other, with curls like blond wood, nodded.

Hands clasped in front of them, they bowed.

The first looked up. His brown eyes, in wry folds. Sparse black hair
stirring in the breeze. "Mister Kent, sir," he said, "may we come in?"

Black boots knocking the porch as they shifted in place.

Awkwardly, Russ stepped back, blinking against the light. As they
passed by him to gather near the stairs, he smelled a sharp, pebbly smell,

like copper and loam, bringing him back, for an instant, to childhood expeditions along the Charles River to hunt for insects, and to early sonatas that had tried to capture the elm and maple, the river mud, the sunset, in colored ink. Shutting the door, he heard the echo of this awkward music in the air, as the two stared at the flagstone and shifted from boot to boot, equipment clinking inside their coats.

"Please," Russ said, gesturing toward the living room. The balding, black-haired one went first. Russ followed the other to the couch. He gestured for them to sit, then carried over a chair and sat down opposite the coffee table.

"My name is Obolus, and this one's Danace."

For the first time the blond one looked up, revealing an ample face and genial blue eyes. Danace looked back down, hands clutched in his lap. Dirt encrusted nails.

"Sir," Obolus said, his voice tremulous and cracked, "Are we alone?"

Russ nodded. "You're diggers. Sandhogs."

A wry smile flitted across little man's face. "Then you know of the glorious empire."

"Yes."

"You're right, sir. Danace and me, we've spent most of our lives downstairs, while the others kept the city going up here."

The coppery smell tickled his nose, and seemed to lead to a question. Tremendously important, if only he could capture it, as the little men watched and said nothing, and the daylight swelled.

Russ managed, "Out on the Oceanview bluff. Why did you run away?"

Obolus shut his eyes briefly. "Sir, we're so sorry, for causing you that injury. We came back to see if you were hurt, but fled like cowards when you revived. It's taken quite a bit of nerve to knock on your door this afternoon."

Russ nodded, and concentrated on the words in his head, to speak them. "Before that, you both were outside, on the sidewalk."

Obolus stared at his hands, and his silence caused the other to look up.

Softly, Obolus said, "We just wanted to . . . pay our respects." His voice broke down, to a whisper. He wheezed in more breath, and got out: "Sir, we are *so* sorry." Clenched hands, knuckles glowing in the dim room.

"What . . ." Russ managed.

"Hesperus is active, sir. Don't doubt our word on that." Obolus looked to Danace, then continued. "Whenever we place a charge to clear an entrance, why, the structure awakens. Its voice is like a thousand voices, and it shines, sir. Like a great roar."

Russ stood up, found himself facing the bay window and the bright street.

The voice, in shadow to his side. "We were digging in a new area that day, sir. Trying to break out of the tower. We didn't think there'd be a problem with the charge. That a minor tremblor would do any harm, you see?"

Russ forced: "What day?"

"On the day she died, Mister Kent. We were trying to break through and Hesperus shifted . . ."

He turned. The two figures were nearly lost in the gloom, in tones of brown and black, and the coppery smell.

"I felt nothing," he said. "There was no earthquake. I didn't fall."

"Oh, but there *was* a tremblor, sir. A localized one. And when we came up, we heard the County sheriff arriving, sir, and we were in shock. We wanted more than anything to apologize, sir, to explain. But they wouldn't let us see you, of course. It was for the good of the town, you see? And then, when you came back, we feared you'd blame us for your wife's death. We lived in torment, sir, and wondered how to approach you, and explain." He exchanged a glance with Danace, then said, "Nobody knows we're here. You see," he glanced up, smiling, "this morning, the *empire* was reached, sir."

Russ remembered the phone ringing that morning, at 6:03, and Peggy's voice.

Megan, wiping sleep from her eyes, barely responding.

"Everyone's down there right now, exploring. And it's as big as Portland, sir!"

Megan, somewhere under the hill. Impossibly remote.

"This is what we needed to tell you, sir. Something good came out of all this misery. The accident wasn't for nothing."

Danace finally spoke. "People," he said quietly.

Obolus nodded. "Well, there's hope, sir. That people will be found."

Russ looked out at the empty street.

"A wild hope, perhaps, sir, but Danace here has heard noises, and we may rescue some of our own. Folks who somehow managed to reach the city, and live there." Obolus smiled, gently shaking his head, then glanced at Danace, and back. "Sir, we should be going, before they find out we came. Danace and me, we won't mention it. Nobody will be the wiser, but now our souls can rest. With Joe's empire finally revealed, we felt it needful to get shriven and done."

Russ nodded, felt faint pinpricks of heat along the back of his head, behind his eyes.

Obolus and Danace stood up. "Thank you, sir. We'll see ourselves out."

Russ stood up, and followed the two to the entry, where Obolus opened the door onto brilliance.

"Good day, sir."

Shutting the door behind them.

Russ stood still. A pain darted down his hip, alive like an electrical current, numbing his left thigh, his calf. He began to walk, wandering the lower floor, wanting to go upstairs, but knowing he couldn't make it.

That time was somehow short.

He walked into the rec room.

The daylight, from the bay window, painfully bright.

While he stood there, sensation left his leg.

He stumbled, nearly fell. He struggled into Megan's room, to the end table, the phone. He lifted the receiver but could not make his fingers work the buttons. He pressed the "0" with his knuckle, walking out to the middle of the room, looking for the snapshot of Jack but finding only his own haggard form in the mirror.

He wore a crown of light.

Glowing tendrils encircled his head. His face was pale, and when he moved his free hand it left behind a layered afterimage, fading from purple to pink.

The operator answered, asked if there was somebody on the line, but he couldn't respond. He couldn't form words. He had forgotten how.

Confusion, like the crown of light, swarmed around his head. Suffocating him. He struggled to make a sound, a moan, and the phone slipped from his hand.

He gazed into his own frightened eyes.

Then he vanished from the mirror.

part three

*t*he mask of orpheus

We have harmonies which you have not, of Quarter Sounds, and lesser Slides of Sounds. Diverse instruments of Musick likewise to you unknowne, some sweeter than you have . . . we make diverse Tremblings and Warblings of Sounds which in their Originalle are Entire.

—*The New Atlantis* (1626) by Francis Bacon

24

Crane fly music

A grandfather clock stood beside the sunlit windows in the library, counting time to the boy on the carpet below.

He sat with legs crossed, an artist's pad on his lap, a yellow pen held loosely in his right hand. Three more pens—blue, green and red—were clipped to the neck of his sweatshirt, with the rest spread out beside him. The page was nearly full. Seven other pages were discarded around him, his first attempts, an afternoon's work of dots and circles, in various colors, with *Crane Fly* written at the top of each. The pages were music. The music was the crane fly at the pond that morning.

A breeze through the open French doors lifted the pages, nearly curling one away until he clamped it with his hand.

Music sounded between his fingers.

That morning, he'd waded in skunk cabbage along the shore of the pond, searching for a toy Viking ship lost the previous summer. The crane fly had appeared skimming the cabbage then dropping to the slack dark water, long legs like strands of hair, leaving a tiny wake behind. Watching it, he had sensed a kind of sudden music in the way the sunlight caught its wings, in the faint ripple as it zigzagged over the water. But how? The flickering wings like tiny quick notes, while the tone, the melody, was really the smell of the skunk cabbage, the feel of sunlight on his arms. While he pondered this, a fleck of silver disturbed the flat water: a bass, gulping down the crane fly, leaving only a ripple, like the moment after the orchestra stopped playing.

His yellow pen now hovered over the page. He was up to the gulp. The notes were close together, a colorful jumble in his own style of notation. Over the summer, his father had taught himself to read it, sitting at the piano, or with the violin. Now, thinking of the quick notes, and his father struggling to play them on the violin, the boy grinned. The last five were brighter, from green to yellow as fish came up; the final note larger than the others, drawn over and over until the ink threatened to soak through.

A mug of coffee had gone cold on the carpet beside the boy. He was nine years old. Both the coffee and the privilege of working in the library were new that summer.

He sat back, looking at the patterned carpet, whose red and black diamonds were like the left-hand Bach music his father liked to play. He listened to the clock. He knew that to put the crane fly into music, he must first put it into the clock, into the pendulum as it tocked from side to side.

The boy sipped cold coffee. His eyes listened. When he looked up his father was approaching.

"Is it done?" His father smiled down.

He nodded, handing up the final page, then stood up with his mug of coffee, and followed his father across the library, watching as the sheet was placed on the music stand, and the violin and bow taken from their case.

The boy had never managed to write the music exactly as he heard it, but this time, as the violin's voice broke the silence, skittering like sunlight, he knew he had it down. His father played as though this were a virtuoso recital, gray eyes following the notes, fingers jumping along the neck, bow jumping, too, on the lowest strings, back and forth, fighting the hollow clock, darting through the pendulum to bring the pond into the room, the ripe smell of skunk cabbage, the ripple of light on the water, up the A string, to the E.

At the end his father added a flourish, an upwards screech like the fish gulping down the fly, bow skating off, leaving only the clock, only the shadow of the windowpanes stretched across the carpet, the pond back where it belonged.

He was drowning. The realization forced his eyes open to a blurry light. He blinked, found a hand lying near the rail of a bed, the wrist braceleted with plastic.

His own hand.

He tried to turn his head but had no energy. His body felt weighted down and strangely weightless at the same time. A while later—though time was vague, and it was only upon consideration that he concluded it was *much* later, for the daylight glare had gone away, and the window reflected the room lights—a woman breached his view, leaning in to smile and ask him simple questions, to which he croaked the simple answers: *Russ Kent. 44 years old. No, I don't remember.*

A needle was tucked into the crook of his arm; he couldn't feel it. Infrequently, something squeezed his upper arm. The room was small, with an anonymous landscape painting beside the window on his left, a white enamel examination lamp over a utility cabinet on his right. A machine beeped and clicked behind his head. Through the open door came the squeak of rubber wheels, murmurous conversations, infrequent laughter, sometimes rising in volume until a nurse ducked into his room to perform various smiling chores, attending machinery somewhere behind his head.

He slept, and woke again to find a different nurse, gray-haired, wearing a floral pantsuit, a bracelet jangling from her wrist. She checked the cuff on his arm: an automatic blood pressure cuff.

"Hello, Mister Kent," she said cheerfully.

He croaked a response.

"Just relax. The doctor's coming by to see you, okay?" She moved around to the other side of the bed. "Now I'm going to take a little blood. You'll feel a pricking."

He nodded, staring up at the tracked ceiling, then at the flowers heaped on the bedside table, and winced. As she brought away the syringe, he looked at the crook of his arm, the blue stain left behind.

He closed his eyes. Sometime later a dry voice said, "Russell?"

A young man in a white coat stood beside his bed. "Hi, Russell. I'm Doctor Barnes." He wore wire-rimmed glasses, and his eyes roamed the equipment over Russ's head. Looking back down, he offered a smile. "How goes it?"

Russ croaked. Then, trying again, said, "Okay."

"Did you have any trouble turning your head just now?"

"No."

"Any pain?" The doctor showed concern by a slight parting of the lips.

"No."

"If you're feeling up to it, I'd like to try a few things."

Russ nodded.

"All very simple," said the doctor, shining a light into Russ's eyes. "Could I get you to count to ten?"

Russ counted, slowly, up to ten.

"Perfect. How about backwards?"

He did so.

The doctor tapped his wrist and knees, asking Russ to name the days of the week, then patted Russ's shoulder. "You're doing great, Russell. Are you tired?"

Russ licked his lips. "Something to drink," he said.

"Sure. How about some orange juice?"

"Yeah."

To the nurse, the doctor said, "Could you get us some ojay, please?"

She nodded, and left the room.

Russ tried to push himself up against the pillow.

"Don't try to move around just yet, Russell. Here, we can raise the bed a bit for you. You're going to get a visitor later today. Your father. He was a concert violinist, I understand?"

"Retired," Russ said.

The doctor smiled. "He serenades us through visiting hours, with Paganini. My nurses love him."

Russ nodded, as the nurse returned with a plastic cup. He was vaguely aware that something awful had happened, something beyond his own injuries.

"Here you go." She handed it over carefully. Russ sipped. The juice had very little flavor.

"Russell, I'll check back in a bit later."

"Okay."

The doctor departed.

When the juice was finished, Russ handed back the cup, then collapsed against the pillow, tremendously tired, and shut his eyes.

Then Ellie was there. He'd been staring vacantly, wondering why this nurse with curly chestnut hair, a gentled face contrasting with keen blue eyes, seemed so familiar. He croaked her name, and she smiled, took his hand.

"Hi. How you doing?"

"Been better."

She had her hair cut shorter than he remembered, revealing the curve of her neck.

"Well, well!" Around the curtain, his father appeared, white hair mussed, dressed in an Oxford shirt and suspenders, wielding his cane. "Good to see you awake," he said, smiling. Ellie brought over a chair and he sat down, nodding as though to himself, searching Russ's face. He hung the handle of his cane on the rail, then reached in and lightly gripped Russ's hand. His eyes caught the light of something flashing above the bed, and they, too, flashed. "I'd ask how you're feeling . . ."

"Great," Russ said.

"The doctor wants to talk to you. Doctor Barnes. He's right behind me." He turned around. "Ellie?"

She looked. A moment later, "Here he comes."

The doctor stepped in, seeming hurried as before. He said hello to Russ's father and Ellie, then once more shone his penlight into Russ's eyes. He stepped back. "Can you remember how you got here, Russell?"

Only childhood memories were vivid, sounds and colors, the pond, the library. Russ shook his head, suddenly upset, aware of a loss: a thing, a person, a place, he couldn't say. Something at the corners of his eyes.

"That's not unusual, Russell. We expect to see your memory returning in several stages. It may take days, or weeks." He turned to Russ's father. "Mister Kent, did you bring the keyboard?"

"Yes. Ellie?"

She picked up something from beside the door, a Casio electronic keyboard, handing it to the doctor. Doctor Barnes placed it on Russ's lap, then elevated the bed. "Russell, your father and I would like you to play something."

Russ stared down at the keys, noticed the plastic bracelet on his wrist as he flipped the power switch. "What do you want to hear?"

He pressed a key, and a metallic D sounded.

Doctor Barnes said, "How about some Bach?"

"I could never . . . play Bach very well."

His father leaned forward, as if shutting the doctor out of the room. "Play the *Crane Fly Music*," he said, smiling. "Slowly. While you were getting better, Russell, I was serenading you with it—*lento*, of course." He smiled.

The notes returned to him, as well as the taste of cold coffee, the sound of the grandfather clock. He began slowly playing the notes, realizing that the doctor was watching his fingers, waiting for him to show disability; to reach for the G, and find the A instead.

But he made it to the end.

"Did you find it difficult to play, in any way?" the doctor asked. With a well-practised casualness, he rolled a stool to the other side of Russ's bed and sat down.

"I could have done better a few days ago."

"But you played all the correct notes?"

"Yes," he said, meeting the doctor's concerned eyes.

"I'm sorry, Russell. I didn't want to discuss the matter until we'd determined a little of your capabilities. And you're doing quite well." He stood, walked toward the door; there came a roll and a clack as the door shut; then silence. Russ turned to his father, who gripped his hand, his eyes intoning: *patience*.

Doctor Barnes returned to his stool. "Russell, you've experienced what's called a *subdural hematoma*, a blood clot between the layers of tissue surrounding your brain. It resulted from the injury to your head. Do you remember that injury?"

Russ tried to remember. He smelled the ocean, then remembered the open French doors in his father's study.

Playing on the carpet, as a kid.

"You fell, according to your father. You hit your head on the sidewalk. And the wound seemed to heal, which is often the case. It was a slow bleed, a hemorrhage. But you should recover completely, with no permanent damage. We've run CAT scans, chest X-rays, angiography, the whole works on you, and we haven't found anything sinister. We use something called the Glasgow Scale—a frame of reference for such injuries—and your score is pretty low. It's likely to heal one hundred percent." He lowered his chin, widening his eyes, as if defying Russ to dispute him. "And this preconcussive amnesia is seldom serious. I've no doubt that your memory will come back. Okay?"

"Okay."

"With some physical therapy and a month or two of rest, we hope to see you back to normal. And we should be able to move you from ICU tomorrow, and discharge you in a week. That makes your father happy, I know."

"It does indeed."

Scratching his chin, Russ was surprised again by bare skin. He stared up at the ceiling. "How long have I been here?"

Doctor Barnes looked at his father, then at Russ. "Yes, you were at Portland General for three weeks, until your father decided to bring you back to Boston. You've been here for nearly three months."

Russ looked out the window at the blue sky, aware that something had gone terribly wrong.

His father leaned toward him, squeezing his hand. "It's March, son. An unusually mild Spring in Boston."

Anna was dead. Later, alone in the room, he remembered this without surprise. The drive down the coastal highway two years ago, the detour off 101. Anna asking to stop, to stretch her legs.

She'd slipped, fallen from the bluff above the water. Blood on the rocks, on the barnacles, and the long wait for an ambulance. Flying with the body back to Boston. The service in the college auditorium, with Vaughn Williams's *Lark Ascending* as accompaniment, though Anna had always hated English pastoral.

He remembered all this clearly as he stared up at the tracked ceiling, and knew—though he could not precisely say how—this wasn't the reason why he felt as though something terrible had happened. It wasn't Anna's death, or his injuries. Trying to remember brought a feeling of helplessness, then anger.

He absently stroked his chin, surprised again by the smooth skin. He tried to remember indirectly, without trying, though the effort was extreme. His heart pounding, and beads of sweat popping out on his forehead.

And what he remembered was really from dreams—from the nightmares that had impelled his second trip to Evening. Anna lost in the trees, calling out. A stretch of coastal rock drained of the ocean, leading to distant black mountains. Tiny blue bones in shards of black. A town underwater, and lost people. Lost, but alive.

His father arrived at noon, the start of visiting hours. The nurse had been bustling about, adjusting equipment, taking his temperature and chatting about the warm weather.

"There he is, always the center of attention."

He carried an oblong package, which he laid against the wall beside the bed, and sat down in the chair, his eyes searching Russ's face. "How do you feel today?"

"I miss the beard."

"Really? You have the Welsh back into your face."

William Kent wore his tweed blazer, and black tie half-knotted; his concert tie.

"You have a gig?" Russ smiled.

"John Wexler and I put on a little show at the college. The first Brahms sonata, and the Ravel. Johnny wants to take it on the road."

"You should."

"Perhaps. Down the coast to our old alma mater. He says hello, by the way."

"Wexler . . . he's the one who loved to boo at Tanglewood, right?"

William Kent smiled. "He regrets that now. He's mellowed with age."

Russ pushed up against the pillow, looked for the remote. His father found it, pressed the button: the bed hummed upward.

"Good?"

"Yeah. Thanks."

"Have you talked to Barnes today?"

Russ nodded. "He was in very quickly."

"I spoke to him over his damned cellular phone. He says you're *on the mend*, and he's happy with your recovery. He promises to release you from ICU tomorrow."

"Great."

"We'll try to get you a single, somewhere in the quiet wing. How did you sleep?" William Kent leaned back in his chair, the padded shoulders of his jacket rising up behind his ears.

A sudden picture came to Russ, of an old man in a black coat, walking toward him across the bluff. The bluff where Anna had died.

He blinked it away. "Nurses are in and out. I slept for a little bit." Russ paused. The old man with gray hair. The witness to the accident. Funny name.

"We're looking into getting a part-time nurse once you're discharged. Therapy nurse. A real drill-sergeant."

Crick.

"Did I mention you have another five bouquets at home? A whole box-ful of cards."

Russ nodded absently, stroking his chin. Crick, consoling Russ, in his house, with the Sheriff.

Crick, who was a Verne fan.

"We can see if the nurse wants to double as your receptionist."

A sudden image of Malcolm in a blue suit with gold buttons. A captain's suit. A captain's hat on his head. And the old man standing beside him.

Crick.

"Dad . . . did Malcolm call?"

"Sure, late in the game. Ellie spoke to him a few weeks ago. When he heard you were on the mend, that was good enough. . . . You're trying to remember, aren't you?"

With an effort, Russ relaxed his shoulders. He wiped his hand across his forehead; it came away slick. "It might help . . ." he began. "Could I get my notebook? The one I brought to Evening?"

"Ellie has it. You can get it when you're released from here. But I think you should let things come as they will. No need to force it."

Russ nodded, listening to the bustle out in the corridor. He thought of Malcolm and the old man. Malcolm, in Evening.

"And as to the project, there's no need to worry about it, Russell. There's complete understanding. All are very worried about you, fore-most."

He nearly mentioned Malcolm, that his librettist had certainly visited Evening. But held back. Not believing it himself. Not yet.

"Now. I have a present, of sorts." William Kent turned in the chair and lifted the oblong box. "Well, a temporary present." He set it gently across the rails, over Russ's lap.

Distracted—an image of Malcolm in the captain's suit holding a green globe to his eye, with green light dancing on his face—Russ lifted the lid. He had to first pry one corner up then lift the length of it, revealing an interior of tissue paper, a gleam of dark wood.

It was a walking stick. His father helped pull back the tissue, revealing the bronze-capped foot, while Russ uncovered the handle, marvelously carved into a wolf's head. A sharp snout, sharp ears, and fangs.

"A dire thing for a father to give to a son, I know. Yet I consider it a celebratory present. You were awfully lucky."

Russ lifted it out. His father took away the box.

"I chose the carving to put you in the right spirit for your recovery."

It had heft, and was cool, with the handle both sharp and smooth to the touch.

The nurse visited with juice and english muffin with ham and eggs, and William Kent sat by, ate some of the eggs and told Russ of friends who had called, and then more about John Wexler. It had been at least a year since he'd had a concert, and it had obviously gone well. He left at two o'clock, promising to call that night.

Running his thumb along the sharp yet smooth wood of the wolf's ears, Russ stared out the window and thought of Malcolm, of the old man, trying to get more from that image of the two of them. Malcolm dressed in a blue suit. Malcolm as a sea captain.

Malcolm had visited the house where Russ had stayed. Stayed with the landlady.

The feeling of sadness was there, immediately. The feeling that something had gone terribly wrong. He tested it, grimly, as he had once poked a toothache with his tongue as a child, thinking of the rooming house, of the landlady with long brown hair.

Why this feeling of sadness, catching in the back of his throat?

It was a ballroom dimly lit by chandeliers, and the pervasive green was really water.

Luminescent fish darted over tables draped in linen that drooped upward, like the mouths of white flowers. China plates floated here and there, glinting gold at the edges. One was knocked sideways by a fish, tumbling to the tall windows, catching on the drapes.

With the water teasing his hair, his beard, he walked, floated to the windows, stopped before the glass, wiping away a layer of scum to find a parking lot below with silted cars, and the glimmering lights of the town beyond. Low buildings encrusted with coral and silt, tended to by schools of fish. Ahead, a hill climbed to the surface of the ocean. Sunlight sparkling there fought down as dim winks on the pine trees and picture windows, and a lime green undulation on the streets.

Evening.

Through the helmet he heard what might have been toy trumpets, faintly piping and warbling.

"Hey, boss." Ellie stepped out onto the porch, waving.

Russ sat in the shade of the deck umbrella, three weeks after his release from the hospital, with the wolf-headed stick hooked on the edge of the table. The afternoon was muggy, the stink of the river mixing with flowers in the garden. He'd been trying to relax, to resist the impulse to remember.

She smiled. "Someone's looking good."

"Looking better, at least."

"Nope. Good as new."

She had just returned from Bermuda. Her tan was deep against the lemon sundress and chestnut curls, which brought out her blue eyes.

As she leaned over to kiss his cheek, he noticed the pack of papers in her hand, and the spiral binding of his notebook.

"Thanks."

"Sorry I couldn't get them to you earlier." She set them on the table. His notebook, its worn blue cover. "Your Dad said the nurse is due soon?"

Russ nodded. "Gloria. If you're lucky, you'll get to meet her." He pulled the notebook toward him. "Want some iced tea? There's a clean glass."

"Sure. Don't move. I'll pour."

He opened the cover. On the first page was a list:

Stravinsky: *Persephone*
Knussen: *Where the Wild Things Are*
Busoni: *Doktor Faust*
Catan: *Rappaccini's Daughter*

Weir: *Blonde Eckbert*
Reimann: *Lear*

Works to inspire *Nemo*, he remembered.

On the next three pages was a rough itinerary for the drive out from Boston, highway routes, motel phone numbers. And at the bottom of the fourth, a stave sketched in pencil, and a thick chord bristling with notes.

Twenty notes. The tone cluster. It had begun there, he remembered. From the dream of Anna on the rocks below, the shimmering crown of sea water.

Russ listened to it, against the clink of ice, and the mosquitoes.

"Remembering more?"

He nodded. Then, "Bits and pieces."

"Like the doc said."

"Yeah."

Closing the notebook, he told her about his recent strange dreams. The drowned town. The ballroom with bits of china floating here and there. Walking the streets in an armored diving suit, trying to reach the house on the hill.

"Don't beat yourself up, Russ. I'd be worried if you *didn't* have nightmares about that town, after what you've been through."

He ventured, carefully, "Did you ever hear from my landlady. Megan Sumner?"

Ellie reached into her pile of papers and pulled out a slip. "Thought you might want to call her yourself. Here's her number." She handed it across to him. "We spoke . . . umm, maybe six weeks ago. Just after you began waking up."

The number was unfamiliar.

"What'd she say?"

"She was so relieved, Russ. What do you think?"

He felt sure that there was more to all this. Again, the certainty that something had gone terribly wrong, tied in with those dream-like bits and pieces.

Malcolm Moore, dressed as Nemo, in a blue suit with gold buttons.

The old man, Crick, walking across the bluff.

It was a kind of motivation, this certainty. Gloria had commended his determination in therapy sessions that left him wiped out, in pain, unable to move.

"When did you talk to Malcolm last?"

She thought for a moment. "About the same time Megan called, maybe a little later. He said he was in Florida, researching a new novel. Didn't seem too upset when I told him the project was on hold."

Russ was somehow sure that Malcolm had been in Evening.

Malcolm, dressed as Nemo, holding a green globe up to his eye.

Russ muttered. ". . . doesn't sound . . ."

"What?"

"That doesn't sound like Malcolm," he said.

Ellie smiled. "He's a jerk, Russ."

Russ became aware of his father practicing in the library. The Bach *Chaconne in D*, the silvery line of it, among the cicadas.

"I'm sorry, but it's true," she added.

Slipping the paper into the notebook, he sat back, relaxing his shoulders. "What did Megan say . . . about how I got the head injury." He remembered tripping on a sidewalk, below the yellow building.

Ellie ran her finger up the condensation on her glass. "The stuff you heard from your dad. It happened on a hill, near the factory. You tripped and fell, and seemed fine for a while. You didn't see a doctor. And a bit later you collapsed. She'd been out for the morning. When she came back you were on the floor."

He glanced at the notebook.

Would the sketches set off more memories—detonations across the page, from that watery crown?

Ellie sipped some iced tea, watching him over the glass.

"So how's your love life, Ellie?"

Smiling—for a moment her eyes entirely disarmed—she told him about her trip with Brian to Bermuda, and plans to go to Europe in the fall.

Inside the library, the violin ceased, leaving only the sounds of insects, and the ice clinking as Ellie sipped her tea. The oppressive air summoned another memory: the cool Pacific breeze, rain in the alder and spruce, and of snow.

Snow falling against the roar of the sea. An icebound landscape.

"Russell!" His father called from the study door. "Guess who's here!"

There came Gloria's bubbly laughter—Dad was charming her again—and then the plump woman poked her head outside and said, "Ready, Mister Kent?"

And his father's retort: "*I'm* Mister Kent, Gloria! He's Russell!"

Two hours later, Russ was exhausted to the bone. The simple series of exercises had grown monstrous on repetition, ending, as usual, with him profoundly fatigued. It had been depressing the first time, but he cautioned himself that it was to be expected, and necessary, if he was to return to Evening.

And he *would* return.

At six P.M., heartened only by the announcement that Gloria wouldn't be able to come the following day, he went to bed. His dad brought him a light dinner, and he fell asleep to the network news.

*s*ome figures

The underwater town.

Silted streets and coral-encrusted buildings, with strange spiny fish swimming under sodium lamps, swatting dully at the water.

He was alone but for a solitary figure in the distance, glinting bronze—an armored diving suit, with silvery bubbles threading up to the surface of the ocean.

Captain Nemo raised his hand in greeting.

The clock glowed: 02:42.

In the dark he sat up and took stock of his body. Moving his right arm, left arm, right leg, left leg; as was the routine. His muscles were sore.

After a moment, he threw back the covers and swung his legs out, then switched on the lamp.

His notebook lay beside the clock. Yawning, he grabbed it and carefully stood, deciding to go downstairs.

The house was quiet. He donned his robe and slippers. Leaving the stick behind—the weeks of therapy had given him confidence, at least while inside the house—he walked slowly into the hall and down the stairs, remembering the other house, and a staircase down to a green fanlight.

In the study, he switched on the lamps set about the room, turned off the main light, and sat in the plush chair by the desk.

Bookcases crowded the walls, full of bound and loose scores, paperbacks, textbooks. Framed photographs took up any empty space: his father with slick black hair and a tux, on stage with Rostropovich; again, his father, even younger, beaming with Kubelik; and Russ's mother, circa 1960, with pale hair and paler eyes.

A bulky reel-to-reel player, a receiver, a CD player and turntable crowded the desktop, with stacks of LPs, a golfing hat, a conductor's baton. In the entire room there were no remnants of those days after Anna's death, the sheets that had covered almost every surface, laid out in tiles on the floor, taped to the shelves, and windows—left behind in Evening.

He powered on the receiver, raised the turntable's lid then flipped through a stack of LPs on the desk. Near the top were some of his own early works on CRI, and three of his father's recordings—the Berg concerto, the Prokofiev 2, and sonatas with Lukas Foss on piano. Then some albums he could remember from the old days: Vivaldi, on RCA; Samuel Barber's *Capricorn Concerto* and *Medea* with the Eastman Rochester Orchestra, conducted by Howard Hanson, on Mercury; Gould's *Fall River Legend* on Mercury; a boxed Korngold opera *Die Tote Stadt*, conducted by Leinsdorf; Stravinsky on Columbia. He nearly picked the Barber, but settled for Vivaldi.

He extracted the inner sleeve from the jacket, and the record from the inner sleeve, then laid it on the platter. He lifted the cartridge arm. His thumb remembered the proper amount of pressure, his eye where to position the cartridge. He pulled a small lever toward him. The needle dropped.

It hissed over vinyl then found the groove. After a few clicks and pops, and a nearly inaudible *whoosh* in the bass, a concerto began, just loud enough.

Russ rubbed his eyes. He yawned, wondering what piece this was. But one Vivaldi was much like the next. The equivalent of wallpaper.

And pleasant enough. A dulcimer thumping out the ground bass, with flutes and strings in something like an arioso. His thoughts soon drifted from it, back to the dream. To Captain Nemo in a bronze helmet, raising a hand in greeting.

That motion, the raising of his hand, carried a sound with it, like an audible warp.

Not through air, but water.

Russ sat up in the chair, looked around at the nearest books for his copy of *20,000 Leagues Under the Sea*. He hadn't taken it to Evening: it was here.

He stood, and limped back into the hall, then made an effort to walk easily into the library. He flicked on a light, approached one of the tall shelves, the colorful, dusty spines, remembering the used bookstore in

Evening, the *Warp and Weft*. It had been one of the first memories to return, pleasant memories of browsing a cigar-shot dimness.

He could see the proprietor's plump face.

He scanned the spines for one with yellow letters on green, as he remembered, passing over the tall books, the paperbacks, the new books.

He didn't find it, and moved to the next case, the top shelf.

Bernard. The bookseller's name—Bernard Something. He tried to remember, scanning the titles, yes, and there it was, the pale green spine with yellow letters *20,000 Leagues Under the Sea*. He pulled it out. An old copy. A cover swimming in green ink, with a quite small, and entirely too-literal submarine, iron gray, casting a watery yellow beam off the page.

Below the author's name, mountainous coral, and the ghostly shape of a gigantic squid.

He walked back to the study, looking at the cover, hearing the tone cluster. Semitones, quarter tones.

He dropped into the chair—aware the Vivaldi had been continuing all ths time; the same piece, perhaps. He opened the book on his lap. To the title page, and the illustration that faced it: three divers in antique diving suits, the foremost holding a trident. *Captain Nemo*.

He paused, staring at the ocean, and snarls of coral in the distance, listening to a choir of double bass, a long, low portamento. More felt than heard. He began to turn the page, then stopped himself, remembering how boring the book had been the first time.

The paintings were the best part.

He shut the book, then stood it on the desk, its cover facing him.

He grabbed the notebook.

Again, the list:

Stravinsky: *Persephone*
Knussen: *Where the Wild Things Are*
Busoni: *Doktor Faust*
Catan: *Rappaccini's Daughter*
Weir: *Blonde Eckbert*
Reimann: *Lear*

Of all those works, it had been Aribert Reimann's *Lear* which had influenced *Nemo* the most. The dense layering of the strings, the intense contrapuntal interplay.

He remembered the underwater scene, written in long score. Vertical swim.

On the third page was Ellie's phone number in gentle cursive, and *Call me every night!* Then the entire cross-country trip mapped out in route numbers, motel numbers.

Then sketches of the tone cluster: done in motel rooms, late at night, through his tiredness, attempts to expand upon those twenty notes, vertically as well as horizontally. Notes, themes, strung out in quarter-tone cantus, in black, blue and red ink—a variety of complimentary motel pens, with no color sense implied.

Reign of the Vertical. A quote from Verne, and beside it: *Descending. Quarter tone? Dense layers?*

Strings in dense layers, mostly descending, and the deep strings like the seabed. Sedimentary layers, almost Stygian, against which the Vivaldi now worked busily, its baroque filigree the clockwork of an engine.

The *Nautilus* soaring over the pine-covered hill.

From a dream.

He flipped ahead; a bit of paper fell to his chest. Megan's number.

He picked it up, glanced over at the clock. *2:58.*

If she *were* in town, she'd be home. Asleep, perhaps, but almost certainly home.

He turned down the music. Startling silence, as he pulled the phone toward him, lifted the handset.

Recalling the second trip—the long drive through the midwest, across the Rockies into Montana and Idaho, with winter ending as he reached the Oregon plain—he dialed. Across that distance now, the line rang.

He pressed his ear to the receiver, listened to static and silence, expecting the line to be picked up. It rang a second time. Megan waking up. Long brown hair, bleary eyes.

A phone by her bed. A rotary. On the third ring, he saw the Wyeth print on the wall, and heard the phone ringing. Not an electronic chirp, but a real bell.

The window behind it looking onto Alder Street.

He remembered her voice, her mellifluous laugh.

Four rings, five.

Another phone upstairs, on his desk. A heavy black rotary. The desk and its straight-backed chair with a diamond-patterned cushion. The view out the window of a classic house across Seventh Street—a Italianate—and the sea beyond.

He was sure, by the tenth ring, that nobody was home.

When he hung up, part of him remained standing there in the upstairs bedroom, in the early morning quiet, beside the corner windows.

Looking at pine trees stepping down the steep hillside to the sea.

But instead of the ocean sounds, he heard the double bass, cellos and violins, each with a separate glissandi, shifting as sunlight shifted on the waves. He listened, recalling the houses down Seventh and Alder, the businesses along First Street, past the *Warp and Weft*, the Cafe, the Laundromat, the Cheese Outlet store. Double bass rumbling, and cellos in dark curves above, with piccolos in harsh cries like the gulls tacking in the breeze, over the pine, as Cheddar Street climbed the hill to a line of alder, and through the trees to a parking lot, a yellow factory. And this was the important area, the hilltop.

He sat entirely still, unaware that the Vivaldi had long ago ended, and the spindle arm had raised itself and swivelled back into its berth. Memories flocking back like gulls to Mrs. Nelson's roof. Megan, and their waltz at the Winter Gathering, lying beside him in bed, under covers, goosebumps on her arms. Peggy Chalmers in a blue blazer. The Victorian Visitor's Center, and the secret group, the Storm Watchers, arrayed like a sinister chorus around the rotund Bernard Dreerson. And the stories told one morning, in Dreerson's upstairs apartment. Of Joseph Evening and the town founders, digging.

Of the dead city under the hill.

"You slept in here?" His father stood outside the study door, in robe and slippers.

Russ sat up in the chair, wincing at a sharp pain in his neck. Everything came back to him—a riot—and he tried to cover it by rubbing his eyes, pretending to yawn.

He'd fallen asleep toward morning.

And the nightmares, it was true, weren't nightmares at all.

"Yeah." He made to stretch, remembering a snowstorm and ancient music, and dark dwarves fleeing up the inland hill.

His father stepped in, his eyes lingering on the notebook next to Russ's hand.

During breakfast, Russ tried maintaining a normal conversation, a cheerful attitude, all the while more depressed; unsure, in the reasonable daylight, how many of those certain memories could be true, and how many the result of his injury. The blood on his brain.

"I'm meeting John Wexler at noon," his father said, buttering some toast.

"Really? Another gig?"

"Perhaps in the near future. Series of little concerts down the coast. Today, it's just some golf, at the club."

His father left at quarter to twelve.

A few minutes later, Russ went into the study, and opened the notebook. Searching the now familiar pages for more clues.

He turned to the last page he'd used, about halfway through. A group of hexachords. Dim, dark music.

Tiny shreds of paper were stuck to the metal spirals. Some pages had been torn out. Tipping the notebook to the window, he noticed impressions on the next blank paper. Using the edge of a soft pencil, he was able to bring out in graphite a series of flicks and curves. They were arranged one after the next, almost like the hexachords on the previous page.

Perhaps just portions of other words, on other pages.

Though they seemed familiar.

A while later, he sat up, looked at the phone then lifted the handset, dialed the local operator, and asked to be connected to Oregon State Information.

"Yes, hello, I'm looking for phone numbers in the town of Evening."

"Just a moment." A pause. Keys being tapped. "I see a Visitor's Center listed. Would you like that?"

"Yes. Thank you."

"One moment."

It almost seemed too easy.

The operator left the line, and a computer voice read him the number. He wrote it down, and in the same fashion got the numbers for the cheese factory, the barbershop, and the *Warp and Weft*.

Then sat looking down at this evidence, getting up the nerve to call.

Nobody answered at the bookstore. No answering machine, either.

The Visitor's Center picked up almost immediately.

"You've reached Evening-by-the-Sea's Visitor's Center," said an eager voice. Peggy Chalmers, in a blue blazer. "We're closed at this time. You can call back, Mondays, one till four, and Fridays, ten till two, or leave a message. If you'd like a brochure, just leave an address. Wait for the beep!"

He hung up, and dialed the next number, which answered on the fifth ring.

"Say Cheese!" said a breezy baritone. "You've reached Evening Cheeses, home of the famous Evening Havarti and spectacular yellow cheddar."

A brawny, balding man behind his desk. Black eyes and a sharp widow's peak. Bob Burle, grinning over the roof of the Evening mansion, carved from cheese. "We're closed at the present, but hey, we'll return your call as soon as possible. For general distribution questions, go ahead and call the Port Rostov Packing Company . . ."

Russ hung up, staring down at the wolf-headed stick.

He nearly called back. To leave a message. A threat.

Instead, he dialed the barbershop.

The line picked up immediately.

Russ jerked straight in the chair.

Someone was breathing on the other end. Expansively. "Evening," said the voice.

"Is this . . . the barber?"

"Yes, it is . . . indeed. How may I help you?"

"You're the mayor, too."

"Well, yes. Yes indeed, I am."

The Barber-Mayor, almost bald, in a white tunic. And in a yellow raincoat, with an umbrella, strolling down the sidewalk.

At the Winter Gathering, his fleshy face, beady eyes roaming Russ's beard.

"Have we had the honor . . ."

"This is Russ Kent."

He could nearly hear a smile, then breath being held, and released. "Yes, Mister Kent. You had an injury. A head wound, as I recall. Terrible thing. Are you all right?"

"I want to know where Megan is."

"Mister Kent, I'm at a loss. I don't have her home phone number handy. But if you hold on, I can look it up for you."

"I know what's going on. Downstairs. In Hesperus."

"Do you, now?" The Barber seemed to sigh. A hand covered the mouthpiece. Murmurs. Was another person in the room? Russ pressed his ear closer to the receiver, then the Barber was back, and his voice had grown cold. "A head wound's a serious thing, Mister Kent. We were all quite worried about you."

Russ hung up. His hand was shaking.

He blinked, wiped his forehead.

It was all true, he told himself.

No need to doubt anymore, it was certainly true.

The plan became clear. It required the utmost effort in his therapy, turning his thoughts away from Evening, applying himself to his sessions, and maintaining a positive face to his father and the few who called on him— his agent, friends and colleagues.

A week later, Gloria remarked to his father, "We're down to the final stretch, Mister Kent. He'll be on his own, back to normal!"

At night, Russ found it hard to sleep, and lay sifting through memories, bright pangs of his time with Megan, and of the stories Dreerson had told, and Malcolm, dressed as Nemo, arriving in town with a reconception of the opera.

Malcolm was still there, in Evening, he was sure.

He wanted to tell his father all of it, or Ellie, but knew their likely reaction. And things were falling into place for his return. His father's friend, John Wexler, dropped by to rehearse. A series of informal concerts down the eastern seaboard, over a three-week period, had been proposed. Happy with his son's therapy, William Kent had agreed. They would leave the next month. "You'll be in Ellie's hands," his father told him. "She's agreed to house-sit if you need the company, or just drop by during the day. And there's always Gloria!"

The final hurdle would be Ellie.

It was a Thursday. She'd said she would drop by that afternoon, around four.

"Russ!?"

"In the library!" he called out, closing the book he'd not been reading, setting it beside him.

Remembering what he must say, must ask.

"You back here?" Ellie appeared, and smiled.

"Hi."

"Hello, yourself."

She sat down on the other end of the couch, folding one leg under her. She had a present. A bottle of homemade blackberry jam. Russ took it, and thanked her.

"Where's your Dad?" She picked up the book, read the spine, then set it down.

"Practicing with John Wexler."

"Oh, right. The concerts. I think that's great. Too bad I won't be able to hear him, since I'll be here, looking after Russell Kent." She smiled.

Russ sat back, hands on his knees. "I have a huge favor to ask, Ellie."

She settled on the couch, turned toward him. "What?"

"I need to go back to Oregon."

Her shoulders sagged. "To Evening?"

"Yes. Alone."

"Really. And your father's okay with that?"

A pause. "I'm not going to tell him. Not until I come back."

She looked at her lap. "If it's to get your car, there's no need, Russ. He arranged for one of his students to drive it back next month." Glancing up, looking evenly at him. "But it's not that, is it?"

He shook his head.

"Is it your landlady? Megan?"

"Yeah. It is. And I won't be gone for more than a week."

With the fingers of her right hand, Ellie played with loose threads on the arm of the couch. "Did something happen there? Beyond your injury?"

"I'm not sure. I need to find out."

"I don't really want to lie to your Dad."

Accepting and rejecting a number of things to say in response, he said nothing.

"That's understandable, Russ. Right?"

"Very," he said.

"You shouldn't go alone."

"Megan's meeting me at the airport. I'll only be alone during the flight. And I'll buy you a ticket in advance. I'll call every night. If I miss a call, you can fly out."

"Nothing good came out of that town."

"Talk to Gloria. I've exceeded her expectations. She says only a few more sessions and I can work on my own."

"What if your Dad calls you?"

"I'm going to give him every reason *not* to call. But if he does, maybe I'm out taking walks, driving into Boston. Maybe Malcolm dropped by, and I'm out with him. If he does, there's the answering machine. I can dial in from Oregon. I can call him back."

She let go of the threads, and rubbed her finger on the material.

"I won't be leaving for a couple weeks, Ellie. Let me prove I'm okay."

She seemed about ready to stand up and leave. Then she looked over. "If you prove it."

*e*vening, oregon

As he'd done last autumn, and two summers before, he took the exit off Highway 101 to Evening, through stands of spruce and alder.

The breeze whistled through the barely-open window, redolent of rain, and mulch.

When Ellie dropped him off at the airport, she'd made him promise to call. "Every day, by noon, Russ. Or the deal's off. I'll hang out at the house during the day. If your dad calls, I'll just say you're out and about, and get his number so you can call him. But you have to call. Promise me."

"I promise."

During the flight from Boston, crowded by business travellers, and the whirlwind of tourists at the airport, his memories of Evening had seemed improbable, even dangerous, the symptoms of a head wound. He wondered if his real duty was to recognize it as an entirely normal town; that all this was a result of his injury.

As expected, the first cottages appeared, to the left and right. Quaint, nestled in their pine, with rhododendron, sunflower and ivy, maybe more overgrown than before, maybe not. Trucks and cars were parked in the driveways.

Then the familiar sign:

Welcome to Evening, Oregon
Home of Evening Cheeses
Population 310

The forest ended. First Street stretched in front of him, with sunlight slanting across the road, onto the red brick barbershop, and the gas station with antique pumps; the further, quaint businesses.

To his right, the bluff and the Evening mansion, in silhouette. To his left the inland hill, brilliant, with windows gleaming in the trees.

He slowed down—the bag of groceries from Portland nearly tumbling from the passenger seat—and tried to see past the glare on the barbershop window. There were cars parked along the curb, but no people in immediate view.

Was it too unusual? For a small town on a Friday afternoon?

On his right, the three-story Victorian appeared against the alder, the sign in lacy black iron:

Evening–by–the–Sea's
Chamber of Commerce and Visitor's Center
Open from noon till five

The yard was well-kept. There were flowers in the garden.

Ahead were the one- and two-story businesses with awnings and overhanging plastic signs.

Yet the sidewalks somehow looked different.

He slowed further. What was it? The lack of people?

No. The windsocks had been taken down. And the iron benches and concrete planters were gone.

Accelerating again, he resisted a thought as startling as the sudden low sunlight in his eyes. That the townspeople were nearby, but impossibly remote, somewhere under the pine-covered inland hill.

On the corner of First and Alder, the gray Victorian looked exactly as he remembered, its windows dim with books. The upper floor was dark. *Closed till we Open* read the sign.

He turned left onto Alder and accelerated up the hill, his heart pounding as he searched the trees at the top, and found the house as remembered, the green Second Empire on the corner of Seventh, its windows—his own windows, there in the corner—flashing with sunlight.

The yard was overgrown. The driveway was empty, and covered in pine needles. His car was gone from the verge.

He parked in the driveway, shut off the engine.

Heart pounding, he grabbed for his walking stick and opened the door, then struggled out, pulling the stick behind him. He retrieved his suitcase from the trunk, with the hillside behind him, and Mrs. Nelson's Italianate, with its peaked roofs and sedate, rounded windows, drowsy against ocean and clouds.

After he shut the car door, the sound echoed back. A gull cried out, piccolo-fierce. It rooted in a spilt garbage can next door, flapping sooty wings.

Another flew overhead.

Russ lugged the suitcase across her yard, trying to avoid the stepping stones hidden in the grass. He carefully climbed the porch stairs. The screen was half-open; it squeaked as he opened it further. He found the key in his pocket and struggled it into the lock. There was a click; he pushed open the door, feeling a surge of relief that vanished as he stepped into the dim hall.

The air was close, musty.

He shut the door behind him, set down the suitcase.

To his left was the living room, sofa and end table; to his right the rec room. Ping-Pong table, covered with brown plants in pots.

The air stank of mold.

"Megan?" Though he knew she wasn't here.

The drowned town, coming back to him now, as he walked slowly into the living room, the stench becoming sharper.

He traced it to the kitchen, and the orange lump on the pie-crust table. Cheese. The cheese bust—of his own head—carved by Bob Burle, now feathered in dust.

Russ stood there leaning on the stick, staring at it. The lines around the eyes and nose. The beard.

The kitchen sink was full of dishes, growing mold spores.

He turned away, walked back through the dining room, the living room, across the entry into the rec room, to her bedroom door.

He gripped the edge of the jamb, recognizing her clothes strewn across the carpet. Tousled bedsheets. Directly ahead, in the dresser mirror, his own reflection, looking furtive, the scar on his forehead invisible.

Jack's photograph was still tucked inside the frame.

Upstairs, he stood at the landing catching his breath, and looked into Malcolm's room. It was empty, and drab, with a beery odor. Russ walked to his own room, remembering how, that first day, Megan had dimmed the light to let him see the ocean.

He pushed open the door. There was the desk, and the corner windows; his bed, made. His old suitcase stood beside the closet, where the tweed jacket still hung.

He walked to the desk. Through dusty glass, the sun glared over the ocean. Shadows nestled in the pine.

The desk itself was bare, the desk drawers were empty but for some pens. His *Nemo* score sheets, the box of sketches from Boston, the libretto, and the fish—the hycopathius—everything was gone.

He sat on the bed, lay back, his head throbbing, as the sights of the empty town settled around him. Eyes darting back and forth, he smiled. He was victorious, in a grim way. He was back, and the town was just as he remembered it.

His nightmares had been real.

He wrapped the bust in newspaper and carried it outside, negotiating the stairs with his walking stick, barely noticing the last of the sunset over the ocean.

As he trudged down, a gull hobbled off toward the verge with something—a scrap of paper—in its beak.

He carried the bust around the corner of the house to Megan's can. The lid was on tight. Leaning his stick against a larch tree, breathing through his mouth, he pulled off the lid and dropped the bust onto a mat of brown lettuce and paper towels, then shut the lid tight.

He fetched the walking stick.

On his way back he detoured to the car, grabbed his bag of groceries from the passenger seat. Bread, peanut butter and jelly, milk, cereal, cold cuts and mayonnaise. He unpacked them in the kitchen, then washed his hands. The tap shuddered, spitting out brown water onto the moldy dishes. He waited for it to clear, and heat up, then set about washing the plates and silverware, and washing his hands.

After a modest meal, he decided to drive around town and look for lights.

The houses near the top of Alder Street were being dismantled. Russ eased on the brake, squinting into the shadows. The roofs were gone, replaced with tarps that fluttered in the breeze. The overgrown lawns were receptacles for lumber and odd pieces of furniture. An ottoman. A bookcase, nested in plastic.

Near the middle of the hill, the houses were in better shape, and after Third Street, they were untouched, with cars in the driveway, and the lawns mown, and everything normal.

He turned onto First. Everything seemed closed for a normal night, not abandoned. The lampposts were lit, the businesses were dark, sidewalks empty.

A flicker of red caught his eye. Brake lights in the distance, further down First Street.

Turning right, up the hill.

Russ accelerated, past the Laundromat, and *Evening Cheese Outlet* store, his eyes set on where the car had disappeared.

Cheddar Street.

He turned, and found the lights up the wide street, winking out of sight, over the rise.

He accelerated, past the well-kept houses on either side. The properties, even those toward the top of this well-travelled street, were maintained.

Through the sentinel line of trees. Slowing down, his headlights sweeping across a parking lot packed with cars.

The building was dark, the "e" sign no longer revolving. The school was also dark. He drove slowly through the lot, finding Megan's Suburban halfway down the middle aisle, near the loading docks, and his Volvo beside it.

No movement, no lights among the cars.

He parked in front of the lobby, in the fire lane. Climbing out, he listened for voices, footsteps, or a door closing. He pulled out the walking stick and walked onto the curb, across the pavement to the door.

The lights were off.

He tested the door: securely locked. He raised the handle of his stick, considered breaking the glass with it, triggering an alarm. He'd wait for people inside to hear it, or down below; or the State Sheriff.

There was a note taped to the glass:

Evening Cheeses is temporarily closed. Our staff is away on a retreat with other Northwest Cheesemakers. Please refer your queries to our Visitor's Center, or for distribution questions, call our new Northwest distributor, Conklin Deliveries, in Port Rostov, Oregon.

He peered past it, into the dark office.

We Provide the Cheese! read a poster, behind Mrs. Nelson's desk.

But he resisted, relaxing his shoulders, stepping back. He returned to the car, deciding to look for lights in houses, see if anyone was home.

Driving back down Cheddar, gazing at the outline of the Evening mansion atop the bluff, he was startled by a gray blur leaping in front of the car.

Russ stomped on the brake pedal, braced his arms as the car skidded, struck the curb. He looked back, adrenaline surging, as the shape trotted into view. A husky.

Ody—Tom Carver's dog—ears sharp, ducking as Russ opened the door.

"Ody!" Russ pulled himself out, shakily. "Hey, boy." Trying to sound calm, holding onto the car door. "You okay?"

Ody studied him with pale blue eyes, then approached, claws clicking on the asphalt, and sniffed his hand. The dog's fur was matted.

"You remember me, Ody?"

Cautiously, Russ scratched him between the ears. "You alone?" Ody wagged his tail, and Russ scratched under him under his collar.

Had Tom abandoned him?

The Carver's house was just down the hill. The chain link fence stood open. The house was completely dark; even the basement windows. And though the breeze stirred in the trees, and sent scraps of paper fluttering across Cheddar, the hill seemed unnaturally quiet.

The wind chimes, he realized. All the chimes were gone.

In the yard behind him, a hose lay half-coiled in the grass.

"You thirsty, boy? Come on."

In the grass, he found the nozzle and carried it back to the spigot. "Let's see if this works."

A dog dish lay overturned in the flower bed. Russ retrieved it, aware only now that he'd left his walking stick in the car. He turned on the water, waiting for the hose to clear. He filled the dish.

While Ody drank, Russ looked toward the ocean. A light was winking on the bluff, at the top of the Evening mansion. A small light in the tower, flickering, lifting up.

*g*hosts

The mansion was a gray silhouette, its bustling roofs and high walls surrounding the horseshoe entrance, a mouth of shadow.

But a light still burned in the tower.

As he drove across the empty lot, Russ leaned forward, trying to see it clearly—a small lamp, or maybe a lantern, casting a glow on the green ceiling.

He parked near the fence and shut off the engine.

Ody, on the passenger seat, watched with glinting eyes.

"Ready, boy?"

Russ opened the door and climbed out, pulling the stick out from behind the seat, planting the foot firmly in the gravel, then straightening.

"Let's go."

The dog bounded across the seat and out. Russ shut the door. He followed the picket fence, noting that the grass was mown, and the fence newly-painted.

The gate swung out on oiled hinges.

Ody stepped through behind him.

Overhead, the Korean pine sprawled against the sky. Something rippling palely in the lower branches. Russ squinted, discerning letters as the fabric played in the breeze. He hooked the thing with his stick. A banner of green silk. Yellow letters. Russ could read the last part: *ning*.

He unfurled more: *of Evening*.

Then the banner came loose, caught in the breeze, floating across the lawn to curl around the fence.

He continued across the lawn and up the porch stairs. Wind whistled through the trellised wall.

At the double doors, he tried one swan-wing handle. It was unlocked. He pushed the door open, and stepped slowly, quietly, inside.

The hall was warm, lit only by a single bulb beside the door.

To his left was the pillared entrance to the ballroom, the floor newly waxed. Another banner was laid out. He stepped inside to read it, in the dim light. *Festival of Evening*.

Just inside, set on an easel, was the portrait of Joseph Evening in its silver sun-burst frame.

He shut the door, aware of the greater silence of the house.

Ody, ears perking, stood beside him.

"Hear anything, boy?"

Ody stared up at him.

A moment later, Russ continued down the Hall of Founders. There were light rectangles on the green-striped wallpaper, marking where portraits had once hung. Brushing his palm along the right-hand side, he felt for the panel, found the latch, and pulled it open.

Cautiously, he stepped inside, fumbled around for a switch, but there was enough light spilling down the spiral stairway.

Ody stayed in the hall.

"Be right back," Russ whispered.

Upon reaching the stairs he gripped the black iron rail and looked up. The half moons and stars impressed in each helical step, just as he remembered it, up to the tower.

A voice drifted down, faint, weary.

Holding the stick to chest, Russ began to climb.

A lantern sat on a low table. The furniture was arranged on the sea-side of the octagonal room, where the voice came from an antique wing-backed chair.

"Hello?" Russ said.

A hand feebly gripped the armrest.

He stepped toward it, seeing the top of an old man's head, spotted, wisped with white hair.

A smell of licorice and wet wool.

"Mister Crick?"

Old Crick stared ahead with sunken eyes. His cheekbones were sharp, sallow. His breath was a dry rasping.

Russ stepped closer.

Pale blue eyes rolled toward Russ, remained for a moment, then returned to the sea. "Why," Old Crick said in a dry cracked voice, "it's Mister Dylan Thomas hisself."

"Mister Crick, I need to know where everybody is. Would you help me?"

"There was once a man in town . . . that was the spittin' image of you. Used to harangue him some. Was a music writer . . . who was stealin' from the great Jules Verne." Old Crick coughed, then looked up at Russ once more. "He had a beard, though. An' was a little fatter."

The old man stared up, lips parting.

"Mister Crick?"

"Lost his wife. Out there on the bluff. I saw it." Old Crick coughed, his upper body shaking with it. "Always told him that he looked like you. 'Cept for the beard. Always tried to catch him up."

"Mister Crick, are they all in Hesperus?"

"Underground city," Old Crick whispered. "No coal down there, but it's the city."

"Who's taking care of you?" Russ knelt, setting the walking stick against the arm of the chair. "How long have you been up here?"

The old man stared down at the stick. He smiled. "When I was a boy, and there was wolves in Wales. . . ." His voice trailed off as he turned back to the window.

Old Crick whispered, "That's all I know of that one."

Russ reached out and touched the man's hand. The skin was a loose glove of flesh over the bones.

Then someone else spoke, from behind Russ. "He can't help you."

Startled, Russ turned.

A figure stood at the top of the stairs, tall, in a black suit and top hat. The lantern caught a red claret tie, a golden watch chain, the white beard tapered to a precise point.

It was the memorial photograph brought to life.

It was Joseph Evening, awake, once again inhabiting the tower.

"I pretty much care for him now."

Russ grabbed his stick and pushed himself up.

"It's me," the figure said, spreading his arms. The eyes were young, and the cheeks were scarred with acne, above a false beard.

Russ said, "Pete?"

"Yeah."

"Ol' Joe Evening!" Old Crick exclaimed. "Ol' Joe . . ."

The young man removed the hat, revealing closely-shorn blond hair, and long bangs, and stepped into the room. "Mayor gave me a haircut," Young Crick said. "Told me it would be an outrage to have a long-haired Joe, but he let me keep my bangs." He pressed the beard against his chin. "Anyway, it's good to see you back, Mister Kent. On two feet, and all."

"Thanks, Pete."

"Came here at a good time. Festival's tomorrow, you know. Few of us had a rehearsal before lunch." With a flourish of his hand, he set the top hat back on his head, leaving a few bangs hanging over his eyes, which he unceremoniously brushed away. "They make me do this for the festival."

"The force that through the green fuse drives the flower," Old Crick said. "That's the way that one goes."

"I lead the parade," Pete explained.

"Parade?"

"The one after the banquet tomorrow night. When we re-bury Joe downstairs. Underground, I mean."

"Goodbye Joe!" Old Crick exclaimed. "Goodbye! Goodbye!"

Russ walked to the windows overlooking the town. The upper hill was entirely dark, except for a light at the southern end; his bedroom light, he decided.

And somewhere under the earth, under the hill . . .

"I'm looking for Megan. Have you seen her?"

"Not lately. But lots of 'em are still down below. Lots don't want to come back up. They want to hold the Festival down there."

Russ turned back to Pete. "Could you help me get in touch with her?"

"Everyone should be up for the festival, Mister Kent. It starts tomorrow, late afternoon. She should be back by then."

"What about Bernard Dreerson?"

Pete laughed. "Yeah, him too, probably. Unless he's really busy. They let him go downstairs. ACL had a truce with the town."

"Tom Carver, too?"

"Yeah, even Mrs. Carver. Not too friendly, just a truce."

"Well, I found Ody. I can't believe Tom just left him behind."

"He didn't. Or I mean, I'm supposed to be watching him, but he ran out on me this morning. He here?"

Russ nodded. "Downstairs."

"Ody hates it below. Hates hanging out with me, too, I guess."

Russ said, "I could watch him for you, Pete. I could use the company."

"Okay. I got the dog chow he likes. Let's go down to my office."

Old Crick mumbled, "That's the way that one goes."

The streetlamps were dark on his end of the hill.

As he pulled into the driveway and killed the headlights, Russ was glad Ody was there.

"We're home, boy."

Once inside, he switched on the hall light and the lamps in the living room—stopping to turn up the heat—then led Ody into the kitchen. He found two mixing bowls, and filled one with water, setting them both down beside the fridge, then poured Ody a full helping of dry food. Ody ate it greedily.

Russ fixed himself a bologna sandwich and brought it into the living room. As he sat down on the couch, he noticed the phone on the end table. He reached over and lifted the receiver, mildly surprised to find a dial tone. He decided to call Ellie, remembering the number (and proud to remember), then wondering what he'd say.

Luckily, her machine answered. He waited for the beep.

"Ellie, I'm here. Hello, you there? Things are going well. I guess I'll call you tomorrow and give you the details." After a pause, he hung up.

Ody approached, sat on his haunches, staring up.

Russ ate his sandwich, giving Ody some of the crust, then cleaned up in the kitchen.

"Okay, dog. It's upstairs for us."

The climb was a chore. The room, however, had become nicely warm, and the sheets weren't too stale. He found a rug for Ody, dropping it beside the bed.

Looking through the chest of drawers for his T-shirts he found a sheet of paper, and unfolded it. A message in Malcolm's jagged hand: *Mobilis in Mobili*.

He sat on the bed, too exhausted to think about his father, or Ellie, but too wired to sleep right away.

Ody had no such problems.

Russ opened his suitcase, unpacked his clothes, then undressed. He pulled on boxers and a T-shirt, and carried the suitcase over to the closet.

After a hesitation, he brought his copy of *20,000 Leagues Under the Sea* to the bed.

With the baseboard heater rattling beside him, he stared at the watery cover, the *Nautilus* throwing its searchlight off the page. He flipped open the cover, turned pages to the first chapter. *Boring* was scrawled at the top, and a few pages further, he'd written *unnecessary scene*.

He remembered Malcolm's libretto, how it had begun with a spoken prologue.

There were slashes through the text. Page after page, then a note reading: *Go to Chapter 7*.

He flipped ahead, reading more comments in the margins—arrows to latitude and longitude numbers prevalent in the text, and in caps *DO THESE MATTER? ASK MALCOLM!* A note urging himself to use the numbers, either chanted by a chorus, or projected onto a screen. He flipped further, faster, stopping at the chapter titled *An Underwater Walk*. This had been the setpiece of the first act. This, and the underwater funeral. He began to read, though his eyes began to blear after the first few pages.

Disappointed, he shut the book, set it on the bedside table.

He turned out the light.

Nearly closing his eyes, he glanced over and down, past the corner of the room, into the dark, and down, picturing movement in the distance, deep under the hill. Familiar faces awake and active. Time was different down there, Dreerson had said. People, awake in the dark, through basalt and shale, below sea level, perhaps *under the sea itself* to a certain extent, all the townspeople at work, with rock beneath and rock above, rock as clouds. Megan, Bernard, Tom Carver. Peggy Chalmers, the Barber-Mayor.

And Jack Sumner?

Had she found him after all, alive?

He shifted on the pillow, as the room reasserted itself around him. The bed, the cracked plaster walls and ceiling. The sound of the baseboard heater, and rain tapping on the shingles, rain falling outside, in the empty town.

He was glad for Ody's company as he sank toward sleep.

He awoke to the rat-tat-tatting of a snare drum.

Remembering where he was, he sat up in bed and pushed away the covers. Another drumroll, more faintly, with the bellow of a trombone causing the window glass to vibrate.

The clock read 7:20.

The room looked smaller in this light.

Carefully, he climbed out of bed, nearly stepping on Ody, who backed up against the bureau, tail wagging.

"Morning." Russ scratched him behind the ears, then leaned toward the window, half-glimpsing a flash of red and gold vanish over the crest of Bluff Street, against a foggy sea.

Everyone was due up today, he remembered.

Trying not to rush, he dressed in sweatshirt and jeans, grabbed his stick and walked downstairs, with Ody behind him. He stepped onto the porch.

A seagull flew over Mrs. Nelson's roof, riding a cold breeze that rustled in the trees.

For an instant, it was a normal morning, before the wind slackened, and the smell of rotting garbage gathered in the porch.

The trombone sliding from A to C.

Russ resisted the urge to get into the car and track it down.

Instead, he went inside, ate some cereal, made coffee, then lay on the couch, watching the morning brighten beyond the windows. He listened. Nearly drifted off to sleep but roused himself, stood, drank some bitter coffee and decided to try and tackle the garbage on the lawn.

He found plastic bags under the sink, and a shovel in the laundry room.

As he carried them onto the porch, Mrs. Nelson's garage door tilted open. A gleam of white, as something floated into view. An elongated head and shoulders of white rock, long segmented arms and legs: a statue, strangely shaped, being carried quite easily by Mrs. Nelson, under her left arm. She wore a yellow pantsuit, and clutched the statue around its waist, carrying it across the lawn.

When she reached the middle she dropped one end. The pedestal struck the grass. Awkwardly, she pushed it up until it stood, arms raised, nearly as tall as the ornamental cupola on her roof.

Twenty feet high? Thirty?

A long face looked toward the inland hill.

Russ climbed down the porch stairs.

Mrs. Nelson was carrying flat rocks from her garden, laying them on the pedestal. The tapping of his stick startled her. She straightened. Her mouth opened, then shut. She raised a hand as if to wave—in curious mimicry of her statue—but the gesture died and she walked backwards to her porch.

Russ crossed the street.

After a glance at the screen door, she leaned forward, squinted at him and said, "It's Mister Kent!" Her voice was nervous. "You're looking well. Of course, we were all so worried." She jogged up the front steps. Only when she had the screen door open did she turn to him. "Isn't the statue lovely? Mister Burle did such a wonderful job. All of us getting ready for the festival! So busy!"

"Have you seen Megan?"

"Megan? Oh, not today. But she should be back. All of us up for the festival, you know!" And she disappeared inside, slamming shut the front door.

Russ approached the statue, gazing up at its features which, foreshortened, appeared vaguely human.

It teetered in the breeze, with a surface pocked with faint flecks of blue.

He reached out, surprised when the statue moved under his fingers, a smooth, pebbly surface, quite familiar.

Styrofoam. Teetering in the breeze.

The curtains parted behind Mrs. Nelson's living room window. She was watching in the shadows. He waved, and after a last look at the Styrofoam statue, turned and walked back to the house.

He tried raking up the garbage, but more gulls had gathered, and were aggressive and noisy, even with Ody nearby. And Ody wasn't bothered by them.

He contented himself with cleaning up the area around the porch, and around the back fence, where he saw a gray rat scrabbling underneath the wood.

Rats in a cheese town, Dreerson had once said.

Rats, or something else, he thought, remembering the tiny blue bones in silver sand.

While he worked, Russ listened to the infrequent sound of the drum and the tuba, being carried somewhere along the hill; and of cars driving nearby.

Faintly, the phone rang.

He grabbed the stick and heaved himself up, hurrying to the phone beside the sofa, with Ody behind him. "Hello?"

"There you are."

Ellie.

"Hi." Rearranging his thoughts for Ellie, and east coast reality.

"So. How are you?"

"Fine. Did you get my message last night?" The tuba bellowed, closer. He walked to the window.

"Of course. You sounded worn out."

Staring at the statue, he said, "I was working in the yard."

"And you *were* going to call this morning, right?"

"Am I late?"

"Does *morning* mean my morning, or yours?"

"Sorry."

"How's Megan?"

He said, "Good. She's good."

"Ah ha. Think you'll stay less than a week?"

"Well . . . Probably not." After another pause, "Has Dad called?"

"Yeah. We talked. I told him you were out at the beach. He just wanted to tell you his first concert went great. Splendidly, he said. And for you not to worry if you don't hear from him for a few days."

"Thanks, Ellie."

"I'm raiding the refrigerator as we speak."

"Take anything you want."

"Call me by noon, tomorrow, Russ. Boston time. If you miss it, you're busted."

A kid rode past on a ten-speed.

"I promise."

There were cars regularly driving past, and people—men, women and children in overalls and hardhats, in regular clothes, in robes—all dishevelled, walking along the sidewalk, tired but cheerful.

A few saw him on the porch, and waved. Russ waved back, though he couldn't recognize them.

The clouds had burned off. The ocean glittered. Every now and then, the curtains twitched in Mrs. Nelson's house.

He was staring at the statue when the blue Suburban appeared, driving along Seventh Street.

At first, he refused to accept it, this familiar truck returning home, pulling onto the verge, and parking. The door opened, and she stepped out. Megan, without doubt, her brown hair blown in the breeze. She wore a T-shirt, jeans and hiking boots, stepped awkwardly down, onto the gravel.

Her arms were white in the sun.

He fumbled for the railing, and pulled himself up.

She had begun walking slowly across the grass but now wearily jogged, saying something he didn't catch. Then she hugged him.

A sharp scent, of minerals and sweat, as he touched her face, kissed her chapped lips.

She made a noise, and held him, nearly falling.

"You okay?"

She stepped inside, nodding.

As he led her into the house, to her bedroom. She unbuttoned her blouse, shrugging it free. Her skin was pale, and her ribs alarmingly gaunt. She kicked off her shoes.

In the shower, she leaned against the wall. She said nothing, staring at the spray through tangled hair, then leaned into it, grimacing as it drummed on her face.

. . .

Later, in bed, damp hair wrapped loosely in a blue towel, she said, "I should've gone back to Boston with you."

He pushed himself up on his elbow, and studied her eyes, which were no longer dull, but had the look of somebody who'd been up for days. He leaned down to kiss her neck. She was warm and smelled of soap, and she stirred, the motion pulling her hair from the towel. Dark strands lay across the pillow.

He kissed her.

"Do you remember me with you in Portland? I went to Portland with you . . . but I had to come back."

"Ellie told me." He added, "Pete said Tom Carver's down there. And Bernard."

She nodded. "We didn't find anyone, Russ." Her eyes tracked something in the air, and she grimaced. "Of course. Just the city, and the river."

"How much has been explored?"

"Miles."

He repeated the word, softly, against her skin. "Miles."

She tugged the towel from her hair and moved against him, making a sound in her throat. Her fingers down his back, to his hip. His skin tingled under her touch. She rubbed her cheek against his chest, and caressed him, taking hold, moving up, her toenails scraping the tops of his feet. She kicked away the blankets and straddled him. Smiling, opening her mouth, she touched his cheeks, his chin.

He kissed her fingers, recognizing the minerals that still lingered. The taste of copper pennies. He found it on her wrist, in the crook of her elbow. When she reached down to slip him inside her, he found it on her neck. He held her hips and tried to push as far as possible inside her while she leaned down, damp hair falling across his face.

Later, she whispered, "Party's tonight. Did you know that?"

"Not even a night's sleep?"

She laughed against him. "We're all on Hesperus time."

"How long since you've slept?"

"A week, maybe." She brushed hair away from her eyes, blinked, looked at the foot of the bed. "I have to go, Russ." She pushed up onto her elbow, and turned to him. "Care to join me?"

"Wouldn't miss it."

She kicked away the covers, looking at dusk through the window. "We're already late. Can you believe it?"

He got out of bed, pleased with how steady he felt. Tired, yet invigorated.

She sat up, and watched him gather his clothes. "You *are* better. Aren't you."

"Don't think I need my walking stick."

She smiled. "Oh, but I was planning to lean against *you*, Russ."

He stepped onto the porch, pulling on his tweed jacket. The little yellow "e" pin from the Winter Gathering was still on the lapel.

The day had stayed clear, and the setting sun had left a wash of pink that faded to cool blue overhead, where the first stars were visible, and a gibbous moon, white as bone.

He looked at Mrs. Nelson's statue. It teetered slightly in the wind, but resembled stone more than Styrofoam.

Its strangely-jointed arms embraced the sky.

He recalled puzzle box and puzzle bones, the miniature creature in Carver's basement.

He became aware of a flickering light. Across Bluff Street a lantern sat beside a telephone pole, shining on a larch tree, a rhododendron.

Curious, he climbed down the stairs and walked to the curb. For an instant he smelled wood smoke, heard voices carried to him on the breeze.

He walked to the corner. Another lantern burned farther down the hill, then another; as he reached the end of the sidewalk a dozen were revealed, bordering either side of Bluff Street, lighting a path down to the sea.

At the far end of the lot, a crowd milled around barbecue grills and pic-nic tables. Some wore green robes, and their faces, glimpsed within their cowls, were orange, yellow, blue, green.

"No spaces left," Megan said.

He parked by the gate and shut off the engine, looking once more at the crowd—robes fluttering in the breeze, their orange, yellow, blue faces entirely too long, lit by the glow from the grills. Masks, to resem-ble the faces of the statues.

Some held paper plates or drinks, or reeled drunkenly around. A few lay on their backs near the gnarled madrona trees.

"They've been up for days, Russ. And now they've had too much beg-gars pudding and brandies. C'mon."

He handed her the keys, then opened his door and stepped carefully down, pulling out the stick.

She waited at the gate. Black skirt, blouse and dark jacket, her hair tied back. He remembered the Gathering last year.

"Feeling up to it?" She took his hand.

"Yes."

Every window of the mansion was alight. Tiny lights entwined the sprawling branches of the Korean Pine, and trailed, sparkling, to the trel-lis porch.

The breeze smelled of woodsmoke and the sea.

"Hey, Megan!"

Behind them, two kids rode mountain bikes across the gravel, their robes fluttering. "Hey!" the first called out again, cowl flinging back to reveal his mask, the narrowed face decorated with stars and white skulls, with red fangs drawn on his chin.

"That's scary, Sammy!" she said after him. "Be careful on the gravel!"

The second rode past without a word.

She squeezed Russ's hand as they walked across the grass. "How's the leg?"

"Okay."

"There's our host." Megan pointed to the horseshoe entrance, where Young Crick stood dressed in top hat and waistcoat.

"Hey!" He hoisted a bottle of Lighthouse in their direction.

She helped Russ up the stairs.

"Hey! Welcome to my party!"

Voices echoed through the open doors, along with the sound of silverware on china, and strange music.

"Mister Kent! Megan!"

It might have been cellos, clarinet, tuba, with strange harmonics, and a slow decay. Perhaps an ondes martenot.

She didn't seem to notice. "You're very good, Peter!"

Pete stepped back, lifted his hat, and with a well-rehearsed but awkward sweep of his arm, gestured toward the door.

Russ asked, "Is Malcolm here?"

Pete replaced the hat on his head. "Nope. Wouldn't expect him either." His collar was undone, a cravat stuffed into his coat pocket. He grinned.

"What about Bernard?"

He shook his head. "Maybe. But he and Tom were busy downstairs."

"The Capt'n . . ." A weary voice spoke in the corner of the porch.

Old Crick sat slumped in a rocking chair, in the gray shadows cast by the trellis. "The Capt'n . . . will be here shortly." He lifted one hand, regarding it with confusion, then swept it down the side of his black felt coat. He squinted up at Russ. "There's trouble . . ." He pursed his lips, blinking blearily. "With the elevator."

"You're right, Pa." Pete drained the rest of his beer, then grinned apologetically at Russ. "But Mister Mayor rode it up, I hear. Anyway, we can't carry Joe down. Ropes aren't long enough!"

"And death shall grant no dominion!" Old Crick declared.

"You two go on in," Pete said. "Maybe see you later."

"Okay, Pete. Bye. Bye, Charles." When Old Crick didn't reply, she pulled Russ into the hall.

To their left was the portrait of Joseph Evening, with bouquets of roses heaped below.

In the ballroom, under green chandeliers, a dozen or so couples slowly waltzed, or stood clutching one another, weaving to the melted tones of a clarinet, cello, tuba, a chiming haze.

Nonetheless, he recognized the largo from Dvorak's *Ninth*.

They walked in.

"Like it?" she asked.

"Where are the musicians?"

"Across the room, I think," she said. "And they're just run-of-the-mill band instruments. With bits of Hesperus wall surrounding them, like a sounding board. You should talk to Tom about the acoustics down there."

Leaning on the wolf-head stick, he tried to find them through the crowd.

"Dogs and cats hate it," she continued. "So do I, really."

To the right was a long table draped in green, under a crop of silver helium balloons. Something lay beneath the green sheet, a humped shape.

"Mister!" At the table beside them, a frail white hand raised. An aged, white face peered up. "Mister . . . Whoozit? Who . . . ?" The voice died away.

"Hello, Arthur," Megan said.

Arthur's prominent nose only drew attention to a starved look in his eyes.

Beside him, his wife dozed.

"Russ Kent," said Russ. "Nice to see you again, Arthur."

The ex-dentist nodded, though not as excitedly as at last year's Gathering. No Frank Sinatra tunes this time. He gazed at the walking stick, then at Russ and Megan's clasped hands, then looked away.

She pulled him on. "There's some free tables."

Walking there, he caught sight of the band in the opposite corner, and Andrea conducting. Seven figures, against shards of glowing green rock. The shards looked about three feet in diameter, roughly hewn. The glow resembled some illusion, as though they were really plugged into the wall, glowing brighter than the ballroom like that.

"This one'll do. Here, Russ."

They sat down at a table beside the windows. The centerpiece was a bouquet of alder sprigs laced with white flowers, and a yellow wafer with the cheese logo, the lowercase "e."

Russ reached for it. Plastic, not cheese.

He turned, and watched the crowd moving to the music, which permeated the room like the watery light.

A figure shuffled by, nodding. Russ turned, looked up at the face within the cowl, fleshy, with thick brown eyebrows. The owner of the Laundromat, rejoining the crowd.

Russ tried to remember his name.

"Who was that?" he asked Megan.

"Clement. I think."

"The Laundromat, right?"

"Very good, Russ. You get an extra point because he had his cowl up." She leaned back, looking very tired once more. "Most everyone's here tonight."

"But not Malcolm."

"Or Bernard, or Tom," she said. "They were off on an expedition. Out in the boonies, downstairs. Crazy as that sounds."

He watched her while she watched the crowd. Her eyes seeming somewhat startled, like those of an insomniac. No doubt, her thoughts were still downstairs.

He asked, "Do you know what they were looking for?"

She shrugged.

He remembered little blue bones. The creature. What had they called it?

"Megan! Russell Kent!"

From out of the dancers a figure in brilliant yellow robes—like a foglight in the green sea—glided toward them, left arm lifted, hand bent up as if in a stylized wave. "You've made it!"

Framed by the loose cowl, Peggy Chalmer's face resembled a fresco, delicately hued, peeling in places, with a faint green glow spun about her animate eyes, and wisps of teal and sapphire on her cheeks and chin.

"It's so *fine* to have you back! Russell, you look wonderful! And without the beard, too!" Her eyes darted to his forehead. The decorative layer cracked, faintly, as she smiled. "Can you sense the joy here tonight?" She floated back and turned in place, arms lifted. Her robe was wrapped in gold thread from which hung bits of green stone. Hesperus stone, clicking together. Little crescent moons and stars.

Russ listened to them. Then said, "I'm looking for Malcolm."

She came to a halt, and laid her fingers lightly on her cowl, each nail darkened with a crescent of dirt. "Our Nemo? No, he isn't here. Or I haven't seen him! I've been dancing, Russell! Waltzing the night away! Listen!" She gazed in the direction of the band. "Oh, they're doing wonderfully! Such troopers!"

The music ended with a triple bleat, slowly decaying under the clinking china, the tired laughter and applause.

The dancers stirred as if from sleepwalking, some moved off the floor; momentarily, Russ could see the shards of rock set up around the instruments; no longer glowing as brightly. Seven, eight . . . ten pieces in view.

A fat boy, scowling at Russ through his gold tuba.

"Hi, Peg!" A woman in yellow robes, tall, with pleated gray hair and a long, green face, hurried past. Her robe trailing across the polished floor.

Yellow for Storm Watcher?

Peggy raised a hand in a peculiar three-fingered gesture. "Praise Joe," she said, as the crowd once more blocked the musicians from sight. "You're both just in time, really. Dessert's about to be served! What about you, Russ? Hungry for raspberry scones and mint tea?"

Russ looked back at the corner, clutched his walking stick, and stood up.

"Russell?"

He stepped past Peggy, into the dancers. Some nodded tiredly to him and moved aside.

". . . the composer."

". . . shaved his beard."

The smell of cinnamon, over the mineral stink of Hesperus.

"Hasty . . . hasty pudding!"

A plump woman wearing a garland crown in blond curls, still dancing, rolled into his path, pressing her large hip against his free arm, forcing him to the side—nearly tripping him—where somebody exclaimed, "Elevators!" A face behind a cowl, gone.

He looked to the corner, for Andrea's hair.

"Lifts'll be working tomorrow."

"By noon," someone else agreed.

"Working now, Mayor says."

Russ stopped, stepped back. A short, barrel-shaped man hemmed in front of him. Georgie Aberfoyle, perhaps, from the gas station. "Fine shindig!"

Russ neared the corner of the room, and the musicians' chairs, occupied by cello, trumpet, clarinet, trombone. The shards of Hesperus rock, fixed to plywood boards, were faintly shimmering with the party noise.

Andrea was there, in a yellow sweater, dark skirt, a baton in her hand. She nodded, watching him with solemn eyes.

The tuba player watched, too. The fat boy with tousled black hair. Beady black eyes watching over the tuba's keys. The very face of the Master Cheesemaker.

"Hi, Andrea." He stopped. Looked at the rock. Shards roughly an inch thick, glowing green.

"Russ," she said, looking down at the floor.

Then the boy blurted out a C, and the sound shook through the air, from the shards. A chromatic chime, against the murmuring crowd.

Bobby Burle grinned.

A heavy hand clapped Russ's shoulder. "Well, hey, it's Mister Kent!" Bob Burle stepped up, more massive than Russ remembered, with the widow's peak shaved and glistening. He smiled damply. "Certainly a pleasure to find you back in town."

Russ nodded, at a loss for a reply; he glanced back at the instruments. The hand hadn't left his shoulder.

"Great timing. Right, son?" Burle looked past Russ, at the tuba.

"Right, Dad," said the boy.

"You ready, son? Give us the fanfare?"

"Sure, Dad."

"Great boy. You just hold on. And Mister Kent—Miss Sumner—how about coming this way. Perfect seat for you, up close and personal."

Megan was beside Russ. She handed him his walking stick.

They followed Burle through the crowd, up to the draped table and its fifty or so silver balloons. The crowd in the ballroom had grown, with more returning from outside, and filing in behind.

The Barber-Mayor, clad in a brilliant white tunic and trousers, and polished black shoes, stepped in front of the table, smiling up.

Reaching into his breast pocket, he withdrew a pair of gold scissors. The blades caught the chandelier light. He snicked them, three times.

Conversation fell in tatters, to silence.

And from the other corner, the tuba sounded an E minor, repeated it, then climbed an octave. A simple fanfare.

"Cit-ehh-sensss . . ." The Mayor paused, as though listening to the E minor shimmer and fade into strange harmonics. "Have to say, these present environs seems a little small nowadays. Such low roofs, such new structures! And you don't even need your earplugs!"

Laughter, and applause.

"We're here on this greatest of all evenings. Which marks the beginning of our *migration*, officially, to the world below. Praise old Joe. If you will direct your attention . . ." He pointed the scissors at the balloons. "We have one balloon here for every founding family. And every founding family must set the eve in motion, like so." He brought the scissors halfway down the nearest string, and deftly snipped.

The balloon hung for an instant, then began to rise, faster, the string fluttering below.

"Praise Joe!" the Mayor proclaimed, as it bumped against the ceiling. Everybody craned their necks, watching it roll, and come to a halt.

"Praise Joe," they murmured. More applause. Cheers.

"Now!" With his free hand, he reached into his breast pocket and withdrew a folded sheet of paper. "I have the roll call."

Holding up the scissors, he smiled his damp smile. "We'll start with the Chalmers. Peggy?"

She was nearly beside him already, and only had to take one step, her bright robes swirling across the floor. Immediately, she turned to the crowd. "I have to say—people!—I have to say it's *your* enthusiasm that's carried us this far! Thank you! Thank *you*!" And she clapped for the crowd, eyes beaming.

The Mayor looked down. His fingers twitched.

"Now . . ." She looked over at the Mayor, who, after prying them from his fingers, offered her the scissors.

"Now, after we break up here, before the parade, we have *dessert*! Can you smell it? I can! Beggar's pudding, and sherbert, and raspberry scones! Oh, what don't we have? I'm hungry! Are you?"

She snipped a string in the center of the table: the balloon took off.

Throwing her cowl back, she watched it, cheeks puffing.

"Praise Joe!" she exclaimed.

The crowd applauded. The Mayor reached for his scissors. "Thank you, Miz Chalmers."

After a pause, she let him take them, and stepped back.

The roll call continued, moving more swiftly as the scissors were passed from one to the next, with the Storm Watchers in their yellow robes always stern and proud—Mrs. Aberfoyle, Mrs. Yarrow, and Patsy Burle-Clarkson, casting a stern glance at Russ as she returned into the crowd.

Russ couldn't fathom any order to the roll-call.

"Sumner!"

Megan didn't move. The Barber-Mayor, holding the scissors by the points, glanced at another woman stepping out of the crowd. Russ had seen her before, on First Street, or at the Gathering. A short, older woman with straight gray hair and bangs, now wearing a long blue dress.

"Claire?" The Mayor offered the scissors.

Jack's aunt?

As she took them, the woman smiled sidelong at Megan. Megan smiled back.

The Mayor pointed out the correct string. With care, she reached out and cut it, not waiting to see the balloon go up.

Russ, leaning on the wolf-head, his knees aching, was left to wonder at it, as the balloons dwindled to five, then four; the crowd shifting anxiously, with more talking than before, until only one remained, and the Mayor raised his scissors. They said: *snick, snick.*

Silence.

He stood at the head of the table, next to the single balloon. "Well, I have one more citizen to bring up here, on this Festival night. We are, all of us, familiar with his handiwork, his artifacts and carvings, his various and sundry cheddars and Camemberts and blues. He has been responsible for maintaining the town's most precious commodity—its illustrious and historic culture. Bob Burle, please." The Mayor gestured.

"Praise Joe!" said Peggy, with echoes through the crowd.

The scissors beckoned.

Bob Burle gingerly stepped out of the crowd, straightening the hang of his robe, and took the proffered instrument. He tossed back his cowl, exposing his black widow's peak and small black eyes. He smiled. Nodding to the mayor, winking at Peggy, he turned to the crowd. "Hey, I got something for you, Evening!"

The audience cheered again, and Bob Burle smiled into it.

"I got a present for Evening, on this momentous night! But first!" He turned and carefully cut the last string. "Think of it, folks!" he called out, over the cheers, as the balloon touched the ceiling. "Just think of it! Tonight, after so many years—hey, we're ready! We can take old Joe downstairs, and say to him, Joe, here you are, your great empire discovered, settled as you envisioned so long ago!"

Russ felt people pressing in behind him, and looked over at Megan, to find her looking at the table, and the humped form.

Burle raised his hand. "Go, son!"

From the other corner of the room, Bobby played another E minor, then repeated it at half the length, warbling up a crude octave and holding the note.

Taps.

Burle gently lifted the sheet (brushing aside the leftover strings) revealing first a yellow top-hat on its side, then the profile—the familiar, serenely shut eyes, noses, peaceful lips and tapered beard of Joseph Evening, all carved from cheese. As the crowd applauded once more, the sheet was pulled away to reveal the shoulders of a waistcoat, the familiar claret tie and vest (Burle pointing out a delicate chain that trailed from vest to inner pocket, to a further surge of applause), then the long legs and jutting, square-toed boots.

"Praise Joe!" he exclaimed, and the audience returned it. The applause rolling now in waves, while the Mayor snicked his scissors and the Master Cheesemaker, his cowl tossed back, bowed solemnly, a raven.

Eventually, the desserts consumed, the sculpture was lifted onto the shoulders of six men and—led by Pete Crick in his period clothes—carried from the ballroom. The crowd followed, to an accompaniment of earthly tuba and snare drum.

The other instruments were gone.

"Old Joe waits at the factory!" the Mayor proclaimed. "C'mon everyone! Let's go say hello!"

Russ sat with Megan at a table watching the withdrawal, the boisterous voices echoing in the Hall, then outside. Cars starting; horns honking.

Claire Sumner was one of the last. Visibly tired, with a cowled figure helping her along, she kissed Megan on the cheek.

"Jack is my brother's boy," she said to Russ, and after shaking his hand, added, "The only one left, now."

Russ wasn't sure if she was talking about Jack, or herself.

When the ballroom was empty, he saw Megan mouth the words, *Praise Joe*.

The last of the cars started up, grinding across gravel down the bluff.

"Ready?" he asked.

She nodded.

Early morning sunshine wandered down the hill, obliterating twilight, and the wet shadows under the alder.

Russ stood on the porch.

The town was quiet. It might have been asleep, with the houses full of exhausted revellers, yet there was an absence in the air. The houses, he knew, were mostly empty. The people were still downstairs for last night's rite, interring Joseph in his kingdom.

Across the street, the Italianate's rounded upper windows began to glare. He squinted at the matted lawn where the statue had stood. The lanterns were gone, too. Everything had been packed away sometime after the procession of cars up Cheddar Street, to the factory.

As a lone gull tracked across the sky, he recalled the acoustics in the ballroom, the easels with their shards of Hesperus wall altering the echoes and overtones. Somehow transforming, restructuring the timbres. Cello, clarinet, tuba, voices.

Next door, a gray shape rustled through the grass. It was Ody, becoming yellow in sunlight between houses.

"You done, boy?"

Tail wagging, Ody clomped up the porch stairs, glancing back as a gull landed by the curb and rooted, noisily, in the tall grass.

"C'mon. Inside."

Russ held open the door, and gently shut it behind them.

Megan was still asleep.

Quietly, he walked upstairs to get the notebook.

This morning's dream had been surprisingly normal, considering. He and Anna in a library or conservatoire, clearly part of the Evening mansion, with the ballroom's glowing green floor visible under throw rugs.

Anna sits forward in an antique chair, practicing; Russ is across from her on a couch. With the graceful neck of her 1721 Montagnana under her left hand, she moves the bow across the strings, playing and replaying portions of Bach's *Fifth Cello Suite*, an intensity—entirely familiar—in the relentlessly repeated measures, in subtle re-phrasings. Engrossed, she only glances over once, and her eyes are distracted, barely taking notice of him.

The pang, as he woke, was palpable, and had kept him from immediately falling back to sleep. It had faded only as he stretched and rose from bed, pulled on his robe.

Nearly tripping over Ody by the door.

He phoned Boston. Ten A.M., Eastern time, and she wasn't home. At the beep he said, "Ellie? This is Russ. Just checking in. Give me a call if you want, or we'll talk tomorrow." A pause. He added, "Things are going well." He hung up, stood there for a moment reasoning that, from a certain perspective, things *were* indeed going well. Megan was back, and it was entirely possible they would leave town.

If not today, then perhaps a few days from now.

But what about Bernard and Tom? And Malcolm?

And the music under the hill?

He brought the notebook into the kitchen.

While the coffee was brewing, he sat down at the table, pencil in hand, and flipped through the pages, past Ellie's note and number, the tone cluster, *Nemo* sketches, more sketches, the hexachords—to the last page, the neumes, as negative shapes in graphite.

He tore out a page from the back. Then, carefully, slowly, he copied out the first neume, making it nearly as large as the page. The shape, with its sharp curves, its six arms at various angles, reminded him in parts of a simplified drawing of a seagull, or eleventh-century Messine notation, though more complex. As he worked, he wondered if his original drawings had been even close to accurate, and whether anything could be learned outside the context of their setting, the arrangement unwinding against blocks of color.

An hour or so later, when Megan shuffled into the kitchen, he had a dozen sheets spread across the table. They had the aura of runes.

"You get any sleep?"

"Enough." He sat back. Looking up, he said, "What about you? Feel better?"

She wore her robe and slippers. Rubbing her eyes with the back of her hand, she nodded. She poured some coffee. "A bit. What's for breakfast? Hi, Ody."

"Breakfast is granola bars and milk, from Portland. Otherwise the cupboards are bare."

"We're not completely out, I bet. Wanna bet?"

He shook his head. "Not a chance."

She opened the cupboard under the sink, knelt, reached back, behind the boxes of detergent and bleach, and retrieved an unopened tub of oatmeal. "Just in case the houseguests consume everything." She lifted out a can of chili, and another of corn. "A landlady's nightmare." She straightened, smiling.

"Clever."

"It's fresh oatmeal. Want some?" She seemed back to normal. Hair loose about her shoulders. Eyes still a bit tired, a bit dazed.

"Later, maybe." He made a pile of his slips of paper. "Last fall, Andrea gave me a folder with some photos. From Hesperus."

Megan nodded. "Captain Nemo took them."

"Malcolm?"

"Yep. When I came back from Portland, I found his room cleared out. Pete told me Charles Crick let Malcolm in on the secret, and Malcolm used your photos to bargain his way downstairs. I think he took your music sheets—your opera, too."

Russ mulled that over. "Do you know Andrea's number?"

"In my little book, by the phone."

He retrieved it, and found the number for *Andrea Yarrow*.

"I'm going to get more food and supplies today, Russ. For you, too, Odysseus."

Ody thumped the floor with his tail.

Writing the number in the notebook, Russ asked, "Where from?"

"The factory."

"No cheese products, I hope."

"Nope. Leftovers from the Festival, and my fair share, per the town charter. Something like that." Yawning, she added, "And I'm going to try and find news about Bennie and Tom. They're supposed to be back upstairs today."

"From where, exactly?"

"Bennie calls it the Far Forty." She lifted out a stainless steel pot from a lower cupboard. "The Avenue's about two miles long, and the Far Forty is what comes after it. I'm worried because it's not very safe. Especially for two old guys. Even if they do have your pal helping them."

Russ nodded, thinking, *Especially if they have Malcolm helping them.*

Past the window above the sink, a flash of gray and white, a gull, flapping up. Gone.

Andrea didn't answer her phone.

At one o'clock he drove to her house, via Seventh Street to Cheddar.

Under cloudy skies, the houses, lawns, piles of lumber, the rhododendron bushes all looked soaked with rain, though the rain hadn't started yet.

Garbage strewn by the breeze was being ransacked by gulls.

Ody watched them from the passenger seat.

At the corner of Aberfoyle and Seventh, Russ saw the only sign of people—a balding, stooped man and his wife lifting an aquamarine bureau into the back of a truck. They were the owners of the Evening Grocery. A child sat on the curb, and wore one of the long-faced orange masks from the Festival, staring as Russ and Ody drove past.

At Cheddar, Russ drove down to 453, parked by the small cottage. He grabbed his walking stick and climbed out, into the first of the rain. Ody hopped down behind him.

Andrea's car wasn't in sight. Her cottage had its drapes nearly closed; the porch light was on. He walked across the well-cut lawn to the door. He knocked, and waited, listening to the gulls farther up the hill. A moment later he stepped off the porch to the window, and peered between the drapes.

As his eyes adjusted, he realized the couch was gone, and the piano in the corner, too.

Down to Hesperus, along with Andrea and most everyone else.

He suddenly thought of Megan, up at the factory. She'd only been upstairs a single day, after all. Why couldn't she disappear again, just as easily? Kidnapped by the Storm Watchers. Taken downstairs. He stood there listening to the gulls, allowing the thought to grow.

If this were an opera, or a melodrama—or a dream—such things would happen. Anna, Megan, lost in the withdrawing tide.

The rain woke him. He blinked against it, and said, "Seen enough, boy?"

Ody trotted back to the car.

By the time they reached the house, the rain was pouring. He jogged across the lawn with Ody at his heels, up the stairs. He wasn't using the walking stick.

Before stepping inside, Ody hesitated.

Nose lifting to the breeze.

Ody sat down.

"Staying out?"

The dog looked back, a measure of patience in his light blue eyes, then turned to regard the rainy street.

"I'll take that as a 'yes.'"

Russ set the stick against the coatrack, and ended up propping the front door partly open with a boot. He went to the kitchen, made a pot of coffee. While waiting, he sifted through the drawings from last night. The shapes like Messine notation.

Or runes.

Close by—on the side of the house—outside—a crash. A spill. Ody barking.

Russ glanced out the window. He hurried to the hall, donned his jacket and stepped outside.

"Ody?"

A gull, startled in the grass, flapped up to the roof of the house next door.

Another bark. From further back.

Russ descended the stairs into the rain, rounded the side of the house. Near the backyard fence, Ody stood facing the hill, ears sharp.

Megan's garbage can was tipped over. Garbage was strewn across the lawn.

"Ody?"

The dog didn't look back.

Rain pattered on the can's lid, on the wet paper and rotten food.

"Chasing birds?"

Ody glanced back, tail wagging. But didn't move.

"If it was a cat, leave it alone."

Russ blinked back the rain, and a memory of water depths, of drowning. He approached the can. Using a piece of cardboard as a shovel, he set about pushing the brown lettuce, the moldy bread, tomatoes and paper towels back inside. Only as he was righting the can did he realize what was missing. He looked near the larches, figuring it might have somehow rolled behind them.

But it hadn't.

The cheese, the bust of his head, was gone.

He recalled dropping it onto wilted lettuce and paper towels, and shutting the lid.

He checked inside the can once more.

Ody trotted back.

"You chase a cat, Ody?"

He looked around again, then reached for the lid.

As he lifted it, dirty water dribbled on his jeans and shoes. He swore, slammed it down, made sure it was on securely. Ody meanwhile walked to the front yard, where the Suburban was pulling into the driveway, tires grinding.

Megan climbed out and down, zipping up her coat. "You should wear a hat, Russ!"

"Only been out for a second!" He made a show of ducking his head against the rain; though his hair, he realized, was soaked.

She carried a flat of cans.

"Is there more?"

"I can manage. Come on. Back inside. Dry off. What were you doing?"

Following her up the stairs, lingering a bit, Russ said, "Garbage can got knocked over."

"Lovely." Megan set down the box on the flagstone. "Ta-da! Free food. And there's more, too." Glancing at Ody, she said, "Would you wipe off his paws, Russ? There's an old towel in the rec room."

"Sure."

After hauling two more flats and three boxes—refusing Russ's help—she unpacked them on the kitchen counter. "So the gulls are getting ornery, huh?"

He nodded, then almost mentioned the cheese bust. "Yeah," he said.

"I got bad news from Pete Crick." She set a can of ravioli in the cupboard. "For the next three nights, they have to cut power upstairs."

"The whole town?"

"Everything but First Street. Ten P.M., each night. Back on by six A.M., to power the Avenue."

"Lamps? Streetlamps?"

She nodded. "Lights of all kinds. Even Christmas lights. Not that they need them. Except for the arc lights they use to charge the walls."

"Any news about Bernard and Tom?"

She shook her head, setting a roll of paper towels by the sink. "Just that they're working in the Far Forty. Somebody saw them yesterday and said they were okay. Busy."

Lunch was canned salmon sandwiches and beggars pudding. While they ate, Russ asked whether there was a direct phone line to Hesperus. "I'd like to talk to Malcolm."

"There's a phone. But I don't think anybody's answering. It might take a while to get through. Phone's in the tower room, which is boring old Hesperus to them. For thirty years. Now everyone's out in the city."

"Huh."

"But when I hear from Bennie, Malcolm should be with him."

"Yeah, you'd think," Russ said.

They spent the afternoon vacuuming, dusting, mopping. Dusk gave way quickly to a rainy dark, and a somewhat normal, somewhat quaint, domestic scene. For dinner they had salmon and applesauce, and mint tea.

She found candles, holders, matches, and set them up in the living room, in preparation. At 9:45 P.M. they retired to the couch, under a down comforter.

She'd poured them two glasses of Zinfandel from the Festival.

"Not too bad, is it?"

"No," he said.

Pulling up the blanket, she lay back against him.

He slipped his hand under the hem of her sweater, palming her soft, warm stomach.

She shivered, then smiled, and sipped her wine.

"This afternoon," she said, "when I saw Pete Crick, I asked about the garbage. If there were any plans to deal with the excess up here." She shifted against him. "Guess there's folk assigned to help him mow the lawns and clean up houses below Third Street. But they're refusing to work farther up the hill, other than Cheddar Street. They say it's just wasted energy."

"They're just going to let the town rot?"

"Oh, no. Of course not. But before they can have shifts upstairs and downstairs, they have to build an elevator for the last leg of the journey. Everyone's complaining about having to make the climb every week. Right now there's just the stairs in the tunnel."

"So in another ten years, things'll be back to normal."

"A month, says Peggy."

At five minutes to ten she lighted the candle on the coffee table, and four minutes later, started a countdown.

"Three," she said. "Two. One." A pause. She smiled. "Zero."

But the lights remained, with the rain dappling the windows.

"Well, you said they lose the concept of time down there."

She smiled, stretched, and had begun to reply when the lights died. They both jumped. She laughed, then softly, "Bravo. Pretty close."

Dark, but for the candle.

"Okay," she said. "This is pleasant. I can do this."

"At least for one night," Russ said.

Near the bay window, Ody was a gray shape with glittering eyes.

He held her as the room, very slowly, seemed to realign itself around the candle. Everything shifting in the wavering glow, around the flame, and Russ suddenly pictured electricity in an underground cavern, a swirl of colored Christmas lights threading the dark, and streetlamps winking on, one by one.

Megan murmured, shifting against him in the warmth of the comforter.

He remembered the garbage can, the spilt garbage. The cheese head.

Had they broken it apart with their beaks? Carried away some of it, at least, strewing the rest on the lawn?

No doubt it was still there. In pieces. Dissolving in the rain.

Her hand trailed down his chest, fingers slipping under the waistband of his jeans. And she whispered.

The sound of the shower woke him. Russ hovered near the edge of sleep, listening to the roar, then the squeal as the tap was turned off.

He sat up, rubbing his eyes. The clock flashed: 5:04. Sunlight filled the window.

He tried to remember any dreams.

A party, in the Evening mansion. In the tower.

"He's awake." She padded out of the bathroom in a swirl of steam. Sunlight made her supple thighs white as paper.

"Good morning." He rubbed his eyes again, and recalled the dream. A crowd in the mansion's tower. Joseph Evening had been there.

"What time is it?"

"After eleven." She tugged on some panties; then, with brisk efficiency, pulled on and fastened her bra.

She smiled. "I'm going to go to Claire's for lunch."

Megan had been in the dream, and Peggy Chalmers. Malcolm, too. Joseph Evening standing on a chair, arms raised, making a speech.

"Her number's in my little book," Megan said.

"Do you suppose Pete Crick's around?"

"Yeah. He said he'd be up at the mansion today."

"I thought he might have some lanterns we could borrow."

"Good idea."

She dressed, and went to make some breakfast. Russ phoned Boston from her bedroom. The line picked up on the second ring. Ellie's voice, vividly close: "Kent residence?"

"Ellie." Surprised to find her there, he sat down on the bed. "I'm late, I know."

"Yeah, but I'll give you extra credit for yesterday. The crack of dawn, I swear. So, how goes it?"

"It goes," he said. "I'll be here for another couple days, at least. How're things there? How's my dad?"

"He called last night. He's been down in Virginia. Awful heat, but a good concert, I guess. And you have four days before he's due back."

Russ tried to comprehend that. Four times twenty-four hours until he was due back in Boston. "Okay. And then I'll make it up to you, Ellie."

"You can do that by being here to greet him. Bring your landlady friend."

Would four days be enough?

After the call, Russ let Ody outside, and walked around the corner of the house, to the garbage can. The lid was still secure. He resisted the urge to open it, or to search the surrounding lawn. Instead, he went in, left the walking stick by the coatrack, got his keys, and stepped outside.

Ody was waiting below the stairs.

"Want to see Pete at the mansion, Ody?"

Tail wagging, the husky followed Russ to the rental, and bounded onto the passenger seat.

Down the hill, the yards were drying out, at least temporarily. He turned right onto First, squinting against the glare. The Warp and Weft was dark. Farther along, the Diner was open, but empty, while a few pedestrians, like actors, roamed the sidewalks.

The sign had changed.

The Evening Mansion: Oregon Historical Landmark Closed for Renovation.

At the top of the bluff, Russ parked in the lot beside an old blue pickup. He climbed out, let Ody jump onto the gravel, and closed the door.

Black wire creaked in the offshore breeze—the Christmas lights suspended over the yard, tangled in the limbs of the Korean pine and along the fence, stretching to the trellis porch.

Remembering wood smoke, and the voices lifting to the dark sky, he opened the gate, and crossed the lawn. Strangely, a black raft lay under the pine. A Zodiac, with wooden oars, a tackle box.

Ody sniffed at it, then followed Russ up the porch stairs, where he resolutely sat down.

"Don't want to go in, huh?"

Ody looked up.

"Okay. Keep watch. I won't be long."

At the double doors, he turned the swan-wing handle. It was unlocked. He went inside.

The Hall of Founders stretched ahead of him, empty, with only the pale squares on the green-striped wallpaper to mark where the portraits had once hung.

In the ballroom, tables were pushed against the wall, leaving an expanse of polished floor.

Russ heard movement.

A scraping sound, a scuff, then the air startled with a bright, rilling chime.

Surprised, he listened to the echo, then followed it.

In the far corner, Pete Crick knelt by a whorl of green glass—one of the chandeliers. Collapsed onto a square of padded linen, it resembled nothing more than some creature of the lower depths, now hauled up on a beach.

A cart waited behind him.

"Moving?"

Pete was folding the linen across it. He looked up. "Hey, Mister Kent." Folding, crimping the corners. "Mayor likes to call it *relocating*."

Russ looked around for easels. For bits of green stone.

"Been trying to do a little bit every day."

"Are you the only one who works in town?"

Pete laughed. "Seems that way."

Russ gestured to the empty floor. "What happened to the bits of rock from the party? The Hesperus pieces?"

"Back downstairs. Mayor's orders." Pete pulled the cart closer.

"Want some help with that?"

"Nah. I got it."

Pete's hair was a mess, and his acne more profuse.

"So, they're installing chandeliers downstairs?"

Wiping sweat from his eyes, Pete said, "Yeah. If you can believe it." He took an industrial stapler from the pocket of his overalls, and secured the flaps. "Makes things more civilized, that's what Mizz Chalmers says."

Pete tried dragging the bundle onto the cart. "Actually could you give me a hand, Mister Kent? Just to lift this up?"

"Sure."

Together they hauled it up. The sound, though muffled, was marvellous.

Russ straightened. "Is it secure?"

"Yeah. I'll run some electrical tape around the edge."

Another chandelier was missing, Russ realized. Only four were left.

"Sorry, Mister Kent, if I was a bit too drunk at the party."

Russ shook his head. "No. Looked like you were having fun." He added, "How's your dad?"

Pete thought for a moment. "Better. He gets along in the downstairs better than upstairs. Makes him feel like he's in one of his Jules Verne books." He grinned. "The Captain helps with that."

"Have you seen Malcolm lately?"

"Not for a few days."

"He's enjoying himself?"

Pete laughed. "Yeah, bit too much. Pisses off Peggy and the mayor. And that's fine with me."

Russ helped him push the cart into the hall. "I came here looking for lanterns, Pete. For the outages."

"Sure. Should've thought to bring some over. Step into my office, Mister Kent."

Russ followed him halfway down the hall, where Pete stopped, and tripped the catch; the door popped out. "Heads up."

Dim light shone down spiral stairs, and glinted on mousetraps in various points of the room.

Russ remembered Carver's basement; the tiny blue skeleton in silver sand.

With his boot, Pete nudged one to the side. "Could say they're for the mayor himself. Not that he'd think to come in here. Sure would be nice, though. See him dancing. Snap, snap." He flicked on the light.

Thinking of the garbage can, the missing cheese, Russ asked, "Have Dreerson and Carver found any . . . evidence, downstairs?"

"You mean for their psycho-whatever?"

Russ nodded.

"Wish they would . . ." He knelt, pushed aside boxes on a lower shelf, and lifted out a Coleman lantern. "Here. Got some flashlights here, too."

Russ took the lantern, then two flashlights. "Could I borrow a few of the traps? What with the blackouts, I'd feel better, somehow . . ."

"Sure, Mister Kent."

But he left the traps in the car.

With Ody bustling beside him, he carried the lantern and two flashlights inside, took off his coat and shoes. He was about to call into Megan's room when he saw her lying on the couch, under a blanket, an arm across her eyes.

"Megan?"

She nodded, rubbed her eyes with the heel of her hand. She patted Ody. "Feeling okay?"

"Headache," she said. "Not enough sleep, I guess. Hi, Ode."

"How'd things go with Claire?"

She shook her head, stretched. "Oh. She's frightened by the outages."

She sat up, and rubbed her eyes again. He noticed a wink of gold at her throat. A necklace. A gold pendant.

He said, "I'm going to feed Ody, and fix some lunch."

She stood up. "I think I'll go lie down."

"Pete gave me a lantern and a couple flashlights. Here." He handed her the flashlight. "Put this one in your room."

"Thanks."

An hour later, he checked in on her. She was asleep. Ody lay on the carpet at the foot of the bed, head between his paws, staring up.

Russ spent the rest of the afternoon alone, pretending to work on the drawings. Ody showed up at dinner, and afterwards sat by Russ on the couch. A flashlight was by his side, in case the outage took him by surprise.

Now that it was night, he was acutely conscious of the sounds outside, and kept an eye on Ody, waiting for those ears to twitch. He thought of the garbage can, the gulls fleeing up to the roof of the house next door, and Ody facing the hillside, ears sharp, barking. And the thoughts grew, in the silence.

An hour later, he found his car keys and walked quietly to the front door. Ody followed him onto the porch, and watched while he retrieved the five mousetraps and set one under her bedroom window, one by the bay window, a third at the dining room window, two more on the porch stairs.

Ody watched as though he'd seen this type of behavior before.

"I'll take them in at first light," Russ told the dog.

At 9:45, Russ peeked in on Megan. She was asleep, on her side in the center of the bed, with the blankets clutched up to her chin.

"Watch her, Ody," he whispered. "I'll be upstairs."

Ody sat down by the door, then laid down, head between his paws.

Russ almost brought the lantern, but settled on a flashlight, two candles and a box of matches.

The sheets on the bed had been changed. He sat down, lit a candle on the desk, and wound up the portable clock. He set the clock to 9:55, undressed into a T-shirt and boxers, and got into bed.

The outage was a few minutes late.

He couldn't sleep. He lay there watching the candlelight on the walls, and listened.

He stands in the midst of a party.

Lanterns set about the room glimmer on smiling faces—Bernard Dreerson and Tom Carver, jovially chatting with Peggy Chalmers and the Barber-Mayor. Megan, in a green dress, laughs with Ellie and Russ's father. The faces are reflected in the five windows surrounding them, in Joseph's tower, and Russ, outside their conversations, slips through, past Bob Burle and Mrs. Nelson, and looks out.

Below is the basalt shore. Farther out, volcanic mountains march to the horizon.

He presses his forehead to the glass. Underneath the voices he can hear a *thrum*, can feel—as Peggy laughs raucously—a deep oscillation through the floor.

On the curved horizon, something trembles. Flecks of silver.

Nobody notices. Even as their drinks begin to slosh and the thrumming grows to a roar, they simply shout above it, while there on the horizon, and closer, the tide, silvery and green, is swallowing up the undersea.

Russ slept deeply, and woke after eleven. He dressed, walked downstairs, and found her at the kitchen table, in a white sweater and jeans. "Morning."

She was gripping a mug of coffee as though to warm her hands. She said quietly, "I found your traps."

"Oh." He wiped his palm across his eyes. "Sorry."

"What were you thinking?"

He shook his head. "Nothing that makes sense."

"We're lucky one of the cats didn't get caught."

"I figured they knew to avoid them," he said, regretting it instantly.

"It was stupid, Russ."

He agreed; still there was no recovering. She went outside to work on the yard, while he mulled over last night, and the causes. The spilt garbage can, Ody barking. The outages. Everything.

He wondered if she'd found *all* the traps.

After a quick breakfast he went out to look. Megan was working with a Weed Eater near the verge, her back to him, with Ody sitting beside a mower. Russ looked along the stairs and the sides of the house: yes, she had found them all.

He made coffee, sat at the kitchen table for a time, then tried to work. Sorting through the drawings, and trying to notate his sound impressions of several, though he was impatient, and a little cramped indoors.

He put on his jacket and went outside.

The breeze was light, leaving a scent of cut grass and sea salt, quite pleasant.

"I'd like to help."

She looked over. Maybe still angry, maybe not. "Want to rake?"

"Sure," he said, descending the stairs, nearly making a joke, something about *The Rake's Progress*. He found the rake at the bottom of the stairs and began work, slowly at first. In fifteen minutes he'd filled a garbage bag and—not finding another—continued with a cardboard box from the factory. He was happy with the exercise, happier still when he realized he'd forgotten the walking stick for a while, and hadn't needed it. He listened to the gulls. Their raucous cries overlapping, up and down the hill.

Antiphonal.

Ody, his head between his paws, paid little attention.

Near the curb, Megan stopped. She leaned on the mower's handle and looked back at what she'd done.

He called out, "I'll take over."

She shook her head. "Almost done."

Ody barked, into the street.

"I gave you the hard work, Russ."

Another bark. She looked over as Ody stood up, raised his ears and barked again.

On Mrs. Nelson's roof, three gulls took flight.

But Ody was peering north, toward Cheddar Street, ears sharp.

"What is it?" Russ met her at the curb. "Birds?"

Rats? he thought.

Monsters?

"Don't think so." She let the mower's handle drop. "Ody?"

Russ said, "You hearing things, boy?"

She brushed hair from her eyes. Her hand was shaking, as though from exertion.

In the distance, the sound of an engine. A flash of metal. A truck was driving down Seventh. An old red pickup truck. Ody began excitedly wagging his tail.

It was Tom Carver's truck, gearing down. The wipers had cleared dust from the front window, over Carver behind the wheel, and Bernard Dreerson slouched in the passenger seat. Glasses winking.

Russ grabbed Ody's collar as the truck pulled up and parked behind the rental sedan.

Malcolm wasn't with them.

"Hi, Tom!" Russ approached the door.

Ody bustled beside him, barked.

"Afternoon, Kent." Carver carefully opened the door, and patted Ody's head, let him lick his hand. "Aww, Ode, got to give me room to get out." Wiry white tufts of hair behind his ears, the bulbous nose. He avoided Russ's eyes as he stepped out, down. Dusty boots, dungarees, gray sweatshirt. He seemed exhausted, though he cracked a smile as he scratched Ody between the ears. "Yeah, dog-dog, I'm glad to see you." He looked up. "Hello, Meg."

Megan hadn't moved closer.

Carver said to the dog, "You change owners on me?"

"Pete let us have him for a while," Russ told him.

Dreerson was extricating himself from the other door, pushing it shut with his elbow. He wore a rumpled, many-pocketed dark coat, similar to those worn by the Stans, but with an "e" pin on the collar. Rounding the hood of the truck he said, "Good to see you back on your feet, Russell."

Russ nodded, with less of a smile than before. "Hello, Bernard."

They shook.

"Good afternoon, Megan."

She barely responded. "Bennie."

Dreerson carried a grocery sack by its twine handle. His jowly face was pale.

"Got some num-nums for you," Carver said quietly, and patted Ody again. "But you'll just have to wait."

The bag didn't seem heavy, yet Dreerson gripped the handle tightly. "Megan, may we go inside?"

Arms folded over her chest, she met Dreerson's gaze, lingering. Then she turned and walked to the porch. He followed, then Carver, while Russ stood unable to move.

Reminded of a dream. Watery air, an antique diving suit.

"Kent?" Carver had paused. He turned back, Ody bustling at his side, and nodded. "Awful glad you took care of him, Kent."

Russ nodded. He managed to say, "Happy to."

"He don't like the sounds downstairs, or the folks. Do you, boy? Let's go, Ody. Follow Bern."

As Tom continued into the house, Russ forced himself to follow; over the lawn, up the porch stairs, with the smell of the ocean and cut grass sharpening into something else, into minerals, into rust and moist earth, from Carver's clothes.

Megan was sitting on the couch. She stared at her clasped hands while Dreerson set the bag on the carpet.

Ody yelped, nails clicking the flagstone.

Tom said, "Gotta calm down there." He laid a hand on Ody's side. "Shush."

Dreerson, leaning over the bag, lifted out a loose stack of papers. He glanced back at Russ. Dusty glasses, and a wandering left eye. He mumbled something.

As Dreerson handed the papers up, Russ recognized the printed staves, his own sketches, of *Nemo*. He took the brittle pages, then looked at the grocery bag, and what remained inside. Folds of gray-green material, a copper stud, a gray lace.

He set the papers on the table.

Dreerson straightened up. "Megan . . ."

His gentle, careful tone had revealed all. Her eyes wavered and looked away.

"I was afraid you might have heard," Dreerson continued, while Megan clasped her hands, knuckles whitening, "before we could be entirely certain. The gossip lines have remained in place. . . . My dear, these are Jack's possessions."

She nodded. Softly, "Claire . . ."

"From the Far Forty. . . ." said Tom, moving up beside Russ.

"Claire was the gossip," said Megan.

Dreerson reached into the bag, came up with a scuffed leather wallet. "Here's his coat, and a few other possessions."

"Much as we could, Meg," said Carver.

"Dear, I'm sorry to bring such news. But I'm also, in a sense, glad to bring you a definitive answer, after all this time."

"Okay." She looked up, and after a pause said, "Thanks, Bennie . . . I . . ."

"You can be proud of him, Meg."

"Yes. He was the first to see the city, its original explorer." Dreerson shook his head. "Jack's dad would have been very proud. As are we all,

Cheese League and non-Cheese League alike." He set the scuffed wallet back into the bag. "But I'm afraid the town has some strong ideas about Jack's remains. They won't let us bring the body upstairs, Megan."

Carver grunted. "Bastards."

She looked down at her hands.

"Tom and I argued quite extensively. A spy from the council had witnessed the discovery, you see, and the town council issued a proclamation that everything in the Far Forty belongs to Hesperus. They've promised not to touch the bones until you decide. But they've offered to lay Jack to rest beside old Joe, with honors. Or wherever you wish, downstairs."

"Bastards'll keep their word, Meg. Bern and me'll see to it."

Briefly, she glanced up. "Thanks." Not meeting his eyes, she gently kissed Dreerson on the cheek. "Thanks Bennie. And Tom." She moved to Carver, stood on tiptoes and kissed him. "Are you hungry? I have breakfast still . . ."

Dreerson shook his head. "At the moment all I need is a long shower and a fresh change of clothes. We'll be off. Though we brought supplies, if you need any."

"We're fine for now."

A tear was tracking down Dreerson's cheek, over wrinkles as much green as gray. "Then perhaps we could share lunch tomorrow? Tom and I have some business to attend to later in the day, otherwise . . ."

She noticed Russ watching her. "Sure. And I'm okay." She looked at him. "Right now I'm going to finish the mowing."

Dreerson raised a hand. "Megan . . ."

"I promise I'm okay. I'll see you at noon, Bennie."

"Very well."

They watched her leave. Dreerson sighed, shook his head. "I could have handled that better, I think."

"You did fine, Bern."

"At least Russell's here for her."

Russ was staring down at the coffee table, at the score sheets.

"That's all I could find." Dreerson gestured to them. "It's your project, isn't it?"

Russ nodded. "You got it from Malcolm?"

"Yes. Though not entirely with his cooperation."

"Bern means he stole it," said Carver.

Ody's claws clicked on the flagstone.

"Yeah, Ode. We can see you."

"So how's Malcolm?"

Dreerson considered, pursing chapped lips. "Well, he's Captain Nemo, isn't he? He's a sort of a fixture by now. His personality, as they say, has grown to fill the house. And he loves nothing more than to shout and carry on, and sometimes sing."

"They keep the ear plugs in, Bern—you notice?"

Dreerson nodded. "I did indeed."

"How can I get a message to him?"

"Tom and I will be returning downstairs in a day or two. Simply write a note, and we'll deliver it. Your subterranean post office."

Dreerson glanced out the window. Megan was once again busy mowing. "Otherwise, Russell, what are your plans?"

Watching her, Russ wondered, remembering the deadline to return to Boston. "Depends on Megan. I'd like to take her back to Boston with me."

"You should."

"Do I have to worry about . . ." Russ tried to phrase the question, ". . . not being allowed to leave?"

Dreerson stared at the carpet. "Most of our citizens are otherwise occupied, Russell. They have a new world ready to receive the imprint of mankind. Without the diurnal rhythms, hours and days and weeks lose their definition. The mind becomes a little . . ." Dreerson looked up. ". . . well, a little flabbergasted by it all. I really don't think they'll notice or care. Certainly they're more concerned with creating their new town, all sorts of ordinances and zoning laws. And when Megan's ready to leave, you should take her away from it all, Russell. I don't think she'll need long. She's been trying to leave for years now."

They fell silent.

Ody wagged his tail, and barked.

Carver said, "Okay, Ode. Let's go see Mother."

Walking with them to the door, Russ asked, "How is Hillary?"

Carver laughed, and began to cough, hack. He shook his head, teary-eyed. "Surprised you didn't hear the ruckus, Kent! She's upstairs. Took her a few hours to climb the stairs and now she says she's never going back down. Says she's moving to Rostov!"

Dreerson offered his hand. Russ shook it.

"Tomorrow around noonish, Russell. Not that I'd be too sad to find you both gone, strange to say."

Russ shook Tom's hand.

"Thanks, Kent."

"Bye, Tom. Ody."

"Ready, dog-dog?"

Russ remained at the door while they returned to the truck. Near the curb, they stopped to talk briefly again with Megan. She hugged them both. Then Ody bounded into the truckbed, and they were off.

She returned to work, and was quickly done. When Russ went out to finish raking, she complained of a headache and went inside, to bed.

Alone, Russ fixed cold salmon and Jell-O, and contemplated leaving town. Back to Boston, via Portland. If and when she was ready to leave. And for now, he faced another night of dark on the hill.

He looked at Dreerson's bag. The gray and green cloth. Shoelace.

He decided it needed to be elsewhere.

He took hold of the twine, lifted it, surprised by how light it was. Boots and a sweatshirt, and shoelaces, and wallet, and what else? He walked to the corner beside the fireplace, and set the bag down. It had left a residue of dust on the carpet. He lifted the score sheets, found green dust on the table. He shook the pages, set them on the couch, then went to the kitchen and returned with a towel, and wiped down the coffee table.

Later, he looked through the *Nemo* sketches. The paper was gritty and brittle. Polyphonic string lines, the pencilled words, the staves, all of it had bled with moisture. And the mineral smell was almost another timbre to the sketch's orchestral fabric.

For a moment, he recalled the neumes, and listened to them in this color.

He ate dinner, checked on Megan to see if she wanted some hot soup. She didn't.

At 9:55 he cranked up the heat, brought out a blanket, lit a candle on the coffee table, and waited. When the power died—a faint click, dark-

ness, and the sodium lights fading through the bay window—he realized
he hadn't Ody for company.

He brought the lantern up to his room and set it on the desk. In bed,
he paged through *20,000 Leagues Under the Sea* and listened carefully for
sounds downstairs.

Rain was thundering on the roof. But it wasn't the rain that woke him.

Uneasy, Russ tossed back the blankets in the dark—chilly air. He
found the flashlight, then his robe on the floor beside the bed, and his
socks. In the wandering beam, he walked downstairs.

Her bedroom door was open.

Faint candlelight shone on the living room carpet. He followed it to a
candle burning on the kitchen table, where Megan sat, with a sweater
over her flannel gown.

She looked over. Tired eyes, hair in a mess.

She held a glass of white wine.

"Did I wake you?"

"Nope. The rain," he said, and clicked off the flashlight.

She wore a gold pendant against her nightgown, on the slender gold
chain he had seen earlier.

"Join me?"

"Sure." He pulled out a chair, sat down, and set the flashlight on the
table.

The pendant was a gold square flickering in the candlelight, with a
steady spark of green in the center.

She sipped her wine, and caught him looking.

He gestured. "Is that new?"

"Nope. Old. From Claire." With thumb and first finger, she lifted it,
then let it drop. "It's a charm." Luminous green. "A chip of Hesperus
rock."

Even in the candlelight, her eyes looked raw.

He discarded several things he might say. Instead, he sat back, listening to the rain; a squall was passing, fading while he sat staring at the
flame.

When she spoke again, it was almost a whisper. "I hate it downstairs."

"Understandable," Russ replied.

"Always hated it. Even before the accident."

She sipped her wine.

"How long had you been a resident, before you were allowed downstairs?"

"Hmmm." She tucked strands of hair behind her ear. "Three months? After the Summer Festival." Relaxing her shoulders. "I didn't really believe him. I was ready for disappointment. Just some small town weirdness, I thought. A big deal to them but not to anyone else."

He looked past her, to shadows trembling on the linoleum, and under the cupboards.

"You ever been to underground Seattle, Russ?"

He shook his head. "I haven't."

"My parents took me when I was a kid." She squared her shoulders, and sat back. "I was expecting this buried city from the 1890s. Old streets and buildings, with gaslight and carriages. Instead it was like a . . . like a movie set built in someone's basement. A real rip-off." She set down the glass. "But that summer, when Jack and Claire took me down, everything was exactly like he'd described. An iron staircase going down into the hill, a mile. Down to the gold wall. Just like he'd said." She looked into her glass. "And inside were the glowing green walls. Victorian staircases, and the elevator, down level after level. I'd never had claustrophobia before." Smiling faintly. "Jack always said it proved I wasn't a native."

Russ remembered the smell of minerals in her hair, on her neck. The taste of copper pennies.

"They'd always had accidents. Everyone was so used to it. People were injured every month, some died. And I always thought about how awful it would be, in one of those pioneer tunnels, the kind Jack was the expert on making." She squinted, then looked up at Russ. "That's what it was tonight. Tom Carver and Bennie were there, helping Jack. And I was holding his lead ropes in my hands. I could hear him, and I knew what was about to happen. I was calling to him, begging him to get out. The dreadful echo. Then the walls were collapsing. The ocean was pouring in. And I woke up."

Staring down into her glass, she said, "Anyway." Lifting the charm. "Claire said this would give me peaceful sleep." Again, the faint smile, as she pulled the necklace over her head, out of her hair, the charm swinging in the candlelight. Then she dropped it in her wineglass.

"You've had them too. The nightmares."

He nodded.

"Close to mine?"

"Variations on a theme."

She looked up. "And you had to come back."

"Twice," he said, remembering his dreams of the underwater town. And what Bernard had told him—how Hesperus brooded into the town, into their dreams.

The rain had almost stopped; the house was quiet.

And as the silence grew, he felt for it. A presence, a pull, from the hill. From Hesperus.

And sensed it. Or told himself he did.

A charge to the air—imagined or not. Under the candlelight. And he didn't move, but remained completely still, holding his breath as the presence exerted a pull under the rustling, crackling candle. Elemental. Russ sought a comparison, and found a simple scale, and the pull of that seventh, penultimate note in an eight-note scale—the *subdominant*, compelling the ear to meet that final note, and the resolution.

Subdominant to tonic.

And here, invisible in the room, under the candlelight, was the moment between those two notes, indefinitely prolonged.

Megan let go her glass. "If I don't go downstairs, one last time, Russ. If I don't see him for myself, then I'll never be able to leave."

Russ watched the candle, wondering if she felt it, too.

"And I need you to come with me, Russ."

Under Evening. Downstairs.

She watched him from across the table, and he tried to nod, to say yes, he would, but something like fear, something like exhilaration, had seized him.

He broke it. Looked away from the candle and said, in a reasonably calm voice, "How about tomorrow."

He knew he wouldn't be able to wait, couldn't have much time to ponder it.

"I'll call Bennie in the morning, let him know."

The moment settled back into silence, both of them watching the candle, and the question occurred to Russ.

Once we're downstairs, why would they let us back up?

Later, in bed with Megan asleep beside him, his thoughts turned, irresistibly, downward. Through basalt and shale, to a city of arching green stone, and familiar faces. The citizens of Evening one by one looking up through clouds of rock to Seventh Street, and smiling.

She had set the alarm for ten A.M.: it woke them both.

While she was showering, he dressed and stepped onto the porch. The sun was breaking through morning clouds, and glittering on the sea.

It would happen today, he told himself. It was impossible, and would happen today. And by tomorrow, they could be out of town, on their way to Boston—Megan meeting his dad, Ellie, his friends; he contemplated that, or tried to. The nearby thoughts were of the dark beneath the hill, the old tunnels and the ancient city.

And, more tantalizingly, the ancient music.

He sat down on the porch and watched sunlight on the pine trees and the ocean, and how the ocean brightened to the blue called cerulean, while the gulls—distant today—wheeled and soared.

When he went inside, Megan was in the kitchen. Bleary-eyed, but awake. She kissed his cheek. "Still want to go today?"

He replied, "Perfect day for a hike."

Hint of a smile. "It's maybe a half hour to climb down. Another couple hours out to the Far Forty. I'll call Bennie and see if someone from the ACL can help us."

"Pete?"

"Or maybe the Stans."

He mulled that over, then asked, "What should I wear?"

"Something warm. Comfortable. Your boots, for sure."

She fixed them oatmeal with apple slices, and Russ added a stale Danish and several cups of coffee. They ate in silence. Russ pondered the hike, which was sure to be wearying. Descending the stairway from the factory—what had she said, a mile? Then down spiral stairs, or via the elevator, down to the city, then out to the Far Forty.

He tried not to think past those details.

Peggy Chalmers, the Barber-Mayor, Andrea, Malcolm. Almost everyone would be there.

And the question reoccurred:

Why would they let us back up?

He pondered taking some kind of weapon. A baseball bat, a steak knife.

The pistol from Carver's basement.

When Megan had finished, she stood up, brought her dishes to the sink, and said, "An hour?"

He had to force the answer: "Okay."

He went upstairs to his room, sat down at the desk.

He stared for a few minutes at the phone, then dialed Boston, bracing himself as the line connected and rang, hoping she wasn't there.

She wasn't.

At the beep, he said, "Ellie. Just checking in." A pause, as he weighed yet again the proper words. He looked up at the bright morning beyond the windows. "Megan and I are going on a day hike. And if I don't call you tomorrow . . . I'd like you to phone the Visitor's Center for me, ask for Peggy Chalmers, and tell her I might be missing, and that I might be *downstairs*. In Hesperus. H-E-S-P-E-R-U-S. Then call the factory, and say the same thing. I know that sounds kind of strange. I'm sorry to worry you . . . it's complicated. But I'll explain more tomorrow." He hesitated, knowing he couldn't take back the words, spooling on the cassette in Boston. "And Malcolm's here, Ellie, in Evening. I'll tell you more tomorrow. Early tomorrow, by ten A.M., your time."

He hung up. He changed into a flannel shirt and corduroys, a sweater, and boots; aware, while he was dressing, of his coordination, remembering the painful, endless exercises with Gloria.

Wondering whether to bring the walking stick.

With a last glance at the neumes—and *20,000 Leagues Under the Sea*—he went downstairs.

In the entry, he took up the stick, ran his thumb over the sharp ears. If not for support, he thought, then at least for protection.

Megan was in the kitchen, loading a bottle of water into a knapsack.

She wore a dark wool sweater, corduroys, hiking boots. Her hair was tied back. "I called Bennie," she said. "He said Pete Crick or the Stans'll meet us downstairs." She zipped up the knapsack, threw it over her shoulder. "Ready?"

Russ smiled. "Mostly," he said.

As she drove slowly along Seventh, the procession of dismantled houses and overgrown yards took hold of him.

How long till it resembles my dream? The town, completely abandoned, overgrown?

She turned right at Cheddar, accelerated up the hill.

Russ almost looked back—a last glance at the sea; then alder was encompassing the road, and ahead, the great yellow building was rising into view.

The "e" sign stood motionless. The lot was nearly empty.

A blue pickup—Pete's—was parked at the entrance.

She pulled in next to it, parked, and stared down at her hand on the wheel for a moment, before yanking out the keys. She grabbed the knapsack from the back seat. "Lock your door."

Clutching the stick, Russ climbed out, stepped down, locked the door before shutting it.

He walked with Megan to the front doors.

There was a new note:

Evening Cheeses is closed for the season. Please refer your queries to our Visitor's Center. For distribution questions please call our new Northwest distributor, Conklin Deliveries, in Port Rostov, Oregon.

She unlocked the door; they stepped inside, and she locked it behind them, then went to deactivate the beeping alarm.

Back in One Hour! read the sign on Mrs. Nelson's desk, next to a stack of perforated invoices weighed down with a tape dispenser.

We Provide the Cheese! proclaimed the poster behind the desk, the words superimposed over a slab of cheddar. The next, with appropriate illustration, read: *Our Cheese has the Blues!*

He remembered stumbling through here, past Mrs. Nelson, into Burle's office. That door—its crystal knob was gone—stood open on an empty room.

They walked down the hall, and onto the factory floor. The halogens were off; ceiling domes admitted a frosty daylight. Some of the machinery and chrome tubs were missing, and the tall racking on the southern wall stood empty.

The air was cold, with only a hint of yeast and cheese.

Russ looked to the far end, and the wide yellow door decorated with the lower-cased "e" logo.

Secondary Storage, read the sign.

The door was heavy steel, set on rollers. At a nearby keypad, Megan tapped in a five-digit code. A bolt clanked; the door shifted. She rolled it back with one hand, onto a room that looked much like the first, though darker, and more cluttered.

They stepped inside.

Ducts trembled overhead. Somewhere, air compressors were chugging. She flipped a switch beside the door: fluorescent lights flickered on, over tall racking and shrink-wrapped pallets, forklifts, a winch, and in the center of the room, what looked like a small, single-car garage, painted bright yellow.

Around it, the concrete floor was scuffed with forklift tracks.

The ducts trailed down to the structure, which had a shuttered steel door.

To his left and right were more pallets. He discerned, under the shrinkwrap, porcelain basins in foam rubber fittings; a plush armchair; a box-spring; a sofa. One pallet overflowed with rhododendron, another with pine.

"Nothing too suspicious," he remarked.

Behind him, a full-length mirror was hung beside the door, and the sign:

WAIT! DO YOU LOOK NORMAL ENOUGH? ARE YOU IN PROPER ATTIRE??

"They used to be more careful," she said.

Street signs were tipped against the wall: familiar green rectangles at right angles. *Avenue* and *Harold Chalmers Way*. *Avenue* and *Burle Blvd*.

They approached the structure—the entrance.

On one side was a desk, with a raised back of mail slots overlooking several clipboards, a telephone, and a cup of pencils. A handwritten sign

read *WOULD THE NEXT ONE DOWN PLEASE TAKE THESE? THANK YOU!*
Tucked into the slots were envelopes and cards, a medicine bottle, sunglasses, two paperback books, each item trailing string and a handwritten
label.

A broom and two mops, similarly labelled, were leaning against the
desk.

Megan found a small sack, shook it open, then loaded in the medicine
bottle, the letters and sunglasses, put the sack into her knapsack, and
zipped the knapsack up. "We all do our part," she said, under her breath.

"I'll take a mop."

"You're exempt. In fact . . . here. Let me carry the walking stick.
The stairs'll trip you up. I can hook it under the knapsack."

He handed it over.

At a panel beside the shuttered door, she used another key to activate
a green light, then pressed a large black button.

A bell rang: the shutter began rolling up.

The noise echoed into a sudden, tantalizing distance.

On threads of cold, coppery air.

Wooden handrails were fixed to walls about twenty feet apart. Two
sets of narrow metal staircases bracketed a ramp fitted with rollers at the
top, and hard-plastic slats over which pallets could be lowered.

Where the ceiling started were metal-grilled lamps, down into dark.

She flipped a switch. And again, on and off. Nothing had happened.

"Power's off." Looking unsurprised, she returned to the desk, knelt,
and retrieved two boxy flashlights.

He took one, pressed the switch. The light shone more weakly than
he'd hoped.

"You take the right-hand stairs, I'll take the left." She nudged the
knapsack—with the walking stick—higher on her shoulder.

He shone his flashlight on the first of the diamond-patterned stairs,
then down dozens, or hundreds, to dark.

"A mile?" he said.

"About."

She stepped down.

Gripping the smooth wood rail with his right hand, he followed. The
stairs rang softly under their boots.

"No need to hurry," she said.

Her flashlight struck a bronze plaque; the tall letters tilting as she moved past it:

EVENING-BY-THE-SEA
TUNNEL PROJECT
CITY OF EVENING, OREGON 1917
OUR EXCAVATION TO THE NEW LANDS

With a careful gait, against a wild echo in the distance, Russ descended into the hill.

*i*n the evening tunnel

It was almost possible to believe, from moment to moment, this was an ordinary walk down a long flight of stairs, with the diamond-grids under his boots and the smooth wooden rail under his hand. Almost possible, at any rate, in the dark, with the flashlights lighting the rusty walls and a sign in large red letters: *No Sliding*.

As the door receded he became increasingly mindful of his actual location in regards to the factory. Wondering whether they had descended below the level of houses on Sixth Street, under the basements, and down, level with Fifth, or Fourth, as the stairs continued materializing out of the dark, ringing under their boots in a nearby echo that covered another, more distant sound.

Megan, on the left-hand stairs, climbed smoothly down, barely grasping the rail, her flashlight on the nearest stairs. Matching her gait, Russ shone his flashlight out and down the silvered stairs and watched the rusty wall panels and lightbulb fixtures rise out of the dark toward them. There were brief sections where the panels had been torn away, revealing old timber beams and sprayed concrete, garish in the light, like some exposed bone.

Glancing over his shoulder, and up, he found the doorway had become a speck of light, high overhead.

Fear broke through. His heart began pounding. The air seemed too close, too stifling, even with the constant breeze. He forced his eyes on the stairs and concentrated on the distant sound, the ringing tones under their ringing boots, certain it was more than a complicated echo, becoming, as he listened, more complex, with faint, bright ripples. He started counting the stairs, but lost track somewhere after one hundred.

He recalled what Dreerson had said about the early days of the dig;

months and years to dig each meter, in the direction laid confidently by Joseph Evening.

Months and years, now easily traversed, as Russ glanced back, and up.

The door was no longer visible, except at the corner of his eye—a tense quivering of light.

While below, the sound—the *sounds*—bloomed in metallic timbres. And his flashlight found a plaque on the right-hand wall.

His light glared across it, the antique font stained green at the edges, as though from algae.

MAY 17, 1927
THE CENTER OF OUR PASSAGE
IN MEMORIAM FOR THE LOST
FOR THE GREATER GLORY OF EVENING

Light collected below. Wet concrete. The stairs ended, becoming a concrete landing before another set of stairs, ramps and rails continued down.

"Rest area?" His voice echoed more loudly than he expected, in alcoves to either side of the landing.

"Yeah. Thirsty?"

"A bit." He caught his breath.

"We'll take a break."

To the left, the low-ceilinged space held a squat winch, a stack of pallets, and a Sani-Can wedged into the corner. To the right, in a similar space, was a table and four folding chairs, boxes, an ottoman covered in plastic.

Carefully, she crossed the ramp, over the slick plastic runners.

Avoiding the steel foot of his stick as she swung past, he followed her to the table.

His boots smacked a puddle of standing water.

He checked the nearest chair, found it dry, and sat heavily down.

She unshouldered her knapsack on the table, leaned his stick against the other chair, then sat down, setting the lamp on the table. It lighted a damp copy of *McCall's* magazine under a chunk of basaltic rock.

"Cosy," Russ said.

She retrieved the bottled water, and handed it over.

He sipped. His ears popped as he swallowed. He yawned to clear them, drank some more, handed back the bottle.

Tasting minerals.

Wiping sweat from his forehead, he said, "The return trip should be fun."

She nodded, sipping. Then wiped her mouth. "You'd see people along the way, usually. Taking their time. And they have a custom made pallet, with chairs for the old folks. Winch them up." She looked over at the landing, and sipped some water.

Forcing another yawn to clear his ear, he leaned forward and read the date on the *McCall's*. Four years old.

"So, how are you feeling, Russ?"

"Surprisingly well." He stretched his legs, felt a slight cramp in his thighs and calves. Manageable. Except for a vague sense of pressure in his eyes, ears and nasal passages.

"They have plans for an automated lift. Ride it like a ski lift up and down."

"In ten years, right?"

He tried to hear more of the distant sounds.

"Ready to get going?"

"Yeah," he said.

How far were they below sea level? Perhaps it was better not knowing.

His knees and calves ached as he stood up. He might have gained a hundred pounds sitting there, though the sensation dissipated as he walked to the next set of stairs.

Again, his flashlight shining down a hundred stairs, easily, and beyond.

The sounds were a lure: he started down. Megan followed.

Once again, he tried to piece out the component timbres of the sounds, but couldn't hear much beyond the ringing of their boots on the stairs. He tried counting the steps, but soon lost track, and focused on the world within their lamplight, the procession of stairs appearing from out of the dark; the walls, railings and ramp, sometimes marked with an incongruous detail his eyes picked out far in advance, descending toward it—a candy bar wrapper stuck within the plastic slats, fluttering; a pack of cigarettes wedged against the wall; a fifty-cent piece on the stairs.

Eventually, just as his ankles began to ache, and he wondered if he needed to ask for another rest, he discerned a vague glow below. Soon, a spot of light directly below—a square of copper light, becoming larger with each step, stretching into a rectangle, the reflection of another light source, on a landing.

The distant sounds no longer so distant, and not quite the metallic bell-tones heard earlier (as though the tunnel itself, to some extent, created that effect). Instead, the sound was muted and forceful, like hundreds of wind instruments heard from outside an auditorium, mixed with rumbles, and faint, bright splashes of sound.

Distracted, he noticed another plaque of green-stained bronze, on the right side:

HESPERUS
THE RIGHTFUL DOMAIN OF CITIZENS OF EVENING
TOWN OF OREGON, AND OF THE
UNITED STATES OF AMERICA
DEC 17, 1937
IN THE NAME OF JOSEPH EVENING.

After the last word, a tiny "e" logo was stuck like a period.

They reached the last of the stairs.

It was strange to stop, with all that momentum. Unpleasant, with all that earth, no longer moving overhead.

"We don't need the flashlights anymore."

Ahead, past another wrapped pallet, was a stretch of dim gold, with a green square in the center, and both, to Russ's eye, formed a simple chord against the distant sounds. And another lure.

The green, he realized, was the chamber beyond. The golden wall, not so luminous as that interior chamber, nonetheless was burnished and lustrous, and seemed to refute the dank tunnel, the dark rock.

It was apart.

Megan handed him his walking stick.

He gripped the wolf head, feeling the sharp ears against the webbing of his thumb and first finger.

He leaned.

Becoming aware now of Megan's agitated breathing. Her mouth was closed; her eyes roamed the wall and the passage, and he could see the claustrophobia settling around her. He, too, felt it; though more so at his back, and the tomb-like stretch of tunnel, the huge mass of the hillside. Forward was the only possible direction, and it would be easy, drawn closer to those sounds.

Straightening, he said, "One last time, Megan."

She looked over, met his eyes.

He offered his free hand, and she took it. Both their palms warm and dry. She let herself be drawn forward.

As they passed between the earth and Hesperus, between what could and could not be, the chamber beyond seemed to dim then brighten, as the air seemed to momentarily thicken against his ears.

There. That was it.

He stopped, blinked. Confused.

Around him, an unusual space of green stone was obscured by the steel and iron grillwork that dominated the center of the chamber. An elevator cage, circa 1940, with reels of cable and electric motors on top, positioned over a portal in the floor.

Empty pallets were tipped on-end, against the wall. A pallet jack, gloves, a hammer, lay beside the elevator.

A handwritten sign, clipped to the grill, read:

> *See Pete Crick to operate elevator!*
> *Do NOT operate it yourself!*

The lift wasn't there. Beyond the grillwork was a drop through five inches of floor. Another chamber was below, and another portal.

A long drop, his ears told him.

Megan had started around the perimeter of the room. Russ followed, to a spiral staircase that jutted from a smaller portal near the wall.

She slung the knapsack farther up her shoulder, and started down.

As Russ followed her onto familiar crescent moon and star patterned stairs, a voice spoke below, in the next chamber. "Saknussen," it said, low and glum, with vivid sibilants. "Maybe thirty minutes."

"An hour," said another, paler voice. "Slower with two, remember."

"Look. It's Miss Sumner."

"Yes." The second voice grew hush. "And here comes Mister Kent."

They stood by the curving wall—Obolus, bald but for a fringe of black hair, and Danace with curls like wet wood.

Their round, gray faces gazing up.

"Evening, Miss Sumner," said Obolus, with a bow. "Mister Kent."

"Miss Sumner. Mister Kent."

Russ greeted them, over the lingering rattle of the staircase.

Both Stans wore long leather coats dusted green at the hem; shirts with antique trim and double-buttoned collars; voluminous brown trousers; tall black boots, as well as metal-framed goggles hanging around their necks.

"We've been expecting you, Miss," said Obolus.

"Indeed, Miss," said Danace; more talkative here, it seemed, than upstairs.

"Thanks. Is the elevator working?"

"It's on the Renworth level, Miss. But it should be free by the time we reach it. Danace . . ."

With surprising alacrity, the Stans gathered up doughboy helmets from a card table beside the stairs, and pushed in their folding chairs. Obolus took a keyring full of keys, and slipped it into his side pocket. "Now's a good time to visit, ma'am. Everyone's busy with the first local batch of cheese."

The clink of metal echoed out, and down.

Russ stepped close to the grillwork, touched the cold iron. A similar chamber lay below, and another below that—no elevator in sight. Cables and counterweights dropping down. More round portals in the floor of each chamber, and the smaller portals on the side, each clockwise from the last.

When he looked back, Megan and Obolus were waiting near the next staircase.

Walking there, Russ touched the glowing jade of the wall. It was cold. His hand looked gray against it.

Danace, behind him, said quietly, "We charge with metal halide lamps, sir, every few days."

Obolus nodded from the stairs. "This chamber's a bit overdue, as you can see. If you're ready, sir and Miss." He started down, followed by Megan.

Russ gripped the black iron rail, the entire staircase swaying. Holding the walking stick high enough to miss the stairs, below and above, he climbed around and down, through the floor.

Into a slightly different acoustic.

The stairs ended on a threadbare Oriental rug.

To his right was a sofa, somewhat dusty, and a table with a pair of Tiffany lamps. Both of the stained glass shades were cracked, and missing some pieces.

Obolus led the way along the wall, past a musty rolltop desk and a bookcase crowded with photographs. Several had toppled. The largest of those standing was a portrait of silver-haired Joseph Evening beside his thuggish partner, Halbert Chalmers.

Next to a portrait of Peggy Chalmers, plump-cheeked and beaming.

A plaque read:

CHALMERS CHAMBER.
IN MEMORIAM HALBERT CHALMERS, FIRST CITIZEN
JANUARY 2, 1961

Russ's eyes only now registered the faint gray shapes on the luminous wall—figures with long, multiply-jointed arms and legs, and elongated heads. Figures like the statue on Mrs. Nelson's lawn, hundreds of them, striking different poses. Limbs raised, lowered, crooked. Figures crouching like spiders.

Obolus said, "Old wallpaper's what I call it, sir."

Russ stopped, and looked around.

Danace, almost knocking into him, ventured, "Sir?"

Russ gestured to the wall, the furniture. The portraits. "Strange," he muttered.

"Strange, sir?"

Russ nodded, looking around. "Everything," he said.

Obolus softly chuckled. "It's strange to find any of you upper folk here, sir." Ducking, and with a placid grin he added, "Farther along, sir, you'll think it's even stranger when you find the rest of the town."

"Aberfoyle Chamber," Obolus announced in the next chamber, as they wended their way through Victorian furniture.

The wall had more of the "wallpaper," though most of it was hidden behind bookcases, a scratched oak ottoman, and a dresser with a vanity mirror, all of which served to dim the green of the chamber, and cast vague shadows.

There were jeweled boxes, more old photographs; a Victrola laid with an old shellac record.

Several photographs had toppled. Obolus righted one as he stepped past.

Down the next staircase, Russ found a maple cabinet stocked with fishing floats, polished pebbles, and driftwood, as well as photographs of resplendently-dressed women: the Storm Watchers, gathered around a punchbowl, at a picnic table, and barefoot on the beach.

CLARKSON CHAMBER

FEBRUARY, 1962

Russ remembered Peggy's friend from the Gathering, and found a portrait of her, next to a portrait of Joe on a cracked vanity—the long-faced woman with platinum hair, and a magisterial gaze: Patricia Burle-Clarkson.

The *Ryan Chamber* was full of plush furniture, as well as various portraits, and—most surprisingly— a dozen of the bristling, blind fish, the hycopathius, posed on a bookshelf. They looked at home among the glowing green stone, but not among the furniture.

The *Burle Chamber* was lined with photographs documenting the construction of the factory—timber spars on the hilltop; a clearing surrounded by thick blackberries and salal; a horse and carriage under a huge "e" sign; white-hatted employees posing before gleaming vats; a young Bob Burle grinning and shaking hands with a young Barber-Mayor, perhaps only a barber then.

Walking past an overstuffed chair, Russ felt the ache in his knees and calves; an urge to sit down into its comfortable cushion. He was getting tired, but wouldn't ask to stop, wouldn't slow Megan down: she was already following Obolus down the next staircase.

They continued, around the circumferences of chambers, past the personal photographs, Obolus or Danace righting those that had fallen over, Obolus leading and Danace lingering behind Russ, as he climbed down, more slowly.

"Yarrow chamber," Obolus announced.

Rounding the staircase, Russ caught only the edge of the stair with his heel. He stumbled, fell back, his elbow hitting the rail, his right hip and thigh striking the stairs.

The pain arrived an instant later, darting up his hip and lower back; he grimaced against it.

"Russ?" She moved back, up the stairs.

"Yeah." He struggled up, and continued down to the next chamber. "I'm okay."

"We're resting, Russ. There's a bench. C'mon."

She took his arm, walking him past a rolltop desk, a water cooler, to an iron bench. Won't rest for long, he told himself. Just catch my breath.

He grabbed the arm of the bench, and sank down, leaned back.

Megan took out the bottle of water, popped the top, handed it to Russ.

He drank—suddenly quite thirsty—then forced himself to stop. He leaned back, shut his eyes.

Megan stood. "Better?"

Clearing his throat, he nodded. Trying to look as though he were just catching his breath. "Yeah."

Perhaps it had been a mistake to sit down. Gravity weighed heavy on his shoulders, his chest, his legs.

How deep?

Remembering that tiny square of light far overhead in the tunnel, he pictured it receding. Daylight and fresh air, rain, the surf.

His throat constricted. He swallowed back the taste of copper and opened his eyes. Megan stood near the wall, staring down at her shoes.

He blinked again.

At what had emerged behind her.

Colors on the green stone.

Groups of color reacting as chords, near and far, as the walls vanished.

He shut his eyes, hearing it linger, and a moment later, looked again.

Strange chordal combinations with the silvery *neumes*—the runes—intensely clear, imprinting the air, weaving among chords near and far, and all of it was an immense processional starting and stopping under his eyes, as he looked from point to point.

Megan, leaning against the wall, was unaware of what surrounded her.

She was looking down at the floor. Past it. He followed her glance: silence snapped over him. Staring at his boots, he gripped the wolf head, felt the ears bite his palm. He stood up.

Danace, behind him, said, "Almost to the elevator, sir."

Nodding, Russ followed Megan to the next stairway, resisting the urge to look back. Climbing down.

"Bicuspids!" announced a voice below.

Russ followed Megan down and around, to another chamber of antique furniture, where an old man sat in a straight-backed chair, facing a desk. Another portrait of Joe stared back.

The cage stood open onto the elevator, a scarred wood platform in a metal frame.

"Mister Renworth, sir?" Obolus approached.

The old man startled, turned. Narrow, wrinkled face, aquiline nose, flat brown eyes. "Hey, Stan-oh!" He grinned.

It was Arthur, the Sinatra fan, in a plaid sweater and checkered slacks.

"Mister Renworth, you're missing the Cheese Taste-athon, sir."

Arthur blinked, past Obolus, and grinned up at Russ. Yellowed dentures. "You're that composer fella."

Russ raised his hand. "Hi, Arthur."

Obolus said, "Mister Renworth, we're going to be taking the lift. Perhaps you'd like to join us? Come back up here tomorrow?"

Russ leaned on his walking stick, tried to surreptitiously catch his breath.

"He was a gentleman," said the old man certainly, then gestured to the portrait.

"Yes," said Obolus, "he certainly was."

Arthur nodded. "Strong anterior teeth. Incisors and cuspids. Though I recall he had an old composite. From an infected root? Eh?"

He looked around, and seemed to notice Danace and Megan for the first time.

Arthur struggled to his feet, with Obolus rushing to help him.

"Can't say the same for you, Stans."

"We do like our sweets, sir."

Arthur squinted down at Obolus. "Good lads, though."

"Yes, sir. You're certainly right. I remember the experience only too well."

Holding him by the elbows, Obolus led Arthur into the lift, where Megan and Danace waited.

Russ followed.

The platform swayed, clanging against the edge of the cage in dolorous D flat.

"Hold on, sirs," Obolus said.

Russ threaded his fingers through the grillwork.

Danace held Arthur's arm.

At the control box, Obolus pushed a big green button; the lift shuddered and dropped, a ratcheting sound far above, as they dropped past the thick, curved portal into another chamber, and down.

As the chambers rose past them—the antique furniture and portraits, against glowing walls—Russ leaned against the grill, and listened.

"I remember you, Danny," Arthur was saying to Danace. "Caries! First and second bicuspids! I recall a third molar. Wisdom tooth. Had to extract it."

"Yes," said Danace, staring down. "You're right, sir. That's a certainty."

The ratcheting and reeling of lines, and its echo, broadening below. Not long now.

Megan stood with her eyes shut, likewise gripping the cage, and the elevator thundered through the last portal—space stretching out on all sides beyond the elevator cage, to vast, vaulted green ceilings and crumbling walls, like a sunken cathedral.

He tried to gauge the size by the maze of a hundred or more pallets and boxes below, the tall racks, the scaffolding on the far wall, where fissures of tumbled green rock were roped off with sawhorses—perhaps the pioneer tunnels, the attempts to break outside the chamber, dozens of them visible.

The elevator clanked down, settling.

Obolus rolled open the door, and stood holding it, while Danace took Mister Renworth's arm. "This way, Mister Renworth. . . ."

The ex-dentist stepped out of the lift. Russ followed, looking down at the scuffed green rock, then at the ceiling, which was vaulted at the edges, and faintly luminous. Nearer the elevator, bundles of wires dropped into pipes that snaked out of sight, or into plastic runners set along the aisles.

There were pallets of Northern Yeast Company boxes, others marked *rennet*, and *Dry Cement*, as well as yellow boxes with the "e" logo, and a portrait of Joe.

Obolus smiled up. "This is all there was to the empire for twenty-eight years."

Just beside the cage, under the electric lines, was a desk, with three rotary phones lined up beside a TV monitor, and an instrument panel marked in black felt pen on masking tape: *Elevator Override Do Not Touch!*; the monitor showed, in flickering gray, the room in the factory upstairs.

Obolus approached the desk. He lifted a clipboard, and the pen attached to its clasp. "I'll have to sign Stan and me in, Miss."

Megan handed him his walking stick.

Russ listened to the distant sound, tried to locate it. Against the far wall, some scaffolding was visible. The sounds came from there, what had at times sounded like faint struck bells, and bass drums, wind instruments, Aeolian harps. Now reverberating, with strange overtones, in the ceiling vaults.

Russ lifted his walking stick, clutched the wolf-head tightly, and brought the steel tip down. The impact tore the air, echoed with an enormous peal around the chamber, trailing warped overtones, strange, like the ondes martenot or theremin, and airy echoes that made little sense to the ear, fading in waves.

As though sounds had been liberated from the ancient rock.

Obolus set down the clipboard. "We got ear plugs for that, Mister Kent."

Listening to the decay, Russ resisted the urge to strike the floor again.

Megan had folded her arms in the din, lowered her head; her pale, almost gray profile staring down at the floor.

Obolus said, "Ready, Miss Sumner?"

She nodded, offered her hand to Russ.

While they wended their way through the maze of pallets—only as fast as Arthur could manage—Russ had time to focus past the mundane foreground, to what loomed on all sides. The towering walls, the vaulted ceiling, aglow. It cast shadows on the path they were following. They seemed to be working their way toward scaffolding, and some of the pioneer tunnels that were now just tumbled rock. They passed a cart of arc lights—"For charging the walls, Mister Kent," Obolus said over his shoulder—and walked around the extracted facade of a yellow-and-creme Craftsman home, towering pitifully in the gargantuan chamber, braced against tall metal racking, its front windows papered. And beyond it, where the path ended, the mouth of a tunnel into the green rock wall, sides laid with slabs of fallen stone, encased in shrink wrap.

The sounds issued from this passage. The ringing, roaring tones.

Obolus slowed. He approached an arrangement of pine branches dotted with white flowers. A metal sculpture, Russ realized. Below the black struts were artfully arranged pieces of driftwood, and in the driftwood were carved names.

Obolus stopped beside it. Arthur, looking a bit lost, stopped too.

Russ recognized the names of familiar families. Fifty, a hundred pieces. Though near the top was a piece reading, *Anna Kent*, and Danace had stopped beside him, shoulders slumped, and bowed his head.

A memorial.

Russ could barely linger at it.

"God bless 'em!" said Arthur.

Both Stans looked up at Russ, with smiles creasing their aged and ageless faces.

"Obolus made it, Mister Kent," said Danace.

"Danace helped me," said Obolus.

"Thanks," Russ said.

"Mister Kent, it was worth it," Obolus said. "You'll see, sir."

He nodded, and looked past it, toward the tunnel, and the shards of rock gathered along the edge.

"This way, sirs, and Miss." Obolus gestured, then continued on, with Arthur beside him.

As the walls and ceiling of hewn stone surrounded them, Arthur looked up and around, and shouted, vibrantly, "An edentulous passageway! To the land of cheddar and havarti!"

*e*vening's empire

The tunnel's end was a flat, faintly luminous square.

From this distance, it revealed no depths to the eye, though to Russ's ear a new acoustic was unfolding. The struck-bell tones, the wind tones, were fluctuating back and forth, near and far, over the *cantus firma* of roaring water—the underground river. Between these two extremes, faint enough to be lost and found again, were voices, laughter, the bark of a small dog, the tattoo of hammers, chisels, mallets striking stone, near and far, and gossamer wind chimes spangling, as the square gained a visible dimension.

A sense of space stretching out, in shades of green and white and gray.

"Flew!" a voice shouted—Old Crick's voice, from the left—echoing to the right, as the group reached the end of the tunnel. The walls and ceiling vanished. A vast space skirted with limestone stretched before them, relieving the sense of claustrophobia, then increasing it. He sought something familiar, found a concrete planter overflowing with sunflowers and green shadows.

"Where's the Taste-a-thon?" croaked Arthur.

They stood on a landing at the top of a wide—tremendously wide— and shallow staircase.

Below, to the right and left, were more concrete planters, and black iron lampposts weighted with concrete blocks. And where the stairs stopped the Avenue began, rectangular slabs of green and gray, marching into the distance.

"Danny, where's the Taste-a-thon?"

"Town Hall, sir," said Danace.

In the distance, a piccolo, or a sea gull, shrieked.

"Too far."

Russ forced his eyes to what loomed on either side. What at first had resembled limestone, faintly glowing, terracing jaggedly down to the Avenue, now bore hints of familiar architecture, a towering repetition of columns and arches, of domes, portals and rooftops over steep, shattered stairways that would have been at home at the Acropolis, or a coral grove on the bottom of the sea.

"Merilee!" A woman's voice, off to the right, echoing to the left, vividly fractured among side streets and structures, joining the bell tones overhead.

Russ listened to the low water. He tried to trace it with his ears, and finally asked Obolus.

The Stan pointed to the right. "Just past the buildings, sir. About a hundred-fifty yards. It joins the Avenue at the other end, heading in our direction."

The mineral breeze carried, fitfully, a scent of apples and baking bread.

"And if you have eyes as good as Danace, Mister Kent, you can see where it gets terribly small out there. Far Forty, we call it."

Arthur was saying to Danace: "Garbage eaters, but I don't care! Nor should you, Danny!"

"You're right, Mister Renworth."

What colors there were projected with startling clarity. On the left, a bright yellow sign with blue letters—*Under Evening Realty*. Roses in a nearby planter, more brown than red. Near an alley on the right-hand side, shreds of yellow and white that were dead rhododendron, heaped. And farther out, indistinct spots of gold, blue and purple.

"Rats with wings!" proclaimed Arthur, being led down the staircase to a bench.

Megan, standing beside Russ, was gazing out into that distance. The Far Forty. She asked Obolus, "How long will it take to get there?"

"About a half-hour one way, Miss. Danace'll be fetching the equipment."

The other Stan overheard. Once Arthur was seated, Danace nodded broadly to Obolus, then jostled off, past the structure on their left—something tumbled in ages past, now little more than a towering scree of glowing stone and a wide landing, over a shattered stairway. Centered

on the landing was a brown leather easy chair. Seated there, as though on
a throne, was Old Crick in a wooly sweater, a scarf and long gray
trousers, his head tilted against his shoulder; perhaps asleep.

Danace ran around the corner, and was gone.

Russ suddenly recognized, from out of the luminous architecture
beyond, a statue. It stood half as high as the ceiling, humanoid—similar
to Mrs. Nelson's statue, and the wallpaper in the tower—though what
remained of its features suggested an alien physiology. Standing with
arms akimbo, its long face time-worn, remote.

Russ noticed a similar statue on the right-hand side, and more, further
along. Like guardians, alive on some geological time scale, as oblivious to
the new tenants as they were to the sudden blaring tone that bounced
from wall to wall—a tuba, in mostly G flat, holding the note against its
own warbling echo, then rising half an octave.

A fanfare.

From his throne, Old Crick leapt to his feet. "Nemo!" he cried,
thrusting a bony arm out to the Avenue. "Nemo! Nemo!"

Russ looked, found a figure in the middle distance, arms folded in a
dark blue suitcoat and trousers, a white turtleneck, black boots. From
here, his face was lost beneath the brim of his hat, but as the fanfare
sounded again, Malcolm tipped back his head and intoned, vibrantly,
"*Adieu, sun! Disappear thou radiant orb!*"

"Amazing! Looking good, Russell! On your feet. Wonderful. Just wonderful."

At the base of the stairs, Malcolm smiled, lightly clapping Russ on the
shoulder, looking him up and down, an eerie intensity in his eyes. "How
you feeling?"

Tatters of fanfare, and of Malcolm's greeting, wandered the nearby
structures.

"That's hard to answer right now."

Malcolm doffed his cap and ran his fingers through tangled hair that
grew past his collar.

"Nemo! Nemo!" Old Crick waved.

"I like the walking stick. Carved, is it?"

Russ lifted it, showed the wolf head, the sharp ears, fangs.

"Looks Eastern European. Not a permanent addition, is it?"

Russ shook his head, set down the stick, and leaned. "Just for long subterranean walks."

Crick cried, against his echoes, "Nemo!"

Malcolm smiled, and raised his hand. "Yes, here I am! Prince Dakkar! Captain Nemo! Nothing!" The sleeve of his blazer was torn, the gold braid untwining.

Crick, hands cupped around his mouth, shouted, "Saw the gull, Captain! Flew right past!"

"Hey-oh!" Arthur half-stood up from the bench. "Same here! Heard it plain as day!"

Malcolm nodded broadly. "Thank you, gentlemen! But we have other business at the moment!" Malcolm donned the cap, and turned to Russ. His beard brushed against the collar of his turtleneck, dusted green. "Tired?"

Russ attempted a shrug.

"You catch the elevator?"

"Most of the way." Russ added, "I'll definitely need it for the trip back."

"Don't worry on that account, sir," said Obolus. "I have the only override key. Even if they try activating it from City Hall, I can take control. Captain, he'll have it on the way back up, sir."

Malcolm smiled. "You have the best guides, Russ. The Stans are practically natives down here. Kin to our jolly green giants."

"Thank you, sir." Obolus beamed. "We try, sir." Patting his heavy brown coat, he added. "Danace is getting the equipment, and we'll be there and back before the Taste-a-thon is over."

Malcolm nodded, slipping a hand into his side pocket, seeming to hold a pose. Captain Nemo, ruminating. Then, in a mock-casual tone, he said, "By the way, Stan, I was out at Saknussen this morning."

"Oh? Really, sir?" Obolus raised his eyebrows. "Was anything out of place, sir?"

"Not at all. Sandwich was on the table, right where I left it."

"Very good, sir."

"Check on it later, though."

"I will, sir."

Megan was waving, hailing someone off to the right. A girl in green robes, waving back, then running toward them, blonde hair like bronze.

"Hi, Megan!" The girl climbed the stairs.

Megan unslung her knapsack and set it down, kneeling beside it. "Could you do me a favor? Give these to your mom?" She drew out the sack of mail and supplies.

Leaning on the stick, Russ studied Malcolm's face, the crooked smile, the eyes, wrinkled at the corners.

Obolus said, "We heard that Misters Carver and Dreerson might be down a bit later, Captain."

"Well, that should work out," said Malcolm. "Perfect timing, really."

"Thanks, Merilee." Megan made sure the girl had a good grip, then let go, and zipped up the knapsack. "Your mom's looking for you, you know."

The girl nodded. "I know. Bye!" She hurried off.

Megan stood up, glanced at Russ, then out into the Avenue.

Malcolm said, "Did Charles ever tell you stories about Old Joe?"

Russ shook his head.

"Bernard and Tom were the storytellers."

"When Charles was a boy, Old Joe gave him his complete collection of Jules Verne, remember?"

"Yeah. You told me that."

"Marvelous books, Russ. And Old Joe told him, 'You ever want to know what Hesperus is like? Want to catch a glimpse, years before we get there? Then you just read this book, and you'll see it, in the corners of your eyes.'" Malcolm reached into his pocket and drew out a green globe—the fishing globe from Megan's living room. He lifted it to his eye. "I certainly know what he meant."

A smile.

With the globe, Malcolm gestured at the nearest structures and statues, and—as Russ feared—intoned from his libretto:

"Before us sprawling
Heaps of tumbled rock;
Shadow forms of castles, temples.
Cromlechs of a prehistoric age.

From somewhere, a tuba began blurting a G-minor arpeggio, in accompaniment to the echoes of Malcolm's voice, if not the voice itself.

A city on the ocean floor,
Drowned before time's dawn.
With new attendants,
Anemone, and shark,
Lingering patrols of a lost empire.

Against the lapping, tidal tones in somewhat-G-minor, the Captain lowered his braided cuff.

"Nemo! Over here!" cried Old Crick.

"Joe gave some of them new names from Verne, you realize? Before the town was incorporated—1905—they became Aberfoyles, and Yarrows, and Nells and Ryans."

Megan had walked a short distance with Obolus. They were talking, both looking to the side street where Danace had gone.

"Dreerson has crazy theories of his own," Malcolm said. He slipped the globe back into his pocket. "You ever read any Ignatius Donnelly, Russ?"

Russ shook his head. "You can tell me about it tomorrow." He added, "Upstairs."

Malcolm smiled, and scratched his beard. "Not tomorrow."

"A few days, then," Russ said.

"Nemo! Over here!"

Malcolm shrugged. "Hard to tell at this point. A situation is developing, Russ. Small town politics, you know the sort. And Nemo has a role in the unfolding drama." He grinned. "Anyway, it's a helluva climb upstairs. I'm waiting for the ski-lift. Yes, Mister Crick! Shortly!"

A metallic squeak and clatter: a cart of giant lamps being dragged, a man in dungarees on the left. It was Georgie Aberfoyle from the gas station. Tugging on the orange power line that whipped and snapped across the expanse of stone.

Obolus approached him, and murmured something. Georgie shook his head, spat, and replied in the same murmuring tones. After conferring with Megan, Obolus jogged back to Russ and Malcolm.

"Recharge about to go, Captain. Mister Kent, you'll have to hide your eyes like this." He briefly thrust his face into the crook of his elbow. "The walls'll take the light, and for a minute everything will be too bright."

Malcolm, with that eerie smile, said, "You'll like this, Russ."

Obolus drew earplugs from his shirt pocket, and stuffed them in place.

"Charging!" Aberfoyle called out.

On his throne, Old Crick flung his arm over his face.

A buzzer sounded, into the distance.

Megan startled, shut her eyes, covered them with her hand.

Russ had his face in the crook of his elbow. A sudden brilliance, as the sounds, the echoes, jolted up by microtones, and he pressed his face tighter into the crook, heat tingling across his exposed skin. Another switch was thrown: the light began to fade, but slowly, lingering.

"Wait, sir," said Obolus, and his voice was three voices, separated by microtones. "Fades quickly in the first minute."

Russ made sure of his balance, then raised the walking stick a few inches, and brought the tip down: the impact tore the air, whirling round. Opening his eyes against the bright fabric of his jacket, he lowered his arm and looked on shining yellow—as the impact, whirling, fading, joined the bell tones overhead.

He blinked.

The others stood covering their eyes. All but Malcolm, the gray Captain, who stood with arms folded, squinting at Russ, smiling. "Quite a concert, right?"

Three voices.

Russ nodded. He added, in a loud voice, "I love it."

Three voices.

He smiled.

Obolus pulled his arm away, blinked; then Megan, squinting, her eyes somewhat startled-looking as she opened them wider.

"Here comes Danace, Miss. We'll be leaving shortly."

Of Obolus's three voices, two had become obvious echoes, with the microtonal split lessening.

Malcolm removed his hat, then wiped his forehead with his sleeve.

"Come along with us, Malcolm."

The Captain shook his head. "I'll see you on the return trip."

Megan touched Russ's arm. "Ready?"

"Are we walking it?"

Malcolm laughed. "Down here we're more civil than that, Russell. Right, Stan?"

"Yes, sir." Obolus gestured, out to the brilliant Avenue, and Danace, who was leading the transportation toward them. "A pair of bicycles built for two."

They were old two-seaters, sturdy, with a chipped blue frame, large square pedals, and sidebags full of equipment. Russ rode with Obolus on the first bicycle, and Megan with Danace on the second.

"I can take it from here, Mister Kent."

Behind them the brilliance had faded, but still cast their vague shadows ahead of them.

No longer in immediate danger of falling, Russ allowed the pedals to revolve under his boots, and glanced around.

On the other bicycle, to his left, Megan sat straight, clutching the handlebars, oblivious to the procession of structures behind her, the shadowless limestone from which emerged columns, arches, portals, buttresses, roofs and towers suggesting, sometimes simultaneously, stolid Egyptian tombs, Grecian temples, Gothic cathedrals, and Antoni Gaudí's Barcelona architecture, and all of it made more strange by the everyday items grafted onto the lower floors. Chintz drapes in an oblong portal. Wooden shutters. White-panelled doors, screen doors. A box planter.

And business signs of varying shape, size and colors—*Under Evening Diner, Parker's Laundromat*—hung above, set beside, the maw-like entrances, with the massive landings furnished with chairs, sofas, lamps, artful arrangements of driftwood, green fishing floats in silvery nets, and all of it in comparative shadow next to the luminous stone.

Street signs, set at the edge of a building, weighed with concrete blocks: *Avenue* and *Burle Street. Avenue* and *Chalmers Blvd.*

Hesperus Grocery (open 24–7). Aberfoyle's Fixit.

To the right, a clutter of garbage cans.

The antique black-iron lampposts were becoming more frequent, marking lanes at the edge of the Avenue, along with familiar mailboxes, and a newspaper dispenser, empty.

New Empire Florist

The side streets looked more like staging areas, crowded with full pallets, ladders, odd pieces of furniture, a forklift, spare doors, cases of bottled water.

To the right, streets terminated in darkness, river roaring, rattling the garbage cans.

And all the streets, so far, had been empty of people. The only inhabitants were the statues; images of the former inhabitants, or perhaps of their gods, the elongated figures, with remote faces that looked even less than human, more reptilian.

Some had colorful fabrics hung from their arms. Some with wind chimes. Most had heaps of objects on their pedestals or on the stairs below: green glass globes, rhododendron, azalea, roses.

Russ looked past Obolus, to the center of the Avenue where, surrounded by lampposts and benches, stood an old-fashioned bandstand with white trellised walls, capped with a gold rooster weathervane. Its stage, set with folding chairs and music stands, was empty.

A banner read: *Taste-a-thon! Taste the first batch! At City Hall!*

The voices—a congregation, distantly cheering.

Russ traced it to the right side of the Avenue, where rows of spruce trees flanked a massive staircase, and a broad, dizzying facade. Vertical seams in the rock, columns and lintels at strange angles jutting into view. It seemed to unfold at their approach, shadowless, revealing a puzzling geometry.

TASTE-A-THON! read the banner overhead, beside another statue.

"Municipal Town Hall," Obolus announced, over his shoulder, as the voices firmly located themselves within the structure's front door, a massive parallelogram framed in blinking Christmas lights.

A statue stood guard beside the door, remote, serene, its clasped hands now fitted with a familiar blue and gold medallion. A Rotary Club shield.

Obolus, then Danace, steered to the far side of the bandstand, around concrete planters and lampposts, past a number of smaller facades facing Town Hall—the *Evening Barber Shop* most prominent, with its barber pole set on the ground beside the oblong door.

Thundering applause, rising and fading from the river noise.

Obolus began to pedal harder; Russ joined him, with Danace and Megan keeping up.

There were fewer lampposts ahead; the structures becoming decrepit, collapsing into rubble.

The river's roar, the bell-tone was receding, echoes oscillating among the ruins.

Ahead, green rock merged with shadow.

First Obolus, and then Danace, switched on their lamps.

Where the light fell the rocky ground took up the glow, so that two wavering trails of light were left behind.

The bicycles bumped off the last of the slabs, onto what looked like hard packed sand. The remaining structures, encroaching from either side, were tumbled, time-worn.

"Far Forty, sir," announced Obolus. His voice had lost the unusual resonance, reduced to familiar fundamentals and overtones.

Silence, or relative silence, descended with the basalt ceiling. The sand shone silver and gray in the lamplight, and retained none of the lamp's glow.

Russ straightened on the seat. He grimaced at a cramp in his thigh.

"Ground's a bit topsy-turvy up ahead, Mister Kent."

Ahead, the ground darkened, and seemed to rise up. Lamplight caught the edge of a swell, blue and silver.

"I see it."

"Miss Sumner," Danace was saying, "You'll have to hold on tight."

She gripped the handlebars, looking past Danace.

The swell loomed.

Russ held on, pedalling harder as the bicycle climbed, five, ten feet, up and over, lamplight swinging out and down—another wave-like swell beyond, silvery blue, and more beyond it, into the dark.

"Mister Dreerson calls them speed-bumps," Obolus said, in the lull before the next one.

Waves, Russ thought, as Obolus started pedalling harder, leaning over the handlebars, and the bicycle began to climb.

There were six more swells, the sand becoming blue in the troughs, silver at the crests, and finally, as they ended, a deep blue under a basaltic ceiling, which was lowering, creating a natural acoustic.

A plain of blue sand, into dark on either side.

Dark ahead, too.

Then the headlamps found something. A card table, and four folding chairs.

Various boxes, a cooler.

Closer, he could see *ACL* scrawled on the boxes. Next to the cooler was a bottled water dispenser, and rolled-up sleeping bags.

A beer bottle stood on the otherwise empty table.

First Danace, then Obolus, applied their brakes. The squeak echoed vibrantly—realistically.

Russ stepped down with his right boot, held the bicycle steady for Obolus, then climbed off.

Obolus extended the kickstand; the bicycle stood at an extreme angle.

Russ stretched, grimacing.

A sign taped to the nearest chair read *Saknussen Point, Oregon*, in Malcolm's jagged handwriting.

Beyond, the sand ended. Volcanic basalt, like a shoreline, growing into stalactites and stalagmites, faintly silvered in the light.

"Russ." She offered the walking stick, and he took it.

"Thanks."

Her face was pale, half of it tinged with green; her eyes, too, glancing to the table and chairs.

"Mister Carver's base camp, Miss," Obolus said.

Looking back, Russ was surprised at how far they'd come.

The Avenue was now a cocoon of brilliant green in the black, its structures tremendously foreshortened.

"Lighthouse at the end of the world, Captain calls it, Miss."

A toy bandstand in the center. Tiny evergreen trees.

The sounds were foreshortened, too.

"How much farther?" She was past the table now, staring into the dark.

"A few hundred yards. Beyond the outcroppings."

Danace glanced at something on the ground nearby.

The remains of a sandwich.

Obolus looked, too. Half the bread was gone, with only a few shreds of roast beef remaining. "But we could bring it out here, Miss," he added. "If you'd like, you and Mister Kent could wait at the camp. There's some snacks in the cooler."

Her eyes were on the basalt. Headlamps shone through it, as if through a forest. "We'll go with you," she said.

Obolus gave a half-nod, and glanced at Danace. "Then it'll be just a moment, Miss."

Russ approached the table. The boxes were full of rope, cans of food, an airhorn, and what looked like climbing equipment.

On the ground beside it was a fishing net.

"Excuse me, sir." Danace lifted the net, whose aluminum handle was taller than him.

Obolus, meanwhile, returned to the bicycles and drew two helmets—bright Evening yellow—from the side bags. Mining lamps were fixed to the brims.

He handed one up to Megan, the other to Russ.

"Mister Kent, if you would put this on, sir."

It was bulky. Ill-fitting. He pushed it firmly down, fumbled for the switch on the brim.

The resulting light was weak: out of focus.

Danace was crouching beside the sandwich, nonchalantly picking it up, and dropping it into his side pocket.

Megan clicked on her lamp.

"If you're ready, Miss."

She nodded.

"Sir, this way." Glancing once last time around the camp, Obolus switched on his flashlight, then led them into the mineral forest.

The lights flared on basaltic rock, leaning through, as Megan followed Obolus, with Russ behind her, and Danace trailing several yards back. Stalactites and stalagmites growing clockwork shadows as they passed by.

He blinked against a dampness in the air, tried to catch glimpses of Megan, the side of her face, widening eyes, watchful.

Danace's flashlight shining past, then out to either side.

Pressure on his eardrums, his throat. He forced a yawn. He began to count the steps, but before he'd reached twenty, he was distracted by Megan's breathing, echoing off the rock.

She was looking down, breathing through clenched teeth.

Quietly: "Megan."

She glanced back. "Yeah." She drew a deep breath, and nodded.

Obolus, slowing down, offered, "It's safer than it looks, Miss. And not much farther."

She adjusted her helmet, which had begun to slide. "It looks old." Louder: "How old is it, Obolus?"

"Old as Earth, maybe, Miss." Obolus was quiet for a few paces, then, as if realizing this wasn't conversation as much as distraction, added, "Mister Carver has all sorts of theories. What with all the measurements and samples he's been taking. He's always telling us about the strata of rock hereabouts, and how it isn't local rock. Not *igneous*, that's the term he uses. Which doesn't make a lot of sense, I think."

Russ glanced right, and left, with the light like water.

Bottom of the sea, he thought.

And Jack Sumner—his body, somewhere ahead.

He swallowed, tasting minerals.

Turning his thoughts.

If this were a Verne book (he told himself) then Jack would have left behind a journal. It would be found near his bones, in dust, and it would explain—would reduce to the mundane—how he'd broken through from the pioneer tunnel. How, alone, in the almost total dark, he'd wandered the ancient streets and beyond, as its first human inhabitant. And here, in the dark, had penned his last entry. A message to Megan. A consolation. A blessing from beyond.

Or a riddle. A cipher.

A drawing.

Thoughts turning.

To his right, a scuffle. The air shook. Movement, a sweep of wings gray and white, at Russ.

Screeching.

Danace cast the net which clattered against the ceiling.

The gull flew off.

"Sir?"

His heart pounded.

An afterimage of the gull's frightened eye, and the sound of its cry, though the cry had faded.

"I'm okay."

Wings rustling in the distance.

"Russ?"

"Yeah." Heart pounding. Struggling for an even tone, he said, "How'd a . . . a gull get down here?" He readjusted his lopsided helmet, wanting to toss it aside.

Danace, gripping the net, was peering ahead of them, out of where the gull had flown.

"It was Miss Chalmers, sir," said Obolus. "She suggested strongly that folks bring down pets, sir. Animals, too, to add a touch of home. We have a raccoon, somewhere, sir. And several trout in the river, though they've died already. All the animals tend to flee into the Far Forty because of the quiet, sir." Then said to Megan, "If you're ready?"

She nodded.

They continued, flashlight beams darting around more suspiciously than before, out and around, shadows sweeping, until the light broke free of basalt, onto another stretch of blue sand, under a vaulted basalt ceiling.

And directly ahead, a glossy yellow tarp, folded over, and an unlit lantern.

Megan tightened her grip on the knapsack.

Obolus stepped clear of the basalt, and to one side, steadying his flashlight on the tarp, and under it, a hint of wood.

She said something. Hesitating there at the edge.

Watching, Russ was reminded of his dreams, of clambering across the ocean floor in a bulky diving suit. She stepped out, and with a similar gait, started across the sand toward it.

Obolus trailed, his flashlight pooling on the tarp, the blond wood of the casket. He knelt, and a moment later the lantern's light raised the nearby sand to turquoise.

Silver flecks glinting in the basalt overhead.

The ground was sloping down, Russ realized. The angle was slight, but there. Dark blue, merging with black.

Obolus drew back the tarp where it was folded over, revealing the open casket, and shadows. The only spot without color. The bones.

She stood, staring down.

Danace joined Obolus on the far side, both lowering their heads, with hands folded in front of them.

Megan took off her helmet. Dropped it on the sand. She unshouldered her knapsack.

Planting the stick in the sand, gripping the wolf, Russ shut his eyes. He remembered a prayer and recited it, aware of rustling sound as Megan knelt, of her saying something under her breath.

Metal jangling, faintly.

He opened his eyes.

The Stans had stepped further back—farther down— and now peered in different directions, aiming their flashlights into the dark.

Russ forced himself forward, and downward, heavily, sluggishly, across the blue sand, bypassing the tarp and casket, toward the Stans, and slightly past them. Aware of another sound, faintly audible, at the bottom of this blue decline.

A thread of river roar. Perhaps the Avenue's river. Or some subterranean cataract.

Entirely black, except for a faint orange mote.

Beside him, Obolus saw it, too. Shone his light there: pale orange. A blob.

Russ whispered, "What . . ."

What is it?

Obolus glanced to Danace, then whispered back, "Wait here, sir."

He set out, clambering down the sand toward it, boots striking with soft plashes, flashlight quivering down blue to the orange blob, settling.

Russ suddenly wanted to call him back.

But Obolus was next to it, looking down. He crouched.

Lifted it.

Then he turned to Russ, held it up for Russ to see—the orange blob—and a moment later started back, clutching the thing, which became recognizable.

Though Russ resisted the idea.

It was the cheese bust.

Obolus, out of breath, said, "Looks like Mister Burle's work, sir."

The face in a hard waxy crust, almost unrecognizable, except for the beard.

Obolus offered it to Russ.

Russ hesitated, then took it with his left hand.

"Burle . . . brought it down here?"

Obolus replied, "Oh, no, sir." He glanced at his partner. "Mister Carver or Mister Dreerson would most likely have to explain, sir."

Russ dropped it. It rolled, and came to a halt face down. "Obolus . . ."

But Obolus and Danace had started back toward Megan. Russ followed.

She was sitting back on her heels, against the Avenue's distant green glow. With her hands on her knees, she stood up. What had been in the knapsack now lay beside the anonymous skull and bones. The portrait of Jack from her bedroom. A sand dollar. A green fishing globe. And Jack's recorder.

Wiping strands of hair from her eyes, she stepped back, then looked up, at Russ.

Her eyes shining in the lamplight. Softly: "Okay." She smiled. "Let's go."

She took his hand.

"Gladly, Miss," said Obolus, grinning.

"Yes, Miss," Danace agreed. "Gladly."

*d*ie tote stadt

The distant Avenue grew steadily larger, its green glow swallowing the basalt, the silver and blue swells, the first of the slabs where trails of lamplight lingered.

The bell tones, the wind tones, oscillated among the first of the ruins, as the structures farther on became clear, with their colorful signs, benches, concrete planters. Directly ahead, the toy bandstand, its gold rooster weathervane winking.

The river roaring to the left, and overhead. The first of the newspaper dispensers. A mailbox.

The bicycles picked up speed. Megan and Danace were almost outpacing them. All the strangeness of the Far Forty, and the Stans' unwillingness to discuss it, became less important in the face of this momentum. It would carry them the length of the Avenue, and further, up the levels of the tower, up the Joseph Evening Memorial Tunnel, to the factory.

Back to the hilltop, and a rainy day.

Which, briefly, seemed fanciful—unreachable in the same way Hesperus had once seemed.

But it wasn't this that made him suddenly uneasy.

It was the stillness ahead.

He listened, and watched the Town Hall unfold its strange facade on their left. No sounds beyond the river's roar, the bell tones, the wind tones, overhead. No sounds wandering the miles of ruins to the right—no hammer strikes, no voices. No sounds of a congregation.

But the citizens weren't gone.

Russ stopped pedalling.

Ahead, stretching from the Hall's staircase, across the Avenue before the bandstand, to the other side, was a banner of mostly green fabric.

Danace glanced over at Obolus. Megan stopped pedalling.

Not a banner, not a bolt of mostly green fabric—but a line of people, mostly in green robes, some in dungarees, in shirts and jeans, standing side by side.

Some with cowls. Others with faces becoming clear, gently smiling.

In the bandstand, musicians were seated on the folding chairs. Andrea, conspicuous by her hair, raised her pale arm.

A tuba sounded an E, a clarinet joined it, and a piano, outlining a slow, up-and-downward stepping melody, the largo from Dvorak's *Ninth*.

"We'll have to stop, sir," Obolus called back.

He applied the brakes. Both bicycles squealed to a halt near the pine trees in their metal stands. After a moment spent watching the crowd— those closest seemed to mouth *hello*—kickstands were deployed.

Glancing at Russ, Megan hung the empty knapsack over the handlebar. She handed him the walking stick.

"Megan!" The voice was hard to track, wobbling right to left. "Megan! Russell!"

At the top of the staircase, Peggy Chalmers strode into view, in a swirl of yellow robes wrapped in gold string. From the string hung sand dollars, bits of carved driftwood: little moons and stars. As she started down they swayed, clacked together. "Megan, *dear*." Her eyes shone in a sapphire cocoon. Her hair, in dozens of bent plaits, jutted out in all directions. "It must have been a *difficult* journey. Oh, you *must* come inside, and sit down for a few minutes. Megan, you both look positively *exhausted*."

Halfway down, she paused, head tilted. "And Russell, you haven't seen our hall. Oh, and the festival is underway—our first batch of native cheddar. You simply *must* try some." Her voice had softened, while her greeting still lapped sharply at the faraway walls.

Megan was looking at the crowd, or past it. Then she called up, "For a little while, Peggy."

"Splendid! This way, this way!"

Trinkets clacking, Peggy whirled around, floated up the stairs.

"We'll wait here, Miss," Obolus said. "And tend the bicycles."

She said, "Won't be long."

Russ climbed, resisting the urge to use the stick. But he was winded halfway up, his knees aching. Peggy was already at the top, standing under the statue with its Rotary Club medallion.

He stopped, leaned, catching his breath. He looked back. The crowd was quietly climbing—stopping now. Staring up.

Some smiling.

Some clutching little plastic knives, or plastic cups.

The music was off-tempo: piano tripping over clarinet and tuba. Andrea was standing at the edge of the bandstand, watching him.

"This way, Russell!"

He continued, using the walking stick, as Andrea turned back to the musicians, recovering the beat with broad sweeps of her arm. When he reached the top, Peggy was rushing through the angle of the trapezoidal entrance where it met the floor. Russ and Megan followed, into a massive space.

Lamps of varying sizes dotted the gloom; a hint of vaults overhead, of twisting staircases and landings, around an open space. His eyes were drawn to the center, and the Christmas lights twinkling on a tall rectangular pedestal of black stone.

Atop, trimmed with rhododendron and pine fronds, was the sculpture of Joseph Evening, arms folded, asleep.

Dozens of dinner tables surrounded it, with candles on the white linen, plates full of cheese, and empty plates, and wineglasses.

Whispers reflecting overhead as the crowd shuffled in, and returned to their chairs. Scrapes of metal on stone, rustling robes, pleased grunts, while in the background, resonating naturally inside, the largo for the *New World* symphony played on.

"This way!" Peggy waited at the other side. "We'll chat in my office!"

Passing the black stone, he read a plaque in the nest of red, green and yellow lights.

Herein Lies Joseph Evening
1876–1959
As he Foretold
His Empire Resplendent

"Watch out for the extension cords!" Peggy cautioned.

Carefully, they followed her along one of the aisles, past citizens in robes and cowls. Russ held the walking stick like a pool cue.

On the far wall were brass squares and vague faces: the portraits from the Hall of Founders.

"Megan, dear." Evie Renworth—Arthur's wife—smiling pearlily up; and across from her, wielding a plastic knife, was the long-faced Patricia Burle-Clarkson in yellow robes, her platinum hair fraying around her shoulders. "Come talk to me afterwards, would you, dear?"

Megan didn't respond.

Other citizens called out, "Megan." "Bless you, Megan." "Joe's blessing."

The cheese smell intensified as they neared tables stocked with trays of cheddar, Swiss, havarti.

Peggy beckoned. "This way, this way!" She passed through a divide in ruffled display curtains.

The backstage. Stacks of boxes labelled *Salt, Calcium Chloride, Anatto, Extract of Rennet*. Pallet jacks. Extra lamps.

Through another curtain they came upon Bob Burle in green robes, cowl flung back from his sharp widow's peak. He held a scalpel. "Peg."

"Oh, there you are, Bob! Oh my! Oh! Look at it!"

She gaped up at a twenty-foot tall statue of herself—Peggy Chalmers in blazer, skirt and high heels, the face eerily recognizable, even from this angle, with its plump-cheeked, wide-eyed grin gazing at the ceiling, or beyond it.

"Oh, I'm a little embarrassed, Bob! You're *supposed* to keep this out of sight!"

Bob's steady eyes looked left, right. "Nobody's been prowling back here but you, Peg." He nodded to Russ. "Mister Kent. Afternoon, Meg."

"Make sure nobody sees it." Peggy smiled, and untangled her trinkets. "We don't want to blow the surprise, do we? I'm holding you to it! This way, Russell, Megan!"

She led them to a gap in the next wall of partitions, floating past several Tiffany lamps that cast colorfully on her robes, into an area roughly five times the size of her old office. The walls were tacked full of notices, pie charts, graphs. Filing cabinets lined one end, with a typing desk, a conference table, stacks of boxes. "Still moving in. All temporary, of course. But so exciting!"

She led them to the far corner, and her desk, with the driftwood sign

Peggy C on a stack of papers. She clicked on a small lamp. Arranging her robes, untangling trinkets, she sat down, folding her arms in front of her, crescent moons and stars collapsing on the blotter, a rill of stones.

Against the backdrop of pie charts and partitions, she was suddenly the only strange thing in sight.

"Russell, please. Megan, please sit down."

A moment later, without unshouldering the knapsack, Megan sat down. Then Russ. The chair was wonderfully comfortable.

Peggy watched them, then reasserted her smile.

Watching Megan over her folded hands, she said softly, "You resent us, Megan, I know. Perhaps you have every right to." She looked down at the blotter. "At this moment, after such an awful trip . . ."

From Megan, a hint of a smile. She wiped hair away from her eyes then shook her head, and the smile was gone.

"Though there's another way to look at it, dear. That Joseph has brought you a gift of peace. And you, too, Russell. In a very real way, Joseph brought you back to Evening, after your tragedy. Brought you to our dear Megan." With the tip of her middle finger, Peggy wiped tears from both eyes; sapphire stained. "Praise Joe." Blinking them away, she said, "What you need to think about now, both of you, is *property*." She straightened in the chair, patted the blotter, then the nearby stacks of paper. "If you'll forgive me for mixing business with pleasure . . ." Grinning, she glanced down at the floor behind her desk, leaned out of sight then re-emerged, holding a large cardboard sheet by the top corners. A blueprint, many narrow white lines on blue, innumerable detail too small to read.

She lifted it onto her lap, and smiled over it.

"You've seen this before, Megan. This is our new layout, Russell. These are the new lots. If I could . . . I want to point out a *lovely* new property that's just become available. Quite roomy, wonderfully Gothic, I think." She tapped a spot with her index finger, near the middle of the blueprint. "It's *perfectly placed*, a few doors south of us here. The cross street is lacking a name at the moment, but I think *Jack Sumner Way* would be ideal, Megan, and I'll be championing the idea in the next zoning committee meeting. As a thank-you gift, from Joseph, and from the town."

Megan smiled again, the slight smile, and brushed her hand across her face. "We're leaving, Peggy."

She stood up.

"But, dear, you have to stay for the afternoon, at least. You'll miss all the fun."

"Bye, Peggy."

Leaning on his walking stick, Russ stood up.

The music, he noticed, was stumbling to a halt.

Peggy sat unmoving, her face a colorful mask. The newfound silence was broken by chairs scraping on the stone floor, clatter, commotion.

A gravelly voice shouted: "*Where is she, huh?! And where's Kent!?*"

Peggy stood abruptly, entangling her arms in sand dollars and crescent moons.

She made a snorting noise, stepped out from behind her desk, and stalked off.

"*Goddamn baboons! Let go of me!*"

Russ and Megan followed her through the partition walls, past the statue now hidden under a dropcloth.

Beyond the stacked supplies they found Bob Burle, peeking through the display curtains.

"Looks like a little brouhaha," he said over his shoulder.

"*Where the hell are they, huh!?*"

Most of the crowd were on their feet, facing the catafalque, and the two figures who stood with their backs to it. Tom Carver, in denim dungarees and fishing boots; and Bernard Dreerson in his overcoat and battered fedora.

Peggy pushed on, trinkets clacking. "Tom! Bernard! *What is the meaning of this interruption!?*"

Carver gestured with a stiff arm. Not at Peggy, but at Megan. "There she is, Bern!"

"Yes, and Russell, too."

Both men held shopping bags with twine handles—Dreerson using both hands. As Peggy stormed toward him, the bookseller smiled, and set his bag on a vacated table nearest the catafalque, holding onto the twine with his black-gloved hands.

Carver shouted, "Got something to show all of you!"

The crowd stirred. They looked back to Peggy, then past her, to the Barber-Mayor stepping through the curtains. He was dressed in white smock, white trousers, and tennis shoes. Large-hewn head with a pleasant sheen of sweat, his tiny black eyes, with a calculated ease, taking in the situation.

Gold scissors in his hand.

"Ha! There he is, Bern! Chief monkey! Decided to show up!"

Peggy stood straighter. "Tom, you have no right to barge in on our Festival!"

"Got momentous news!"

The Mayor approached. "Misters Carver, and Dreerson." His voice sibilantly echoing overhead. He made a slow backwards sweep with his scissor hand. "Perhaps you'd join me in my office to *discusss* whatever concerns you. Just brewed up some Ovaltine."

Peggy shot a glance at Bob Burle, while Tom shouted, "Damn you and your office, baboon! Time's here and now!" Tom raised his bag.

"Tom!" Peggy's tone was now amused, and she stood with her head canted, hands up, below her chin. "This is an *organized* event. A *Taste-a-thon*! And we can't have you just barging in here, and taking over, can we?"

The yellow-robed Storm Watchers, scattered through the front ranks of the crowd, nodded vigorously.

"Don't have to have no permit! Don't need one!"

Dreerson chuckled. He raised his hand, and said loudly, to Tom, "If I may? Miss Chalmers?"

"Absolutely not! There are proper channels . . ."

The Mayor held up the scissors.

Peggy stiffened, glancing at Burle.

"Mister Dreerson, why don't you go ahead and speak your piece." The Mayor smiled at Peggy, then Burle. "*Fill us in* on the brouhaha, as they say. Citizens, let's hear him out."

Snick, snick said the scissors.

The crowd fell silent.

With all the attention, Dreerson did nothing but glance up at the catafalque and its twinkling lights, and the sculpture on top.

He stared for a time, then chuckled, shook his head. "It really *is* a good likeness, Bob."

Burle, skulking through the back of the crowd, froze. He nodded non-committally.

Dreerson continued, "Really rather good, yes, though some detail is lost from this angle. Nonetheless, there he is, good old Joseph, looking much as he looked one dreadful day in 1959. Oblivious to us, wouldn't you say?"

A pregnant pause, while some of the crowd studied the sculpture, and some sipped their wine, nibbled their cheese. Others—among them Clement Parker from the Laundromat, and Georgie Aberfoyle—gathered behind the Barber-Mayor, and were now glancing at the yellow-robed Watchers.

In a more subdued tone, Dreerson continued. "As all of you surely know, Tom and I found Jack Sumner's remains a few days ago."

Murmured assents, bowed heads.

"There's a story behind it. One that can be told, now that Megan has returned." Dreerson looked over at Megan and Russ, and smiled. "It started with Mister Russell Kent. Really, it wouldn't have happened without him."

Some of the crowd turned to look at Megan, and Russ.

"We live—you and I, and this effigy here—in the Land of the Gray Owl, revealed to Joseph many years ago during his solitary sojourn down the coast. Joe knew it, and soon we all knew it, or rather, had the patience to work toward it. Recall those days of toil and drudgery in the mundane world, when our lives were perched on the rocky shore, by the sea. The upstairs."

Peggy, off to the side, raised an arm, crooked a leg, resembling one of the poses in the tower's wallpaper: ancient semaphore, being answered now by one of the other Storm Watchers, with bent arms, crooked neck.

"We had patience back then, and the faith to look beyond, to what would come. Patience, as the empire was reached, and Joe's dream was found. Well, perhaps now we've forgotten that patience is still required. For truths continue to emerge." With something of a distracted smile, Dreerson continued, "The heart of the matter is this, Tom and I weren't

responsible at all for finding dear Jack Sumner's remains. We had . . .
some rather unusual help."

Dreerson nodded at Carver. Carver opened his bag.

The Mayor twitched his scissors.

"We were helped, I dare say, by the *very same thing* that led Joseph
Evening to Hesperus!"

Peggy glared at the Barber-Mayor then inflated further, rising on her
toes. "Bernard, you have no right to stand up there and . . . and *spew*
such nonsense! People!" She raised her arms—her left entangling in
string and sand dollars, which she shook off. "People, let's return to our
festivities! There's the new Hesperus green cheddar to sample, and we
have a few more surprises, don't we, girls!"

The Watchers nodded.

Dreerson, fingering the twine handle, smiled. "This time, Peggy, we
simply have *undeniable proof*."

"Proof, you baboons!" Tom shouted.

"No right!" Peggy shrilled. "You had no right to barge in! None at all!
And no official *permit*! This should *not be allowed*, Mister Mayor!"

"Permit," echoed some in the crowd.

"Permits, Tom!"

"Permits!"

"Imagine, people!" Dreerson called out, over the din, and gestured
over and behind him, at the catafalque. "Imagine Joseph awakening to
this nightmare. Picture it, the poor man waking up, shaking off the rhododendron. Why, he'd be rather shocked to see all of you reduced to
such a state, and looking . . . well, quite ridiculous."

Peggy, her features seized in apoplexy, finally cried, "*How dare . . .
how dare you speak for Joseph Evening!*"

"Joseph Evening, rest his soul, never imagined the likes of you! Look
at you! Look at your hair, Peggy! What have you done to it?"

She grimaced, and blinked twice. "It's the local style!"

The crowd had grown noisier, and Dreerson shouted above them:
"*Ladies and Gentlemen! We have made a great discovery in the Far Forty!*"

Carver reached inside his grocery bag, and lifted out an old shoe box.
He removed the lid and turned it toward the crowd—who calmed
down, who peered. Shards of puzzle box on tissue paper, black and glittering blue. "This here was found by Kent, along the shore."

"Another find!" Peggy exclaimed, one arm raised. "We know all about your *so-called finds*, Tom. . . ."

"Oh, we know!" said another voice, against echoing laughter.

A light shone on the box: Patricia Burle-Clarkson held a flashlight.

Peggy turned to the Barber-Mayor. "Put a stop to this! Or I will!"

"A stop!"

"Stop!"

The Barber-Mayor stepped toward the box. He peered inside. Rustling robes and whispers. A moment later, he stepped back. "Appears to be animal bones," he said calmly, raising his eyebrows. A moment later, "I believe the hue is called *cerulean*."

"People!" Peggy raised her arms. "This is pointless! Let's return to our party! Ignore all this silly chatter! Sit down, everyone! Everyone!"

"It's your doom!" Tom yelled.

The din swelled, crowned by Peggy's laughter and a sudden swamping tuba blaring in A flat, wobbling up to D.

In its wake, a voice proclaimed: "Enough!"

The crowd, hushing, turned to the entrance, and the figure standing against the green. Dark coat with glimmering gold buttons, dark trousers and boots.

Captain Nemo, arms folded.

"Enough!"

The noise died down, became murmurs, shuffling robes.

Peggy, glaring at her cohorts in yellow.

Even at this distance, Russ could see Malcolm's ugly grin.

"They listening to you, Tom?"

"Nope!" Tom shouted.

"He has big news, folks." As Malcolm stepped forward, Burle appeared a few yards behind him. Scalpel glinting in his hand. "Stow away the cheese and hang up your hats, there's something new on the horizon." Glancing over his shoulder, he added, "Something you'll be interested in, Mister Burle. I guarantee it."

Burle froze, as Malcolm unfolded his arms.

In his left hand he held a .45 Smith and Wesson—the pistol from Carver's basement.

"Beneath the costumes, the melodramatic trappings, we have dire business." Malcolm grinned. "Yes, Miss Chalmers, you're right! I have no right for such action! But I have the *piece*—as I love to call it—and for the next ten minutes or so, Captain Nemo will be ruler of Hesperus."

Behind him, Burle lowered the scalpel. "Okay by me." He smiled icily. "As long as you don't sing."

Malcolm stepped up to the table. "Very good. The floor is yours, Tom."

Carver nodded. "Now . . ." He cleared his throat, while beside him Dreerson glanced down at his bag.

"Now, Kent here's the one who found it." Carver squared his shoulders, and nodded at Russ in the crowd. "Down there below the Ocean-view bluff. And he brought it to me. Or Bern brought it. Bern and Kent come over, and we opened it up, and found this here."

The flashlight beam played over the bones and bits of puzzle box.

Most of the crowd was still looking at Malcolm, who was looking at Burle.

"Now, then." Carver rubbed the side of his nose with his thumb. "This here creature's not one-of-a-kind. Its fellows have been here thousands of years. Things we found upstairs—real goddamn things you all said was nothing. Things me and Bern told you Joe told us! Well, they were true!"

Peggy's eyes had been darting from the bones to Carver, and now they widened brightly. "Tom, you say Russell *found it in the water!* In my book, that means it's *not from here!* Am I right?!" She looked to the Watchers, who nodded vigorously. "Maybe it's something you picked up in Mexico, Tom. We *do* remember past instances, don't we girls?"

They laughed behind their hands.

"You'll not slander my methods!"

"What methods! From the bottle?!"

As Malcolm raised the gun, the crowd quieted.

"The teller tells his tale," Malcolm said, sighting the barrel of his gun on Peggy's forehead. She grimaced, decorously. "And the audience listens, without interruption. No coughing. No eating, drinking. No need to riffle through your program books. No talking with your seatmates."

Dreerson stepped forward and shouted: *"Psychopomps!"*

Some jumped. Some grimaced, and the Storm Watchers spoke behind their hands as Dreerson waited for the attention to return to him. Then waited a little longer. "That's what Joe decided to call them: *psychopomps*. Guides to the underworld of Oregon. And yes, the shards of brilliant material you see there, around the bones, were once a container, or a sarcophagi. Not from Mexico, or Timbuktu, but from *here*." He glanced down at the bones in Carver's hands. "Look closely, and you'll note the extra joints in the arms and legs. Not quite like our statues, or I dare say, our original inhabitants of this city. Yes, look closely at the skull! This creature is certainly an adult. Note the sutures! It's a native, but it's from—relatively speaking—*downstairs*."

There was silence, though Peggy was building to another outburst—eyebrows jutting up, mouth turning down. She exclaimed: "It's a rat!"

Echoed the other Storm Watchers: "Rat!"

"*Rat!*"

"Not a rat," said Carver. "Biped!"

Laughter.

"Rat! Rat!"

The voices multiplied, and Carver angrily shook his fist and shouted above them, "Harpies!", broken by seasick B flat, tuba, somewhere behind the catafalque.

Startled, the crowd looked not to Bobby, but to Malcolm.

The Captain slipped his free hand into his blazer pocket. "Thanks."

Carver nodded, stepped back, and lost the flashlight beam.

Malcolm smiled. "Bernard, I can take it from here."

Leaving his bag on the table, Dreerson stepped back to the catafalque, and the vines of twinkling lights.

"Gentlemen and Ladies," Malcolm projected. "Tom just wanted to tell you some big news." He stopped, glancing sideways at the women in yellow robes, who froze in mid-semaphore. His gun moved to them. "Ladies? Could the Captain have your complete attention?"

They relaxed their poses.

Peggy shot a glance at Burle, who shook his head.

"Being the scientist," Malcolm continued, "Tom wanted to lay out the whys and the wherefores. A lucid lecture, in the manner of the great Jules Verne. Monsieur Verne liked to stop and lecture, something I found charming in many, many of his novels. But not my collaborator . . ."

Malcolm searched the crowd with his eyes, found Russ, and smiled. "Russ . . . he grew tired of it. Though in opera they're called arias, and every character should get at least one. To *tell us* instead of *show us*. Or, in the case of Verne, to *lecture us*." Casually, Malcolm slipped the revolver into his pocket.

"My friends," he said, a smile tugging at his lips. "I'm not here to lecture." With both hands, Malcolm reached into Dreerson's bag, and lifted.

The crowd almost imperceptibly leaned forward, staring at the mouth of the bag, and Malcolm's hands lifting out a wire cage, in which something whirled, bounding.

Dark blue. Chitinous.

Russ resisted the urge to step forward. Squinting.

Megan tensed up beside him.

Claws scrabbling on metal.

Some in the crowd gasped, as the flashlight beam twitched over it.

Calmly, Malcolm said, "Keep the light off its eyes."

Knocking the empty bag onto the floor, he set the cage onto the table. Inside, a blue and black thing, rattling, round and round.

Some of the crowd backed up, hands to mouths; while the Storm Watchers in brilliant yellow gathered their robes about them, leaned, squinting.

Peggy, with her arms raised, fingers splayed, glared at it.

Dreerson said to the crowd, "It was more calm when we caught it, two days ago, in the Weft. Now it's no doubt feeling rather threatened by all the strange creatures looming around it."

Russ gripped the wolf head, felt the sharp ears on the web of his thumb.

"Perhaps you saw them in the shadows, and convinced yourself you'd seen a rat. They're curious creatures. They've travelled to our upstairs on a number of occasions, smart enough to evade our traps. They rather like Tillamook cheese, more than the local variety, which shows a certain level of intelligence. Otherwise, they took nothing, and never *left* anything for us until a few days ago, when Tom and I discovered Jack's remains in one of their upper tunnels."

The crowd was murmuring. Some cried out, staggered back. Harsh whispers.

"A thing!"

"A monster!"

Another voice: "Far Forty!"

"Today, like good neighbors," Dreerson added, "we are returning it, along with the remains of its comrade, to the entrance of its world, where the same creatures left Jack's body for us."

Nodding, Carver replaced the cover on the shoe box, and gently lowered it into his sack.

"The fact must be faced, ladies and gentlemen, that this new realm of ours, called Hesperus, can be also nicknamed the *new* upstairs, to their downstairs."

Peggy gathered her robes close to her, tipped back her head. "Bernard, you will take *no further actions* in the Far Forty!"

"No further actions!" echoed the Watchers.

With a Medusan intensity, she glared over the sweep of her cheeks. "The *Far Forty* is now *off-limits!*"

"Off-limits!" "Off-limits!"

The Mayor was advancing—but whether toward Malcolm, or Peggy, was uncertain, and not to be resolved any time soon.

Malcolm lifted the hinged door on the front of the cage, and stepped back.

The door clattered open. The thing, whirling sharply, bounded out.

Wails burbled into shrieks, into screams, as it leapt onto the table. Crouching, almost spider-like, in the flashlight beam. Its claws twitching the tablecloth, tearing it, as the creature turned and turned again. Its blueness more like rock than flesh, as its claws tucked into the tablecloth.

As it shrieked, piercingly bright—gull-like.

"No lights!" Dreerson shouted. "No need to be afraid of it! They're intelligent!"

Then the thing jumped surprisingly high, came down in a crouch, claws tangling the tablecloth. A wineglass dropped over the edge, shattered.

Giving another piercing cry, it bounded across the table, knocking aside plates, tipping over wineglasses, then stopping beside a plate of cheese, straightening. It plucked up a toothpick, brandished like a short spear, crouched at the edge of the table then sprang to the catafalque, catching the vines of lights in its claws, scrambling up.

Over Joseph's shoulder, onto his chest. The creature whirled.

Bits of cheese being torn and flung.

"Down from there!" Peggy shouted, flapping her arms. Others were stumbling back, under the barrage. Peggy rounded about, stamped her foot. "Bob, get it!"

Burle stepped back. "Going to have to decline that request, Peg."

"Megan, dear." Dreerson was suddenly beside them, gesturing. "Russell! This way! Quickly! Come along!"

She took Russ's hand, pulled him after Dreerson, along the edges of the panicking crowd, to Malcolm.

"Hurry!" Malcolm lost his hat, lunged for it then let it go. "Outside, Russell!"

Clutching the satchel to his chest, heart pounding, Russ stepped dizzily out into the Avenue, which was broad and bright and quiet against the noise at his back. Megan pulled him toward the stairs, and down.

Among the spruce below, Obolus waved. Something in his hand. "Sir! Here, sir, Miss!" He waved. "Special transportation." He bowed briskly to Malcolm as the group tromped down the stairs.

Megan said something Russ didn't quite catch, as Obolus passed the satchel to him. "Here, sir," he said, rushing ahead once Russ took it. Over his shoulder: "Those're from Miss Yarrow, sir. Color music, she said. And that you were to have them." Obolus rounded the corner of the Town Hall, and hurried down the side street.

Russ looked back for her, saw a figure in the bandstand. Then rounded the corner.

The river's roar was upon them.

the black river

"*Allez vite!*" Malcolm shouted, waving Obolus ahead of him.

"Malcolm!"

But Malcolm tramped past a line of garbage cans, kicked through a drift of shredded paper.

"Hold on!"

"We're taking the river, Russ!"

"Why not the bikes?!"

Over his shoulder: "River's faster!" A grin. "*Mobilis in mobili!*"

The light from the Avenue grew faint. Clutching the satchel, Russ followed Nemo into the dark, with Megan and Dreerson hurrying behind. The roar grew louder as the walls narrowed, then suddenly dissipated as they ended, stretching into splashes, into rills against a nearby shore, over the boom of deeper currents.

Icy particles thrumming in the air.

A light flared beyond Obolus—a lantern, lifted by Pete Crick, sending their shadows backwards. "Watch your step, Captain! Mister Kent!"

They had reached a landing of wet black stone, a quay of sorts, with a low wall stretching off to either side.

"How'd it go, Mister Dreerson?"

"More complicated than we had hoped! But still along the lines of our initial plan!"

Russ gripped the wolf head, planted the steel foot. He leaned, looked back at Dreerson. "Tom going to be okay?!"

Dreerson nodded, though with a tenseness in his expression, a twinge above his nose. "Yes." Louder: "He's not alone, Russell!"

"Boat's ready to go!" Pete turned to Obolus. "Just needs to be lowered over!"

Obolus nodded broadly. "Good, sir!" He said something to Danace.

They clambered over coils of rope, to a black pontoon raft— the Zodiac from upstairs.

"In addition, Russell, he's armed with a spanner wrench! And he has a tremendous right hook!"

Russ looked out beyond the low wall, discerning movement in the dark, left to right.

The ground shook with it.

He shouted: "Why take the river!?"

"Swift currents, Russ!" Malcolm replied.

Dreerson, wiping his lenses on his shirt sleeves, nodded. "Yes, swifter than you'd think!"

"Don't worry, Russ! I've made the trip three times!"

"Megan!" Dreerson stepped close to her, spoke in her ear, while the Stans unloaded from the raft a ladder, an aluminum box, and bulky life jackets, leaving behind wooden oars.

"Mister Crick!" Obolus waved.

"Sure! Hey, Captain?! Could you hold this!?"

Nodding, Malcolm unfolded his arms, took the lantern from Pete, and lifted it to his chest. The light fired the gold buttons on his coat, sent the tousled shadow of his beard up over his smile, his eyes asquint above its gleam.

Russ tried to muster his argument.

"Don't worry, Russ! Stans are excellent river men!"

With one hand in his blazer pocket, Nemo stood watching the activity, shifting from boot to boot. Finally, he joined the others.

Russ, in near dark, stepped up to the wall, tried to see the water. Gray and black movement, left to right, and the watery air moving with it.

"Heave, now! All together!" The Zodiac was lifted up at Malcolm's command.

Russ stared directly down. Blinking against the spray, he wondered at the river's breadth, and how a boat could possibly navigate it; while to the right, the Zodiac nosed down in lamplight for perhaps a dozen yards over silver currents, then hit, skipped, being buffeted then lying flat, tethered by a yellow line. The light moved away from it, brightened the nearby wall.

"Russell!" A hand tapped his shoulder. Dreerson stepped close, clutching the lantern, blinking like a mole. "Russell! I must say goodbye here!"

The Stans had flashlights. They were securing lines.

Russ shook his head. "You and Tom should come with us! Upstairs!"

"Too much for my age!" Dreerson gestured out, and made a dipping motion with his hand. "We'll be up eventually! But right now, we'll try to help and guide the others!" Droplets of water obscured his glasses. He took them off, and wiped them, shouting, "Odd to say, Russell! But we in the ACL have been working toward this for years! Contact with the native population! Investigation of the origins of this city, and the worlds below it! Joe always knew the day would come!" He gazed on the structures, and offered a smile. "What Joe didn't count on were the Peggys and the Patricias, and the Bob Burles, steering the town into the land of cheese!"

Danace handed Russ a bulky life jacket. "Sir!"

Russ took it, switching the satchel under his arm, then under his coat, letting the stick balance against his hip, where it nearly toppled.

Megan took the stick.

"Russell, as I told Megan, we've all had it so easy up till now! Compared to our forefathers, at least! And I feel I owe them something!" Dreerson looked over at her. "I owe it to those who suffered in the winter cold for years, before the first property was platted! When all this was just an unlikely prospect, for which they sacrificed their comfort and their futures!" Dreerson smiled in the upward light, thick gray bangs riffling in the breeze. "At any rate, I was *born* in Evening! So was Tom! And Peggy, and the rest of the rabble! But not you! And not you, Megan! And it's time for you both to leave!" He offered his plump hand, and shook Russ's, firmly. "Don't wait around upstairs! Go back to Boston! The east coast! *Anywhere but Delaware*, that's my motto! Megan, dear!"

She hugged him, and kissed his cheek. "Call!"

"I promise! I have the number!"

Danace handed out a life jacket to Megan, while Obolus—already wearing his—boosted himself up on the wall, stepped over to the hanging ladder, and began climbing down.

"Careful!" shouted Dreerson.

"Yes, absolutely, sir!" Obolus grinned, nodded. "We'll meet you and Mister Carver at the prearranged site! Very soon!"

He disappeared from view.

Struggling into his vest, Russ stepped closer to the wall, and watched Obolus climb down against dark currents, to the boat that was nearly invisible.

Pete shouted: "Megan, you're next, okay?! Then Mister Kent! And you, Captain!"

Malcolm replied: "Very good!"

Megan stepped close to the wall.

Russ said, "You've done this before?"

She shook her head, wiped hair from her eyes. "First time for everything."

Pete Crick climbed up on the wall, grabbed the top of the ladder, stepped over, down, onto the rungs, shifted his weight, and slowly climbed down. He had little difficulty. The ladder was steady; the rungs were large enough; and Obolus held the ladder until he reached the deck.

Once down, he shouted: "Megan!"

Tightening the vest, she glanced back at Russ. "Piece of cake!"

She hugged Dreerson again. "In a week, Bennie!"

"Yes! I promise I'll call! Be careful, dear!"

Using the toolbox as a step, she climbed up onto the wall. Russ and Dreerson were ready to lunge for her as she grabbed hold of the ladder, shifted over, stepped down, finding the rung.

She climbed carefully down.

Russ counted fifteen steps before she reached the boat, and dropped between Pete and Obolus.

She waved up.

Dreerson tapped his arm. "Go, Russell!"

"Goodbye, Bernard!"

They shook hands. "I'll call you both in a week! At the Boston number! Tom has . . . Russell, he has a wristwatch that plays Yankee Doodle every twenty-four hours! And a little calendar window! I won't miss it—barring any unforeseen developments! But don't mention that to Megan, please!"

Russ nodded. "Be careful!"

With the satchel stuffed under his coat and vest, he climbed onto the wall, trying not to look down, as he reached for the ladder, gripped the icy aluminum, made sure he was steady then stepped out, with the roaring, booming water at his back.

Dizzy. He held on tight.

"Easy does it, Russell!"

He nodded to Dreerson, situating himself on the ladder, and started down.

The smell of minerals intensified, as the black rock of the wall became turquoise. His shadow leaning up as he climbed down, through a realm of roaring water, ten rungs, twelve.

Megan's voice: "Down!"

Her hands took hold of his coat, his arm. He stepped, jumped on the rocking deck, with Megan helping him to sit down.

Malcolm hurried down, clambered off the ladder, hair and jacket whipping in the breeze. "Everybody settle in!" He moved to the stern. "Ready, Stans?!"

"Yes, sir, Captain!"

"Yes, Captain!"

Russ was staring out into the waters to their left as Megan took hold of him, and they lay in the empty space between the benches.

Wind howled. Where the sliding lamplight touched the turquoise, there was no remnant glow. Overhead was dark rock, and Dreerson's pale face gazing down, worriedly, his hand waving.

The Stans took up the oars. Pete, with an electric lamp, stretched out, settled in the bow, while from overhead the line went slack, came down.

Dreerson waving, as the boat soared away from the quay.

Megan settled in the crook of his shoulder. "Lie back," she said, close to his ear, as the currents took hold.

Thundering in the air, and under the hull.

He turned his head, looked up at Obolus looming on the bench, easily wielding the oars. Noticing Russ, Obolus nodded, smiled gently. Beyond, in sepulchral gloom, the structures drifted past, separated by vertical flashes of green that were the alleys or side streets.

Here was momentum again, as flashes quickened. He relaxed his shoulders, gave in to tiredness, as had the rest of them, comforted, assured in the Stans' ability to guide the boat. All the day's climbing, walking, riding now descending like a weight, and he looked at Megan, the curve of her forehead, the half circles of her shut eyes, her nose, her smile.

The warmth of her body holding off the dark beyond the boat.

Hard to keep his eyes from closing.

He shut them. Only to be woken by the boat knocking to a halt. A quay loomed overhead.

Danace was tugging on a line, drawing their boat close, against the currents. Tying it.

Obolus, leaning moon-faced overhead: "Here we are, sir. Miss Sumner, wake up."

"Watch your step, sir!"
Obolus helped him up and over another wall, onto another quay. Russ was light-headed.

He tasted minerals, and the cold, and wondered about what had just happened. Had the journey been so strange? Nobody else was remarking on it. Yawning, Megan took off her life jacket. Malcolm had already discarded his, and now stamped his boots on the stone, and shook his arms.

Russ untied his life jacket, shrugged it off. He pulled out the satchel, slightly surprised to find it still there.

Had the journey been strange, or merely quick?

"Best to get moving!" shouted Malcolm. "Double time!"

They set off for the Avenue, now a column of bright green anchored by a cluster of tiny garbage cans and a tiny black-iron bench. It was good to be walking; not just walking but *striding*, with the Stans hurrying alongside, and the breeze at their backs.

Coldness, tiredness, falling away with every step.

"Great job, Stan!"

Obolus nodded. "Captain, it's the boat that makes it, sir! Durable fiberglass and pontoon support, is what they call it!"

Danace said something to Obolus, who shouted to Malcolm, "Danace hears a crowd, sir!"

"No worries. We'll beat them!"

What Russ heard, as the roar diminished, was a variety of tones that was the breeze wending through structures, through cracks and fissures, windows, doorways, as if through embouchures and ducts of ancient stone, gathering as they neared the Avenue in gentle oscillation, lingering, becoming the struck-bell tones, the wind tones.

Across from them was the first of the structures, the crumbled summit, and an easy chair, where Old Crick now slept in a woolen sweater.

Megan had to steer him around a garbage can.

Streetlamps, mailboxes, signs, drapery.

And voices. Hundreds of voices, or remnants of voices on either side, antiphonal, like voluntaries, against a sudden massed outcry in the distance.

Russ squinted. In the relative shade was movement, a glinting dark green wave that was swarming around, swallowing up, the newspaper stands, the lamps, in slow motion.

Voices in ragged congregation.

Obolus and Danace hurried up the wide staircase, followed by Pete, and Malcolm.

Old Crick lifted his head, then his arm. "Nemo!"

Malcolm ignored him. "No time for sightseeing, Russ!"

The green wave was people running down the Avenue. He could see faces, open mouths. Those in the front were on bicycles, weaving back and forth, and shouting.

"Nemo, Nemo!"

"C'mon!" Megan tugged his arm, and he climbed with her, after the Captain, whose blazer flapped as he jogged up, across the landing, into the tunnel. The river roar, the bell tones, the wind tones, reducing as the tunnel enclosed them, and they neared the other side; all but the voices.

At the far end, Arthur stepped out in checkered slacks. He peered. "Big crowd?"

They ran past him, into the tower room, following the maze-like lanes of pallets and shelving. Winded, Russ jogged past the Craftsman facade, a thicket of street signs, into the center.

Directly ahead, the elevator cage rose through the ceiling. Empty.

No car in sight.

Obolus grunted. He dropped into the chair behind the desk, while Danace, using a great ring of gold keys, opened a panel beside it. He tripped some switches.

Russ and Megan walked to the cage, while Captain Nemo, arms folded, hair in wild curls, surveyed the scene. "Mister Crick, get us some big lights!" He glanced up, and with less authority, said, "So where's the elevator?"

Obolus said, "Town Hall sent it to the top, Captain."

"Thought we cut the lines."

"They must've rewired, sir." He glanced at Danace, who nodded. Obolus smiled. "But as of now . . . we've patched over their override, sir."

Danace tripped some more switches. In the cage, there was a ratcheting sound. Steel lines twanging through pulleys and wheels.

"Car's on its way, but it will take as much as four minutes, I'm afraid." Obolus looked up, as the voices began to echo in the chamber.

Megan hooked her fingers in the grillwork, staring up. "Bring it down to the fourth level. We can climb up, meet it there."

Obolus nodded. "That can certainly be done, Miss." He went to work at the panel.

Pete was dragging out a cart of lamps that trailed power lines across the floor, while Malcolm grabbed a pallet jack, rolled it over to a pallet of *Dry Cement*, jacked it up, then pulled the entire load nearly against the staircase entrance.

"Hey-oh!" Arthur hobbled into view, waving. "Big crowd coming!"

"Stand-by!"

"Okay, Captain!"

Malcolm reached into his pocket, pulled out the revolver.

"Follow us up, Malcolm," said Russ. "Watch our backs."

Malcolm looked over. "Upstairs can't be compared to this." He cocked his head, smiled at the choral onslaught. "Nemo has a role here, Russ. To keep the natives from capturing you, by conjuring terrible wonders." He shouted: "Goodbye to the upstairs! Goodbye, mankind! At least for a few months! Meg, get him up those stairs! Go, both of you! When you hear me call out, both of you shut your eyes! *Don't look back!*"

Megan said, "What'll you do?"

"I'm not quite sure." He grinned. "But it will be *loud!*"

Russ approached the staircase. With Megan's hand on the small of his back, he grabbed the iron rail, and began to climb, jogging up. Behind them, Malcolm jammed the pallet up against the stairwell's entrance, lowered it, then yanked out the jack. Pushed it, sent it careering down an aisle.

"Who knows, Russ!" He shouted. "One day, back in Boston, we can pick up the project!" He boosted himself to the top of the cement pile, and straightened. "Something inspired by all that stuff in that satchel! Something to shock the ears at Salzburg, eh!"

Arthur shouted: "All the rotten teeth! Here they come!"

Megan's hand steady on his back as he climbed, up and around, trying not to stumble as the staircase began to sway.

The crowd surged into view, waving, pointing. Their shouts were indecipherable, except for "*Down!*" and "*Stop!*"

Some tripped, pushed by those in yellow robes—by Bob Burle, and by Peggy, the prickly, sapphire-spotted flower, shoving to the forefront, glaring up.

She stabbed her arm toward the stairs, her voice rising, "Thieves!"

Malcolm raised the pistol, and shouted over the others: "Lights!"

A switch was thrown. Twelve lamps flared up, searing the walls to bright green, to yellow, white.

The crowd cried out, voices rising in alarm, even as their echoes—in triple layers—cried out after them, in disturbing harmonies, over which Peggy's voice soared, wobbled, "Stop them, Bob! Get them down!"

Gray figures, struggling against the glare.

Russ reached the ceiling, climbed up and around to the last stair, and the lowest of the tower chambers. The glare was sweeping up through Victorian grillwork, over dusty boxes and portraits.

Below, Malcolm was a gray figure over a sea of gray, over pale faces, grasping arms, and Peggy, stiffening, her voice swooping: "*Take him!*"

Hands reaching out—one caught his boot.

The raised pistol fired.

Dust trembled off the cage as the air shuddered. An enormous peal unfolding. Russ felt it in his bones; Megan, too, grabbing the cage as the echo volleyed brightly up and down the tower, shaking iron, and wood of furniture, gold of picture frames, ceramics, the steel and glass—shattering glass—as the entire structure whirled with quarter-tone echoes, and the light subsided.

The crowd, cowering, had dropped to their knees.

Even Peggy Chalmers, hands in her bristling hair.

All except for the Captain, whose suit looked more black than blue, standing with arms folded.

"I can see it!" Megan was close by Russ, staring up. Shining eyes. She pulled him to the next staircase, which was still resonating with the peal.

"Almost there," she said.

They climbed, over lingering tatters of sound like cubist fanfares. And the voice of Captain Nemo, intoning, "*Okay, folks. Enough's enough.*

*e*ntra'acte

Outside the factory they found daylight, clouds, a trace of rain; a marvelously normal morning.

The breeze revitalized him. He followed her to the truck, squinting. Her wristwatch read *3:30*, but this was neither early morning nor midafternoon. *11:50*, according to the truck's clock. More than a day had passed.

Russ was almost too tired to be surprised. "Sky always this bright?"

"Yep," she said, settling in her seat. She looked equally tired, hair in a mess, clothes, like Russ's, dusted green. "You'll be squinting till tomorrow."

With no signs of pursuit, they had taken their time climbing the Memorial Tunnel, stopping halfway up at the rest area—*The Center of Our Passage*, as the plaque read. There at the damp table and chairs, Russ had wanted to stay longer than an hour. Perhaps, without realizing it, they had.

Time works strangely down there, Dreerson had said.

Once past the parking lot and the sentinel line of alder, they were greeted by the expanse of sea and sky, and the Evening mansion sitting like a green and white toy on the bluff.

The dismantled homes along Seventh Street were similarly reduced by the sky.

Russ rolled down the window, inhaled the cool, salty breeze.

Over the lower hill, gulls swooped and dived.

"Hey, look who it is." Megan pointed. On the sidewalk to their right trotted Ody, with lowered head rising, ears sharpening, tail wagging.

Megan stopped beside him, set the brake and climbed out.

"Ody. Just wandering around? C'mon. Up."

Ody bounded up into the seat beside Russ.

"Hey, Ode."

"Maybe he snuck away from Hillary," she said, climbing back in. "I'll call her."

"Or Hillary's left town?"

"Maybe."

Once home, she took Ody into the kitchen for food and water, while Russ trudged upstairs to his room.

He resisted the urge to sit down, sure that he'd have difficulty getting up any time soon. By the desk, with one hand clutching the back of the chair, he lifted the phone's handset, found a dial tone, and called Ellie.

She answered on the second ring.

"Hi, Ellie."

"Russ? So everything's okay?"

"Yeah."

"And now's the time when you tell me what it's about?"

"Tomorrow, in person. I promise. We're leaving here in two hours."

"Home tonight?"

"Yeah. Do you think you could book two seats from Portland to Logan? Sometime after six P.M. And a cargo seat for a dog?"

"For Malcolm?"

"For Ody. Me and Megan for sure, and probably Ody. And I'll explain everything later."

Or try to, he thought.

After giving further promises, Russ hung up, took a shower, dialing the water cold toward the end to wake him up. He changed into the last of his clean clothes then packed everything else into the two suitcases. Or nearly everything. He left his copy of *20,000 Leagues Under the Sea* in the desk drawer, a sort of Gideon bible for future tenants.

"Comfortable, Ody?" Less than two hours later, in the rental sedan, Megan switched on the wipers and adjusted her seat belt. "Is there enough room for him?"

Ody sat on a blanket in the back seat, by a box of clothes.

His tail thumped against the cardboard.

"Yeah. He has room to lie down."

"Hillary said they'd be leaving by five. I made her promise."

"To Port Rostov?"

She nodded, familiarizing herself with the instrument panel, trying out the blinkers, hazard lights. She turned up the defroster. "Claire has an old friend there. In the big city. She and Hillary can stay for a while if they have to."

Outside, the rain was pouring. Heat was blasting condensation from the windows.

Russ grasped a thermos of coffee and a bag of sandwiches—leftovers from their hearty lunch. He looked over his shoulder. "Ready, Ode?"

The dog, panting, seemed to nod with his solemn blue eyes.

"He's sad to go." She glanced in the rearview. "Aren't you, Odysseus?" She released the parking brake, put the car into gear. A smooth jolt: then they were in motion, tires grinding across the gravel verge as she cranked the wheel, turning them around in the middle of Seventh, back to Alder. "Say goodbye, Ody." She waved at the house. Softly: "Bye, house."

At Alder, she turned right and drove slowly down the hill.

The dismantled cottages leaned with the leaning fences, with the rhododendron, morning glory and fern in a frozen spill. Looking, Russ was really looking somewhere past it, under and down, in the distance, *there*.

Hearing the lingering echoes.

He wondered what was happening, right now.

At the bottom of the hill she braked beside the Warp and Weft, peered up at the second floor windows, which were dark like the first floor.

Closed till we Open, read the sign.

"A week, Bennie," she said, under her breath, and turned onto First Street.

It might have been a lazy Sunday afternoon. A few cars were parked along the curbs. The businesses looked open but empty, with the Evening mansion watchful on the bluff, glaring with cloudlight.

In front of the Diner, in the downpour, sooty gulls were squabbling over shreds of paper towels and lettuce. Three more dropped swift and sharply down as she braked slowly at the first stoplight, then accelerated through.

Farther along, near Aberfoyle, gulls sailed up the hill, to where a garbage can had toppled and scattered garbage along the curb.

Russ looked up the side streets, into the depths of greenery, waiting for something impossible to appear. Close by, the facades of the Cheese Outlet, Grocery, the Beauty Salon were perhaps open for business, perhaps closed, with the empty sidewalks reminding him of the black-iron benches and concrete planters, now elsewhere.

The windows of the Evening Barber Shop were soaped over except for a placard, *Open 11 to 5 Sundays.*

". . . right off," Megan said, staring out her side window.

Approaching on the left, the Victorian Visitor's Center loomed against hemlock.

Evening-by-the-Sea's
Chamber of Commerce and Visitor's Center
Open Mondays from noon till five

"Huh?"

She faced forward. "Breeze," she said. "The offshore breeze. Knocked the tiles right off."

But the Visitor's Center was intact, far as he could tell, along with the brick barbershop, and the gas station with its sign *Try Again Tomorrow, Folks.* He glanced back over his shoulder, but by then they'd left the town behind for the trees.